Nicole squirmed in his arms, pushing away from his chest. "Put me down," she whimpered, her words barely audible over the rasp of his breathing. He set her down rather than let her fall from his arms, but she sank to the grass, curling into a ball of misery, surrendering to the pain—her magic trying to tear its way free.

"No—Nicole. We need to find the portal," he insisted, pulling her back up by the arm.

She stood, the effort shaking her body, unable to straighten up completely as she nodded. She put a hand on his shoulder and straightened herself up with some renewed strength.

"It was there," she said. She reached out, stepped away from him, and swayed on unsteady legs.

His grip caught her arm as she leaned too far forward. Her momentum pulled him off balance, and they fell through the portal.

The Hidden Magic Series

Hidden Magic

Lost Prophecy

Dragon King

Hidden
MAGIC
THE PORTAL OPENS

C.C. RAE

C.C. Rae Books

HIDDEN MAGIC
THE PORTAL OPENS

This is a work of fiction. All the characters, names, incidents, organi-zations, and dialog in this novel are either the products of the au-thor's imagination or are used fictitiously.

C.C. Rae Books titles may be ordered through booksellers or at www.ccrae.com

ISBN: 978-0-578-45288-3 (hc)
ISBN: 978-0-578-45285-2 (sc)
ISBN: 978-0-578-45287-6 (e)

Acknowledgments

To my freshman English teacher and editor Karmen Leggett, thank you for opening the door to the world of literature. I will be forever grateful for your lessons and your friendship. A big thank you to Monique Manifold, for starting me on my publishing journey and encouraging my love of English for two wonderful years in high school. To the other incredible instructors I have had: Ted McLoof, Timothy Dyke, and Portia Moore. I couldn't have had better teachers. Thank you to all my family and friends who read every version of this changing story through the years and encouraged me to keep chasing this crazy dream. Most impotantly thank you to my sister, Renee, for being my lifelong partner in weirdness and never growing up.

To my dad. Thank you for everything—for
believing in me and for the running shoes
that started this whole story.

☙❧

One

Raiden sat slouched in his chair, his feet resting up on the desk. He was close to dozing after a night without sleep and a day of waiting. Most of the desk was piled with books pushed away from the corner where his feet rested. The diffuse gray light of a cloudy day barely made it through the dusty window.

A high-pitched ringing pierced the room, and he lurched upright, dragging his feet off the desk. He fumbled among the books, cringing against the sharp sound until he found it: a tiny conch shell the size of his thumb. In the dim room, the shell glowed faintly with magic—the charm he fashioned to alert him when his target left the island.

"Etena." He spoke the command, and the charm's ringing ceased.

His wait was over. He snatched his coat from the back of the chair. As he slipped his arms into the sleeves, his gaze dropped to the sword with a hilt of folded silver wings that leaned against the door. The aged leather of the sheath was familiar against the callous skin of his hand. With a huff, he swung it behind him and adjusted the wide strap over his shoulder.

He stepped out into the icy air of an overcast afternoon, the

1

winter sun hidden. His breath rolled from his mouth in white puffs. The night without sleep did not lessen the strength of his stride. Even before he began this waiting game, he had become accustomed to going without sleep. He wouldn't have slept at all if he had the choice. He had no control over what passed through his mind while he slept. Too often, he dreamed of things he would rather forget. But even worse were the visions. The Sight often woke him; glimpses of some future, with their stunning vividness, clear and sharp, were so unlike dreams—so much worse. The Sight had a funny way of doubling the senses and visions wrenched him violently from sleep.

He was always grateful to be awake. His lungs shivered with each inhalation of icy air. The door whined as it closed behind him, and he set the lock out of habit rather than need. There was no one around who would try wandering into his hiding place. It had been a home once, the house where he grew up, but not anymore.

A white envelope at his feet hopped up off the damp stoop as though it were alive. He snatched it off the ground. The edges were a little soggy, and the black ink was slightly smudged. His name, looked like it was about to drip from the paper—Raiden Aldor Cael. The people who had given him that name were long gone, and the only people who knew it now were in Atrium, the capital on the mainland.

His hand closed on the envelope, and the sound of it creasing in his grip filled the uncanny silence of the empty city hanging around him.

"Your first contact with a living being outside of Cantis in nearly ten years, and you don't even want to read it?" The cold voice of the death keeper came as little surprise to Raiden. There was a time when the disembodied voice made Raiden jump out of his skin. But nothing startled him anymore.

"I don't care what the Council has to say to me." His hoarse voice grated against his ears. When was the last time he had spoken aloud? He buried the letter in the deep pocket of his coat and strode to the low gate, stepped over it, and turned onto the street.

"No, you don't seem to care about anything anymore." The cold voice of the death keeper followed, its speaker still unseen. "Your song has grown rather dull, Raiden. Pity."

"I cannot say I'm sorry to disappoint you, Amarth," Raiden muttered.

"People who cannot feel do not make good music. You had so much promise years ago, such passion as a boy. It would be a shame to end on such a flat note."

"Are you saying I'm going to die tonight?"

"Look for yourself, Raiden. You have the Sight."

"And you know I don't use it," he said.

"Was that a spark of feeling I just heard?" The voice chuckled. "Perhaps you should, Raiden, since it's the only thing that stirs any emotion in you these days. A man who feels nothing might as well be dead already."

"Why don't you follow the others if my lack of emotion is so abhorrent?" Raiden huffed, his hot breath forming a white puff in the darkness of the empty streets.

"Follow? They cower in their holes. I cannot follow someone who does not move. Besides, one can only stomach so much fear. You could say you cleanse the palate."

"Glad I could be of service," he muttered. He kept his eyes forward as he walked. It was easier to move through the silent city when he didn't look around. If he did, he would see the emptiness and find himself remembering what it should have been—the cart full of bread on the corner outside the bakery or the red glow and hot fragrance of rack upon rack of loaves and rolls waiting in the window instead of the collapsed pile of wood. If he looked, he wouldn't just see the empty storefronts. His memory would fill in the space with the people who should be bustling in and out of those doors, chiming the threshold bells into a kind of music over the constant din of customers and shopkeepers and friends greeting one another in passing. He didn't particularly like to recall those lost people—

"Your mother—she had quite a song," said Amarth.

—especially her.

"Oh, there it is again," Amarth said. "There's hope for you yet, Raiden, still a chance to recover your heart."

Raiden's jaw clenched. Existing was easier without feeling, and it was easier to feel nothing if he didn't think about his mother. *Just keep walking,* he told himself. Emotions got in the way of what he needed to do. Longing for company made the silence maddening. Greif made him indifferent to his physical needs. Anger made him hasty and impulsive. Fear made him doubt himself. To survive, to plan and prepare he needed the numbness. He wouldn't need it anymore if he succeeded today. He could let himself feel again, maybe find new people to care about, live again.

Amarth materialized before his eyes, blocking his path. Raiden stopped, forced to look the death keeper in the eye. Amarth was a pale, ageless being, no more like a human than a person's shadow. His presence was faint and the hazy gray daylight passed through him. He still looked precisely the same as he had when Raiden first beheld him standing beside his mother: a slight boy of fourteen or so with eyes that had seen centuries pass. Looking directly at Amarth made resisting the Sight difficult. Raiden didn't fully understand why, but he found himself squinting and looking away every time to keep the Sight at bay.

"Maybe it is better you die tonight. You put your mother's gift to shame."

"Why should that be any of your concern, Amarth?"

Silence reigned for a moment, and the death keeper flickered, partly transparent in the corner of Raiden's eye.

"Read the letter, Raiden."

Raiden closed his eyes and walked straight ahead. He met no resistance. Death keepers can't interact with the living—not physically at least. Amarth said nothing further. Whether he followed unseen, Raiden could never be sure.

Determination lengthened Raiden's stride and straightened his spine despite his inclination to hunch against the cold. He didn't care if he shamed the Sight. The Sight was no gift to him. His mother had not seen it as a gift either. The Sight was a curse revered by people who failed to understand the price paid by those who used it. Apparently, even death keepers considered it a crime to waste it.

Raiden didn't have time for visions. He didn't have time for memories or death keepers or letters from the Council. Today he would finally get the justice for the silence, and if he was alive tomorrow—well, he wasn't entirely sure what he'd do. In nine years, he had thought only about what he would do today. Beyond the occasional unwanted vision, not once had he spared a thought for what might come next.

His trek through the forest was familiar; sometimes it felt too familiar as he moved through the endless slender trees. Their white bark made them seem ghostly where they stood in the remains of their golden canopies, recently shed.

The forest looked unchanged after nearly ten years, and he half expected to see his friend Caeruleus step out from behind a tree, still thirteen years old, with that grin that could penetrate gloom like an audible laugh. Caeruleus was lucky; he and his father had left the island of Cantis. The idea of his old friend kindled a feeble spark of hope, perhaps he would see him again someday.

It was such a welcome distraction that he struggled to suppress it. Pining too much for the future was a surefire way to summon the Sight, so he focused his mind and eyes on what lie ahead of him. Soon he could see through the bare canopies and make out the small castle atop the mountain looming ahead. It was the only trace left of the Candhrid monarchy, empty since the realm united under the Council. Now it was no more than a headstone. Even after so many decades of neglect, it was still obnoxiously ornate; it never suited the modest island chosen as the royal seat of Candhrid. Soon it would be a tomb, but he didn't dare use the Sight to learn if it would be his or not.

Before long, he found himself on the old dirt road leading up to the castle. He stood here once before and even made it all the way to the top. That had been a time when he was full of pain and anger—but mostly fear. It was for the best that his unruly emotions had hindered his pursuit of justice then. He hadn't spent nine years mastering numbness. That boy with the tear-stained face would have died like the rest of them. Today he had every scrap of knowledge he could dig out of the rubble of Cantis and carry away from empty homes. He had nine years of fending for himself, practicing the magic he needed to take on a monster. Numbness was the only way he could focus. When the task was done, he could afford to feel again. Whether or not he would be able to was another matter for another day.

His mother's voice called out from his memories. *What are you up to today, my Ray of sunshine?* She had asked him that same question every day when she was alive.

He stood before the tall, narrow doors and took one last look around him, wondering if he might see her somewhere. On the neighboring mountain stood the black pillar of a tower, the broken stone bridge between it and the castle like two arms forever reaching for each other over the forest in the valley below. A whisper from the sea of pale trees reminded him now was not the time to think of her.

There was no fear to stop him this time, but he didn't have any anger to propel him forward either. He didn't feel weak, but he didn't feel strong. This was what he had to do though; it was the reason he woke up every day. Now—it had to be now or return to his hole and become a shadow for the remainder of his life like the few people left cowering in Cantis. He opened the door enough to slip inside and marched into the cold halls of the tomb.

Two

Nicole hurried down the stairs, pulling her hoodie down with one hand, her backpack hanging from the other. Her running shoes thudded against the carpeted steps; she had to wear them if she was going to make it to class on time. An electric guitar riff rang from her backpack, and she retrieved her cell phone before swinging the bag onto her shoulder.

Glancing at the screen, she saw the picture of her friend Roxanne, a cascade of blonde waves around her face and blue eyes peering over a rainbow birthday cupcake.

Nicole answered, "I'm on my way."

"Where are you?" Roxanne demanded.

"I'm heading out the door now—I swear," Nicole said, rushing into the kitchen to snatch the Tupperware bowl containing her lunch off the counter. She stuffed it into her backpack before opening the fridge to grab her shaker bottle.

"You know Barkin is reassigning seats today. If you aren't here, you won't get first choice with the rest of the As." Nicole could hear Roxanne's anxious bouncing that jarred her words.

Nicole downed the last of the protein shake and smiled. "I'll be there," she said as she grabbed a half-eaten cashew-butter-and-banana sandwich she had stopped halfway through her breakfast to take a shower.

"So why are you running late *this* morning?" Roxanne's tone hovered somewhere between humor and annoyance.

"Just a little morning workout," Nicole said and took a large bite of her breakfast as she strode from the kitchen to the back door. As the sound of the door opening and closing passed through the phone, she heard Roxanne gasp with the realization that she'd been lied to.

"You *just* walked out the door, didn't you?"

"Roxie"—Nicole paused to force down her mouthful of food—"I'll be over the back wall in thirty seconds. You know it only takes me two minutes to get to class from here."

"The bell is going to ring in five minutes," she warned.

"Then I'll have three whole minutes to catch my breath," Nicole said.

Roxanne let out a groan.

Nicole laughed. "I'll be right there," she said, taking another bite.

"Yeah, yeah," Roxanne said and hung up.

Nicole turned off her phone and stuffed it back into her backpack. Just as she put the last of her sandwich in her mouth, the back door opened behind her.

The man standing there was tall, framed by the doorway, his dark hair scattered with white strands to the point that it looked marble gray, matching his eyes.

"Hey, Dad," she mumbled though her food with a guilty grin.

"You're going to be late," he said lightly, a challenge. He stepped outside, followed by a long-legged, shaggy black dog.

"No, I'm not," she countered, her words still muffled by masticated bread, banana, and cashew butter. The dog trotted across the yard, and she took long strides away from the house. Her feet sank deep into the thick green lawn. It had just been mowed a few days before yet seemed overgrown by weeks this morning. The whole yard was this way, far more lush and green than a yard in Yuma,

Arizona, had any right to be. The rosebushes along the east wall had been sad scraggly things in October. Then in November everything in the yard was suddenly growing with a fervor that baffled Nicole and her father. Now, by January, their backyard looked like an unkempt botanical garden.

Nicole made her way across the yard, heading for the south wall, the only barrier between her and the student parking lot behind her high school. On mornings when she didn't have time to walk out the front door, past four houses and around the corner out of the neighborhood to get the school—which was most mornings—she cut through their backyard and hopped the redbrick fence just like her two older brothers always had. Much to their parents' duress, anything her brothers did, Nicole would follow suit.

Bandit, their dog—who at sixteen years old had been showing his age in more than just his whitened muzzle—also seemed strangely invigorated since November. He lurched to a halt in the grass, alerted by something. His hackles bristled, and a low, guttural growl rose up in his throat just as Nicole passed. She stopped and looked around, alarmed.

When the dog bolted, Nicole was left standing there dumbfounded.

Her father chuckled from the patio. "What was that all about?"

"I don't know," she said before letting out a nervous laugh.

Then, in the middle of the yard as she turned back toward her course for second period English, something hit her hard and knocked her completely off her feet. Growing up with brothers for eighteen years, Nicole knew too well that she'd been tackled, and although she couldn't fathom who had hit her, she could guess he was about the size of her brother Mitchell. They hit the ground together.

Air flooded back into her lungs in a gasp and she coughed it out again. She heard him curse under his breath. His weight rolled away from her, and she turned onto her side, still trying to catch her breath. Bandit's barking crashed around inside her head.

"My sincerest apologies." He was breathless too and managed

little more than a whisper. It was not her brother's voice or any voice she knew—there was a strangeness to his vowels, some accent she couldn't place. Before she could get a good look at him, he had her by the hand and pulled her to her feet as he stood.

For a moment they were face-to-face, only inches apart, and all she could see were his piercing, blue-green eyes and the auburn hair hanging around them. She couldn't even get a sense of his face—just those eyes. She was startled by that closeness more than being tackled, and she was relieved by the distance between their noses as he straightened up. Instinctively, she stepped back. Finally, she could see the guy who had nearly flattened her.

She couldn't help gawking, only partly because he had undoubtedly come out of thin air. His skin was warm and dark. His eyes were like pools of tropical waters. His nose was straight, and his hair hung around his temples and halfway down the back of his neck. Attractive, she thought, and then dismissed it with a little scowl.

"Where the hell did you come from?"

"I don't think you want to know that," he said, glancing over his shoulder.

The barking hadn't stopped.

"*Bandit*—I'm pretty sure I do." The dog fell silent. "And since you did just tackle me, I think I'm entitled to an answer." She was light and giddy from shock or disbelief or the adrenaline still surging through her. This had to be a dream. *Did I fall back asleep…slip in the shower?*

"Well, it would seem I accidentally ran through a portal."

Her lips parted to speak but froze, she had no words.

"Did he say portal?" her dad asked from the patio.

Of all the things pinging around in her head, what came out was, "How do you accidentally run through a portal?"

"Do you see any portal around here?" He presented the yard around them with a sweep of his hand.

Nicole looked around, patio, Bandit, rose bushes, pool, grass, stranger—nothing else.

"No."

"Precisely."

She scrutinized him for the span of several sharp heartbeats as Bandit approached him curiously, circling and sniffing him thoroughly. Nicole watched her dog inspect his boots and then the bottom of his coat. She half expected him vanish at any moment. She looked back at her dad for affirmation, and the wide-eyed shock on his face confirmed—she hoped—that he had seen what she had seen. In the back of her mind, she realized her dad might have that same look if he were watching her talk to an imaginary person, but she didn't want to go there. He stood there looking as confounded as she felt. Actually, he looked almost catatonic. She turned back to the stranger from the portal, and her dad came closer, his steps slow but steady.

Bandit jumped up, standing on his hind legs and placing his front paws on the stranger's chest. Nicole studied his reaction, seeing the slightest smile as he scratched both sides of the dog's head. Bandit dropped back down to all fours, and those blue-green eyes shifted once again to her and she was at a loss for a proper response.

Then the air quivered like a mirage behind him. A sudden spitting snarl hit her ears, and a twisted, blackened creature crawled through the rippling portal behind the stranger. He jumped away from the creature, nearly pressing his back against her.

"Whoa!" Her dad lurched into reverse, stumbling.

The creature stood on all fours, back arched, like a disfigured primate as tall as the stranger's waist. He took another step back, bumping into her. Until that moment, she hadn't noticed the sword against his back. Now his hand appeared over his shoulder, whipping the sword out of its sheath with a silver flash. She jerked away, startled.

With one swing of the sword, he severed the nearest limb at the creature's shoulder. To Nicole's horror, its flesh merged back together. Another creature emerged from the portal, followed by two more. They did not hesitate. The strange beasts sprang into pursuit of anything that moved.

Nicole wheeled around instinctively as one charged at her. Its weight hit her from behind, knocking her to the ground. She scrambled on her hands and knees beneath its weight, frantically wrestling off her backpack and shedding the creature as she stumbled to her feet. Her heart raced.

At the sound of a yelp, she searched the yard, and her panicked eyes spotted two black beasts tangled together in the grass—one of the strange creatures and her dog. Dread struck her chest, and she could feel her heartbeat crashing inside her skull. Another twisted beast ran for her, gnarled clawed hands tearing through the grass as it sprang at her.

A shrill sound rang in her head and she doubled over, cringing and covering her ears but the sound was inside her, a million tuning rods and nails on chalkboards. Her head pounded with the endless ringing. Had she been hit? She couldn't feel anything. Finally, her head cleared, it was silent. Reluctantly, she pried her eyes open to the bright sunshine and the vivid green grass. The creatures were gone as suddenly as they had appeared. Now there was only a few piles of what looked like soot sitting in the grass. Bandit stood and shook; a cascade of black dust fell from his fur.

"What happened?" Nicole asked.

"They just ... deteriorated," the stranger answered, returning his sword to the sheath on his back. "The magic that made them must have died once they came through the portal."

Nicole frowned, her head still throbbing. She was still confused. What was that awful sound in her head? What did he mean the magic died?

"Nicole! Are you okay?" Her father crossed the yard and scrutinized Nicole with anxious fire in his eyes. He put his hands on her shoulders and turned her around and then back, apparently looking for wounds.

"I'm fine, I promise," she said, gently peeling his hands away. "What were those things?"

"Golems," the stranger answered.

Her dad turned to him. "Golems?"

"Do you have a name?" Nicole wondered.

"Raiden," he said, pushing his hand back through his hair.

"I'm—" why wasn't her name coming to her.

"Nicole?" Raiden guessed with the slightest curl in the corner of his mouth.

"Yeah," she said, flushing. "This is my dad."

"Michael Jameson," Nicole's dad said with such conviction she wondered if he was clinging to the last thing he could be sure he knew.

"I apologize for the trouble I've caused," Raiden said, looking around at the remains of the golems.

From over the back wall of the yard, the forlorn toll of the intercom bell sending students toward their classes reminded Nicole of where she had been going only minutes ago. It sounded much farther away than it ever had on those mornings when she was late and it had signaled her to sprint across the parking lot. Her backpack was a sad, shredded heap in the grass.

She moved toward the bag, her legs weak with much more than physical exertion as she came upon her things. For three and a half years, she practically lived out of that backpack. Binders, books, meals—it contained everything her life was at school and even at home; most of her waking hours were devoted to the contents of that bag. Now it lay ripped and scattered at her feet. Yet to see it destroyed somehow brought to her an absolute, inexplicable relief. The undeniable fact that her life was irrevocably altered—that her monotony had been shattered into fantastic oblivion—left her reeling with giddy anticipation.

Nicole exhaled a laugh only she heard. Without bothering to gather up her things, she scanned the yard and counted black piles scattered around the grass like the remains of small campfires. Eight. More than she remembered seeing as they appeared.

"So," her dad's voice pulled her back to him and Raiden standing there, "should we be expecting any more of those things?"

"They're like puppets, and that was all of them."

"What about you?" Nicole said.

"Me?" There was a hint of amusement in his voice.

"What are you?" She thought it was a valid question given current events. "Better yet, *who* are you?"

"I'm a human—just a nobody from a quiet place called Cantis who happened upon a portal."

"You're the first person from another realm *I've* ever met; I would hardly call you *a nobody*," she said with a nervous laugh. Saying things like this out loud in all seriousness made her feel like reality would start melting around her at any second. *Either this is a coma dream or I'm unhinged.*

"Likewise," he said through a distraction of his own: studying the yard around him, the stuccoed house with its tile roof, the workshop behind her, and her. "I mean"—his eyes sharpened, his focus returning—"It's surreal. This is not at all what I expected today, but it's nice to meet you."

He offered her his hand with a little reluctance, and she didn't hesitate to take it—to know he was tangible.

Three

Raiden took Nicole's hand and fell into a torrent of visions. He caught glimpses of places he did not recognize so quickly that each flash he saw drowned out the last. He tumbled through noise and scenes, grasping for anything, a single moment to focus on, a chance to stop falling, spinning out of control. He saw flash after flash of Nicole, her expression changing. With each glimpse of her, he was drawn toward her eyes, two pools of honey. A flash of brilliant green light washed her away, and he spiraled into darkness and silence, struck repeatedly by sharp bursts of sound and sudden bursts of light. Shards of the future glinting harshly in his eyes as they flew by him so swiftly he could barely register the images—his sword falling bloodied to the ground, Nicole's shocked face, a vast desert plain, Nicole dropping to her knees, so many flashes of blood that his vision went entirely red. And then it stopped.

He saw Nicole again, standing before him. His legs were sturdy beneath him, his feet still planted in the grass, his hand clutching hers. Just once, he shut his eyes hard. The visions were gone; the Sight receded.

"You all right?"

"Yes." He forced a smile, releasing her from his grip. "This is all a little overwhelming."

"Don't get a lot of strangers where you're from?" Michael asked.

The question was heavy and he shifted under its weight. "Not at all."

"And where is it you came from, exactly?" Michael asked.

"That portal will take you to the realm of Veil as we call it. But more specifically, Cantis. It's an island fairly isolated from the mainland."

Michael nodded thoughtfully for a moment. "I see...and when exactly does all this go away and things go back to normal?" There was an uneasy edge to his voice.

Raiden frowned. Back to normal, for him that was an empty city, alone, seeking justice and failing at it. Whatever normal was for Nicole and her father, Raiden had certainly destroyed it. The people in the old world didn't know about Veil—but he couldn't undo shattering their understanding of the world.

"I'm sorry, but I don't know how this portal got here in the first place."

"Do you know how to make it go away?" Michael asked.

Nicole stood there listening and when her eyes shifted from her father to him he found himself thinking of visions instead of answers.

"I, uh, suppose it will go away on its own. Portals aren't common at all anymore, but that's usually how it goes."

"How much time?" Michael pressed.

Raiden pulled his eyes away from the fervent glean in Michael's gaze and instinctually looked back to Nicole. Was that disappointment he saw as they waited for his response?

"It's hard to say. It could be a matter of days or as long as a week before it closes on its own."

Michael's face fell. "I don't have days or a week to sit here worrying about a hole in reality or whatever the hell—I've got the Castillo kitchen behind schedule and Ramon is on paternity leave this month—"

"Dad." Nicole's voice steadied her father a little. "You don't have to sit here worrying about it, what's that going to do?" She turned to Raiden and he blinked, feeling like he'd been caught staring. "Is anything else going to come out of that thing?"

Raiden thought of the desolate island on the other side of the portal. There was literally nothing left there to wander through this portal besides him. Well, and maybe one other person who would certainly be looking for him. Nicole craned her head toward him and raised her eyebrows expectantly for the answer her father needed to hear.

"Nothing," he said.

"There," she said, looking back to her father. "So you can stay home and freak out or go to work where everything make sense."

Michael considered this through a deepening frown. "You're right. I need to do something, but that thing's still…here."

"We'll stay and babysit…portalsit," she said. "We can figure out what to do when you get home?"

Raiden watched as her father scanned the yard, looked at his daughter through several slow breaths. He looked to be gathering up everything he'd seen in the last five minutes and closing it in a box.

"Right," he answered, snapping out of his trance. "That sounds good, kiddo. I'll see you later. I've got my phone," he said, "you know."

"Yeah, I know," she answered.

"Okay, good," Michael said with a curt nod and turned toward the house. His stride was one to escape. He waved as he reached the door, not even turning back to look at them lest the illusion break and he remember. "Be careful."

"I will," she said.

"Okay," he said once more and disappeared into the house.

Nicole shook her head. "This is gonna be tough for him to wrap his head around."

"And what about you?" Raiden wondered.

"I'm still working on it," she admitted, taking it all in again with a look around the yard. "Doesn't seem hard at all for you," she remarked.

"I suppose that's because the existence of the two realms is common knowledge in Veil. Although I certainly wasn't prepared for this visit," he said.

"Do you have to be getting back?" she asked.

Raiden looked over his shoulder at where the portal was, invisible to the eye except for the slightest glimmer of light. "No," he answered, surprising himself. He didn't belong here, but he didn't want to leave. He could stay a while.

"Really? You sure came through that portal hard and fast," she said.

He cringed. "Did I? In my defense, there was a pack of golems on my heels, but I am very sorry about that."

"I grew up with two older brothers," she said a with chuckle. "I couldn't afford to be fragile. Still"—she paused to give him a devious smile—"I think you owe me for that."

He was a little surprised with himself as a smile spread across his face. She had infected him somehow. "Like what?" He laughed. Had it always been so easy to feel like this? He couldn't remember. Not even an hour ago, he had wondered if he was still capable of such things.

"I'll think of something," she promised.

ⲉⲝ

Within the castle of Cantis, an agonized shriek disturbed the silence. It echoed through every cold corridor and wavered through the air of magic-laced halls. Moira stood in the middle of her chamber. The fireplace was bare, all the soot gone, meaning her golems had been awakened. Someone had disturbed her private chamber. There was no trace of her golems anywhere in the room, no remnants of their soot, no body of a slain intruder, but worst of all was what lie at the far end of her chamber—or rather what did not lie where it should have been. Against the far wall stood a pedestal, but absolutely nothing sat upon it.

She crossed the room, trembling as she drew nearer, her greatest fear becoming undeniably clear. Her most precious possession had been stolen. She couldn't fathom who might have done it. The last time she had angered her master had been more than twenty years ago; he certainly had no need to punish her further. There was only a sad handful of people left in Cantis; would any of them even have dared to come here and provoke her after what she and her master had set loose upon the city a decade ago?

At a loss for the answer, she turned to the corner beside the empty pedestal where a tall, narrow mirror leaned, watching the room. She stumbled up to the looking glass, where she saw herself: she was slight—nearly lost in her layers of dark robes—and her long blonde hair, lackluster and graying, lay twisted and draped over her shoulder. For a moment her eyes lingered, gazing into themselves; she had lost so much more than her youth.

With a heavy sigh, she waved her reflection away with a flick of her wrist. The mirror rippled and then revealed the room once more, only she did not see herself before the mirror. She saw the room as it had been while she was away on the mainland. She twirled her finger impatiently to speed up the time as it passed in the mirror. The only indication of time's passage was the uncanny speed at which the candles shrank upon her worktable.

At last she saw the chamber door open in the mirror, and she put up her hand in haste just as a man came into the room. His quickened steps slowed to their natural pace. He looked around the room cautiously. In the fireplace the soot promptly stirred, swelling and taking form, spilling out onto the floor. The intruder reacted quickly, jumping back and casting some defensive spell that slowed his enemy to near stillness. Moira knew this spell and knew it wouldn't last long. He appeared to know that fact all too well. He looked around more anxiously. Was he making the decision to retreat or fight? Then his gaze halted in the direction of the mirror and the pedestal.

While the golems crawled painfully slowly from the fireplace, the stranger walked across the chamber with interest burning in his eyes. Moira inhaled stiffly. *What was this man thinking?* she agonized. *Why was he here?* He slipped mostly from the reflection in the mirror as he approached the pedestal. When he backed into the mirror's reflection once more, his fist contained a smooth, milky white stone. The sight of it wrenched Moira's heart.

The man looked down at the stone, his face crumpled beneath emotions she couldn't read. Then he turned, running for the door as her golems gradually regained their natural momentum. He reached the door, and the golems tore away from the fireplace in pursuit of the thief. Her mirror could show her no more of the past than what it had reflected within the room. She heaved a shaky sigh and waved her hand before the mirror once more. This time the mirror went dark, allowing her to gaze into the tower. She could not see the prisoner, but she heard deep rumbling breaths in the silence and the heavy moan of a large metal chain shifting in the shadows. Her charge was still safe, but that mattered to her master, not her. Now what mattered most was retrieving the stone, her beloved.

❧

"So what *did* you have planned for today before you ended up on the other side of a portal?" Nicole asked. She stooped to retrieve the ripped backpack and redeposit her stuff inside.

"Well, I was trying to get rid of problem but that didn't turn out so well. Most days I spent my time studying spells and putting them to practice. Honestly, that's been my life for almost ten years." Raiden crouched down to assist her, picking up her cell phone and looking at it for a moment.

"Ten years of independent study," Nicole said. "Sounds like more fun than high school. Thank you," she added as he handed her the phone and her sketchbook. "If only spell casting was an elective," she laughed as she slipped her things into the bag and closed the ripped ends together with a firm grip.

"Your hand." Raiden pointed.

She lifted her right hand to examine it. There were angry red scratches and tiny cuts across the knuckles. Soot had clogged most of the bleeding by now. She was astonished that she hadn't noticed. Then again, the rush of adrenaline had not yet receded; her heart was still racing.

"That isn't pretty," she said. "There's a sink in the shop." She lifted the bag in her hand toward the shop—a square building that occupied a quarter of the backyard, with the same peach-painted stucco and burgundy roof tiles as the house.

She opened the door and went inside, Raiden following behind her. As they entered, they passed the worktable to the left and the shoulder-high toolbox. To the right of the door there was a long couch against the wall and in the corner a large, plush chair. What had started as a workshop for her dad had turned into a quasi-pool-house-gym over the years. Nicole tossed her backpack onto the couch, and its contents slid out across the cushion. She proceeded past the red tool box to a large, white sink, while Raiden trailed behind her.

Workout equipment occupied the back half of the shop: a large barbell rack and many black plates, an adjustable bench, and a set of dumbbells ranging from five pounds to fifty.

"What is all that?" he asked.

Nicole turned the knob beside the faucet and put her hand beneath the stream of cold water. "Weights, workout stuff," she answered as she scrubbed her hand gently. "It's for training—building strength, balance, coordination. You know—exercise."

"I see," he said.

She turned off the water and held her hand up once more. It looked even redder and angrier than before now that the soot was gone and the skin was irritated from scrubbing. *Now* the cuts panged and twinged with angry heat. She sighed.

"May I see?" Raiden asked, holding his palm up and waiting for her hand. "I didn't want to distress your father anymore than he was, but that portal out there means there's magic here…somewhere," he explained as she presented her hand and he took it, "and if there's magic here, then I should be able to do this—*haelan*."

The back of Nicole's hand grew warm, tingling to the point of itching furiously. The cuts shrank, the scratches faded, and the redness waned. Her hand appeared perfectly unscathed.

She yanked her hand back to examine it more closely. "That's incredible." She let out a laugh. "Thank you," she added quietly.

"My pleasure," he replied.

"Even with proof like that—" she held up her hand. "—you, those things, that's so hard to believe," she said, shaking her head. "Magic. Here."

"I wouldn't be here if there wasn't," he said.

Nicole couldn't stop marveling at her hand. "Nothing even remotely magical has ever happened here before," she said.

"That makes sense. There isn't usually magic in this realm—hasn't been for a long time."

"I don't understand. Where did it come from then?"

"That's a good question," he said. "Are you sure nothing out of the ordinary has happened recently?"

"You mean besides you, the portal, and our golem friends?"

He smiled. "Right, besides that."

"No—I mean—well, our yard never used to be so green," she said.

He looked out the window behind her at the lush vegetation, looking unimpressed by the lush scene.

She explained. "This is Yuma, Arizona. We're in the middle of the desert. Even for a well-watered yard in the mild winter, that's an unnatural amount of foliage."

"Oh. When did that change?"

"In November—two months ago. The yard started growing like crazy." The more she thought about odd things the more she could list. "Bandit is acting like a puppy again," she said. "The lights in the house have been flickering a lot. Dad has been changing bulbs and chasing wiring problems for weeks. Do you think it's related?"

"I couldn't offer you any other explanation. There has to be a source of magic here for a portal to open between the realms, plain and simple," he said.

"What kind of source are we talking?" She backed up to the

worktable and hopped up, seating herself.

"The last time portals were opening they were caused by colonies of magic folk converging here. There aren't many of them left, but eventually they manage to gather into isolated communities. With enough of them in one place, their combined magic has a tendency to cause natural portals."

Nicole frowned. "What do you mean, left? How did they leave?"

"They weren't wanted in this world. The old religions that had cherished and protected the ways of magic and its denizens were gradually left behind in favor of a new religion. In the beginning, it adopted many of the old religions' celebrations, and as its popularity grew, people drifted away from the old ways. The more powerful this new religion became, the more it sought to attack the old beliefs. It demonized the fey and condemned practitioners of magic as evil. Human belief is a powerful thing. What one man perceives is real to him, and when the majority of men share the same perception ... well, what can the minority do?"

"Are we by any chance talking about Christianity?"

Raiden let out a short, breathy laugh. "Is that what Christendom calls itself now? I suppose it shouldn't be surprising to hear it's alive and well after so many centuries."

"Is this when you tell me about all the creatures and people hunted by Christendom?" she asked, scrunching her nose.

"No," he answered softly. "They left before the hunt could begin. It wasn't hard to see what was coming. People stopped practicing magic openly and banded together for support. The fey retreated deeper into the forests where they would not be found. They left the human world farther and farther behind, and the magic went with them. As they congregated, something strange happened. They started slipping away from this world."

"So magic disappeared," Nicole said.

"And Veil was born," he added with a nod. "Veil was constantly changing those first few centuries. It was possible to travel between the realms as though they were neighboring lands. But as the environment here grew more hostile toward their kind, more and more of them retreated to the safety of Veil. They actually called it Veiligland, the safe land. The more of them retreated into Veil, the less magic there was left here, and it became ... difficult to return. Most people in Veil realized it was for the best."

"Most," Nicole repeated with a curious tone. "Not everyone thought so?"

"In the early days, there were those who saw Veil as a sort of exile. As centuries passed, Veil became home to new generations who knew nothing of the old realm. Hardly anyone spares a thought for the old days now. We learn about Veil's origin in primary school, of course, but few people harbor any illusions about things going back to the way they were."

"Christianity really boomed around the sixth century," Nicole said. "So that would make Veil something like"—she paused to do the math—"fifteen hundred years old?"

"Thereabouts," he agreed. "I'm no historian, I leave that to the books. Most of my studies favor the natural sciences, spell theory, casting—that sort of thing."

"Wow." The word whooshed out of her mouth on a sigh. "I can't believe I'm sitting here having this conversation." She shook her head dreamily.

"I'm still disoriented myself to be honest," he said, glancing out the window once more toward the portal.

"Wait." Nicole's voice went up an octave, and she straightened where she sat. "We have a portal in the middle of our yard. Wouldn't we notice an entire community of magical folk somewhere nearby?" She felt a little disappointed, like something spectacular had been under her nose this whole time and she was the fool completely unaware, incapable of seeing magic. She had always thought of herself as someone who would, her heart always aching for something different.

"I dare say you would. The portal would indicate the epicenter of magical activity. So whatever the cause, it has to be *here*," he said.

"Here," she repeated. Nicole looked around the silent interior of the shop. Nothing moved. Even now with her newfound knowledge, nothing around her appeared strange. Her eyes swept the entire room until they came back to Raiden. "It can't be you—you just got here," she said, meaning she was the only other option, and the thought made her laugh. "It can't be me, because let's face it—I think in eighteen years I would have noticed something that interesting about myself."

"I don't even know that it could be just one person," he mused. "That would make them … immensely powerful. It usually takes hundreds of fey living together to open a portal. At least that's what the books say."

"Hundreds of fey? Are they really that good at hiding that they could be right on top of us, or below us and we'd never know?"

"I'm not sure that is what we're dealing with here." He shook his head.

"Then I guess it's time to start looking," she said.

"I suppose so," he said. "You are probably a far better judge of what is normal and what is out of the ordinary here."

"That's me. Normal girl ordinaire," she said as she hopped down from the counter. "If there's anything I know well, it's all things unremarkable," she said with a sigh as they went back outside together.

Four

R aiden couldn't understand why there was nothing to be found anywhere around the portal.

"Are you satisfied yet? There is nothing magical here other than an overgrown yard and a portal," Nicole said with a sigh as they finished their third circuit of the backyard. There hadn't been a single sign of even a nymph, fairy, or gnome—he couldn't understand it.

"Maybe they're further away," he mused to himself. "More spread out around this focal point, beyond these walls."

The vision he had experienced upon meeting Nicole kept slithering back into his mind, troubling him. Something was going on around here, something had caused that portal to open, and somehow it would lead to—well, he wasn't entirely sure; but he knew there was chaos and spilled blood in Nicole's future.

"That's the only possibility that makes sense," Raiden muttered. His shoulders sagged. They drifted onto the patio and sank into a couple of chairs arranged around a fire pit.

"What about possibilities that don't make sense?" Nicole leaned back and tipped her chair back onto its rear legs.

He watched her long brown curls swaying behind her as she rocked, her gaze lost somewhere in the sky above. Then she gasped and let the chair drop onto all four legs.

"A dragon," Nicole said with bright eyes.

"Sorry, but that's even less likely than a fairy court," he said with a dry laugh.

"Oh," she said with such a look of disappointment that he couldn't help being intrigued by her expression. "Don't mind me. You didn't just crush a childhood dream or anything," she said, waving her hand.

"Really? Dragons? Of all things you dreamed of dragons?" He wondered if he should tell her.

"They can breathe fire and fly," she said. "What can I say? I grew up with brothers," she added with a nostalgic laugh.

"They don't all do those things," he said.

"Fine," she said. "If it can't be a dragon, what else?"

"I don't know." He drew out the last word in frustration. Abandoning logic and reason did not come easily to him. He sighed and then remembered a possibility. "There is something," he said but immediately doubted the idea.

"Let's hear it," Nicole said.

"Several decades ago there was a"—he searched for the right word—"nuisance in Veil. A number of dangerous beings with too much power to control were wreaking havoc anywhere they went. They were called the fera. The books say they were a danger to themselves and others; but the Council took care of that problem. They're gone now."

"You sound skeptical," Nicole said. "Do you think they really took care of it?"

"I believe they're gone. All accounts say they were so volatile they could hardly hide for long without causing a disturbance, and there hasn't been any sign of them since. But I do wonder about the truth in the Council's reasoning for what had to be done. When all the sources insist it was done to protect the people of Veil … well, I can't help questioning that. Either way, it could be possible—if any fera were still out there—that one found its way here in an attempt to escape. It would explain the sudden changes around here."

"If this Council of yours is out to get the fera, does that make it a friend or foe?" Nicole asked.

Raiden frowned, inclined to consider any foe of the Council a friend of his, but the stories about the fera were terrible. He could honestly say, "A fera is not someone you want as a foe."

"Friend it is then," Nicole said. "How do we know it when we see it?"

"That's one of the problems. They look like ordinary people. But as long as it's been since a fera has been sighted, it would have to be quite old, I would think. Very little is known about them, I honestly can't tell you much more," he said.

He hated that he couldn't figure this out, that he couldn't help her after throwing her world into complete upheaval. The thought of saying goodbye to her, leaving her and her father here with the source of the portal unknown, it troubled him more than his unfinished business back in Cantis. He had no way of knowing if it was better for her if he stayed or if he left. He didn't know if the danger in her future followed him through the portal or was no fault of his own. Even if it wasn't his fault, having seen those things in her future weighed him down with a sense of responsibility to try to change it.

"Isn't that great," she muttered.

"For all we know, it could be gone already, or the cause could be something else entirely," he offered hopefully.

"Dad will be happy to hear that," Nicole said with false cheer.

He sighed. "There's still a portal here, and that's a problem."

"It's not your fault," she said, shaking her head. "Just because you stumbled upon it doesn't make it your responsibility."

"But I'd like to help. I could stay—to keep an eye on the portal, find out what's going on here." If he was being honest with himself, he didn't want this to slip away as suddenly as it had happened. He enjoyed this—conversation with a living person, laughing again—and he didn't want to leave if something potentially dangerous might be lurking near Nicole and her family.

"You won't hear me complain," she said with a shrug. "When

you leave and that portal goes away, life goes back to normal."

"You don't like normal."

"It's fine. But I think I like this more. Frankly, I expect to wake up in the hospital. We could go upstairs and see if my body is unconscious in the bathroom."

She perplexed him in a way that made him want to smile. "You lost me."

She chuckled. "Or we could just sit here and babysit the portal until Dad gets home."

Raiden bobbed his head in approval. "All right then." Spending a day with her could be a risk, could Moira find him here? But maybe it couldn't hurt, and he was selfish enough to risk it because he liked this surreal escape from the world he had known. Even when their conversation fell quiet it was nothing like the silence waiting for him back home.

❧

"There's no way to get rid of it?" Michael asked with a frown. When he had returned home at five thirty there had been optimism in his voice. Raiden felt guilty for having to dash it so swiftly. The three of them stood facing each other on the patio.

"There's a way to close it," Raiden said, "but without knowing the cause, you might just end up with another one two days later."

"The good news is there aren't any magical creatures in the backyard and nothing has come through the portal all day," Nicole added.

"We could close the portal and see if it stays closed, then it's likely whatever it is has already moved on." And a portal wouldn't open again, he wouldn't see Nicole again. "However, if another were to open, then we would know the source is still nearby," Raiden said.

"I just want to know what's going on here," Michael said. "We can't ignore this and go about our lives." The frown on his face hardened.

"Dad," Nicole said, placing a hand on his shoulder, "we'll figure this out." She turned to Raiden with a question in her eyes. "Right?"

"Of course," he said. "I can retrieve the books I have on portals tomorrow."

"Tomorrow," Michael repeated. "Good. Uh … I guess that means you'll need a place to sleep tonight?" He scratched his head, looking unsure. "There's a couch in the shop there," he suggested with a nod toward the shop.

Nicole gave her father a swift look of surprise and Raiden pretended not to see. He supposed the offer was balanced precariously between mistrusting a stranger and fearing the presence of the portal without someone around who knew what to do.

"That's perfect," Raiden accepted. "That way I'll be close to the portal in case anything were to happen—not that I think anything will," he insisted.

"That's settled then," Nicole said, coaxing her dad on to some other thought. "What do you think, Dad—should we have a fire tonight?"

"Oh, sure," he said, nodding. His gaze was far away.

"What about dinner?" she asked.

Raiden hadn't realized how hungry he was until now. How had he spent all day with her without noticing he hadn't eaten?

"Dinner. Right." Michael sounded defeated. "How about we order a pizza?"

Nicole smiled. "We have definitely earned pizza."

"Two large veggie monsters?" His voice perked up, and his smile finally broke through his trance of worry.

"Perfect," she agreed with a nod.

Michael pulled a small device like the one Nicole had from his pocket and began tapping it. Raiden watched him for a moment, trying to understand the rectangular mirror producing shapes and color in reaction to his touch.

"What is pizza?" Raiden asked, repeating the unfamiliar word awkwardly.

"It's a big round, flat bread with tomato sauce and all sorts of toppings on it. Easy on the cheese, Dad," she said, raising her voice to Michael. He acknowledged with a nod and a little wave.

"Yes, extra veggies and easy on the cheese." Michael bobbed his head as he listened.

"You'll see." Nicole turned back to Raiden. "Everyone likes pizza. It's even better the next day when it's cold, right out of the fridge."

Raiden just nodded through his confusion. "I'll take your word for it."

"All right then. Pizza should be here in twenty minutes," Michael announced. "Let's get this fire going, shall we?"

The sun was down, and the temperature dropped swiftly as the wood in the pit caught fire. Nicole and Raiden stood close, waiting for the flames to grow. As its heat expanded, they stepped back and each pulled a chair into place. Nicole sat across the fire from him, and kept her eyes directed at the flames hoping to burn away their interest in him. Occasionally, she glanced up at Raiden and watched the flames in his eyes.

Raiden looked up and caught her gaze before she could drop it back into the fire. She scooted her chair a little farther away from the fire as the flames grew hotter. Her dad returned with two pizza boxes and placed them on the nearby picnic table.

"Come get it while it's hot," Michael said as he opened the top box.

"Thanks Dad," Nicole said, hopping up to grab a slice and sit back down.

"Raiden," Michael said, waving him over.

"It's not too often you get to see someone trying pizza for the first time ever," Nicole remarked as Raiden got up and took a slice of pizza for himself. Michael took a slice for himself, holding his slice of pizza slightly folded in one hand. Raiden mimicked him and took a bite.

"Well, what do you think?" her dad asked.

Raiden nodded, eyes round, and Nicole laughed.

"Pizza never fails," Michael said before taking a bite for himself.

They sat around the fire, listening to the spits and crackles of the perishing wood over the sound of their chewing. The smell of wood smoke and pizza mingled in the cold air. The warm peace around the fire seemed even more unreal than the events of the day. Nicole wasn't sure if she should trust it.

Michael looked up at what stars managed to shrine through the street lights and pointed out Orion. Raiden and Nicole looked up. She wondered if the stars in the other realm were the same as the ones overhead, or were there entirely different constellations there?

As the fire reduced to red embers, they all pulled their chairs closer to the shrinking heat. It was silent without the whispers of the flames.

Michael broke the silence. "Why is it you're so interested in helping us, Raiden?"

Nicole lifted her chin off her knees and looked curiously at Raiden as he met Michael's eye.

"There was a time when things took a turn toward the worse, and there was no one there to help me and my mother," Raiden answered and then dropped his gaze back to the dying fire.

Michael raised his hand. "Say no more." There was gentle gratitude in his silence, but she could still hear her father's discomfort. Raiden came from another realm, her dad didn't want to know what horrors might have come for them; knowing would make that nightmare too real, give it the power to come for him and his daughter. There was a fragile sense of safety in not knowing what was out there. "I think I'm gonna call it a night." He stood up slowly.

"See you in the morning," Nicole said and leaned her head back.

Michael bent over her and planted a kiss on her forehead. "Good night, hon."

"Night, Dad," she replied.

Michael disappeared into the house, leaving Nicole and Raiden to the silence of the embers.

"It seems weird," Nicole said, "to just go to bed like normal after such a bizarre day." Truth be told she didn't want to risk going to sleep and waking up to find herself back where she started this morning, another day like every other day with nothing to offer her but the same path forward, a tunnel with no windows or doors.

"Hopefully, tomorrow we'll figure out what's going on here." Raiden sounded optimistic to Nicole, but the way he frowned at the fire's remnants made her wonder if it would be as easy as saying so. His answer lingered in her head, churning a curiosity to know more about him. Something happened to him and his mother that made him want to help total strangers, she wondered how bad that something had to be to care so much about people he didn't know, to leave behind his home, and take on something as big as this mysterious portal. Her gaze lingered on his face until he glanced up at her and she blamed the fire for the heat in her face as she pulled her gaze away.

Five

Nicole turned over beneath her blanket for what had to be the hundredth time. From the moment she laid her head on her pillow, she worried that sleep might erase all traces of the day's events from her world and her memory. She did not want to wake up to find her life was unchanged. Somehow, despite exhaustion thick in her head, her body hummed with restlessness, her skin itched. The best she could do was doze in short bursts, her mind resisting peace, racing through the day again and again until her heart raced too. At long last, she heaved a sigh of frustration and decided it was time to abandon her bed.

The darkness before dawn was familiar to Nicole. Even though it was the middle of the night, she fell easily into her usual routine. What could she do? Her body was restless and would not let her sleep. She thought maybe a little run might do the trick. Muscle memory guided her to her clothes and her shoes in the dark of her room. She had no desire to flood her eyes with light, they were adjusted enough to what little light crept through her window from the neighborhood streetlights. If she was lucky, after a couple miles at the best pace she could muster, she might be capable of collapsing into sleep.

As she crept down the stairs, the digital clock glowed blue over the stove in the kitchen. It was four o'clock, only two hours earlier than her usual wake-up time.

Lying back on the couch in the shop, Raiden peered up at the ceiling. He'd been lying in the dark for hours—nearly every night for years, actually. He was comfortable in the dark. He could stare into it forever, but he was always leery about closing his eyes. His body pleaded for rest, but desperation to put off sleep propelled him upright and off the couch. Outside in the yard, a street lamp on the other side of the wall dropped its orange glow into the yard.

As he stood outside in the chill of the lamplight, he heard a doorknob turn and hinges creak.

"All right, come on then." It was Nicole's hushed voice accompanied by the faint jingle Raiden recognized as the dog's collar.

He didn't know what time it was—it was either extremely late or very early. "Nicole?"

There came a short gasp. The street lamp flickered, and Bandit gave a low woof.

"What are you doing out here?" she hissed through the quiet night.

"The same thing as you," he said. "Not sleeping. Is something wrong?"

"I've been tossing and turning all night, so I gave up trying." She took a deep breath and let it out. "Then Bandit wanted to go out, and you scared the life out of me."

"Sorry about that."

"No worries, I was planning on getting my heart rate up anyway," she said with a soft laugh. "You mind if he sticks with you while I'm gone?" She nodded toward Bandit, a black shadow in the darkness sniffing around Raiden's feet.

"Not at all," Raiden answered. "Where are you going at this hour?"

"Oh, just around," she said with a shrug. "To run a few miles. I take that street behind the house around the school and over to the canal nearby."

"To run?"

"Yes," she said.

"For no other reason?"

Her laugh permeated the darkness. "None other than to be alone with my thoughts, sweat out my frustrations, or in this case to escape this weird buzzing feeling that's kept me up all night."

"I see. Well, be careful. There's still an unknown source of magic out there."

"I'll keep my eye out for anything strange," she promised with a chuckle. She turned, and her shadowy form disappeared around the side of the house.

"Well then," Raiden said to Bandit, "let's find something to do." The dog followed him back into the shop, where he turned on the light. He was blinded by the white brightness flickering into full force. Bandit jumped onto the couch where Raiden's coat lay draped over the armrest. The sound of paper crinkling beneath the dog's weight reminded Raiden of the letter from the Council. Curiosity drew him in, calling his hand to retrieve it.

Whatever it was the Council wanted, Raiden already knew he wanted no part of it, but he did wonder what they wanted from him. What request, or demands, would he have the pleasure of refusing? The wet edges of the paper were long dry and he opened the envelope, he plucked the letter from inside and shook it open brusquely.

Raiden Aldor Cael,

We are pleased to honor you with an invitation to serve the realm as one of the Council's soldiers of peace.

Invitation—that was a joke. Everybody knew that the Council conscripted whoever they pleased. They had deluded plenty of men and women into thinking everything the Council did was righteous. So why did they want him? Was it because his father had been one of them? Or did they know he had the Sight? No, if they knew, he would be in the courts by now, no letters. Most of the seers in the realm belonged to the Council. He continued reading.

> An urgent matter has arisen that requires our involvement in Cantis. Under these pressing circumstances, you will be considered an active agent without introductory training. It has come to our attention that a portal between the two realms has opened, or will do so in the immediate future. Although the precise time is unknown to our seers, the location is clear. We are quite certain that the source of this portal is an individual of terrible potential. We require your assistance in escorting this entity to Atrium. Due to the severe nature of this situation, we can reveal that this person is a threat to both realms. Although it is widely accepted that the beings known as fera were dealt with years ago, we can confirm in the strictest confidence that there remains one that evaded our grasp. It has been the pursuit of the Council since the fera's first appearance to nullify the threat their kind poses to innocent people. As the Council takes responsibility for beings of magic in both realms, it will be your duty to safely transport the fera in question into the custody of the Council.
>
> For your diligence under these unique conditions, you will be permitted to bypass initial training and be immediately assigned to patrol a district here in Atrium. We look forward to your arrival and wish you fortune in this endeavor.
>
> Council Scribe Office
> Atrium City Courts

His hands, still clutching the letter, fell limp into his lap—his mind revived the vision he had seen when he met Nicole. Unease spread through his chest like a pestilence. It had to be her, but if she really was a fera, how could she not know? How could anyone live eighteen years without knowing—without discovering—unless it had been hidden from her this whole time, her power contained somehow. That had to mean it was now surfacing.

Raiden dropped the letter and jumped to his feet. He wrenched the door open and plunged into the night after Nicole. As he rounded the back corner of the house and sprinted toward the gate, his heart sank with dread; he had no way of knowing which direction she had gone. The metal gate whined. As he pulled, the gate seemed to resist him, and when he released it, it pulled itself shut with the help of a metal spring. A sharp clang from the closing gate rang out behind him as he ran into the street. His frantic gaze swept from one end of the street to the other past the fronts of quiet houses. He saw no movement.

Then the flicker of a street lamp called his attention to the left. The lamp at the far end of the street flickered again, and something lay slumped in the road in the pool of its failing light. He bolted, appalled that his eyes had slipped right past her the first time.

She was four houses away, and all Raiden could fathom was that something terrible was happening now. What would happen to a body containing hidden power as it overcame its bounds? As his feet struck the ground and air rasped in his lungs, he felt dread weighing him down. He could see her writhe in the light, and as it flickered her movements flashed in his eyes. His stomach clenched with vertigo as he ran and fought the Sight trying to crawl into his head. Her agony was obvious, answering his question, her body might not withstand this power emerging. It took only seconds to reach her, but each one felt too slow. If he had read that letter sooner, could she have avoided this?

"Nicole." Her name came hushed between his heaving breaths.

She struggled against the pain, trying to pick herself up. He took her arm and placed it around his neck, and as he stood, she rose alongside him. He couldn't walk her back, so he held tight to her and let the desperate need to get her to the portal spark the magic that pulled them into the ether together—but as they slipped through the ether he felt a violent shudder and they emerged outside the gate. His thoughts jarred with confusion—she had disrupted their shifting to the portal.

"Nicole, can you hear me?"

Her slow nod was her only response as she cringed. Her head hung forward.

"We need to get to the portal. Do you understand?"

"Why?" Her voice was little more than a whimper.

"You're the one who opened the portal, Nicole, and I think your magic is trying to get free," he explained.

He set her down reluctantly so that he could open the gate, fumbling with the unfamiliar latch. Her legs buckled, and her whole body sank he lurched to catch her and scooped her up into his arms entirely. She shuddered in his arms and a hot wave of crackling energy rolled out of her, crashing through him like a current of wildfire. He felt the heat of it all the way to his bones—this was the magic attempting to force its way out. He nearly collapsed under Nicole's weight as he endured the burn of her power.

He pushed the gate open and stumbled for a couple strides as he heaved her weight higher against his chest. Another convulsion and pulse of heat hit him. He almost sank to the ground again, leaning against the wall for a moment of support. The wave of heat passed. He could feel the cold air against his skin again. Clutching her in his arms, he ran as fast as he could. As he crossed the grass the streetlight peering over the back wall went out with a ferocious pop and the darkness snapped shut around them. There was no clue to the portal's presence in the air.

Nicole squirmed in his arms, pushing away from his chest. "Put me down," she whimpered, her words barely audible over the rasp of his breathing. He set her down rather than let her fall from his arms, but she sank to the grass, curling into a ball of misery, surrendering to the pain—her magic trying to tear its way free.

"No—Nicole. We need to find the portal," he insisted, pulling her back up by the arm.

She stood, the effort shaking her body, unable to straighten up completely as she nodded. She put a hand on his shoulder and straightened herself up with some renewed strength.

"It was there," she said. She reached out, stepped away from him, and swayed on unsteady legs.

His grip caught her arm as she leaned too far forward. Her momentum pulled him off balance, and they fell through the portal.

The next thing Nicole knew she was on the ground, gasping. The cold air flooded her lungs. She heard Raiden's sigh of relief beside her and, from the corner of her eye, saw him sink to the ground in exhaustion. The air slithered through her clothes like breaths of ice, chilling her to the bone despite the morning light pouring over them—its warmth was thin and weak. A shiver shook her. She took a deep breath; every cell, every molecule of her body ached. Another shudder against the cold rattled her, awakening a primal force within her. A soothing wave of drowsy warmth bloomed from her core, spreading through her like a balm, and her body stopped aching—no more coursing pain, no more buzzing restlessness.

Somewhere in the back of her mind, she knew she should not allow herself to sleep—they were outside lying in the dirt—but her limbs were too heavy to move, exhaustion was thick in her head, and the strange new force inside her swept her up into an inescapable slumber.

❦

In the castle above, a tremor of magic made the walls shudder, and Moira lifted her head off her worktable. She had been up all night, unable to sleep through her distress. Suspicious, she stood and moved stiffly to the window. There was nothing to see out in the forest except the sea of leafless branches in the morning light. A gentle, icy breeze wafted up from below. Then, suddenly, the biting air became warm against her face, and she felt heavy and groggy. She knew magic when it hit her, and her long night left her too weak to resist the strange sleeping spell that slithered in on the wind. She turned toward her bed and dragged her feet across the chamber. She barely made it, falling across the foot of the bed before the drowsy magic dragged her mind down into slumber.

ↄ

Nicole surfaced from a strange dream. Before she even opened her eyes, she knew she'd overslept. It was bright. Light turned the inside of her eyelids red. As she moved, her senses returned to her. Shoes on her feet and the snug compression of running tights hugging her legs left her confused. Instead of sliding against soft sheets, her hand felt a layer of cool dirt. Her fingers closed around a handful of fine, silky fine earth.

She opened her eyes to a blue sky. As she positioned her hands to push herself up, her palm pressed against a stone. Curious, she closed her fingers around it and turned it over in her hand. It was oblong and smooth like a river stone. Still groggy, she wasn't sure she could trust her senses. This stone, although firm in her hand, appeared to move like swirling smoke trapped within a transparent prison—she had to be asleep still.

A cold gust of wind rustled her hair. She shivered, looking around. Her posture went rigid in surprise when she saw Raiden lying beside her, asleep. Her memories surfaced from the muck of sleep with a jolt at the sight of him—everything that happened yesterday, the portal, him, the golems. It all came back to her—waking up in the middle of the night, getting dressed, finding Raiden outside, leaving to run, and then …

She looked down at the peculiar stone again before tucking it safely into the pocket of her running jacket—why not keep a peculiar souvenir for a bizarre day.

"Raiden," she whispered, and then wondered what need she had for whispering. "Raiden," she said clearly, pressing her fingertips against his chest for a moment.

Her jerked upright, his eyes wide and blinking. She yanked her hand back and leaned away.

"Nicole," he said, confusion in his voice.

"How did we fall *asleep* here?" she wondered, standing up and swatting the dirt off her clothes.

"I would guess it has something to do with the residue of magic

41

in my eyes." He rubbed his eye with his knuckle.

"You mean like a sleeping spell?" she joked, offering her hand.

"Exactly," he said as he took her hand and she helped him up.

"How can you tell?" she asked, her attention slipping as she noticed his eyes scanning around them.

"There's a kind of glimmer in your vision when you first wake up from a spell-induced sleep," he said. She heard him but found herself preoccupied with her surroundings. She knew they were outside, but it only now occurred to her that they weren't in Yuma, they were in Veil. She was standing in another realm. An unstable laugh expanded in her lungs and swelled up her throat but stopped behind her lips.

As she turned around, she was confronted by a vast wall of gray rock that seemed to reach upward for miles. Great, swirling veins of minerals turned a door-sized spot on the cliff face into a smooth painted canvas of stone. Her eyes followed the anomaly upward to the rough rock above and on to the top; then her gaze was lost above in the bluest sky she'd ever seen.

She shook her head in disbelief as she turned around and saw the forest of tall, slender trees with smooth white bark. A golden carpet of leaves covered the ground, still newly fallen. The wintery breeze rustled the leaves, and though the air was cold, it felt strangely welcoming to Nicole. She felt revived. In a way she could not define, her body seemed entirely new.

"Nicole?" Raiden's voice broke through her reverie.

"Hmm?" She looked at him and got the feeling he'd said her name more than once.

"I asked if you're feeling all right," he said.

"I feel fine," she answered. That was an understatement; actually, she felt incredible—invigorated. "How did we get here?"

"You don't remember?"

"I remember running down the street, and my body just … seized up in pain. It felt like my bones were burning. That's it—it was like waves of fire. Then it just stopped, and I remember being achy, cold, and tired," she said with a sigh.

"I think it's safe to say who cast that sleep spell," he said, brushing the dirt from his arms.

"I did that?"

He smiled. "Not bad for your first spell."

"Me," she said, still not believing. The idea was both absolutely absurd and perfectly wonderful. She laughed. "Wait. *What?*"

"You're the one who caused all this portal trouble," he said. "Sure seems like we're dealing with a fera after all."

"No, but—I've never—what does that even mean? What am I now?"

"What do you mean? You're exactly what you were yesterday," he said.

"No," she said, shaking her head. "Yesterday I was a senior in high school; I was a girl like any other girl, living the same life, following the same path to a high school diploma and a state university." Her heart pounded. Her blood raced. Here she stood in another world, another life. Today she was someone—something?—different.

"What I meant is this is what you've always been; you just didn't know until now," he said carefully.

Nicole shook her head. "You think you know who you are…"

"I know the feeling," he muttered.

"I guess I've got a lot to learn about myself."

Raiden smiled at her. "Might as well start now, right?"

Six

Nicole took in the forest before her, a scene right out of a story book, and she couldn't help smiling. "So this is Veil."

He nodded. "This is Veil."

"It's so quiet," she remarked. "Where do you live? In a cottage in the woods?"

"In a way I live in the woods," he said with a laugh. "I spend a lot of time out there in the trees, but if you mean to ask where I eat and sleep, that's in the city."

"Where is that?" She looked around and saw only the expanse of bare trees extending before her.

"You won't see it from here. It's beyond the woods." He raised his hand and pointed in the direction of the city.

"Let's go then," she said, marching into the trees without hesitation, leaves hissing and crunching under her feet.

Raiden lurched after her and caught her by the hand. "It's not a pleasant place to be."

"Neither is Yuma in the summer," she scoffed, rolling her eyes.

"It's empty, Nicole. There's no one there." His hand remained locked on hers, anchoring her to him.

"But you live there," she said. Their arms were taut between them, caught between her desire to go and his to make her stay.

"Yes, I do."

"You're telling me you live in an empty city all alone?"

He nodded.

"Care to explain?"

Raiden released her hand. He turned and looked up over his shoulder. Behind them towered the great cliff, and now Nicole could see that an old castle stood at the top.

He turned away from the castle and faced her. "Everyone was killed," he said. As he proceeded into the woods, she noticed he wasn't heading toward the city; in fact, his path seemed deliberately angled away from the direction he had indicated just minutes ago.

Her shock fell from her mouth on an exhale. She shook it off and followed. "That's awful. When did it happen?"

"Nine years ago," he said.

"But—who would do that? Why?" her voice trembled with outrage.

"I resigned myself to never knowing the reason. The person who did it, however, happens to live right up there." He nodded his head back at the castle behind them. Farther from the cliff now, they had a much better view of the deteriorating structure, still spectacular and strangely sinister with its opulence glinting in the sunlight. Raiden continued and Nicole noticed his voice had faded with distance. She pulled her gaze away from the hypnotic pull of the castle's crumbling beauty and jogged to catch up.

"The castle was abandoned during the Dragon Wars. After the wars passed, the kingdoms of Veil united and abolished their monarchies to form the Order of the Council. Cantis, however, had no royal family left and was mostly forgotten."

They wove around the slender white trunks of the trees. Nicole watched Raiden touch each one as though acknowledging a dear old friend. The unseen path he followed curved so that Nicole only had to turn her head up to the left to see the castle now. As they walked, she shifted her gaze periodically to look with distrust toward the gilded spires watching them from atop the cliff. The magnificent structure, despite its inhabitant, still held a compelling attraction for Nicole.

"It's important to know that Cantis is an island and the farthest, most secluded region in Veil. Those seeking refuge from the Council found their way here. Remember those people I told you about, the ones who think of this realm as exile from the old world?"

"Yes," she replied, looking down to match her footsteps to his as they navigated through an outcrop of large rocks.

"That belief is still firmly held by a syndicate of sorcery which calls itself Dawn. They arrived in Cantis ten years ago and appropriated the old castle for their purposes."

The earth sloped downward for several strides and then back up to a small ridge that looked over a stream. Raiden sat down at the edge, letting his feet dangle over the ridge. Nicole sat beside him, swinging her feet somberly and waiting for him to continue.

"They were here almost a year. Residents who had been unnerved by Dawn's presence began to relax and accept it. Some people who had been concerned with Dawn's activity left Cantis altogether, if they could afford to. For the most part, Cantis lay beyond the influence of the Council on the mainland."

"How do you forget about an entire place?" Nicole muttered in disbelief.

"War does that to people. They can only see their own hardships. After the wars, the people here had no desire to uproot themselves. Other than losing its royal family, Cantis suffered relatively little since they put up no fight when the dragons arrived, and other than the disposal of the royal family, there was little violence needed to seize control here. After Cantis fell, the rest of Veil knew what was coming and naturally they prepared to fight. The other kingdoms suffered far greater hardships and an incredible loss of lives.

"After the wars, people in Cantis thought they were lucky and safe out here. Being forgotten mattered little to their way of life. They didn't have to deal with the changes of the Council. As far as I know, only one person knew what lay in store for the people here, and she kept it to herself. Perhaps she thought no one would believe her, or she didn't see it coming until it was too late. She even kept it from me, and I don't know if I will ever forgive my mother for that," he confessed quietly.

Nicole looked at him, but he kept his gaze in the distance. "She saved you." She felt compelled to say it, to appreciate it.

"Yes, she protected me from sharing her fate and secured a life of solitude among the dead for me. She left me completely alone." Nicole was studying his profile when he turned his face to her and looked into her eyes. She had no choice but to look directly into his.

She noted every ridge and valley of his turquoise irises. As her gaze shifted from one eye to the other, she saw his eyes make the same subtle shifts as he studied her back—their gazes locked for only a second or two. Then he turned away and looked back out over the stream.

Nicole couldn't stand to hear anymore, it felt cruel to make him relive it. He'd spent nine years with those ghosts and he looked defeated by them.

"You're the first living person I've known since then," he said with a laugh that came without a smile.

"Is human company everything you remember it to be?" she asked, hoping that was the right turn in the conversation.

"Far better, actually," he said, and a timid smile spread across his face, only half of which Nicole could see. The heavy silence of his last nine years seemed to live in his face, but his smile was transformative.

Suddenly, a frightening thought crossed her mind. "Am I still human?"

Raiden laughed; the sound instantly eased the tension in her shoulders. "Of course you are," his tone was aghast, and he finally looked at her.

"You can't blame me for wondering," she said, folding her arms against the chill in the air.

Nicole leaned forward to peer over the ridge. From where her feet dangled, it was only a short distance to the stream bank below.

She positioned her hands at the edge of the ridge and heaved her weight forward, dropping no more than four feet.

"How does someone like that—like me—end up in a realm without magic, anyway?" she wondered.

Raiden dropped down beside her; the stones clicked and grumbled under his feet.

"I *was* born there," she added, "unless my dad has been keeping something from me."

"You are not the only person in your realm capable of magic. You were just too powerful for that world to suppress. Any number of people born in the other realm could have some magic in them, and they might discover it if they had the opportunity. Just because people stopped using magic in favor of new beliefs doesn't mean the ability died with the practice."

"I haven't been practicing anything. It came out of nowhere. How does that happen?"

"Some people just have a natural affinity for things embedded deep in who they are. And as I've read, the soul—like any living thing—does not live and die just once. Every living organism lives again in some form or another after it dies. Death is just Life changing form."

"You're talking about reincarnation," she said.

"Precisely," he answered.

She folded her arms and raised her eyebrows. "That's a real thing?"

"Well, I've read a few necromancers' studies and autobiographies. Not to mention I've had the displeasure of a death keeper's company for nearly a decade."

"A death keeper?"

"Yes. I believe Christendom would have referred to him as an angel of death, a being who guides the souls of those who've passed into death. The Christians fancied that every magical being was either an angel of their God or a devil. Most magic folk and creatures were unfortunate to be considered devils, with the exception of the flying fey." He stopped to chuckle. "They didn't leave the old realm before they were dubbed angels of 'the one true god.' They never much cared for the name as I understand it."

"Who?" she asked.

"The *solis filiis*, the celestial fey, flying folk—they have many names, but they rather despised being called angels, as it means 'messenger.' They are beings of absolute freedom, lovers of the winds. They didn't appreciate being considered the servants of humanity's newest god. Frankly, I think they were so used to being revered as gods themselves that they resented the demotion." He laughed, and Nicole couldn't help laughing too.

"I guess I don't blame them. But I am a little surprised at how well acquainted you seem to be with Christianity for someone who claims not to be a history buff."

"I think most people in Veil know this well enough. A group of people will not easily forget injustices or their transgressors. It's the type of history that endures the passing of generations. In the beginning, it's what united them all. Veil began as a place of safety and hope. They even erected a shining palace, believing it was the start of a peaceful kingdom for them … huh," he said, "maybe I *have* spent too much time with books."

Nicole smiled, holding back a laugh.

"Well, either way, that ideology didn't last," he admitted.

"Let me guess—it ended right about when they finished and realized they had to decide who was going to be king?" She knew the scenario well enough. She and her brothers could work together to build a great couch fort, but the moment it was finished, the arguing about who got the best spot inside would begin.

"Exactly," he said with slant on his mouth. "Before long, the realm divided into nine kingdoms."

They came to a loud rushing as the rocky ground shot upward and the streamed met a pile of smooth, water-worn boulders. The water gurgled and tumbled over the falls from a height just over their heads.

"When have people ever been able to avoid conflict?" Nicole mused, watching the water cascade over the rocks.

"Never," he said. "That was the downfall of Veil. The kingdoms bickered constantly and fought frequently. At a time when several kingdoms were at odds with one another, the dragon king saw his opportunity and took advantage of their instability."

A frown darkened Nicole's face. She knew history that had nothing to do with her shouldn't hang so heavy on her heart, not for the selfish and childish reason of hearing dragons were the enemy. Countless people died and her heart mourned the destruction of a childhood fantasy.

"What happened to the palace they built?"

"It's still there," he answered with a shrug.

"What, just sitting there empty?"

"As far as I know—nobody can get inside."

"How is that?" Nicole asked, stepping closer to the waterfall.

"That's the funny thing about magic; it's working even when you don't realize it. It's everywhere—in the wind, in the sunlight, in the trees. When they built that palace, so many people came together to craft something magnificent. There is a special kind of magic created when people share a dream. Their effort of unity and resilience in the shadow of uncertainty was embedded in the very stone. They had an unspoken pact to stand together and, when they broke it, they could no longer gain access to the palace or the keys inside."

"Sounds like a pretty clear message to me," she said as droplets of water splashed against her cheeks. She reached out to catch some of the falling water in her cupped hands. "You'd think they would have figured it out and reconciled their differences then and there."

"Yes, you'd think," Raiden agreed. "But it only made matters worse—and after all they went through, driven from their homes into a realm hidden in the shadows only to be barred from the very fruits of their labors. It is an unfortunate truth: magic cannot always be controlled. Their bond was broken, and the palace has been sealed shut ever since."

"Does that ever happen to you?"

"What?"

"Do you ever have trouble controlling magic?" She turned to him and waited intently for his answer.

"I do," he said.

"How so?"

"I was unfortunate enough to be born with the Sight," he confessed.

Her eyelids peeled back. "You mean you see the future?"

"It's not as marvelous a gift as you may think," he countered.

She cocked her head to the side. "Why not?"

"Mastering the Sight comes at a steep price. Those who do spend most of their time in visions of the future and quite literally lose sight of the present. Their eyesight deteriorates and they go blind."

"Oh." Her voice was tinged with dismay. "So you don't practice it then?" There was an edge of concern in her words.

He smiled. "No, but that doesn't mean I am free of it either. I am unpracticed, so if and when the Sight comes to me ... well, let's just say I'm like a leaf caught in a storm."

"That doesn't sound pleasant," she admitted.

"I can steel myself against it for the most part. I much prefer spell craft."

"You're a seer, but you choose to practice spells instead. Can anyone learn how to cast spells then? Does everyone have some kind of gift, like you with the Sight? How does that work?" She had a hundred more questions, and she could barely stop herself.

He chuckled at her exuberant interrogation.

"Not everyone is born with a particular gift, and not everyone is born with an affinity for magic either. Some people are just ... magically inclined. There are children who struggle with spells and those who excel like in any subject. I'm not very good with potions. To be honest, I hated them in school," he said with a shake of his head.

"But how does someone know if they have one of the special gifts, or what it is? I don't know that I feel that different from yesterday. You said I must have so much power, and yet it doesn't seem like it."

Raiden smiled at her. Then his eyes drifted past her, behind her. "I wouldn't be so sure about that."

Nicole gave him a quizzical look before turning around. In the path she had walked along the stream, delicate wild flowers sprouted up from the rich soil at the water's edge. Polished stones she had tread on had been liberated from gravity's hold and were spinning freely in the air. Not far down the stream, she could see the place where she and Raiden had been sitting on the ridge, because there was a distinct patch of brilliant green grass, but everywhere else the grass was sparse and gray.

She let out a breathy laugh, unable to find words. Then a tiny digital beep rang out from her wrist, and she raised her arm to look at her watch. The chronometer was still running, started when she had left the house for her impromptu run.

She gasped. "Three hours!" Aghast, she switched her watch to the time and understood why it had beeped. It was seven in the morning back home. Nicole was usually up by six to turn on the coffeemaker. Her dad's alarm went off at six thirty.

"We need to get back," she insisted.

"All right." He turned and invited her to lead the way with a wave, moving swiftly back the way they had come.

Nicole's heart raced at she imagined her dad getting out of bed to no aroma of coffee in the house, finding the kitchen dark and the coffeemaker quiet. She knew he would wonder immediately where his daughter might be—thinking she could have overslept. As she hurried along the stream, she watched the ground and noticed more stones were sent spinning off the ground, twirling like tops.

"This way," he insisted, stopping at the low ridge with its bright green patch of grass.

She stopped and realized she'd hurried right past it. Then she wondered why they would climb over the ridge when they could follow the stream until the ridge sank back into the earth and smoothed into a gentle slope. Nicole looked down the stream for a moment. Raiden seemed to understand her unspoken confusion.

"A kelpie lives in that stretch of the stream. It's unwise to wander into its territory." He placed his hand on the ridge and gestured for her to proceed.

The word *kelpie* stuck in her mind, and she jumped forward to hop up and heave herself up and over the ridge. Raiden managed the same feat with ease thanks to his height. Nicole's heart gave a hard thud of relief as they left the stream behind. Once she was on her feet she was running, sure her dad had already discovered her empty bed and was sinking into a state of panic.

"When you say kelpie," she said easily as they ran, "do you mean the water horse, like the kind that drowns people?"

"Well," said Raiden. His speech came between heavy breaths; he wasn't used to running and talking like Nicole. "They don't drown … only people … but I worry … about this one … because it hasn't … had much sport … in the last nine years."

Nicole shuddered at his words.

As Raiden led them through the forest, she noticed the single tower looming high on the neighboring mountain across from the castle. Their feet crunched through the desiccated leaves beneath them. Nicole's adrenaline radiated from her as she ran. A hissing sound behind her made her look over her shoulder to see the leaves behind her tumbling upward.

They reached the edge of the forest and came upon the dirt road leading around the cliff and up to the castle. The only clue as to where the portal stood was in the disturbed dirt where they had fallen and trodden earlier.

Nicole hesitated, her momentum slowing as they approached the rocky wall and the cloud of leaves behind her settled back down to the forest floor. Stepping through that portal with this new power humming inside her meant destroying her dad's hope that life would go back to normal.

"After you," he said, raising his hand toward the unseen portal.

With resolute strides, she pressed on and mustered up her confidence as she came to the portal. There was a tingle in the air that met her nose first and washed over her as she stepped through. Although she knew she was only taking a single step, her body felt as though it were rushing forward at such an incredible speed that her stomach churned with nausea and her head spun.

Any thought in her mind was dashed by the sudden vertigo. She stepped into her backyard feeling ill and disoriented by the abrupt change from bright daylight to dim dawn. Trying to settle her head and stomach, she stopped where she was just as Raiden stepped through the portal behind her, bumping into her.

"Pardon me," he murmured.

She pressed her temples. "Ugh, did you feel like this when you came through yesterday?" The air around her, although cool against her face, tasted stale and felt thicker in her lungs. The crisp dawn that she usually found refreshing felt anything but.

"It will pass," he promised, placing a reassuring hand on her shoulder. After a few breaths, though, the drastic change in atmosphere dulled until it was near imperceptible. The acclimation of her senses almost seemed to come with the pressure of Raiden's hand.

A sharp sound startled them: the swift turn of the backdoor knob and the door being yanked open—Raiden pulled his hand away.

"Nicole—" Her father's voice shifted quickly from a frantic call to a frustrated sigh when he laid eyes on her. "There you are. Did you go out for a run?"

Nicole couldn't see his face well enough, but the panic lingered in his tone. He managed to keep it together yesterday, and he thought this would all go away soon. But it wouldn't. This was just the start of it. There was no 'back to normal' for them like he wanted and she didn't know how to tell him that.

"Not exactly," she confessed.

"We found the source of your portal," Raiden explained.

"Oh?" Michael stepped forward and crossed his arms. "What is it?"

Nicole raised her hand like a timid schoolgirl with the answer,

"Me."

Michael laughed nervously, no doubt hoping it was a joke. "What do you mean?"

Nicole huffed. "There's no going back to normal, Dad."

The humor melted from Michael's face, leaving a stricken expression behind, one she hadn't seen since he and her mom sat her and her brothers down to say they were getting divorced.

"Let's take this conversation inside," he suggested.

Seven

Nicole followed her dad, and she stopped at the door, dreading the task of destroying her dad's reality, taking away his normal like her mom had. She looked back to see Raiden standing uncertainly in the yard. After witnessing what her magic had done back in the forest without any intention from her, she worried what it might do inside. How would her dad take all this?

"Raiden?" Now wasn't the time to notice that she liked the sound of his name. "Will you help me explain this to him?"

Some swift emotion pinched his somber expression quicker than she could understand it. He tromped through the grass and crossed the patio to join her. She wasn't even aware of the expression on her own face until he frowned at her.

"What's wrong?" Raiden asked quietly.

"Nothing." She tried to convince herself of that and forced herself to step over the threshold.

Raiden stepped inside behind her and closed the door after him. She felt trapped.

"All right, what's going on?" Michael asked from the kitchen.

Nicole looked to Raiden with beseeching eyes; she didn't know how to explain.

"The source of the portal is apparently Nicole," Raiden said. "It seems she has been harboring magic for quite some time."

Michael shook his head slowly. "How is that possible?"

Raiden gave Nicole a quick look and an almost imperceptible smile. "Well, some people don't come into their abilities until later in life. In Veil, lots of children have abilities from the time they're born but find they develop further as they get older. This realm would normally suffocate the magic in most people born here. Since Nicole has lived her whole life in this realm, any early manifestation of her power was buried—so her magic remained concealed inside her until it couldn't be contained anymore."

"So it's always been there, getting stronger?" Nicole looked at him because she didn't want to look at her dad and see horror on his face.

"Until the point when this realm couldn't suppress it any longer. Likely the same time as everything started grow in your backyard," Raiden suggested.

"After your brothers visited…for your birthday." Her dad looked at her with understanding in his eyes. "The yard got greener. Bandit started acting differently." His words hastened as he made all the connections for himself. The dog came trotting into the kitchen at the sound of his name.

"Great, I'm the girl who didn't hit puberty until eighteen," Nicole muttered to herself.

Her dad gave her an exasperated look. "I don't know how to handle this, Nicole."

"Neither do I, Dad," she confessed with an anxious laugh. If she didn't laugh, her fear would come out as tears instead. "We take it one day at a time, I guess."

"I should warn you," Raiden interjected, "even after this portal closes, there will always be another. Nicole will be a constant link between this realm and Veil."

"I see, but"—Michael took a careful breath—"what does this magic … entail, exactly?" He chose his words carefully, and Nicole flushed with gratitude, guilt and uncertainty still racing through her blood.

"Well," said Raiden, his eyes sweeping the living room.

Nicole and her father's eyes did the same. Objects all around the room drifted toward the ceiling. Lamps were tethered down by their cords. Throw pillows hovered over the couch. As a tennis ball lifted off the floor, Bandit charged forward and snatched it from the air eagerly.

"I'm still trying to work that out myself," Raiden said with a chuckle. "There's no telling what she can do."

"May I remind you I've only known about this for"—she looked at her watch—"less than an hour?" She wasn't entirely sure. How long had they been asleep in Veil and how much time had they spent in the forest talking? Why did that thought make her cheeks burn?

"Okay," Michael said, his voice higher than normal, "you're not going to school today."

"Aye aye," Nicole acknowledged with a playful salute.

"And you've got to figure out how to control this, pronto," Michael added.

"That might be easier said than done," Nicole warned. "I don't think I'm going to find video tutorials on this."

"I might be able to help you with that," Raiden volunteered. "Edwende," he commanded.

Everything that had been disturbed by Nicole's unruly powers drifted back down to its rightful place.

Nicole looked to her dad, and she could see fatherly gears turning behind his gray eyes and firm mouth. "Do *you* know any other people who have experience with magic?" she asked him before he could reject the idea. She knew she had him there. What other option did they really have?

"Okay," Michael said, his shoulders sagging. "I guess that means you'll be with us for a little while then, Raiden."

"Does he still have to sleep in the shop?" Nicole asked disapprovingly.

"No," he answered in defeat, rubbing his eyes and pinching the bridge of his nose. "He can stay in Anthony's room while he's here. Why don't you show him around?"

Nicole eyed her dad suspiciously; he seemed suddenly eager to shoo them off upstairs when just moments ago he'd been unsure about the man from another realm sleeping in the same house. "All right," she agreed and waved Raiden to follow as she moved toward the stairs. They reached the landing in silence, and Nicole took one last look down at her dad in the kitchen. He looked up at her with a smile that betrayed nothing.

"So," she said, raising her hand to the right, "my room is at the end, and the bathroom is the first door on the left. Your room is this way," she turned to the hall left of the landing where they stood and led him past the first door on the right. "That's Mitchell's room," she said in passing before opening the door at the end of the hall. Anthony's door was perpendicular to Mitchell's door. "This is your room." She presented the tidy sparse room with a sweep of her hand.

Raiden was quiet as he surveyed the room—bed on the right-hand wall, closet in the back corner, window across from the doorway, dresser on the left. Nicole knew Raiden probably only saw an empty room, but this room was where she confided in her oldest brother, where she always found him when she needed help studying or when she was just looking for a reason to smile.

Nicole cleared her throat. "So, uh, would you like a change of clothes?"

Raiden turned to her, and his eyes lit up with more enthusiasm than she expected. "Yes, I would greatly appreciate it."

She suppressed a laugh. "Be right back," she said, holding up her finger. Backing out of the room, she turned to Mitchell's door and went inside. She lowered herself to the floor beside the bed and reached beneath it for the box of clothes Mitchell never wore. When she returned to the other room, Raiden was standing at the dresser studying a picture of her and her brothers at ages ten, twelve, and fifteen.

"Here you go," she said, dropping the box on the bed.

"Whose are all these?" Raiden asked when he opened it.

"Mitchell's. He never wears them—not exactly his style," she said with a shrug.

"Well, thank you. I think I'll change now, if you don't mind," he said.

She nodded. "Right, I'll just ..." She hiked her thumb over her shoulder. "Yeah." He shut the door—mostly—but before she could turn away, she caught a glimpse of skin as he pulled the shirt off his back. She knew she should turn right around, but her feet wouldn't move and her eyes were locked on the movement of muscles in his back. At last she wrenched her gaze away, her cheeks hot with embarrassment, and she forced herself down the hall toward the bathroom. She glanced downstairs as she passed the landing, but her dad was no longer in the kitchen.

In the bathroom, she sat down to pee and couldn't help thinking of Raiden—a complete stranger sleeping at the other end of the hall. Did she really need him to be that close to help her figure all this out? He has had a perfectly good place to sleep until ending up here—then she reminded herself that he lived in an empty city. *He's been alone for nine years,* she shook her head in dismay. She flushed the toilet and she turned on the faucet, washed her hands, and rinsed the oil and dirt from her face. Then she pressed her face into the plush towel hanging beside the sink and groaned, annoyed that she couldn't get that glimpse of Raiden's bare back out of her mind. With a huff, she prepared herself to step out into the hall once more.

She could handle this. He was attractive—what did it matter? *Not a big deal,* she insisted to herself as she crossed the hall, confident he would be done changing. But when she reached the door, she peeked through the opening and saw that he only had a pair of jeans on. Then he turned toward the door.

With a gasp, the tension in her body snapped like a rubber band, and she jumped like a startled cat. Her muscles seized under false alarm. Every picture frame down the length of the hallway was caught in an unseen gust of energy, as though someone ran down the hall dragging her hands along the walls. Nicole's knees buckled in her surprise. She sank to the carpet and reached for the nearest picture frame.

Raiden came out of the room in the act of pulling a gray, long-sleeved shirt down, and Nicole turned her guilty eyes away from the glimpse of his abdomen to hide the embarrassment hot on her face.

"What's going on up there?" Michael called from downstairs.

Nicole's eyes widened, and the heat drained from her cheeks. She sure as hell wasn't going to tell her dad she was startled because she'd been peeping on Raiden changing. "Just—uh—a little … magic accident." She cringed, realizing those were probably the silliest words she'd ever spoken.

"You need some help up there?" The strain in her dad's voice almost made her laugh, and she wondered if he was more worried about the destruction or the magic.

"It's fine, Dad," she called before picking up a frame and looking at it coldly. "The glass is broken," she said quietly, disappointed.

"Here," Raiden stepped closer and took the frame. It passed from her hand to his; once there, he pressed his other hand over the glass. "*Renovo*," he said softly.

The glass fractured in reverse, cracks fusing together without leaving behind even the faintest scratch. The picture beneath the glass became clear. Nicole felt like she hardly knew those people, the younger version of her father, her six-year-old self on his shoulders, the woman with light brown hair and dark eyes standing proudly behind her brothers with her hands on their shoulders.

Nicole put it back on the wall with indifference.

Raiden waved his hand and commanded, "Edwende." All the fallen frames jumped back to their places on the walls.

"It's nice to have someone around to help me clean up my messes," she laughed. "I suppose I'll be making a lot of them now."

"What fun would life be without a few messes?" he said with a smile.

She nodded, smiling as her dread turned to relief. "In that case, I'm in for a hell of a lot of fun."

"Don't you mean *we?*"

She stopped to look at him seriously, her mouth stuck somewhere between a smile and a confounded grimace. "We haven't even known each other for twenty-four hours. It seems wrong to commandeer your life with my problems." There was sympathy in her voice.

"I came from an empty city, remember? I didn't leave behind a life; I left behind a tomb." His serious words broke into a chuckle.

He doesn't want to be alone anymore. Her heart felt heavy.

"Nicole?" Michael called again.

"He's just going to come up here," she whispered through an exasperated smile before pivoting toward the landing. "It was nothing, Dad. Just a few pictures fell."

Raiden was right behind her.

"Oh—I see you found him some clothes," Michael noted as they came down the stairs. "I suppose I should get going, or the crew will beat me to work again," he said, looking over his shoulder at the clock in the kitchen.

"Okay," Nicole responded.

"Don't destroy the house," he added.

"You'll never know what was broken and what wasn't," Raiden said, and Nicole tried to hide her smile behind her hand when her dad looked more troubled than amused.

"Right, I'll see you later," Michael said, pecking Nicole with a kiss. "Raiden," he added with a feeble smile, "don't let her do anything dangerous."

Nicole let her arms drop in annoyance.

"I won't." Raiden avoided her glare.

"Responsible eighteen-year-old honor student standing right here," she announced, glaring at her father.

"I have every right as a father to worry, magic or no magic." He took one last look from Nicole to Raiden before adding, "Oh, and Mitch is on his way home, so just remember that." He pressed his lips together and raised his brows, looking directly at Nicole.

Nicole's mouth pressed into an annoyed line. So that's what he had been doing while she and Raiden were upstairs—calling in reinforcements.

"I've got my phone if anything happens—and, you know, to check in on you," he finished with a nod.

"Bye, Dad," Nicole said, hoping to expedite his departure before he added any awkwardly obvious reminders about keeping her wits about her and the young stranger in the house. He was right, she conceded silently, just because Raiden was handsome didn't make him any less of a stranger. This was definitely a little crazy, maybe utterly insane. Were they both still expecting to wake up?

"Right, good-bye," he said and turned toward the door.

Once he was out the front door, Nicole sagged with relief.

"I can't decide if he trusts me or not," Raiden murmured with a hint of chagrin.

Nicole laughed, completely unembarrassed. "Probably a little of both. Wait until you meet Mitchell."

Eight

Nicole and Raiden sat with their empty breakfast bowls in front of them.

"Well?" Nicole was waiting for an answer.

"Best porridge I've had in years," Raiden said.

A little swell of laughter slipped past her lips.

He smiled, her laugh was infectious. "What?"

"Porridge," she replied through her broad smile. "I'm sorry. You're from a different realm and all. I don't really hear the word *porridge* too often."

"What was it you called it?"

"Oatmeal," she said.

"Then it's the best *oatmeal* I've had in years," he clarified.

"Thank you," she said with a little bow.

"Are you sure it's always been this good? Magic can do many things," he said, nodding at the bowls.

She looked at him with a tiny gasp. "Of course it's always this good," she said with another laugh, but she looked down at her bowl. "How do I know if I'm using my magic or not?"

He chuckled. "I'm teasing. You would know."

"But so far everything has been out of my control. Back in the forest, in the living room, up in the hallway." Her face puckered with a frown.

"What's wrong?"

"Yesterday," she said, looking up at him with her honey-brown eyes, "you told me about something—what did you call it?" She thought for a moment. "The fera?"

Raiden's chest tensed with anxiety. "That's right."

"And you said they were dangerous, that they were hunted down because of it," she said, her gaze unwavering.

"That's true. The Council would have Veil believe they were successful and the fera are merely a piece of history now, but—"

"But it's the only likely explanation, isn't it? That's what I am," she said.

He hesitated. How could he tell her what he knew when the Council themselves were the messengers? "There's no other likely possibility, but even that isn't much of an explanation, I'm afraid. There's so little information about them. The few references to them I've come across in my reading only mention the fera vaguely."

"I don't care what the books have to say about the fera. I'll find out for myself what I am. What I'm worried about is this Council of yours. Do they think the fera are gone, or are they going to come looking for me?"

Raiden shook his head. "They might be looking for you."

"Do you think they know?"

"I—" Could he lie and tell her 'no' to grant her a sense of safety? Could he hide her from the Council when they had every seer in the realm at their disposal looking for what they wanted to find? They already knew about her appearance in Cantis. "—would assume they do."

She took a deep breath. "So I guess I better figure out this whole magic business...if people are going to come after me." She shrugged, and her smile looked strained.

"We can get started as soon as you like," Raiden said, swallowing back the guilt in his mouth as he cursed the Council silently, because if it weren't for their letter he might not have found Nicole in time, but there was no way she would trust him with such a damning connection to the people out to get her.

"No time like the present," she said as she stood up. "But first, if you're gonna stay in this house, you should know if you don't make the meal, you do the dishes." She stacked their bowls and presented them to him.

He smiled. "Fair enough." How quickly he could go from being a stranger to a part of the household washing the dishes. Until now, his life had been nothing but lost happiness and the dust of the dead lingering in the gutters of every empty street and silent house. He had tasted a small morsel happiness again—he couldn't just throw that away. The Council knew all about Nicole, but he could help her. They would come looking for her, but Nicole would be ready. For all he knew, she was nothing like the other fera. Maybe she could control her powers like the others couldn't. Nothing about her seemed dangerous to him. How could someone like her be anything like the stories told about the fera?

He finished rinsing the second bowl and laid it beside the first on the rack to dry.

"Ready?" She came down the stairs with a soft red hooded jacket on, carrying another garment over her shoulder.

"Absolutely," he said, drying his hands before falling into step beside Nicole. She handed him a beige jacket which he pulled on over the gray sleeved shirt he had on. He hoped he could help her control her magic. Raiden had learned young about the terror of having no control, unable to keep his father from leaving, unable to protect his mother from monsters. He refused to see the same happen to Nicole, to see her condemned by the stories of the other fera.

Bandit brushed past their legs as they stepped outside into the crisp morning air. Their breaths were white wisps that drifted away. Raiden watched Nicole bury her hands deep into the pouch of her coat. Her black trousers were like a second skin from hip to ankle, and occasionally he caught his eyes traveling the curves of her legs.

"So, where exactly do we start?" she asked, turning around to face him.

He wrenched his gaze up, hoping the heat in his face didn't show. "Near the portal. If we're going to be using magic, it would be best to keep it close and not risk opening another entrance into Veil." If every portal was a rift in the barrier between realms, multiple portals near enough to one another could cause massive deterioration of the barrier—maybe even completely unravel it. He wasn't entirely sure he could teach a fera to control her power. He couldn't even imagine having the two realms collide in the process.

"So why not eliminate that risk entirely and practice in Veil?" Nicole asked.

"Given what we've already seen when you aren't even trying, it would be best to practice here and avoid unwanted attention," Raiden said, his heart pounding again. If he could just keep her here, away from where the Council's seers could find her, maybe she would have a chance.

"Good point," she said with a sober nod.

Raiden felt his shoulders ease with relief.

"All right." She tromped out into the grass and positioned herself in front of the portal, at least two long strides away. "Now what?"

"Just try to connect with it, get to know where it is, what it feels like."

"Like the mind-muscle connection—can't be too different, right?" she said with uncertainty dripping from her words. "All right." She nodded and closed her eyes.

Raiden waited patiently, free to ponder her face and wonder if she could ever become what the tales of the fera described. He tried to picture her unbridled, violent, and destructive. What could possibly push someone like her to that place? He doubted the truth of those accounts regarding the fera, and the Council's actions only grew even more ominous as he pondered them coming for Nicole. Disposing of wild, violent, irrational creatures to protect the people of Veil was indeed noble. Hunting down misunderstood individuals who needed help bearing the burden of their powers was brutal, unjust, and self-serving. What reason did the Council have for disposing of the fera if not to keep the citizens of Veil safe?

Just as that troubling thought hardened his face, a gentle charge wafted through the air. The prickle of magic radiated from Nicole, and around her the grass trembled, growing at a perceptible rate.

"It looks you don't have any trouble tapping into your magic," he said with a chuckle.

She opened her eyes and looked down in shock as the grass inched farther up around her ankles and shins.

"Again with the—is this sort of thing common in Veil?" She looked up at Raiden.

"Not at all." A laugh broke through his words.

"This isn't funny," she insisted with a smile, stepping sideways into shorter grass, which only proceeded to grow around her feet.

He smiled and crossed his arms. "Your laughter would indicate otherwise."

Once more, she jumped to shorter grass, landing on one foot as though less contact with the earth would lessen the effects.

Nicole laughed. "So even by Veil's standards I'm a freak of nature?"

"I wouldn't say that," Raiden said. "A force of nature perhaps, I don't know how easy this is going to be."

"Thank you? That's the strangest compliment I've ever received." She switched feet, and the blades of grass still reached eagerly for her.

Raiden did not want to influence her perception of her powers. Believing her magic was innately dangerous could change everything. He had every reason to believe the fate of the fera was a self-fulfilling prophecy. He would not put the idea in her head that her magic was uncontrollable—that it had any kind of inherent nature aside from that which she gave it.

"Consider what you've already experienced," he suggested. "What does it mean to you?"

"It does whatever the hell it wants!" she cried. Her dance to evade the growing grass brought her closer to where he stood.

"I think if you don't give it form, it will take the nearest and simplest form it can. When you aren't thinking about it, it becomes an extension of your reflexes, and plants can use it more readily than the energy from the sun."

"Is that ... a bad thing?" she asked. The grass reached up around both of them, creeping up their ankles.

"That is the nature of magic—it is the individual who gives it form. Some people cannot help what form their magic takes— people like seers, shape-shifters, flyers, elementals. Maybe you're dealing with utterly raw, unformed magic, and having more than most people makes it...a little unruly."

"Sounds bad to me," she said, looking down at the grass brushing her knees. She stepped over it gingerly and skipped back to the edge of the patio.

"But it doesn't have to be."

"How is magic that acts on its own not a bad thing?"

"It's not acting on its own. It's reacting to you, whether you make a conscious decision or not. The particular quality that makes magic so troublesome is that it's affected by emotion."

"You do realize you're talking to an eighteen-year-old girl, right? I don't even want to know what's going to happen when PMS hits."

"For now, let's focus on today."

"How about you—what happens to you when you get emotional?"

"Me?" He was ashamed to admit that he didn't know, that he'd lived numb for so long he had become proficient at spell casting without any of the supplementation or limitation that emotions might bring. Sudden dread struck his heart. Emotions very well might render him no better than a novice.

"Yeah, you," she said, blinking expectantly at him. "You said you're a seer. Can't emotions mess with what you see?"

He had to think for a moment. His childhood felt almost beyond his recollection, lost in the years of seclusion he'd only so recently escaped.

"I suffered uncontrollable visions as a boy. My mother taught me how to block it out. She didn't want me to train it, but I figured out how to tap into it on my own. I knew how she felt about it, that she refused to practice. I kept my dabbling a secret. I was thirteen when I finally renounced it; but by then, I think, I had given the Sight too much of myself to ever escape it. I don't usually have a problem keeping the Sight at bay, at least when I'm awake, and I think it has a lot to do with being so empty for all this time, so focused on day-to-day. If I felt nothing, I saw nothing of the future. Visions still find me in my sleep though."

"What kind of things do you see then?"

"Most of the time its the same vision." He wanted to leave it at that—and leave that vision of the future in his past—but Nicole's eyes lit up with interest.

"What kind of vision? Let's hear it," she insisted. "You must know it by heart now."

He sighed. "It's a vision of a woman—"

"Is that so? Please continue." She wore a wry smile on her mouth.

"It's brief. All I really see is myself holding a woman with long silver hair," he said with a shrug.

"You've analyzed this more than you're letting on," Nicole said, folding her arms.

"It was the closest thing to human contact I got for nine years," Raiden said frankly.

"So when do you think you'll meet her?"

"I saw glimpses of a woman from a point in my life when I had different plans. There's no telling if that vision is still viable. The future is constantly changing."

"But do you want that future to change?" she asked.

A troubled huff escaped his lungs.

She straightened up. "I seem to detect a little anxiety."

"I try not to give visions sway over me. We control our futures, not the other way around, which is why we're out here. Can we continue?"

"You can't reveal that you've been dreaming about someone for a decade and expect the conversation to just move on like that," Nicole said.

"It's nothing like a dream. She's not some fantasy born from a lonely heart," he scoffed. "Visions are not hazy, flimsy images like dreams. With the Sight, you're *there*. You can feel, hear, and smell it with unnatural intensity. I've *held* her. I know the smell of her hair. I've heard her sigh in my ear."

"Wow, you've got it bad." Nicole looked at him as if he were a condemned man.

"I beg your pardon?"

"Love," she said.

He let out a huff of conflict from his chest. Was that what he felt in that brief vision, that moment with his arms around a woman without a name, holding her desperately, feeling his entire being shed the weight of sorrow in her arms? What did it matter? That was the future, not *now*. For all he knew his future was different now, having met Nicole. "Isn't that what everyone is looking for?"

Nicole's face pinched with a frown. "No," she said, "not everyone."

Raiden studied her hard brows and mouth before she could soften her features. Her eyes remained—annoyed, he thought. He was perplexed by her reaction, but glad the topic had finally changed.

"Practicing is more important now," Raiden said.

"What exactly am I supposed to practice? I don't know any spells."

"You don't necessarily need spells to practice."

"So do I just point a finger … or clap my hands?" She folded her arms.

"It's your magic, not mine. You can channel it however you want, through your hands or through a wand if you like."

She put up her hands to stop him. "Hold on. People really use wands?"

"Of course. Although, mostly the older generations use them— last I knew. It fell out of style."

"So people don't need them to cast spells?"

"The wand itself doesn't have any power. It's merely a tool. It concentrates and directs the magic from within the wielder, allowing for more precise aim if you're casting at a distance. Those who prefer wands have a tendency to think those who do not are unrefined. I've never used one myself, but I've always been curious about the advantages."

"Could we make one ourselves if we wanted?"

"Wand crafting is nothing short of an art. They're more than just polished sticks; the materials are chosen for their conductivity. Certain materials can withstand greater power than others. On top of that, you have to find the one that best fits you—the materials that combine best with you and your magic. Here." He stooped to pick up a stick from the pile of scrap wood they kept for fires. "Try something and see for yourself."

A grin spread across her face as she took the stick and held it like a wand. It was mostly straight, with a single bend at the end where Nicole grasped it.

"Go on then. Try something," he said.

"What?"

"How about this? *Ilumina*," he said, holding his hand out. A little orb of light blinked into existence and bobbed over his open hand. "Try channeling it through your makeshift wand." He let the light shrink away and nodded at her.

Nine

Nicole closed her eyes and thought of that tiny orb of light in Raiden's hand. She spoke the word to summon it: "Ilumina."

A warm electric sensation bloomed in her core and moved through her veins. A wave of magic flooded her and rolled down her arm. Her hand filled with heat, and her fingers burned as the energy surged through them into the stick. The wood trembled. It grew hot, blackened, and cracked, and the end of it sparked. She released the stick, yanking her hand away as it burst.

"Shit!" She gave her hand a frantic shake, and her fingers escaped unscathed. Her whole body hummed, buzzing with heat deep in her bones. That soft whisper of magic inside her swelled into a barrage of power. Adrenaline raced through her, and her instinct was to let it out to relieve the pressure. But somewhere between her quickened heartbeats, a note of fear rang high and sharp.

"See," he chuckled, "even a well-crafted wand can suffer the same fate if it isn't strong enough to stand up to the user's magic."

She hardly heard him. Her mind was stuck on replay, seeing the stick blacken and combust again and again. Magic had done that— her magic. For all the possibilities that lay before her, she couldn't get past the idea that her magic might be able to do that to her. It burned, and the heat lingered in her hand, cooling slowly. Each beat of her heart made her painfully aware of the energy coursing through her, looking for a way out. A caged animal was trapped in her veins, searching for a way to break free, even if it had to destroy its prison in the process.

"Nicole."

"Huh?"

"Is something wrong?"

"Oh—just letting my imagination get a little carried away." She forced out a laugh and convinced herself that was the case.

"At least you have no problem tapping into your magic. That can be the hardest part for beginners."

Nicole suspected it would never be a struggle to tap into her magic. If anything, the hard part would be resisting it. It felt alive— capable of taking advantage of her; anything could open the door and let it out. *Stop it,* she told herself, taking a deep breath. This was new to her. It was ridiculous to expect control so immediately.

She remembered the first time she rode a dirt bike. When her dad showed her how to click the toe-shifter into first gear and go, she had no idea how responsive the throttle would be. The first twist she gave it was heavy-handed, and the bike lurched forward and her heartbeat accelerated like a maniac. Her hand released the throttle so quickly that she stalled the bike to a stop. For a minute, she had been too startled to realize the bike hadn't been out of her control at all. It had done precisely what she told it to. She lacked practice. All she needed to do was figure out how the controls worked. She mastered the motorcycle, albeit not without throwing herself over the handlebars countless times. She could master the power inside her as well.

She nodded in self-encouragement. Raiden seemed to think she was responding to his comment.

"Let's try something with the light charm."

Raiden held out his hand again, and the light charm bloomed to life, this time without him speaking a word. "Let the light grow and then subside again," he instructed. The light hovering over his palm grew and shrank, fluctuating several times before he closed his hand and let the light die. "Try it."

She took a careful breath. "Ilumina," she said, opening her hand as warmth coursed through muscle, vein, and bone.

The air sparked over her palm, and a soft marble of light formed and then expanded into a golf-ball-sized orb. The light remained as the heat of magic receded from her hand, slinking back into her core like a beast recoiling into its den. But as she focused on the light, she willed that sensation to emerge again, welling up swifter and hotter than it had the first time. The entirety of her arm tensed as magic moved through it, flooding the tiny light in her hand. It grew, expanding into a small sun the size of a bowling ball so rapidly that it popped into beads of sunshine.

"Oops," she said. Nicole opened and closed her hand, easing rigor from her tendons. Her fingers tingled with the residual burn of her power.

Still a little heavy-handed on the throttle, she could hear her dad saying.

"Try again," Raiden encouraged her.

Nicole sighed, cupping her hands together, hoping it would mean twice the control and perhaps half the intensity of the heat. With a deep breath, she thought of the light, and her magic surged before she could say the word. There was a spark of fear in her chest as the light bloomed in her cupped hands. She knew she would have to smother that feeling before it could grow to consume her.

How could she control something inside her if she feared it? She let her magic expand with each inhalation and quell with each exhalation. In her hands, the bubble of light pulsed in sync with her breathing.

Raiden nodded with approval. "I was right about you."

She answered with a grin, "What if you had been wrong?"

"Who is to say? Does it matter?"

"I guess not." She shrugged. "So are you going to join me or just stand there watching? I feel like a performing monkey here."

He smiled. "All right. Now that you and your magic are better acquainted, let's try some spells."

"I like the sound of that."

"Let me think." Raiden looked around at the lush, green yard. "Why not some garden spells?"

"Sure," she agreed.

"What shall we grow?"

"Clover," she said, beaming. "I love clover."

"First try this: *belar lurzorua bueltan*."

"What bizarre language was that?" The alien words slipped from her mind almost instantly.

"Basque I think. Magic has been around as long as language has, and it's been used by many peoples. Just like there's a word for the sun and the sky in every language, there are spells that originate from different places. Many spells are Latin—the expansion of the Roman empire penetrated many cultures. But you'll hear spells in other old languages: Welsh, Basque, and even Galician. Over the centuries, some spells were even combined as people shared and borrowed one another's languages."

"Can you repeat that last one then? I'm new to Basque."

"Belar lurzorua bueltan," he said slowly for her.

Unsure what she was casting, she repeated his words, "Belar lurzorua bueltan."

The thick carpet of grass across the yard browned, withered, and shrank into the earth, leaving nothing but dark, moist soil.

"Whoa." Her mouth fell open.

"Now then. You wanted clover."

She nodded absently, still stunned to see fresh bare earth where there had been untamable grass for weeks.

"Feithrin meillion," Raiden said with a commanding nod of his head. A small section of the earth closest to his feet changed. A multitude of tiny sprouts erupted from the soil and opened into a patch of bright green clover that spread nearly three square feet.

A laugh fell from Nicole's mouth.

"Your turn." He gestured toward the ground in invitation.

"Feithrin meillion," she said, almost laughing, unable to take herself seriously saying spells in languages she didn't know. Her body grew hot with the magic swelling within her, sinking into the ground beneath her feet. It seeped into every last inch of dark soil. Sprouts broke through, and the clover opened in emerald flourishes. Nicole's hands clapped shut against her face, and she peeked over her fingertips in amazement.

"That was far too easy for you," Raiden said as he folded his arms. "Maybe I should give you something more challenging."

Nicole could not help crouching down to touch the clover. Expecting them to be cool against her skin, she was surprised to feel they were warm. As she pressed her hand into the plush ground cover, she could feel the tingle of magic against her skin. It was her magic lingering in the new growth. Without a thought, she sank to her knees and laid herself down, rolling onto her back. She sighed.

"Enjoying yourself?"

She rolled her head side to side. "You have no idea." She looked up to see a look of confusion on Raiden's face. She laughed.

"What, you've never just laid on the ground for the hell of it?"

"No," he said and then lowered himself to the ground and lay down beside her.

"Well?" Nicole kept her gaze up in the sky above them.

He took a deep breath and huffed. "I'm not entirely sure what you've done to me. I knew who I was yesterday. I've never been so unsure of who I am or what I'm doing, and yet somehow I'm completely content."

She was silent a moment. "Huh, that's funny … yesterday I knew exactly where I was going, following the plan. Keep your GPA up, apply for scholarships, apply to colleges, decide on a major with good career options. I've been following a formula forever, but I felt utterly panicked, like walking a balance beam, only one way to go. Now I have no idea what's going to happen or where the hell all this will lead me, but I'm okay with that. In a weird way not knowing is a relief."

"We sound like a genuine pair of fools," he said.

"And we probably look like it too." She chuckled and sat up.

"Well then," he said, sitting up too, "what should we try next? No more easy spells—I think you're ready for something more advanced."

They stood up in unison.

"You know what I've always wanted to do?" She sent her mind back to childhood dreams without shame.

"What is that?"

"Fly."

A soft smile formed on his lips. "Who wouldn't?"

"Do you think I could?"

"That's up to you."

She inhaled until her lungs were stretched full and held her breath for a second. The buzz of magic pulsed just below the surface, humming like bees. When she exhaled, she released the building magic. Its warmth chased away the chill of the January morning, and gravity dispersed like a fog. Her weight lifted from the earth, and she wobbled in midair only a few inches above the patio.

A cry of shock and delight broke from her lips, and she dropped back to the concrete. "I did it!" There was a touch of hysteria in her voice, and she laughed.

"You did it." He sounded as stunned as she felt. "Try again."

"Okay." She swallowed the lump in her throat and decided this time she'd jump.

Her magic rushed through her as she hopped up; it caught her more powerfully than before, like a kite in the wind. She lurched forward, floundering in the air, trying to right herself like she was in water. But flying was nothing like swimming. Moving her arms and legs did not stabilize her, and she dropped back down to the ground, heart racing. She pitched forward past her center of gravity and right into Raiden.

He caught her, taking only a small step back to absorb her momentum. Their laughter mingled together, hers bright and nervous, his quiet and warm.

"Maybe a little more practice on landing." He propped her back up on her own feet.

"There's no point really. Even if I get the hang of it, it's not like I can fly anywhere I want. That is not the sort of thing people can just shrug off around here."

"When you master flying, then I'll teach you the invisibility spell," he said.

"Deal!" She leaped with exuberance, turning toward the portal. She froze for a moment, surprised by the sudden clarity with which she could see it.

"What are you looking at?"

"The portal. It's different today." Curiosity subdued her excitement as she moved toward it for a closer look.

"How so?" He stepped up beside her.

She studied the portal now; it shimmered in the air like a spiderweb catching the sunlight. Beyond it she could see not her yard but the realm that lay past it. She moved closer until her nose was just a foot away from the surface.

"It's more distinct." She traced the portal in the air with her index finger. "I can see through it. The forest and the dirt road."

"Really?" He leaned closer and squinted at the portal. "I only see a glimmer from the corner of my eye."

"It's pretty clear when I look through the portal, but ..." When she unfocused her gaze, the other realm became visible, barely, like a dim shadow. "When I don't look at the portal, I can almost see Veil if I unfocus my eyes. It's difficult to see—like the portal is a lens that makes it clear."

"The realms are closer to each other than most people realize."

"They're right on top of each other." She blinked her eyes back into focus and saw Raiden clearly beside her.

Raiden looked down at their feet, and she followed his gaze to see the clover quivering around her, tiny white flowers trembling open.

"I'm not going to be able to go anywhere if plants react like this."

"Make it stop then."

Make it stop? Since she knew how to let her magic out now, she supposed that was the key to understanding how to hold it in. She tensed up and noticed the smallest current of magic moving through her. It halted. It was a lot like holding her breath—increasingly uncomfortable but manageable for a time.

"It's a strange feeling." Her head buzzed with the trapped magic, and she was dizzy for a moment. Releasing it, she sighed, relaxing.

Raiden frowned. "You've lived your whole life with your magic pent up inside you. Maybe you shouldn't try to contain it; channeling it may be the best option. If you try to hold it back, it will just build up and inevitably slip by you, misdirected. Ensuring that you control the form it takes should prevent accidents."

"In other words, keep practicing," she said with a huff and looked around for inspiration. Her eyes fell on the fire pit again. So she trotted over to it and picked a chunk of wood—one of many scraps of various sizes from the shop. The block fit on her hand, and she could cover it completely with the other. With her hands cupped together, encasing the wood, she thought of the stone she had found, her souvenir from Veil.

Warmth rushed down her arms and prickled in her hands until they almost burned. The sharp corners of the block digging into her skin softened. The rough grain became smooth as glass. Her hands opened, and the oblong stone was there. It was egg shaped and cloudy but not quite pale enough, and the shape wasn't right. A tiny wave of magic rolled into her hand, and the iridescent gray stone became white as a pearl, just how she remembered it. Now it was elliptical, a perfect imitation.

From the corner of her eye, she noticed Raiden gawking, his eyes round.

"What?" she laughed.

"You just performed a transmutation like it was nothing."

She opened and closed her right hand. "It burned a little, to be honest. Why is that so impressive?"

"That's alchemy, only you did it without all the work that usually comes with alchemy."

"I'm sorry, what?"

"Alchemy turns magic into a formula, employing written symbols. It's the only kind of magic immune to emotional influence. It's an extremely difficult craft to learn and takes nearly a lifetime to master. Few people devote themselves to it anymore. Truth be told, it's a dying art."

"Do you know what that sounds like to me? Math." She lifted her lip.

"I don't think you appreciate the magnitude of what you just did."

"Come on—I turned wood into a rock," she laughed. "It's a natural process."

"You're already doing advanced magic, and this is your first day."

"And?"

"Magic, like everything else in life, is accomplished gradually—like mastering your body. You crawl, stand, walk, and then run and so on. In terms of magic, you've only just gotten to your feet, and you're sprinting."

"Is that bad? I have a lot of catching up to do, don't I?"

"Yes, and I want you to learn as much and as fast as possible, but I let myself forget that magic is still physically taxing and just because it comes easily to you doesn't mean your body is used to this yet."

"What if I don't have time to take it slow?"

"Nicole, that pain you described—just because a spell is cast as easily as speaking it doesn't mean it can't be too much to handle. I've done it. I've spoken a spell without enough endurance and it nearly destroyed my voice. I couldn't utter another spell for almost a month."

She wondered if that had been recent, if it was why his voice was slightly gravely, why she liked the sound of it when he said her name. Her face went hot.

"Being prepared for the Council is important but not more important than your physical wellbeing."

"I guess you haven't heard the saying, 'No pain, no gain.'"

"Please trust me on this."

81

"All right," she agreed. "I will."

Ten

Raiden stared at the perfect replica of the stone he had stolen from Moira and lost. "May I see that?"

Nicole set the copy onto his open palm. He closed his hand around it, turned it around in the light, ran his fingers across the smooth surface. It was no illusion. Any transfiguration spell could accomplish the same thing but would only change the surface of the thing, not the substance of it. Shape and appearance would be altered, yet it would still have the lightness of wood. The stone in his hand had the same weight of stone he remembered, pressing against the center of his palm with the certainty that the wood had been wholly changed.

There was a difference though. This stone retained the heat of his hand. The true stone had remained cold even after minutes trapped in his fist. He felt haunted. He had been happy to forget about that foolish impulsive change to his plan, about his years of cold hate and that madwoman whose murderous nature seemed to infect the very air hanging over Cantis. How had Nicole known what it looked like? How could she, unless she had seen it ... or found it? The thought made his heart race.

"Why did you to create this particular stone?" he wondered

83

aloud.

"I just copied this stone I found earlier when we were back in Veil. I thought it would make a good memento."

"This stone." He held up her replica. "You brought it back here?"

"Yeah." She shrugged and pulled it from her pocket. Now there were two identical stones, one in her hand and the other in his.

She'll come for this, and for me. Raiden knew his transgression could not be undone. Returning the stone wouldn't help. There would be no forgiveness from Moira. He had sealed his fate when he stole the clearly precious object, and she would try to kill him whether she got her stone back or not. For now he hoped he was safe in his hiding place, so long as Moira didn't find the portal. He looked down at the false stone. He felt possessed by the same need Nicole had felt in finding the real stone: to have a memento, a reminder of the foolish man he had become and who he chose to be today.

"May I keep this?"

"Sure." She laughed and tucked the real stone back into her pocket.

Raiden felt a little baffled by the passing of time with Nicole. Her determination to master flying in a single day, conversation about spells, little jokes, laughter, her annoyance as she struggled was endearing—it all whittled away the time in a haze of pleasant surrealism.

The more frustrated she became, the more she struggled until she finally conceded to go back inside for coffee. As they advanced toward the back door, every few steps she took, she hopped into the air and drifted along the length of a longer stride. He watched with a discreet smile on his face.

"I can't imagine why I thought flying would be easy." She turned toward him, walking backward as they entered the house.

"It's one of the rarest natural gifts there is, next to the Sight." He watched her feet hover above the floor for a few seconds.

"Hey!" A man's voice brought Raiden's eyes back up.

Nicole plopped immediately to the floor. Her knees almost buckled. She wheeled around to face the tall figure she had just bumped into. "Mitchell!"

"Hey, I heard you missed me already," he said. Mitchell's smile was the same as Nicole's, a little broader and more mischievous maybe.

"You got me. I don't know what to do without you." Nicole put on a charming smile as she hugged him, and Raiden wondered if her brother had seen her floating.

"Don't mind me. I didn't mean to interrupt," Mitchell said lifted his eyebrows repeatedly at Nicole when she stepped away from his embrace. "I can't believe you of all people are playing hookie *with a date*." Raiden was perplexed by the phrase, even more so when she elbowed Mitchell's abdomen in response.

"Ow!" He laughed and caught Nicole's neck in his arm and bent her over in a headlock.

"Mitch, come on, stop." Her laughter had a nervous edge to it as her hands pulled at his arm.

Raiden felt the tiny surge of magic before it hit. It prickled his skin and had the hair on his neck standing alert. The back of Mitchell's shirt flew up over his head, and his pants dropped to the floor. He released her. His hands threw back his shirt and snatched up his waistband from around his ankles, yanking his pants back up over his loud orange underpants.

"How did you—what the hell was that?"

"It's called self-defense," Nicole answered with a scowl.

"You know what I mean, Nikki." He pointed a finger at her nose.

"You mean this?" she said. With a devious smile on her face, another pulse of magic moved through the room. Mitchell's pants dropped again.

Nicole giggled, and Raiden tried not to laugh.

"What the hell? How are you doing that?" Mitchell's outrage was compromised by laughter and confusion.

"Dad didn't tell you anything?" She let out an incredulous laugh.

"He just said come home, Nikki needs to be supervised," he said, pushing his chin out.

Nicole scowled at him.

"Please, tell me your secrets," he said with a sad pleading expression.

She huffed, letting her hands fall to her sides with a slap. "It was magic."

"Come on, I want to know."

"I'm not joking," she said, straight-faced.

Mitchell laughed. "All right, good one. Seriously, though."

"I told you. *Magic.*"

"Fine, keep your—"

"I'll show you." She gave her brother a curt glance, frustration and determination mingling in her eyes.

Raiden masked his smile behind his hand as he watched Nicole. She gave her brother a twisted grin and put out her hands expectantly. Mitchell's pants dropped to his ankles and flew off his feet, pulling his legs out from under him. His shirt flipped over his head and off his back as he toppled backward onto the carpet wearing nothing but his bright orange underpants and a look of shock upon his face.

"Still don't believe me?" Nicole stood there, his shirt and pants captive in her arms and triumph on her lips.

"All right! All right, I believe you," Mitchell insisted, fearfully grabbing the waistband of his last remaining garment as he stood. "Can I have my clothes back?"

Nicole handed over her brother's wad of clothes with absolute satisfaction brimming from her eyes and a mischievous smile on her lips.

Mitchell stepped into his jeans with a suspicious glare. Then he gave his shirt a hearty shake and pulled it back on.

"Magic." He tested the sound of the word.

"Yep," she said lightly.

Skepticism crept into his voice. "Magic," he repeated.

"That's right," Nicole persisted.

"Magic." His voice was incredulous this time.

"Yes," Nicole groaned, the word turning into a cry of exasperation. She looked up and huffed.

"When did this *happen*?" he demanded.

Nicole crossed her arms and turned her gaze to Raiden. "Care to help me explain? It is partly your fault."

"Actually, the portal was all your fault. I just accidentally ran through it." Raiden crossed his own arms, resisting the urge to smile as he looked her in the eye.

"I'm sorry. Who are you?" Mitchell finally seemed to remember Raiden's presence.

"Raiden," he said, extending his hand. "I came through the portal yesterday."

Mitchell nodded slowly, his eyes glazing over with disbelief, accepting Raiden's hand in greeting.

"So," said Mitchell, swinging his arms and snapping his fingers before his hands met in a clap, "apparently I missed a lot since last week."

Raiden studied Mitchell's expression, trying to understand how he could react so differently than his father to all this. Where their father's gaze seemed to drift far away to escape what his mind couldn't assimilate into its understanding of the world, Mitchell's took it all in a hasty superficial glance, shrugged and carried on, accepting the situation but perhaps not the reality of it.

"That's an understatement for the books," Nicole said, rolling her eyes and dropping her face into her hand for just a moment.

"Are those the clothes Mom bought me?" Mitchell's brown eyes looked Raiden up and down.

"He's staying to help us sort all this madness out and he needed something other than Renaissance wear."

"Right," Mitchell said, his voice skeptical.

He gave scrutinized Raiden another second longer then glanced at Nicole, her mouth pressed into a flat unreadable line, her lower lip tucked under her teeth and—Raiden noticed with an urge to smile—a flush in her face. She turned away from their gazes, wandering toward the kitchen.

"So," Mitchell said, casting a suspicious look at Raiden now. "You into my sister?" His his head twitched to one side like he'd been smacked. "Hey!" He whirled around, but Nicole was in the kitchen biting into an apple. "That's not fair," he said as he rubbed his head.

"Life isn't fair, Mitch."

"Can you at least teach me how to do that?"

"I don't think so," she answered.

"Come on, you can't spare a little pixie dust or whatever?"

"You're hilarious. I don't think I could if I wanted to. Besides, even if I could, I don't think I would." She took another bite of her apple.

"We share the same genes—I could have a little magic in me, don't you think? Ray?"

Raiden hadn't heard that moniker since the last time he'd seen his childhood friend Caeruleus and it caught him off guard. He cleared his throat. "Everyone's capacity for it varies, but most people can learn to use magic."

"Ha! See?" Mitchell turned a smug scowl back at Nicole.

She gave him a skeptical look. "You're going to start studying magic now, Mitch?"

"Maybe—if you teach me."

"I just learned about all this last night—this morning." She took a devastating bite from the apple. "Beginners don't exactly make good teachers," she said around the chunk of apple tucked into her cheek.

"Rain check then."

She laughed. "Sure."

Raiden's mind latched onto what Nicole had said. Could he really teach her what she needed to know? He wasn't a novice by any means, but now he had his doubts. Nicole was starting out so advanced, maybe she would be better off learning from the books themselves than from him. Of course, there wasn't a worse idea than going back to Cantis now. He supposed he could go later tonight. If he was quick about it, conservative in his choice of material …

"So what else can you do with it?" Mitchell's voice pulled Raiden back.

Nicole's broad smile beamed. "I've been trying my hand at flying."

"Don't you just need to think happy thoughts?"

"Turns out it's a lot more difficult than that."

Mitchell hooked his arm around Nicole's shoulders. "Everyone"—he gestured to an imaginary group of people and Raiden— "I'd like you to meet Nicole, my magical flying sister."

They laughed, and Raiden smiled. At least Nicole's family were surprisingly adaptive about it all. Nicole wriggled, clutching the half-eaten apple protectively. Mitchell refused to let go, and their playful embrace evolved into a wrestling match. Mitchell chuckled when Nicole finally escaped, and Raiden watched with a pang of jealousy, wondering what life with a sibling would have been like. As Nicole bit into her apple again, her brother wandered into the kitchen.

"Oh man," Mitchell said as he opened the refrigerator. "I can't wait to mess with Anthony. He doesn't know yet, does he?" His head popped up from behind the open door.

Nicole shook her head. "Do you think Dad and I called him up this morning and told him over the phone? You barely believed me, and you saw it firsthand."

"Good point," he admitted and ducked back into the fridge.

Mitchell rummaged inside for a minute before he came out with the foil-wrapped pizza slices from the night before. "Is this pizza?" His eyes were wide with excitement.

"Oh yeah, I forgot about that." Nicole lunged toward the kitchen.

Mitchell held the pizza high over his head, where he clearly assumed Nicole couldn't reach it. Raiden could see in her eyes what was about to happen. The air prickled with magic. She hopped into the air and snatched it, drifting back down to the ground triumphantly.

"The tables have turned, Mitch," she declared with a laugh. "Your reign of terror is over." She scowled at him and then turned a smile to Raiden. "Would you like some pizza?"

"I would," he said.

At Nicole and Mitchell's insistence, he ate the pizza cold like they did. As they ate together, he wondered why he should ever go back to Cantis, back to Veil. What was there for him there anymore? He liked it here with Nicole and her family. It was nice to be warm again, to smile, to laugh. He must have gone the past decade without laughing once. But he worried about the stone potentially leading danger through the portal and the Council growing impatient. How long would it take them to realize he wasn't going to bring Nicole to Atrium?

Mitchell disappeared with a half-eaten piece of pizza in his hand, leaving Raiden and Nicole alone in the kitchen.

"I was thinking. You could really use a better teacher when it comes to magic." He studied the teeth marks on his pizza.

"What?"

"There are books that might help you understand magic far better than I can. You could practice the smaller spells and work your way up, build your strength."

A smile transformed her face and a pang in his chest made him want to put the pizza down, but he swallowed back the fluttering in his stomach.

"Books about magic," she said wistfully.

"I'd just have to go get them—"

"Can I come too?"

"I don't know if that's such a good idea." He knew he didn't need to say why—her smile faltered for just a moment and he felt bad for reminding her that there was danger out there waiting for her, searching for her.

"We won't be there long, right? I just want to see more of Veil, and we won't be practicing any magic, so what could possibly draw their attention?"

He was tempted to explain—the Council had most of the realm's seers at their disposal. Nicole's mere presence in Veil put her within their Sight. But would they be looking for her now if they thought he was taking care of their mission? If anything, they would see Nicole and see Raiden with her, surely that would convince them their plans were unfolding as intended, at least long enough for him and Nicole to make a quick trip to Cantis. He didn't want her to worry more than she needed to for a few measly hours. Mostly, he just didn't want to talk about the Council if he could help it, he wanted to bury the connection he had to them. He wanted to forget about that letter. He was not their man and he didn't want Nicole to wonder why he knew so much about them.

"All right, we'll go together. Maybe we should go now before it gets dark in Cantis." He was certain it was sometime in the afternoon back home. If they were to encounter anything, he would rather see it coming, be it a golem searching for him or the Council's next underling looking for Nicole. He did have an advantage over anyone else the Council might send; Raiden knew Cantis and the forest better than anyone alive.

Nicole jumped into the air with an almost inaudible cheer of triumph. He knew he should be more concerned about the trip, but he found it difficult in the light of her enthusiasm. He didn't want gloom and shadows anymore. He wanted to close the portal, close the door on that life and keep this instead. Maybe he was the one who would wake up soon.

∾

On the rocky shore of Cantis, Sinnrick Stultus wobbled on his feet, landing just ashore, the heels of his leather boots right at the water's edge. The Council couldn't have cut it any closer, making him wonder: was their aim really that good or just lucky? He really had to get the hang of ether-shifting on his own, he wasn't sure he wanted to trust the courts transportation anymore. He tromped across the smoothed stones and up the beach, his sights set on the not-too-distant buildings of Cantis. Only five minutes had passed since he received his orders to leave for Cantis.

Despite starting his training only a week before, he had been told he was chosen for this very important assignment because he had showed so much promise in such a short time. The mission would be considered a training mission, the completion of which would allow him to bypass the remainder of the standard training regimen. Upon his return to Atrium, he was to be promoted to a patrol somewhere in the city, and if he did well, he might even earn his wings.

Sinnrick could imagine himself with wings—flying above the crowded streets; seeing the long, straight roadways that divided the city into its districts like the spokes of a wagon wheel; and watching the currents of people moving like urgent blood through Atrium's cobblestone veins. He looked forward to patroling one of those districts, but mostly he thought about wings. He wondered how they felt, what it was like when the Council bestowed that incredible honor, earned only by the most trusted of their agents. It was a powerful kind of magic (blood magic—he knew that much), and it seemed to be the dividing line between those suspicious of the prerequisite blood sample taken at orientation and those who thought it was harmless. True, there were many terrible things blood magic could do, and perhaps it was knowing what the Council could do to its men with that kind of power that made them all so obedient—though no one would admit it. Ultimately, for Sinnrick and many of his fellow recruits, the prospect of wings outweighed those fears.

He sighed, he was getting ahead of himself. He had a job to do first, and he still hadn't quite shaken his disbelief after receiving his instructions. Somewhere in Cantis a man named Raiden had been conscripted by the Council. It was Raiden's task that now fell to Sinnrick. The Council had yet to hear from Raiden, and while the assignment was quite urgent, there was concern that something could have happened to him when he slipped from the seers' Sight.

Sinnrick's orders were clear: he was to determine Raiden's whereabouts, and the two of them would proceed together to complete the mission. Sinnrick shook his head and almost laughed out loud just thinking of the task—it still sounded like a joke. Find the fera. If there was one thing he had learned in his week of basic training, it was this: when the Council said to fight, you fought; when the Council said retreat, you retreated. So when the Council said the fera were still at large, you accepted the task without question. Everyone knew the fera's deadly reputation.

Eleven

U pstairs in her room, Nicole practically dove into her closet to find an old retired backpack and her fleece-lined denim jacket. Raiden had gone to the shop to retrieve his own coat. She changed into jeans and pulled on a pair of running shoes. She hopped on one foot as she pulled on the second shoe, nearly tripping over the clutter on her floor. There was no way she could go to another realm and not be prepared to run—she had golems on the brain. The empty backpack hanging from her shoulder was barely noticeable. She couldn't wait to feel the weight of foreign books in it. As much as this mysterious Council worried her, she couldn't quell her hunger to see more of Veil.

Nicole tromped down the stairs and hopped off the fourth step from the bottom, drifting to the floor.

"You're getting better," Raiden noted from where he waited at the door.

"Where are you two going?" Mitchell asked, stepping into the living room with an overstuffed sack of dirty clothes over his shoulder.

"We're going for a walk," she answered through an innocent smile.

"With a sword?" Mitch nodded toward Raiden, who had his sword on his shoulder.

"We're going for a walk in Veil, all right?" she clarified, folding her arms.

Mitchell dropped his chin to emphasize the look he gave her. "The place with the monsters?"

"Golems," Nicole corrected.

"It's very unlikely we'll see anything," Raiden said. "The sword is just a precaution. We shouldn't be gone more than an hour."

Nicole nodded in agreement.

"Yeah, okay. One hour," Mitchell reiterated.

"Yes, *Dad*." She feigned an obedient tone, rolling her eyes as she marched toward the backdoor.

"Your time starts now," Mitchell added as she opened the door.

Once the door closed behind Raiden and they were safely out of earshot, Nicole sighed, shaking her head with humor on her lips. "I never thought I'd see them act so suspicious." They crossed the yard, heading for the portal at a leisurely pace. "I guess, to be fair, you are a stranger carrying a sword...and they're used to seeing me chase guys away." She laughed and stepped through the portal without hesitation.

Raiden was right behind her. "Really?"

"Yeah." She tried to keep her voice upbeat as she realized how wrong He had been about the time in Veil—it was dark already. "I wonder what's more weird to them, magic, monsters and strangers with swords, or seeing me with a guy," she said with a laugh.

He sighed. "Well, safe to say my internal clock is completely unreliable." His voice was heavy with disappointment and worry. "Maybe we should come back tomorrow."

"We're here now. Might as well get it over with, right?"

The sound of a heavy sigh preceded his words. "You're right. We'll make this quick."

"Let's go then," Nicole said.

They made their way into the forest. At first Nicole cringed at every crunch of their footsteps on the leaves, screaming *here they are, here they are!* Her eyes wandered around the forest of straight white trees that seemed to glow in the soft light of the rising moon. Moonlight drifted down through the bare canopies. To her right, she caught the black shape of a beast not far off. Then her eyes understood the shape. The creature was not unlike a deer or a horse. She froze. Logic would have had her relax at the familiar animal, but it was, in fact, the thought of a horse—or rather something like it—that struck her heart with a pang of fear. Raiden stopped as well, spotting the same figure that had startled her.

"Is that what I think it is?" she asked, keeping her voice soft.

His hand clamped around hers—the answer was *yes*, then. He pulled her to the left, in the opposite direction of the still, dark animal.

"Come on." His voice was low.

Their pace quickened, the dry leaves hissing as they waded through them. Not until Raiden slowed and they were far away from the dark shape did she feel safe enough to ask again. Uttering its name might stir some dangerous magic in the night, like it could summon the creature out of the shadows.

"Raiden, was that a kelpie?"

"Yes. It's nothing to worry about. We're just giving it a wide berth," he said, though he did not release her hand. Was he lying to make her feel better? "It won't bother us; they rarely stray from their streams. Kelpies may be dark creatures, but they are strictly opportunistic killers."

Nicole swallowed hard; those last words were heavy with personal pain.

"You all right?" Raiden asked.

He squeezed her hand, and she realized she had his in a firm grip.

"Oh." She loosened her anxious grip. "Yeah. You?"

"I'll feel much better when we get back," he said with a bitter laugh.

Nicole could understand why he didn't want to be here—she knew there were too many reasons for her heart to fathom. Her fears paled in comparison to his memories.

They hiked. The contours of the land rose and fell as though they were walking over a sleeping face. She grew to appreciate the sound of their steps. The shushing of their feet through the leaves provided relief from the eerie silence.

The trees began to thin, and they came upon the few houses at the outskirts of the city. They were dark and quiet, but the stillness did not sound like sleep. As they walked, the number of houses increased, pressed closer together until they were nearly on top of one another. Each one was completely dark. Shops and buildings grew taller the farther they went. They left the houses behind, wandering through a maze where the walls were shop fronts, flats and apartment buildings. Nicole didn't count more than five stories for the tallest buildings. Surviving window panes were clouded in a death-shroud of dust and grime. Glass long broken and gone left windows gaping open, filled with darkness like faces without eyes.

"Raiden," she said, keeping her voice quiet, uncomfortable with disturbing the vast silence of the city, "how long did you say you lived here?"

"My whole life. But it has been like this for nine years." He didn't look around him, instead he kept his eyes forward.

"Only you?" she questioned, still disbelieving anyone could be so alone and endure it for that many years. He did not seem like the product of such a life.

"There were a few others, but I haven't seen a trace of them in years." He stopped and stepped over a low fence.

"How does a whole city—" she stopped herself, horrified she would even utter the question.

"Golems."

Nicole swallowed the dismay in her throat and followed, trying not to imagine the golems from yesterday and refusing to let her imagination conjure up the horrible day when they had fallen upon these streets. Curiosity nagged at her. How many golems had there been, when had they come—in the night, or during a deceptively bright day? But she didn't dare to ask those things. He had spent nine years in the wreckage of that day; he shouldn't have to relive it again for the sake of her morbid curiosity—she felt ashamed.

"What did you do here for fun—I mean, before—" She looked around, letting the silence finish her question for her. Even her attempt to change the subject to something brighter struck another dismal chord in the quiet streets around them.

"I had a friend named Caeruleus," Raiden said, his voice lifting out of the gloom.

Nicole realized with sudden dread that his friend must be dead too, like his mother, like everyone. She felt worse than before now.

"Ruleus was lucky," Raiden continued. "He and his father left Cantis before it happened."

Nicole's shoulders sank with relief as her heart lifted her back up. She couldn't help but rejoice that Raiden had someone he hadn't lost. She noticed, then, that they had arrived at a house. It was only two stories tall, sandwiched between two five-story tall flats.

It stood on a small foundation, a quaint home with a small yard separating it from the once-bustling street. They approached the house in silence. She was so distracted by the incongruous house that she bumped into Raiden when he stopped.

She let out a nervous laugh. "Sorry."

He returned a soft smile and then stooped just in front of the door to pick up something white—Nicole could have sworn it was an envelope, but who would send him mail? *A letter from Caeruleus?* He certainly didn't seem happy about it—his shoulders were tense. Whatever it was, he buried it in his pocket and opened the door to the dark house.

They stepped inside and Nicole was surprised to find the silence could get thicker still. Raiden shut the door, and the faint moonlight disappeared. Nothing existed—nothing but black. His hand found her shoulder, and she responded with an instinctive jerk.

"It's me." His murmur was barely audible and his hand found hers to lead her through the house.

She eased her hand out of his, annoyed that his touch made her cheeks burn. *Ilumina* flitted through her mind, and in her hand bloomed a small light. "I—" She felt the need to explain, as shameful as it felt to admit it. "I don't like the dark."

"I don't blame you."

Her light shone on his face. While his words were gentle, his mouth was firm. He turned away, proceeding down a hall.

When the creak of an opening door broke the silence, she relaxed a little, following Raiden through a narrow doorway into a room. Soon enough, light blossomed in the room. The shadows rolled back into the corners, retracting like curtains to reveal the books. Books were everywhere—columns, stacks, piles against every wall. It was a nest of knowledge with a bed and a nightstand in its center and a desk beside the door, almost buried under books. Raiden closed the door behind them.

Nicole spotted the window and noticed that they were on the second floor, but she knew they had not climbed any stairs.

"Weren't we on the first floor?"

"We were, but my safe haven is up here. I fashioned a transporting spell to the closet door downstairs. It took me a few years to get it right, but it was a necessary precaution. The few other survivors in the city were not beneath stealing from one another to get by. Once I had the spell working and only I could activate it, I destroyed the staircase so they couldn't get up here."

"Protecting your books?" She smiled, half at him, half at the expanse of books around them.

"I don't think they would see the books as anything more than rubble." He shrugged. "They stole my food store several times before I could work out this system."

"I just can't understand how a city can become ... this."

"Veil has many cities like this. It's still fragile—even though decades have passed since the Dragon Wars." He spoke matter-of-factly.

"Oh, don't say Dragon Wars, please." Nicole felt herself sink with disappointment at the thought.

"Why?"

"I've loved dragons since I was a kid. If there was ever something I desperately wanted to be real, it was dragons."

He chuckled. It was a sardonic sound. "You might want to keep your enthusiasm to yourself when you're in Veil."

"Oh, are you afraid I'm going to offend all your neighbors?" She crossed her arms.

He answered with another chuckle. "These books are my only neighbors."

"In that case I'm sure they don't mind that I love dragons. Books understand," she said, laying her hand on a book affectionately.

They each turned to a pile of books, Raiden searching for particular titles and Nicole looking with aimless curiosity. On the spine of a book just three from the top, she spotted a title that provoked her interest: *The World Divided.* She carefully pulled the book from its spot in the stack and opened it. Scanning the words of the page quickly at first, she didn't make any sense of the words until she slowed her eyes and realized it looked like the English of *The Canterbury Tales* her class studied last semester—Middle English. One word leaped out from the page: *portal.* It was a book all about the division and relationship between the separated realms. She brushed a few pages farther and saw a passage that mentioned those seeking to return to the old world. There was a spell to open a portal—and on the next page was a spell to close one.

Eagerly, she shut the book and stuffed it into her backpack. "What made you start collecting books?" she asked as she continued perusing.

"I needed to find the funeral pyre spell for my mother. The flames only burn the deceased. I knew where to find it; there's a small bookshop two streets over. I didn't leave the house for two days. I was afraid to walk out that door. But I finally worked up enough courage to find the book I needed. On my way there, I saw the rest of them everywhere. I must have taken care of the bodies for weeks. It just became a part of my daily routine. I had to search shops and homes for food and supplies. I couldn't go anywhere without coming across someone.

"As the months passed, I found fewer remains. I started collecting the books. One here, one there, armfuls from the bookstores and mastery shops. I needed spells to help me get by and take care of myself. I anticipated needing to defend myself in case the golems came again. But the city has been silent ever since, and the books eventually became a habit—a way to pass the time."

He stood up and plucked a book off the very top of a column with a huff of annoyance. Nicole stifled a laugh; he must have expected it to be at the bottom of the stack.

"How old were you?"

"Thirteen." He placed the book beside the others on the bed.

That made him twenty-two now. She looked up at him. She was eighteen, and she couldn't fathom pulling herself together after something like that, let alone as a thirteen-year-old. There wasn't even a hint of pain on his face. His mouth was relaxed, his brows undisturbed, his eyes clear.

"I can't understand how there could be other survivors and they didn't want to help each other, help you."

"They were afraid, more afraid of golems and dying than their conscience. I don't think they ever walk through the streets or the forest like I do, or fish at the docks. They hide, and they do it well. I only learned there *were* others by the absence of my supplies."

"You never tried to get away from here in all that time?"

"To be honest, I could have left years ago. But by the time I might have been able to shift to the mainland I had already decided there was something I had to do or no one else would," his voice grew quiet.

Nicole understood. "You wanted revenge. Someone sent those golems."

"I had nothing but time to plan, prepare, get stronger." He sighed. "It was all I had to live for. I thought about leaving once or twice, but I felt like if I left, then Cantis would truly be a forgotten place. I wanted to stay. I wanted justice. I became quite comfortable with being alone, not having to feel—it's easier than you may think to forget."

Nicole knew she would want revenge if someone took her dad and her brothers from her. She shuddered at the thought of losing them like that. Her mind raced through all the information she had now, rifling through it and shuffling each piece into chronological order. The golems came nine years ago. Yesterday, golems had followed Raiden through the portal, but then he had been sure no more would follow. Did that mean he'd taken care of the culprit before they met? No—he had said the person was still there.

"They're still up there?" she asked, needing to be sure.

"She is," he said. "Moira. I don't know why everyone in Cantis had to die, why she would stay in the castle all this time."

"Do you mind if I ask what exactly happened yesterday before you happened upon the portal?" She could smile now, remembering their abrupt collision.

"I guess you could say after nine years I found out what kind of man I turned out to be," he said with a shake of his head.

"What kind of man is that?" she asked.

His mouth twisted in a bitter smile, a sneer. "A coward … I managed to get into the castle, get through her spells, and find her chamber. But when I triggered the magic that woke the golems, I panicked. I should have held my ground and waited for Moira to return. Instead, I chose petty thievery as my retribution, and I ran."

"What did you steal from her?" She couldn't help but wonder what a person like that could possibly treasure.

"It doesn't matter, really. I lost it in all the excitement yesterday."

Nicole felt his desire to change the subject, and she was content enough to let it go now. Her mind felt swollen with the details, her heart heavy with the pain in them. Was it all real? There was no one to confirm his story, just the empty city that couldn't dispute it. The golems had been real, though, they had been after him. Wasn't that proof of his honesty? The room fell quiet. She usually enjoyed a little quiet, but she didn't like the silence here in Cantis.

"So these are your friends, huh?" Her eyes swept the room of books, and she stood up. Enough gloom, enough silence—they were here for books, not nightmares.

"All the friends I've ever had besides Caeruleus and you."

She turned away from him, heat flooding her cheeks. What motive could he have to lie, to call her a friend when he barely knew her? There was a sad earnestness in his voice, in his eyes, in the way he turned his books over respectfully in his hands.

"You've read them all?"

"At least once."

"What's on all these pages?" Her hand found a book, which opened eagerly, but there was no English on the page.

"Some are spell books, magical theory, history, encyclopedias, memoirs." He moved slowly along the stacks, scanning the embossed titles on the worn cloth spines.

"But these aren't all in English. You can read this?"

"The people of this realm didn't come from just one country. There are a few prominent languages here. Dutch is about as common as English. The fey primarily speak a form of Gaelic or Welsh I believe, but you won't hear that particularly often in the cities."

"That's incredible."

"It's turned into a muddled conglomerate of them all over time. A large arrival of old world refugees almost eighty years ago, and lots of people got curious about the old world. I don't know where it opened precisely, many speaking English arrived. Since an old form of English survived here, many took to it easily enough. I think some liked to imagine Veil is still a part of that world, so they tried to preserve some connection to it."

"To think," she said, kneeling down beside the bed, her eyes making their way down the stacked spines toward the floor, "all this is in your head."

"I've read them all, but I certainly couldn't remember each one word for word," he chuckled.

"Downplay it all you want; it's still impressive." She nearly pressed her face to the floor to read the spines of the books at the very bottom.

"You're welcome to take anything you like." He handed her the backpack, having added three books to it.

"Thank you." She took the bag absently, her eyes on the dark form of a book in the shadows under the bed. How did this one end up here? She reached in and grabbed it. It was small and pliable, unlike the hardbound books around the room. She felt soft, aged leather against her hand. As she pulled the book out, the back of her hand scraped against something rough and cold.

She studied the pink scratches across the skin of her knuckles as she placed the unknown book into the backpack. Out of curiosity, she reached under the bed once more, searching for the rough object. Her hand closed around what felt like concrete.

Twelve

Nicole stood up, holding a heavy building stone in her hand. "What's this?"

"Hmm?" Raiden looked over his shoulder, his eyes focusing with recognition. "It's an old project of mine. That's a shift token."

"A what?"

"It's a more secure way to ether shift, using a token or object from a specific location. It can only take you to the place where the token came from, so it's like an anchor. If you aren't focused on shifting you can end up somewhere between where you left and where you want to go. Tokens make it easy. Many people carry one tied to their home, activated by a simple movement."

"Like what?"

"That won't work unless you tap it and turn it over, you don't want shift tokens to be activated too easily."

"Does this bring you home?"

"No. That takes you far from this room—somewhere you really don't want to go." She set it on the stack of books beside her carefully.

Suddenly, they heard the distant knock of knuckles against wood. They turned to each other, frozen, their eyes locked together.

"What are the chances that's one of your extremely reclusive neighbors?" Nicole whispered.

"Stay here." His harsh tone left no room for disagreement. He slipped out the door before she could even object.

"Raiden," she hissed, but the door shut on her hushed voice.

A flash of white caught her eye as an envelope fell to the floor. She looked at the envelope for a moment, but she turned back to the bed anxioulsy to zip her backpack closed and get ready to leave.

The sound of paper sliding along the wood floor caught her attention, and she turned to see the letter slip across the room and bump against the sole of her shoe. Written on the envelope was the word *urgent,* compelling her hand to retrieve it. When she touched the letters with her fingertips, a prickle of magic made the letter jump, alerted by her touch.

She wondered why Raiden would ignore it as she tried to snatch the twitching thing off the floor. When at last she caught it and stood up, the envelope yanked itself from her hand and split open. The letter inside jumped out and unfolded, falling into her hands. She suupposed her touch had activated its response.

Her curious eyes couldn't help seeing the words that filled the paper in her hands.

Raiden,

For fear that the first letter we sent may have been intercepted or lost, we write again with the utmost urgency and hope this message finds you before our window of opportunity passes. If you, indeed, received and read our first correspondence, our seers suspect the portal between Veil and the old realm has already opened. It arrived far sooner than first anticipated, and it is imperative that you locate the fera. Without knowledge of who this individual is, we can only implore you to proceed with caution and escort the fera safely to Atrium at the soonest possible opportunity.

Nicole's mind stitched together the words as she read. As it mentioned a first letter, this had to be the second. The Council did know about her then, but had Raiden gotten the first letter or not—had he known all along? *Is he helping them?* She shook her head slowly, but it was all too easy to believe.

Nicole's grip tightened on the paper, crushing the sides. Her heart bludgeoned her rib cage. Was that why he had brought her here? She looked around the room at all the books and felt like she was surrounded by lies.

The sound of the paper crumpling brought her gaze back to the letter. She was partly confused by the sound until she realized her hands were shaking, threatening to tear the page in two. There was still more to read, so she stilled her hands and continued.

> This letter will be followed by one of our most trustworthy agents to assist you should anyone try to impede your delivery of the fera to Atrium. We cannot stress the magnitude of this mission's importance. If left unregulated, the fera could do irreparable damage in the other realm, including disturbing the delicate balance that sustains the barrier and preserves the separation of our two realms. Thus, our responsibility falls to you, Raiden, to protect not only this precious realm, haven to magic and all her denizens, but the realm which we left behind as well. May fortune be with you.

> Official Scribe to the Council of Veil

A seal was affixed below the scribe's signature. A flourished eternity knot hung over a pair of keys encircled in a wreath. The gold seal glinted in the light, but Nicole was oblivious to all except her heart falling into a pit of fear within her. Raiden had closed the door only a minute ago, maybe two. The knocking from downstairs echoed fresh in her mind with a whole new meaning. It had to be the Council's man—their second man, if Raiden was the first.

She found herself recalling everything he had said to her, questioning it all, her heart aching with betrayal. But she had to wrestle her mind away from such foolish sadness. She'd known him a day, a mere twenty-four hours. How many lies she'd been told didn't matter. This was no great tragedy. There was no relationship to mourn. Now was not the time to feel—it was the time to think, because the only way out was through that door, and now there were two obstacles instead of one.

Raiden moved soundlessly down the hall from the closet door, a skill earned with years of practice, sneaking around the house without alerting his mother. He sacrificed the silence by pulling his sword from the sheath on his back. The blade's ringing sang into the darkness, and he could only hope whoever stood on the other side of the front door didn't hear it. What stranger would knock on any door in Cantis unless he or she knew there was someone still calling the place home? The answer was just a few feet and the turn of a doorknob away.

"Hello?" said a muffled voice from outside. "Anyone here? This is Sinnrick Stultus, I was sent by the Council. Raiden, are you there?"

His heart clenched. The Council had sent someone after all. He wasn't sure if he should open the door and try to mislead him or just wait until he left. If he did speak to the man, he might not be able shake him. This Sinnrick might not let him out of his sight and might insist on retrieving Nicole at once. But if Raiden left him to walk away, what was to stop him from finding the portal on his own? Raiden couldn't be sure how far this man would go to bring Nicole to the Council.

It occurred to him that the most prudent choice would be to open the door and kill Sinnrick where he stood. He was prepared, sword in hand, but he froze. He was certain that two days ago he could have dispatched this stranger if he had to, so he should be fully able to do so now.

Raiden tightened his grip on the sword and took a deep breath. His priority should be getting Nicole back through the portal. She was at too much risk in Veil. This man was a completely unpredictable entity. Raiden couldn't risk failing and alerting him, and ultimately the Council, that he was working against them. Even worse, if this man had means to communicate with the Council from Cantis, Nicole's presence in Veil could be exposed.

His breath went stale in his lungs, but he did not exhale until he heard the sound of fading footsteps turn away from the front stoop and follow the path back to the street.

He spun on his heels and hastened down the hall, securing the sword back into the scabbard on his back. His hand closed around the knob of the closet door, and it swung open as he strode into the room without slowing.

Nicole stood right where he had left her. Then he spotted the shift token in her hand. When she tapped the upward face of the stone, his heart dropped, and he lurched forward.

"Nicole," his warning trailed off as she turned the brick over on her palm. He grabbed her arm, but the room turned over as the stone did in her hands, and they fell into darkness.

Thirteen

For a sickening moment in the weightless dread of falling, Raiden swore the Sight had taken hold of him. They dropped together onto an icy stone floor, jarring him from the grip of the fleeting vision. Immediate relief soothed his heart at having caught Nicole as she activated the token, but his relief was short-lived. Raiden would have preferred letting Sinnrick into the house to being here.

As they picked themselves up, Nicole turned on him, jerking away so violently that she nearly tripped herself. "Get the hell away from me."

"Nicole," he said softly, confused, "it's just me." For a moment he supposed that she must have thought he was the stranger who knocked on the door. Now that she was looking, she would see who he was.

"Were you going to take me home, Raiden, or were you taking me to Atrium? Would you have told me, or would I have woken up there one morning?"

She hurled a crumpled page of paper at him. He knew exactly what it was as he pressed his hand to the outside of his pocket where he had tucked the letter. He hardly felt the light wad of paper tap against his abdomen, but it struck his heart with a nauseating blow.

His mind raced to find the right words—the swiftest words—torn between the importance of convincing her that she could trust him and the need to leave this place as quickly as possible.

"I never accepted the Council's task, Nicole. I can explain everything, I swear to you, but we have to leave this place immediately. Please."

Extending a gentle hand, he took a step toward her. She matched his step, preserving the distance between them.

"I'm not going anywhere with you." Her voice was quiet, but it shook with such intensity that the stones underfoot trembled, and he almost backed away. For a split second he saw the fera, felt the danger the Council had described.

The cold dark air crackled with magic, raising the hair on the back of his neck.

"Nicole," he tried again. If he was going to get her out of here, he would have to convince her. He would have to tell her everything.

She looked around, taking in their surroundings. Her eyes followed the walls around the circle of the tower, took in the stone floor, and then peered up toward the open sky through the absence of a roof.

For a twisted second, Raiden was glad they stood where they did. He might not have had the chance to convince her if they weren't here. As long as she didn't know the way out, she had to listen.

"I was oblivious to the Council's request when I met you. I received the letter, but I hadn't even opened it. Everything happened so fast yesterday. You remember. I didn't read it until this morning."

She glared at him with distrust in her eyes. He couldn't really blame her, but now he had to convince her how much he despised the Council. This problem had been created by his secrets. He took a deep breath, bracing himself.

"The Council destroyed my family." He couldn't remember saying that aloud before now, not even to Caeruleus.

Nicole's face softened for a moment when their eyes met. She shook her head and scowled again.

"My father was one of them—one of the Council's men. He'd be gone for days, weeks sometimes, on their errands. The Council—whatever they were asking of him—was more important than our family. More times than I could count, he left my mother and me to answer their call, until one day he left and never returned. We never received a thing from the Council—no support, no condolences, not a word. Their men are disposable to them, and my father let them use him. There is only one person I hate more than them, and I vowed long ago never to be like him."

Her stony face didn't soften.

"I should have told you about that letter. But before I even had a chance to think, your magic surfaced, and—"

A chilling grumble moved through the shadows, and Nicole turned her head, searching for the source of the sound. The last thing he needed now was for her to go looking for more trouble.

"Nicole?"

She jerked her glare back to him. "So I'm supposed to believe that you aren't working with them and lying to me right now?" she asked.

"The Council took my father from me and left Cantis to its fate. I lost everything because of them. I would sooner die than serve them." His words trembled with sincerity. "Look, you've seen the golems, the city, where I've spent the last nine years of my life. I've told you everything." He swallowed the lump in his throat. Now, thanks to the Council, he might very well lose her too. Why couldn't they have left what remained of his life alone?

"Why didn't you just tell me everything before?"

"I didn't want the Council's claims to convince you that you were something you aren't. I thought you deserved the chance to figure that out yourself without their accusations."

"What if you're wrong and I'm exactly what they think I am?" Fear shook her hard words. "Will you change your mind?"

"No," he said sternly.

She looked at him expectantly, like she was waiting for something more.

"I don't know what more to say, Nicole," he said with a sigh.

Nicole inhaled. "Start with where the hell we are and how we get out."

"The tower. It stands on the neighboring mountain across from the castle." He lifted his hand to gesture the direction of the castle as though they could see the stone.

Within the circular walls, they could barely see each other now. Even in the darkness, though, he could sense her eyes piercing him; he could practically hear her thoughts connecting. She knew the whole story now: what had happened in Cantis, why he had wanted to get into the castle all those years, the degradation of his vendetta into petty thievery.

"Why have a token to this place?"

"It was my first attempt to get into the castle. I thought I could cross the bridge that leads to the tower, but it wasn't sound. The entire structure nearly came down; my token only brought me to a dead end."

Nicole looked up and let out an exasperated sigh.

"Can we continue this elsewhere?" He wanted to get back to the portal, to get Nicole away from here. Sinnrick lurked in the back of his mind. How long would it take him to find the portal? What would he do when he found Raiden and Nicole? Were his instructions to deceive Nicole into accompanying him peacefully or to use whatever force was necessary? Raiden shouldn't have brought her here; even Cantis, sitting at the very fringes of Veil, was far too close to the Council. Too many threats were coming from different directions.

"Fine," she agreed with a sigh.

Another grumbling breath crept out of the darkness followed by the moan of moving chains. She jumped. "What was that?"

Raiden knew he could afford no more secrets, so he confessed something he'd known since before their unfortunate trip. "We're not exactly alone in this tower."

He could see her stiffen and knew what she must be imagining: golems or, worse, Moira. "Trust me," he said. "It's not what you're thinking. Nor is it anything to worry about."

"Not exactly alone? Who's here?"

Raiden could feel her anger already; maybe it was the Sight in his mind. "It's not really a who ... it's a dragon."

"What? Where?" She looked around.

He was reluctant to tell her. "Below us."

"What is a dragon doing down there?"

"You would have to ask Moira that question; I don't have the answer."

"Ilumina," Nicole said. Her hand blossomed with light, the magic of the spell trapped beneath her skin, which cast a yellow glow. The room lit up, and she spotted the dark opening that led down below. She turned and marched resolutely toward the stairway.

Raiden followed several steps behind her, hurrying to catch up.

They neared the bottom of the stairs. With every step she took, the shadows crawled back into the recesses of the chamber, vermin running from the light of her hand. The darkness slipped away like a black sheet, revealing the large beast lying curled up on the stone floor.

"It really is a dragon," she whispered as though the sound of her voice might shatter the reality.

There was a huge metal collar around its neck that weighed it down to the floor. Its breathing shuddered with weakness, but even that didn't make it safe to approach. Its head rested upon the stone floor, and its eyes remained closed.

Nicole stepped toward it.

"Don't." He lurched forward, erasing some of the distance between them, almost close enough to take her hand.

"Don't you see what I'm seeing?" She raised her hand toward the beast, and her light glinted off its scales.

"You don't understand, Nicole. They can't be trusted after—"

A bitter laugh fell from her mouth. "I think you're the last person who should be talking about trust right now."

"You don't know their kind—"

114

"Raiden," she interrupted gently, "yesterday we were perfect strangers and I trusted you. You know all the horrible things about my kind and you trust me. Why is this creature any different? Why doesn't he deserve help or trust?"

"Nicole, this is far more complicated—"

"No. Tell me—why didn't you believe everything the Council said about me?"

"Because I got to know you first, all right?" he answered with swift frustration.

"Because *some* dragons did horrible things in the past, I should condemn *this* dragon? Like the Council would have you condemn me for what other fera have done?"

He understood what she was implying. "You and that dragon are not the same, Nicole. Don't make this about you."

"You don't get it," she said with an angry laugh.

"Help me understand then," he pleaded, exasperated and desperate.

"It's not about what I am or what he is." She extended her hand toward the dragon. "This is wrong. If he was anything but a dragon, you would see that."

Raiden opened his mouth but could think of nothing to say.

"I'm not leaving him here." She shook her head.

"Nicole, there are consequences—"

"You mean like saving a life?" She stepped past him, swinging her path away from him, keeping him farther than arm's length. "I don't need your permission."

The dragon opened its eyes, and the light of her hand reflected in its vibrant violet gaze. A rough, heavy sigh rumbled in the dragon's chest, and Raiden saw Nicole's hand hesitate over its muzzle. In the light it was clear just how large it was, its body long and lean, the slender neck weighed down by the collar beneath its horse-like head. Its scales were dark and iridescent like oil. It had shaggy fur like a mane behind its head and partway down its forelegs. Halfway down its tail was more fur. It looked more mammalian than reptilian despite the scales.

Raiden cringed as Nicole set her hand against its forehead. All he had to do was grab her hand. She reached for the collar. Raiden lunged forward, but he caught her hand too late. As Nicole unclasped the metal fastener, a screaming wave of heat burst from the collar, lifting them off their feet and throwing them back across the chamber.

Nicole's hand was wrenched from his grip as they skidded into the wall. Her light went out, and the darkness snapped shut around them. He scrambled on his hands and knees, searching for her.

"Nicole?"

A cough.

His hand found her, her back, her shoulder; then he caught her arm. Touching her somehow gave him a charge. He called his magic, but he could swear it was Nicole's that surged forward, propelling them through space. They slipped into the ether, shifting easily back into the book-filled room, dropping onto the bed as though they had fallen through the ceiling.

He rolled off the bed and jumped to his feet. He adjusted his sword, positioning the strap across his chest. "We have to leave. Now."

☙

The dragon picked himself up off the cold, wet stones, weak but without pain. With every second that passed, his strength crept back into his bones and sinews. A deep, unburdened breath rumbled in his chest, and the heat of his power rekindled in his lungs. Then a new sensation awakened in his chest, like a tether around his heart, pulling him.

He knew he should change. Being bound to her would be easier in his secondary form. He didn't particularly like the human shape—too compact, uncomfortable, restricting—but a decade in that cursed shackle put that discomfor in perspective. His bones shifted and popped. He shrank, his wings trapped beneath the skin of his tiny torso, itching with confinement. The human neck was so short he could barely look over his shoulders. No wonder they made such easy prey.

As the dragon transformed, he could feel the pull toward her. He was free of his chains and bound by an even stronger force—a debt to the one who freed him. It was natural to despise the prospect of his debt, but he could not help wondering about her. She had not shied away from him. She had seen him clearly for what he was, and still she had helped him. Why hadn't she reacted like her companion?

Across the valley in the castle, a shrieking alarm pierced Moira's prolonged slumber. She jolted upright in a panic at that sound.

"No," she exhaled, scrambling off her bed and stumbling to the corner where her looking glass waited. She waved her reflection away to look into the tower. There were only chains left lying on the floor, the collar open and empty.

"No, no, no!" Each successive cry grew louder. The dragon was gone—she needed golems! This was precisely why she stored the ashes and soot of her decade living here. It was a completely dead medium, not a speck of life or magic left in it to interfere with the magic that formed the golems and propelled them. She learned that long ago when she had been a young gifted apprentice to her master.

She rushed to her worktable and rifled through scraps of paper until she found the right illustration: a golem tall and swift with the sharpest of talons. This would do nicely. The page almost burned with the spell laced into the image. In a blink, she shifted through the ether from her chamber to the cold, dark room where her medium had accumulated all these years. The door moaned open, revealing a room filled with great mounds of fireplace soot. With an angry flick of her wrist, she threw the rigid parchment into the nearest pile of ash, where it ignited, and the spell awakened.

Fourteen

Nicole sat up with a hand pressed against her head, dizzy from shifting between the tower and Raiden's home.

"Why did we come back here?" She swallowed hard and stood up, stooping to grab the backpack from the floor. In the back of her mind she told herself she should leave it, she could run faster without it, but she needed them.

"Think of it like throwing a rock into a still pond. Our ether shifting will not go unnoticed. If I had gone directly to the portal, she would know where to send the golems, and your backyard would be swarming with them. It might attract Sinnrick as well."

"Who?"

"The Council's agent. The one who knocked at the door."

Her heart pounded, and her stomach clenched with the impulse to run. This had to be her opportunity. All she had to do was cooperate long enough to get out the front door. He had said himself that ether shifting would lead trouble right to him, so she could use the only advantage she knew she had over him—running. She couldn't believe how glad she was that she had put on her racing shoes.

He pulled Nicole through the dark house. Her heart reeled at his touch. She now had a total of three threats to worry about—one had her by the hand.

Nicole had to make a decision and make it fast. Her pulse was racing. She recalled the book she had found on portals. If she could make it back home and close the portal, no one could come after her—not the Council ... and not Raiden. A twinge of sadness struck her. She was torn. Deep down she didn't doubt his sincerity. But he had kept secrets, and she didn't *want* to trust him anymore. He would be better off without whatever responsibility he thought he had to her. She could give him his life back—hopefully now he was ready to move on and live it.

He opened the front door, and Nicole's heart lurched. Her stomach twisted with nervous anticipation far greater than any she'd experienced at the starting line at track meets, waiting for the pop of the gun to go off. This was a whole new game, a race unlike any other. Her competition would be not only behind her but potentially all around her.

They stepped over the threshold, walked down the little path to the gate. He opened it and, in her head, the gun went off.

She leaned forward into a sprint.

"Nicole!" he called.

She was halfway down the street already, rounding the corner, her feet almost slipping out from under her as she turned. She was a hundred feet away before he could pull himself from his shock to chase her.

Adrenaline and fear were so thick in her chest that her heart was pounding in her throat. She pushed her legs harder still, hoping that Raiden was shrinking into the distance behind her and that he wouldn't risk ether shifting. She could make out the black, blocky shapes of the buildings as she followed the streets, scanning as best she could for a human form or the hunched, gangly shape of golems. The last thing she should do was cast any light, but she knew she would need it as soon as she reached the end of the paved roads and entered the forest. She tried to keep her mind out ahead of her, on her stride, her breathing, her plan—away from what she was leaving behind her and the weight in her heart as she thought of never seeing him again.

Far behind her, Raiden cursed himself for yelling her name into the night where Sinnrick was looking for them. Still, his heart conjured up her name in his lungs again and he had to resist. He ran, dumbfounded by Nicole's speed. At this rate, she would lose him; and if he used a tracking spell to follow, he risked leading enemies right to her. He knew precisely where she was headed anyway, but she didn't know her way through the forest and he needed to make sure she made it home, make sure nothing followed her through the portal even if he didn't either.

Sinnrick was out there somewhere, and it was very likely golems would soon join the hunt. He couldn't allow them to track her back to the old world. He had to catch Nicole first without seeming like an enemy himself. A groan of frustration slipped from his mouth as he decided he'd have to risk the tracking spell.

"Onthullen troed," he said, his voice harsh, magic warming his throat as he spoke.

Blue phosphorescence on the stones of the street appeared at every footstep Nicole had made. What should have been a subtle glow grew bright with the trace of magic Nicole had left behind her. The trail leading to her extended into the black night, signaling anything in the vicinity to follow. He could only hope that he was the sole tracer of her trail and that he could catch her—the trail would only disappear when he reached her.

Nicole's breathing quickened as she reached the edge of the city. "Ilumina," she exhaled, and an orb of light burst into being just ahead of her, hovering with her at the level of her waist as she ran, lighting the forest floor. Her mind was consumed with the engine of her muscles, her breathing, navigating the terrain that lay before her, her legs bound for the portal.

With the book about portals in her backpack, she hoped she could figure out how to close the portal before Raiden managed to catch up.

A sharp snap somewhere in the trees jerked her gaze to the left, but she could discern nothing except the few trees revealed by her light and the black shadows filling the space between them. Something wasn't right. Her muscles seized up, and she skidded to a halt, ankle-deep in leaves. She thought she saw the shadows move beside her.

"Shit!" With explosive instinct, she turned completely around and ran. Up ahead, the blackness between the trees moved toward her.

"No," she cried, turning again, a quarter turn to the right. How many golems could there be? She stopped cold; her heart dropped into a well of dread. The shadows just ahead writhed with artificial life.

Just as she turned back toward the city, she noticed a blue glow welling up beneath the leaves. She slowed, distracted by the strange sight. When she nearly ran right into a tree, she dodged it, and instead her shoulder clipped Raiden's. They both fell. Her immediate reaction was relief at the sight of Raiden.

She staggered to her feet, her legs still programmed to get away.

"Nicole, wait," he cried as he picked himself up.

Her words tumbled from her mouth: "Your friends are back."

"What?"

She heard his confusion, but it was only a matter of seconds before she heard him curse followed by the hissing of his feet running through the leaves behind her. He caught up with her, which meant her speed was waning.

"Nicole, stop!" he begged.

The forest ahead filled with unnatural black forms. Once more she stopped, nearly sinking into fatigue. The familiar sound of Raiden's sword ringing free from its scabbard struck a chord of comfort amid the cacophony of fear drumming in her chest.

Magic churned deep within her, kindled with panic, fueled by adrenaline. The golems crept forward into the light of her spell, still hovering over her shoulder. They were twice as big as before, hunched, spindly things taller than Raiden with gangly limbs. Now they stood upright.

Raiden heaved a tremendous sigh. "If they're focused on me you can get back. It's time for you to go, Nicole."

"There's nowhere to go—"

"That way." He pointed up. "Go."

"I could barely keep my feet off the ground before." Her words trembled. "You know I can't."

"Now." His voice boomed with the force of a spell that caught her up like a leaf in the wind and threw her into the air. The thin branches of the canopy snapped around her as she tumbled into the sky.

"Raiden!" she screamed, angry and startled as she pitched and wobbled in the air over the treetops.

A blade of light cut through the tangle of bare branches. Nicole saw every swing of his sword but nothing else as the golems screeched.

"Raiden!" she shouted, concern and irritation dueling in her vocal chords.

He had given her the chance she needed to leave him behind, to go home and close the portal, but now—faced with the guarantee that she could never see him again, leave him here to face the golems, to his quarrel with Moira, to face the people who took his father and could have prevented his mother's fate all on his own— she squirmed at the thought of being the kind of person who leaves. She couldn't be that person. She wished she could forget the sincerity in his voice when he had called her his only friend since Caeruleus. She had people on her side: her dad, her brothers, her best friend. Raiden had no one. She let out a groan of annoyance; her instincts conflicting with her better judgement.

"Go home, Nicole!" His strained voice rose above the fray.

She hated being told what to do and she wasn't about to start by listening to this jerk—picking fights with mass murderers, keeping stupid secrets—even if it made her just as idiotic as him. Maybe that dragon had done horrible things after all, but helping it was still right, she wouldn't change her mind about that and helping Raiden was right too, even if he was a jerk. She would have liked to deny it, but truth be told, she like that he called her his friend, she wanted that to be true.

She struggled to catch a glimpse of him through the trees, but could only see the blue light of his sword blinking through the black mass of golems and shadows like a ship beacon through the night. Then a golem burst from the canopy, latching onto her with sharp claws. Her control over gravity slipped from her grasp. She fell, crashing into branches. Her stomach knotted as she tried to push gravity away once more. Too slow. The ground stopped her. Her light went out. A shower of broken twigs rained down around her.

The golem persisted, dragging claws through the denim of her jacket. It was a flurry of movement. She pushed it away, holding it at arm's length, but its arms were longer. She kicked frantically. Her heart pounded furiously. The strange new presence in her body swelled out of her core, a prickling energy ripped through her veins. Every cell in her body screamed with heat. Power flooded her arms and escaped through her hands. A cloud of soot collapsed on top of her, and she lay there trembling.

The shadows moved around her. Her body wanted to lie there in shock, but she forced it to move, get up, to run. She strained her eyes to see through the darkness. Every sound seized her attention. She needed light but was afraid to set a beacon for the enemy. Was it a golem or her feet snapping twigs beneath the leaves? For all she knew, the forest went on endlessly in every direction. Where were the golems? She looked behind her again and again. Where was Raiden?

She stopped to look closely all around her, unable to discern even the faintest flash from his sword in any direction. It occurred to her that the golems probably had no problem navigating in the dark. Maintaining her disadvantage did her more harm than good. A spark of light bloomed into a hovering sphere with only a thought. The spell was easier every time.

Her thoughts jumped to Sinnrick. The golems might not be the worst thing in the forest. A snap—she was sure it came from directly behind her. Her heart leaped forward, and so did she, lurching into a mindless run. Sweeping her gaze around her as she ran, she searched the night with frantic eyes. But something caught her foot, and she fell forward, crashing into water and river rock with a frigid splash.

Her body shook with the cold, muscle fibers seizing. Struggling to move her shivering limbs, she scrambled to get to her feet. Water flowed around her knees, turning her legs and feet to ice. Her heart stopped, frozen with the realization of where she was. Both up and down the stream, however, there was no sign of any form, not animal or golem or human. Trembling violently, she paused a second to take in a deep breath, a puff of white in the night. She turned to wade toward dry ground only to come face-to-face with a dark horse with a pair of piercing black eyes.

She threw herself back, away from the kelpie, crashing into the water again. Somehow, without seeming to move, it came closer, standing over her, pressing its face nearer to hers. Its gaze was so utterly black that moonlight did not even reflect in the dark orbs. As its head loomed closer, she leaned away, crawling awkwardly through the water numbing her limbs. The kelpie's eyes held hers. They were voids, black holes pulling her into their depths. Her thoughts were lost in them. Unable to think, unable to look away, all she had left was the instinct in her limbs to lean away from it, lying back into the water.

Not even the shock of the icy current rushing over her face could jar her away from the kelpie's stare. Her lips shut tight, trapping the last precious breath in her lungs. Ideas crept into her mind from the black voids. What would it be like to part her lips and inhale that dark water? Could it really be so bad to let the numbness flood her? If anything, it promised relief from a world ready to come crashing down on her.

As her lungs burned, a familiar spark reignited in her core, raging into an inferno. Inside her frozen form, she burned. The heat of this force called magic frightened her. Perhaps all she had to do to put it out was to open her mouth, let the cold smother the conflagration before it could erupt, before it could consume her. *Open your mouth, take a deep breath, you'll feel better*—that's all she could think with those bottomless black eyes peering into her. The piercing cold became numbness but not fast enough. Somewhere deep in her mind, she knew these thoughts were wrong. She squirmed against them. But she had no sway over her heavy limbs. There was no calling for help without letting those black currents into her lungs. Her choice was either let the fire out or let the water in.

Raiden tired, swing after swing, even with a sword so light. His blade cut through countless limbs and torsos. The golems regenerated. It was all he could do to keep them back, but he had yet to discover the point of weakness in their forms. So many golems. There were too many to count, too many to keep back. While he hacked at one after another, the others clawed and slashed at him. A set of talons raked across the back of his leg, another his shoulder, tearing through jacket, sleeve and skin. He doubled over, ducking away from swinging talons, and the golems closed in, piling onto him.

Then the Sight came, rolling into his mind and turning his stomach with the urge to vomit. His eyesight went blurry, and a vision overtook him. Everything was dark and frigid, sounds distorted and muffled. A freezing shudder rolled up his spine; the cold was real, and there was a face, her face. Cheeks pale and lips blue. Nicole. The vision slipped away like it was caught in a stream. His eyes cleared.

He was on his back, golems weighing him to the ground. Frantic determination seized his body. There was no way for him to know just how far in the future that vision might be. It could be minutes. It could be seconds. He cursed the uncertainty of his gift, but for now he was grateful for it.

He heaved himself from the ground and tore through the golems. He kicked, slashed, stabbed until he regained his footing. The golems fell away to reform. He ran without concern that the golems might still be coming. Pain at wrenched his legs into a desperate stride, carrying him as fast as they could.

The vision left his head spinning, and he was unsure which way he was running for the first few dozen strides. *The stream.* The vision had made that much sense at least.

He never tripped in the forest, even on moonless nights. But something caught his foot, and he fell forward into the dried leaves. Before he was even on his feet again, his hand found the object—Nicole's backpack. The rustling of the pursuing swarm of golems drew near. Panic clenched his hand tight onto the bag. He jumped to his feet and charged toward the stream.

The stream came into view. First, he saw an orb of light hovering over the water, revealing the black shape of a horse—its neck stretched abnormally long, head beneath the water. The light flickered, weakened, and went out.

His heart lurched and he staggered forward. Suddenly, the dark water glowed. A column of white light erupted from the stream, slicing up through the night, and erupting into a wave that spread through the forest. The force caught him like a sail, lifting him and pushing him back. He leaned into it. His toes scraped along the ground. He managed to remain upright. As the surge of magic died, he stumbled forward.

The forest was as warm as a spring afternoon. The trees glowed with a residue of magic. There was no sign of the kelpie's form anywhere as stream water rained down. He looked around and saw no sign of the golems. The sound of coughing and splashing jarred him out of his stunned stupor. He propelled himself into an unsteady run.

Nicole scrambled out of the stream, slipping on the slick stones. She fell twice before she finally made it to her feet, swaying dangerously as she attempted to run.

Raiden wasn't sure she saw him until he heaved her name from his chest. She stumbled full tilt away from the stream, looking ready to crumple under the weight of her weight clothes. His arms were ready to catch her, and her body sagged immediately, but he did not let her fall.

"Are you all right?" He could barely breathe the words through his waning panic.

She was soaked, her hair dripping, her clothes clinging heavily to her shivering form. She shook so hard that his body shook too. It was more than a powerful tremble from the cold. He could see it in her eyes when he eased her back, holding her at arm's length.

Her head nodded, but her eyes were dark. She wasn't there.

"Nicole?"

"Hmm?" She raised her gaze to his, and this time her eyes were clear. "I'm fine."

He didn't believe her.

"My, my." A cold voice came to Raiden's ear. It sent a chill down his back—he hadn't felt that response to Amarth in a long time. Although it was not a pleasant sensation, he was strangely grateful to feel it again. "Quite a song this one has—intriguing. Where did you find her, Raiden?"

There he was, like a figure out of time, pale and nearly transparent. Amarth stood beside a tree with that same face and smug adolescent mouth. Raiden preferred not to look at him. The death keeper's perpetual youth threatened to send Raiden back to the moment he first saw Amarth standing over his mother with a casual acknowledgement that she was gone. Raiden looked to Nicole, wondering if she saw Amarth too.

"She cannot see me, Raiden."

Still, Raiden felt uneasy, fearing she would somehow see or hear the death keeper. This time Raiden refused to engage in conversation. Amarth persisted despite Raiden's silence.

"She came extremely close—an impressive crescendo—had me convinced her time was near."

"We should get out of here." Raiden said quietly to Nicole.

"You should have read the letter, Raiden."

Raiden's arms tensed around her as he guided her toward the portal.

"Or perhaps you have ... ah, I see—and you don't shy away from her." Amarth never moved, never actually followed. He repeatedly appeared in their path as they walked.

Raiden took a careful breath and steered Nicole through the trees, stooping to pick up the backpack. He couldn't remember when he had dropped it.

"I would be wary if I were you." Amarth's mocking coldness was ever at Raiden's ear. Once again, he materialized beside a tree just before Nicole and Raiden passed it. "It is not too late to disentangle yourself."

Raiden clenched his teeth against the urge to call the death keeper every foul name he could summon. All he could do was ignore it and get Nicole back through the portal before any straggling golems found them—or worse, Sinnrick. She leaned against him and nearly slipped to the ground every several steps. When he stole a glance at her, he caught her wincing.

Amarth would not be left behind. "If you could only hear her song."

Raiden inhaled carefully, suppressing the urge to sneer and curse at something Nicole could not see or hear.

"You're sure you're all right?" Raiden murmured in her ear, tempted to scoop her up—whether she liked it or not—to get her through the portal faster.

"Yeah."

"You saw what she did to that kelpie." Amarth's usually dull tone now sounded intrigued—impressed even. "She put out a candle with a hurricane. You should worry less about her and more about yourself, Raiden."

The portal was at the base of the castle's cliff. Once he could see past the edge of the trees, he took an easy breath. Nicole gave a weak wave to the exact location, and he wondered what it was like to see the portal as clearly as she seemed to.

Amarth continued, "Your friend—what was his name? Sinnrick? He nearly caught up with the two of you. You're lucky those golems got in his way. But how long will your luck last, Raiden?

You can't rely on it forever." He came into view again, leaning against a tree, his arms folded.

A faint laugh lingered in the forest as they crossed the dirt track that led up to the castle. Raiden didn't want to know what amused the death keeper so much. He'd never once heard Amarth laugh. The sound moved like ice down his spine.

"Good luck, Raiden."

Raiden threw a scowl over his shoulder in the direction of the forest and turned to step through the portal with his arm around Nicole.

The dragon watched as the pair stepped out from the scant shelter of the withered forest. The girl was near collapsing, but her companion looked back. He was sure the man's eyes couldn't pierce the darkness and distance like his could, yet that hard, despising look seemed to be directed right at him. Perhaps he knew the dragon was following in the shadows.

His debt to her pulled at his body like a physical tether. It led him through the forest and when he finally came upon her caught in that stream beneath the kelpie, he thought he couldn't possibly be so lucky as to repay his debt in the same night he incurred it. Before he could intervene, however, the kelpie and his opportunity vanished in a blinding flash of profound power.

He knew he should regret missing his chance. Instead, he kept thinking about the compassion she had shown him back in the tower. As he followed, he couldn't help looking up suspiciously at the castle above the forest and wondering why they headed toward it.

They disappeared. A portal. Many of his kind were old enough to remember the days before the world was torn, he knew that world in another life. In this life, in this world, not much had really changed, not anything that mattered anyway. He wondered if the old world had changed in all that time, if it had changed at all. Curiosity added to the pull toward the portal and the girl.

Fifteen

"You're late." Mitchell's voice greeted Nicole and Raiden as they walked through the back door. Then he looked up and studied them. "You look like hell."

Nicole dropped her gaze down to see what he meant. Raiden was covered in soot; she was soaked and blackened by soot all down her front, their clothes were torn in countless places.

She was exhausted, hoping her brother couldn't see that she was barely walking on her own. At least she wasn't burning anymore. The lingering heat of her magic had finally faded away, leaving her limbs filled with lead. The cold from the stream seemed to have caught up with her. A shiver rippled out from her core. She could have collapsed right there if she hadn't been so cold and if Mitchell wasn't watching. What she needed most of all was a long, warm shower.

Thankfully, Raiden apparently knew she still needed help. The pressure of his hand against the small of her back was a discreet re-minder that he saw the wobble in her stride and wasn't going to let her fall. He trailed a pace behind her as she heaved herself up every step, relying heavily on the rail for support.

At the landing, she was so torn between a hot shower and her bed that she could have cried. But her pause only lasted a moment, because Raiden planted his hands firmly on her shoulders and steered her toward the bathroom.

"You should get out of those wet clothes and warm up." He hesitated a moment. "I—I'm truly sorry about everything. You need only say so, and I'll go."

She closed her eyes for a moment, feeling capable of slipping into unconsciousness while she teetered there on her feet. When she opened her eyes, she huffed, frustrated with her completely il-logical instincts about him. "Stay." Half a smile was the best she could muster.

The tension in his shoulders released.

"For some reason, I'm inclined to trust you," she mumbled, too tired to smile anymore before shutting the door in his face.

She peeled off her soggy clothes. It was especially difficult to wrestle off the soaked denim jacket. Every muscle ached as she struggled, but she finally freed herself. It was torn to shreds and she droppd it with a sigh. Each piece of clothing slopped to the floor. Slowly, she managed to get into the shower. For the first few mi-nutes, she just stood under the warm water. She didn't turn it up too hot; it reminded her too much of that fire inside her. If it hadn't been for her exhaustion, she would have stayed under that warmth for hours, but she couldn't bear standing much longer. She needed to sink into the floor and never return.

She wrapped herself in the biggest towel she had and then shuf-fled into her room. There she found herself a pair of sweatpants, a tank top, and a clean sweater. She didn't even bother with under-wear—she'd fall right over if she tried to step into a pair of panties now; it required far too much coordination to aim for those small openings. Loose, baggy sweats were difficult enough.

Dragging her feet, she tried to return her towel to the bathroom, but it wasn't going to happen. Her body would take no more. She gave up. Lowering herself to the floor was the only thing she could do—gravity overpowered what little strength she had left.

Raiden appeared at the top of the stairs and stopped. He had a plate with a sandwich in his hand. The sight of him still filthy and holding a plate like a restaurant server was so strange that she couldn't hold back a laugh.

"What are you doing?" she asked through her laughter.

"I should be asking you the same question."

"I couldn't make it back to the bathroom," she confessed. Her laugh turned into a sob.

He chuckled. "Here." He handed her the plate.

How had he known she was hungry? She was famished actually—it was an unusual hunger. She was burned out, empty, and the hole got deeper every second. If she didn't throw something into that pit, she'd implode.

She took the plate with one hand and the sandwich with the other. Her ravenous bite tore through the soft sandwich. Cashew butter and banana.

"Mitch said to bring that to you, and that it's your favorite." Raiden spread out her damp towel and sat beside her. Soot fell off him as if he were a chimney sweep.

The ache in her stomach faded to a whisper with that first bite, and with another bite it went silent.

"I feel much better," she said after forcing down that mouthful. "Thanks." She sighed. "You don't have to babysit me, you know. I'm not going anywhere."

"I don't know—the last time I thought things were all right, you took off at a sprint."

"I couldn't if I wanted to now."

"I am sorry, Nicole, that I gave you any reason not to trust me."

"I know. Don't take it personally. I was sort of caught up in the surrealism of it all. When I read that letter, everything just caught up with me, like it hadn't quite sunk in that there's someone out there who wants to kidnap me ... and kill me, I guess."

"I understand." His turquoise eyes were intensely bright against his soot-covered face.

"Seriously," she said, laughing, "you look ridiculous. Go take a shower."

His grin flashed, his teeth even whiter as his smile emerged from his blackened face, which only made her laugh harder.

"All right, all right."

He disappeared into the bathroom as she relished another bite of cashew butter and banana. Nothing could have tasted better. Sitting on the floor in the hallway, she ate, listening to the water run behind the bathroom door. Once the sandwich was gone, she picked herself up with less effort than she anticipated. She scooped up the towel and hung it on her bedroom door since the bathroom was now occupied.

The only thing on her mind was a glass of milk until she turned around and stepped right into Raiden. He was mostly dry, a towel around his waist, a few beads of water clinging to his chest. His skin was the warm, creamy brown of a latte. Her eyes fixated on three angry claw-marks across his shoulder. For a split second she imagined pressing her lips to those red marks and her face went hot. *Where the hell did that come from!?*

She cleared her throat of her chagrin. "Sorry," she murmured, hurrying past him and practically falling down the stairs to get away. Her movements were slow and halting as she eased herself downstairs, relying heavily on the railing.

"You're looking better," Mitchell said from the kitchen, leaning against the counter with a glass of water in his hand.

Nicole hoped her flustered thoughts didn't still show on her face. "Tons," she managed to say while taking the last two steps carefully.

"What the hell were you two doing anyway? Slaying dragons?"

A satisfied smile spread across her mouth. "No," she said and set her sights on the backpack of books, which she had dropped beside the backdoor. "No. Just went to pick up a few books."

Mitchell folded his arms. "From the most dangerous library in the world? Come on."

"I'm serious. We went for books." She stooped to pick up the bag.

He gave her an exaggerated wink. "Right, I get it. *Books.*"

"Shut up, Mitch." Nicole reached into the bag and pulled out a book. "See?"

"No worries. Your secret's safe with me, sis. It's about time you—"

"Don't even go there." She swatted him with the book before tucking it back into the backpack.

Mitchell laughed, and then his smile fell. "Really, if Dad saw you two walk in like that he would have had a heart attack."

She swallowed a growing lump of shame. "Yeah."

"What happened?"

"We ran into a snag—I guess a lot of snags. There are people who might be looking for me," she said, trying to soften the truth and feeling guilty about it.

"Why?"

"They don't like that I opened a portal between the realms, they think it puts everyone on both sides at risk," she said, it wasn't a lie of omission if she planned on telling him the rest. She would, just not all right now. "Then I made someone very angry by letting their prisoner go and we didn't have an easy time getting back to the portal."

She cringed, watching her brother's face as he nodded. "You're not going back there."

"Excuse me?" she let out an unamused laugh—a reminder that he knew better.

He huffed. "Are you?" he asked, altering his command into a concern.

She sighed. "No, of course not, Mitch."

"And what about Raiden?" he asked quietly.

"What about him?"

"We're really gonna do this? Trust this guy? I mean, I get that he's—" Mitchell nodded with appreciation and Nicole shook her head.

"If anything that's the main reason I shouldn't trust him," she muttered. "But I think he needs us as much as I need help with this whole magic thing. He has no one, Mitch...literally no one, and he's put himself at risk to help me."

It was strange to have such fresh memories at her back, less than an hour ago, from the middle of a strange night when outside the daylight insisted *no, no, that can't be true, just a dream.* But none of it faded like a dream, the golems were all sharp edges in her mind, her body went cold at the thought of black eyes peering into her own.

"You all right?"

"Yeah," she said.

"Hey," Mitchell said, catching her shoulder and pulling her into a hug. "Don't lie to me."

"I will be. I just have to process this," she admitted.

He nodded and released her.

Nicole opened the back door. She was anxious to stand in the sunlight and chase away those black eyes and dark waters from her mind. As she approached the clovers, they all leaned toward her as if she were the sun. The power in her core felt gentle, sleepy, and tame for the time being. Now she knew its true intensity, how hot it could blaze, like the midday summer sun.

Raiden felt entirely new wearing fresh clothes. He walked down the stairs in a daze. This world, a home still alive and warm, was surreal to him. Downstairs Mitchell sat on the couch in the living room. Raiden wasn't sure what to say.

"Where's Nicole?" he wondered.

"Outside," Mitchell answered, barely glancing at him. "She didn't want to give up many details. Are there people out there looking for her?" He sat up, leaned forward and cast his eyes down at the carpet between his feet.

"Yes," Raiden answered.

"And what's the deal with this prisoner she set free? I don't understand."

Raiden sighed. "She let a dragon go."

An incredulous huff escaped Mitchell's mouth. "No shit?"

"I couldn't really do anything about it. They're—they can be very dangerous, but she wouldn't hear a word of it," he said with a shrug.

Mitchell chuckled. "No, can't imagine she would."

Raiden looked out the window of the back door for a moment to see Nicole standing at the edge of the patio.

"I'd leave her alone for a while if I were you. She had that look on her face when she went out there," Mitchell said.

"'That look'?"

"I take it you don't have a sister." Mitchell's eyes did not blink under his cocked brows, one low, one high.

"I don't have any siblings." Raiden felt sure the envy in his voice was audible.

"Some advice, especially if you're gonna look at her like that— when she wants to be alone, leave her alone. She can and will argue you into a coma. And don't try to tell her what to do." Mitchell sat back with a smile on his face.

The way I look at her, Raiden wasn't sure how he looked at her— he caught himself before he looked out the window again. "What was she like growing up?" He felt like he'd known her longer than a day, was it some trick of stepping back and forth between two realms, between day and night in a single step.

"You mean has she always been stubborn as hell and nothing but trouble?" Mitchell laughed. "Yeah. She's always been determined to do anything and everything Tony and me did. You could never tell her to slow down because she was younger or especially because she was a girl. She was determined to keep up with us, and she always managed to get hurt doing it. Mom really tried to raise a little lady, put her in skirts and dresses, bought her dolls. But Nikki preferred to follow us. Mom was always so mad when she came home with her dresses filthy." He laughed. "I can't tell you how many times Tony or I had to patch her up. But she refused to be left behind. If we told her that she couldn't come with us, she came anyway."

There was fondness in Mitchell's voice despite his carefully feigned annoyance. Raiden could hear the protective tone in his words.

Mitchell stood up. "Good luck," he said, shaking his head with a wry smile on his mouth as he crossed the room and passed Raiden on his way into the kitchen.

Heat flooded Raiden's face, but he couldn't be sure where that flush was coming from. She was the first friend he had had in almost ten years—the first real person to exist in his world, to step inside, look around, see every broken thing, and stay. Why shouldn't he hold on to that? She chose to trust him when she had every right to trust no one, especially him.

He looked out the window again and considered what Mitchell said about leaving her alone. He survived his solitude by burying how much he hated being alone in the numbness. He didn't want to be alone anymore, so maybe she would forgive him for intruding for a minute or two, to apologize, to thank her, to be near her.

Nicole stared across the yard, her arms crossed firm against her.

"It's a little strange to be here again after going back." Raiden's voice came from behind her. She hadn't even heard the door open or close and she wondered how much time she'd spent adrift in her daze.

"I know what you mean. Good thing I've got an achy body and a bag of books to prove that it wasn't some strange dream."

"It would probably be better for both of us if this was all just a dream," he said quietly.

She turned to look at him, trying to understand his expression. "It would, but I don't think I want it to be. I still want to see Veil again," she confessed with a dry laugh.

"Even after all that?" he asked with an astonished laugh. There was an unbitten apple in his hand. He turned it over endlessly in his palms.

"The kelpie wasn't pleasant, I'll admit."

"Or the dragon," he said with distaste in his voice.

She rolled her eyes. "None of it was the dragon's fault." She folded her arms. "If I'm not mistaken, that was all a culmination of your secrets."

"I can't really deny that, can I?" His smile couldn't conceal the shame in its corners.

"No, you can't." She rubbed her shoulders to warm herself against the fresh memory of it all. She believed him, but she could still feel the betrayal like a bruise. There was a sliver of doubt deep in her heart. Would her body force it out and heal—she wondered—or would that splinter fester and ruin…whatever this was? He wasn't on the Council's side now, but what if he changed his mind about her?

He warned in a quiet voice, "In all seriousness, we can't go back."

"Oh please, is it really any safer here from them? They know the portal is somewhere in Cantis, and they've already sent someone else to find it—to find me. Isn't it just a matter of time?"

"We could close the portal, but with all your magic here I don't even know if it would stay closed. The best thing you can do is learn how to control your powers and, from now on, be careful whom you trust."

"You mean you or dragons?"

Raiden folded his arms. "Like it or not, the dragons proved they are untrustworthy. That's just how it is, Nicole. You don't know why it was there, or that it didn't deserve to be locked up."

"And you don't know that it did," she retorted. "Just because a creature can be dangerous doesn't mean its life is worth any less. Nothing deserves to be treated like that."

Her heart struck a tempo of defiance against her ribs. She knew she'd done the right thing, and she was prepared to defend it until she went blue in the face. It wasn't just the dragon she was defending.

"I only ask that you start thinking about the risks you take."

"You saw what happened with the kelpie." She kept a wary eye on the portal. "Maybe you should start thinking about risks too. Helping some stranger that might turn into some kind of monster."

"All right, fine, consider me as reckless as you then." He

shrugged.

She couldn't help smiling.

A rogue cloud crept in front of the sun. The air grew colder. Even though it was only noon, she wanted to hide, curl up, and sleep. How long had she been awake—a year?

"Nicole?"

"Yeah?"

"Nothing the Council says could ever change what I think of you. They can promise me the highest rank, try to persuade me, give me wings and honors—it doesn't matter. You'll always be Nicole. They can't make me think of you any other way."

Heat flooded in her face. She dropped her gaze to the ground only to see a blush of tiny flowers blooming through the clover she had grown herself.

"Can they really give someone wings?"

"It's what they do. To them, wings represent the kind of non-violent justice they strive for. It's how they brainwash their men. They inflate their egos and make them into a force that will stand up for the Council no matter the threat. They've stolen the image of the celestial fey to imply they stand for the same ideals."

"Ideals? You mean like freedom?"

"The celengels make their home on the winds and among the clouds. They were the only ones who remained untouched during the Dragon Wars. They watched in safety above as Veil fell. They could clearly see that the people of Veil had fallen victim to the dragon king because they had divided themselves. From the sky there is only one land—Veil—and the winged fey saw one people. As the story goes, one of their own grew tired of watching the dragons' reign spread to every corner of the realm and descended to defeat the dragon king. It's said that his voice could be heard through all of Veil when he admonished them for bringing war upon themselves, for forgetting that they were one people. But that's how the Council tells the story. Who's to say what really happened that day?" Raiden shrugged. "The Council likes to claim that they were founded by the celengels, by freedom, by the very sword that had slain the dragon king. I dare say it's an elaborate story, soaring rhetoric to instill faith in the people."

"I'm sure life is easier for those who believe it."

"That was never an option for me—not before I knew you and especially not now."

She laughed. "I can honestly say I've never had someone willing to give up wings for me."

Raiden dropped his chin to his shoulder, turning a smile away from her before he turned entirely back to the house.

Sixteen

Nicole shivered, the warmth of the sun captive behind a long cloud. She sighed with exhaustion, ready to go inside and collapse on the couch, or even the floor. As she turned toward the house, something felt off to her. An almost imperceptible wiggle in the air, the feeling of being watched. Instinctively, her eyes swept the yard—left and right before tilting upward. That's when she saw him sitting on the roof like it was as ordinary as her standing on the ground. His form was lank and lean; even folded up like he was, she could see he was quite tall.

The human figure on the roof caught her by surprise but only for an instant. After portals and golems this seemed rather ordinary. He stood and stepped off the roof so suddenly that Nicole gasped, lurching toward him. He landed with the lightness of a cat, and she froze, foolishness flushing her cheeks. What was she going to do—catch him? Couldn't this person be Sinnrick? When he straightened up just a couple feet away her heart sputtered.

She knew his eyes—those violet eyes with a sharp slit of a pupil. Though much smaller now, their brilliance still stunned her. She'd have known that dragon's eyes anywhere, in any form. Once she recognized him, her shock turned into a sort of bewildered joy.

Nothing about him looked or felt threatening to her. Maybe it was because—deep down—she knew there was nothing more dangerous than her.

"Hi." She wasn't sure what else to say to someone who had just stepped off her roof, let alone to a mythical creature disguised as a human.

His clothes alone made him seem like he was from another world or at least another time. The loose linen tunic he wore rippled in the breeze, clinging to him now and then to reveal his lank build. He had on simple trousers that looked like loungewear. His feet were bare, and from where she stood, his skin looked almost gray. If her eyes were not mistaken, there seemed to be a purple tinge to his complexion. Ink-black hair fell in straight sheets around his neck and shoulders, shining with a luster that her peers at school would have killed for.

As she studied him, he seemed to do the same to her. "You're not like other people." His quiet words made her tense. "Few would have done what you did for me. I owe you a debt."

She relaxed. "You don't owe me anything."

"It's a natural law I cannot break. You saved my life, so I am bound to you."

Her face pinched with confusion, and she tried to make her slow mind work faster. "Bound to me?"

"My life is yours until I can repay you." He did not look at her but looked across the yard as if he expected to see something. "What harms you will hurt me. If you die, I die—unless the debt is paid, of course."

Her eyes shifted to his neck and the dark, deep scar there. He would wear that iron collar forever. "I guess that means you aren't dangerous."

"Whatever your companion has told you about my kind is true."

Nicole frowned.

"Dragons have done terrible things—"

"I know, I know—the Dragon Wars," she dropped her head

back.

"It is dangerous to align yourself with dragons. We are still the enemy, and you will bear the animosity warranted by our crimes. That is why what you did is foolish."

"I'm sure you've noticed by now that I'm not from Veil, so why would you think I care about their prejudices?"

"I hope you have the courage to stand by that conviction when you're surrounded by those who disagree." His eyes shifted toward her but flashed away as soon as he caught her gaze. "There may come a day when you regret having me beside you."

"Not a chance." It was that simple to her, as naïve as it may be to think so.

He gave her a perplexed look.

"There it is again," his voice was even softer, nearly inaudible.

"What?"

He spoke as frankly as someone making an observation about the sky. "When you found me in the cell, it was unmistakable. I was shocked at how suddenly and wholly you could care for me."

Her face flooded with a fresh wave of heat.

"I've never experienced that before. It's quite intriguing," he mused.

"How could you possibly know what I was feeling? Are you some kind of mind reader?"

"No," he chuckled. "Most dragons have a knack for seeing things others cannot. It is different for each of us. I happen to see the truth within others' hearts. You could think of it like reading the soul if you like, feeling what you feel."

"You mean an empath."

"Precisely."

"Is that why you won't look me in the eye?" She tried to move her gaze into his line of sight.

"You're smarter than I gave you credit for. I thought you were just foolish when you reached for that shackle. Forgive me."

"Thank you?"

"Looking into your eyes would be like looking directly into the sun. With that said, I do not rely on my eyes to understand what lies in someone's heart."

For some reason, his words had her blushing, and she was appalled at herself for feeling so giddy.

"Are you just going to hang out on rooftops the entire time you're stuck with me? You could come in—"

"It's best if my presence remains unnoticed by your loved ones, especially Raiden."

"Oh, he's not—"

"For now, at least, I will stay out of sight."

"You mean just for them, right? I don't mind seeing you. Actually, I wouldn't mind having you around."

"It would be best for everyone if … attachments were avoided. But regardless, I will be near, whether you see me or not."

"Wait, don't you have a name? I can't just call you 'the dragon.'"

He was silent for a moment. "Then you can call me Gordan."

"All right, Gordan. See you around." She nodded with satisfaction and turned toward the house, cherishing her new secret.

Nicole opened the back door to find Raiden and Mitchell just inside. They were silent, and she gave them a suspicious glare. Bandit—who lay belly up beside Mitchell—rolled onto his legs and sprang up to greet her.

She patted the dog's head absently. "What are you two talking about?"

"You," Mitchell answered with ease.

"Oh good," she said with a sarcastic laugh. "I feel like I need to sleep for a month. I'll see you guys later." She shuffled toward the stairs, pausing at the first step in a moment of self-pity. As she looked up at the landing, it seemed so much farther away than she remembered.

"You know, I could—" Raiden's offer was cut off.

"Don't waste your breath, Ray," Mitchell said. "She doesn't ask for help, won't accept help, and above all hates being picked up. Right, little sister?"

"Pick me up, and I will bite you." Her playful words were flat with exhaustion, which made her sound dead serious as she heaved herself up the stairs one step at a time. Bandit was at her heels, pausing happily as he followed her halting progress.

"See?" Mitchell hiked his thumb back at her and shrugged.

Nicole let out a triumphant sigh of relief at the landing.

"Good luck getting up to your bed," Mitchell called up to her, laughing.

She gave her brother the finger from the landing. Raiden started up the stairs, and she turned toward her room with a heavy sigh, shuffling down the hall.

When Nicole reached her bed, all she could do was look up at the rungs and groan. She put her hand on the plank just at her shoulder, but it was a wishful gesture. She knew she wasn't going to make it up one step, let alone to the top. She sighed, resigned to just curling up on the floor and sleeping on the soft carpet. It was good enough for Bandit, after all. She sank to her knees.

"What are you doing?" Raiden asked from behind her in the doorway.

"I can't get up there," she said, shaking her head with a laugh that felt more like a sob.

"There's a bed down the hall, you know. Come on," he said, plucking her hand off her bed and pulling her to her feet. The dog scrambled to get up and stick loyally to Nicole's side.

Once she was on her feet, she pulled her hand free of his and walked unassisted out of her room. She didn't notice the sway in her gait until Raiden's hands dropped onto her shoulders and steered her in a straight line through the door of his room and to the bed. She had nothing left, not even for words, as she sagged onto the bed without even pulling the blanket back, already half asleep. Bandit turned around a couple of times beside the bed before lying down with a huff.

Raiden pushed his fingers back through his thick auburn hair and sighed. How were the two of them supposed to stand up against the Council? What was he supposed to do—prepare her for war?

Looking at her and cringing against a surge of the Sight, he wanted to believe it wouldn't come to that. But something told him the Council would not be convinced to treat Nicole differently from the other fera. The portal loomed in the back of his mind, becoming ever more ominous as their enemies seemed to multiply behind it. Would Sinnrick find it? Had the dragon? Would Moira come after them?

Nicole's home gave the illusion of safety, but that comfort seemed to curdle in his chest as it mixed with his anxiety. They weren't really safe, only temporarily hidden. As she lay there sleeping, he could feel a gentle charge in the air around her. He wondered if that aura of magic could protect her while she slept, because he couldn't always stand watch. Sleep would come for him too eventually. For now, though, he could wait.

❧

Moira stood staring at the limp chains and empty shackle left behind in the tower. How the dragon had broken the curse and removed the shackle was beyond her comprehension. Her one task had been to keep it here. It was simple yet crucial. Cantis had been chosen as the hiding place, an ideal location, and all Moira had to do was stand watch. First her most treasured possession had been stolen, and now her mission was a complete failure.

She paced up the stone stairway to the upper floor. Her life depended on that dragon. Her master would have her head. The golems had failed to ensnare the petty thief yesterday and a weak dragon tonight. How could that be? Was there another factor she didn't know about? Overhead, the sky glowed red through the open tower. The forest was burning, but there was still nothing to find. The slippers on her feet tapped softly against the stones as she paced. Then something crunched under her step. She lifted her foot and snatched a wad of paper from the floor. Her eager fingers pulled it open, and she read.

A letter from the Council. They had a man in Cantis—no, two. Her heart seized; had the Council become suspicious of the activities of Dawn? Her master was adamant that the machinations of their organization remain undiscovered by Veil's leaders, inadequate though they may be, the Council could still complicate Dawn's initiative. If they had men in Cantis, that might explain how her golems had failed. What if they already found and killed the dragon for straying from the Wastelands? From the sound of this letter, there had only been one for a time. Had he been searching for information on Dawn's objectives in her chamber, some way to gain the upper hand against her?

"No," she said in disbelief at what she read next. A fera and a portal. It was the fera that had brought the Council's agents here. Her dragon was gone, but the very thing Dawn was searching for had turned up in Cantis!

"Me amosar fortiden." She swept her hand through the air, and two faint phantasms appeared. A young man and a young woman stood here. She saw them, standing apart, arguing, their words indiscernible. Him! He had to be the Council's Raiden—she recognized him, he was the thief! She looked back to the girl. She had to be the fera.

As the fera turned and disappeared down the stairs, Moira followed her like a shadow, her heart racing. Could she be so fortunate? Would this shadow from the past show her what she so desperately hoped? Yes—the fera approached the dragon. She knew that dragon couldn't have freed itself. It had help. The fera released the latch and broke the curse that restrained the weakened beast.

She held in a delicious laugh, savoring her luck. The dragon and the fera were bound together. Not only could she recapture the dragon, but she might very well obtain the fera for her master before the Council could get to it first. The Council would *not* destroy this one like they had all the others. She watched with satisfaction as the wisps of these two people picked themselves up and flitted away.

She glanced through the narrow window at the burning glow in the sky, knowing it would be several hours before the cinders were ready for a new batch of golems. Until then, she had plenty to do. There was a portal to locate. If the fera came from the other realm, then that was where she would be hiding. However, Moira had one other nuisance to find. The Council's second man had not been with the fera and the other. If he was in Cantis, she would find him.

Seventeen

Raiden glanced up at Nicole, still asleep on the bed. The dog had claimed the space beside her not long after she fell asleep. He dropped his gaze back down to the paper in his hands. Sitting on the floor beside the bed, he leaned against the bedside table and re-read the Council's first letter.

The paper collapsed in Raiden's grip. There was nothing more he could glean from these words than he already had. He stared furiously into that paper, hoping to see the hidden intentions through their disguise of responsibility and concern for the greater well-being of all. It was difficult to keep in mind the advantage he had: The Council still assumed he was on their side. Sinnrick's muffled voice had addressed Raiden as a friend even though they'd never met. But he couldn't stop seething about how the Council wrote of Nicole. They wrote as if she weren't human—as if he would be capable of looking at her with that same indifference. Could he possibly have seen her that way if he read the letter that morning, before he knew her name, her smile, her laugh?

Nicole's words pierced his thoughts. He really had treated the dragon as coldly as the Council was prepared to treat her. Nevertheless, he could not ignore the truths the Council had told, truths

149

he could see for himself. Her presence in this realm put the barrier between the realms at risk. If she could weaken the barrier and create portals with no effort, then might she compromise the barrier enough to destroy it entirely? As long as she remained in this realm, she put the barrier at risk. But why did that matter? Why not bring the two worlds back together? He sighed. Nicole deserved to be seen for what she was: compassionate, determined, and kind—a person, despite the terrible power she was capable of.

Unfortunately, it was clear from the fact that they had sent someone else so soon they were growing impatient. He wondered how much information Sinnrick had been given. Was it more than they had given to Raiden? Or did he know just as little about their plans for the fera?

His fist tightened around the paper, and he wished the Council could suffer that crushing force.

"Hey." Her quiet voice crept over his shoulder.

"Feel better?" He dropped the letter beside him.

"Yeah. Sorry we commandeered your bed." She scrubbed Bandit's head affectionately. "He's used to sleeping up here with Anthony."

"That's all right. Sleep would only bring on visions if I closed my eyes now." He smiled reassuringly.

He could feel the Sight on the fringes of his senses. This was always the case after any accidental submission to the Sight. One vision always seemed to bring more, tripping him at the top of a very steep slope that could be impossible to reconquer—and he had had several visions in the last twenty-four hours.

His vision during the frenzy of golems in the forest still made him shudder. Nicole's cold, pale face in those black waters would not be easy to forget. Any time the Sight managed to seize him, it seemed to grow stronger. It was best not to sleep now; otherwise those visions would wreak havoc on him.

"You can't not sleep forever, you know." She pulled her legs up to her chest.

"No, not forever. The Sight builds momentum in a way. I just need to wait it out, concentrate on keeping it at bay until it subsides a little."

"Oh," she said.

Raiden couldn't deny he was curious, tempted to let the Sight creep in and show him something. He would hope to see something to do with the Council, something to help Nicole. Unfortunately, the Sight would likely show him what it usually showed him; and he was in no mood to see some glimpse of a happy embrace with that silver-haired woman. He wanted to remain in this house and this moment.

"Tell me about the Sight." She straightened up and crossed her ankles. "How does it work?" She punctuated her inquiry with an eager bounce that moved the whole bed, disturbing Bandit, who lifted his head.

"Well," he began, standing up and sitting on the edge of the bed with one leg folded in front of him and other remaining on the floor. He suspected they were both tempted by the same thought: knowing. "It's hard to explain. I don't know everything there is to know about it myself."

He had never told anyone about the effect his visions had on him. No one knew, except Caeruleus. He and his mother were in hiding and no one could know they had the Sight. When his mother had been alive, she had given him steadfast support. The Sight mostly troubled him as strange dreams in his sleep and she had always been there to ease his distress. But as he grew older and stronger through the years, so did the Sight.

"It didn't worry me when I was younger. When I did get the occasional vision, they rarely made sense. I trifled with it some as a boy. I was usually persuaded to use it by Caeruleus, and it mostly got us into trouble. After I lost my mother, I regretted not taking her warnings about the Sight to heart. Visions became sad reminders that she wasn't around to help me anymore."

"What about your mystery girl? When did you start having visions of her?" Nicole asked.

"Oh." He had to force a smile. "I suppose that vision first came about five years ago? Forgive me; the last nine years are a blur of books."

"I understand," she said.

"There were times I was grateful for that vision, I'll admit. It felt like proof I was still alive, that I had a future ahead of me and wouldn't always be alone. I suppose it allowed me to accept the numbness all those years." He shook his head before lifting his gaze to Nicole's.

"I have one more question—I swear I will never ask you to use the Sight for me, but is there any chance you've had any visions since you met me? Anything that might help me understand where all this is going?"

His brow furrowed. His thoughts rekindled the two unsettling visions. Recalling them sent his heart racing. They had been flurries of fleeting moments he could not analyze. All he had gotten from them was a nauseating dread deep in his gut. He couldn't bring himself to share such ominous and unclear visions with her and expect her not to take them as some kind guarantee that something terrible awaited her. There was hope in one of his visions, the one that had not come to pass—proof that a vision was by no means an unchangeable future.

"I have," he admitted reluctantly. "I had one back in Cantis, actually." A shudder rolled down his spine, and he hoped she didn't notice.

"Really?"

"When we were in the forest." He caught the way she stiffened, sitting up straighter than before. "I saw you in the water. Your face was white and your lips blue. It was like seeing you through the kelpie's eyes. It was horrible. I was watching you die. It couldn't have been more than a few seconds, but I felt trapped in that moment for much longer than that. I didn't know how far in the future that moment was. It could have been minutes, or it could have been mere seconds. When I got there, you were in the stream, and all I could see was the kelpie standing over you."

He didn't need to tell her the rest—she knew it. Not one word parted her lips. When he looked into her eyes, he wondered if she was in those dark waters again.

"Nicole?" His hand found hers, and she jumped, but her eyes were bright again.

"Sorry. I wasn't expecting to live through that from two perspectives. One was plenty." She gave him a nervous laugh and a pained smile.

He frowned.

She smiled. "I asked, didn't I?"

"You shouldn't have had to go through that."

"Come on—a little trauma is worth the excitement in my life. I'll have it repressed in no time."

"Do you mind if I ask *you* something?" Raiden ventured.

"Not at all," she said with a shrug.

"What happened in the stream?"

She fidgeted. "It's ... hard to say. It was like having something else's thoughts in your head. It had me thinking I should just give up—and then ..."

"You overcame it," Raiden guessed.

She shook her head. "No, I was ready to inhale those waters and..." He watched her swallow back the discomfort in her throat. "I tried, but my magic came out instead. I can't even describe that force, but it swallowed the kelpie and for a split second I could hear its cells separating, feel it burning into nothing. I don't know if I can control something like that."

Raiden fought the urge pull her into his arms. Knowing the kelpie had forced such darkness into her mind, a darkness that had been his own company throughout the years—he couldn't stand it. "Of course you can—you will. It takes time, Nicole. You can't expect it to happen in a day. You do realize it's only *been* a day."

She sighed. "Yeah. It just feels like so much time has passed since we met."

"I know the feeling. Trust me—your strength will grow with practice."

She smiled, but her gaze fell to the bedspread between them.

"Thanks."

"Maybe I can prove to you that things get better?" As much as he wanted to resist the Sight now, he had to give Nicole something. He knew she could do it, and she needed to know too. How much harm could one more little vision cause?

"Didn't you just finish telling me visions make it harder to resist the Sight? Don't you ever want to sleep again?"

He laughed. "One more won't hurt," he said, hoping he was right. "May I?" He held out his hand, suddenly unsure of himself. He'd never tried to call the Sight for someone else. The last few times, he'd had no control over the visions. Nicole scrutinized his face for a second before giving him her hand.

For a second, he studied the feel of her, the warmth of her skin against his. There were calluses on her palm, and he noticed a faint pale scar on her knuckle. He almost didn't want to let a vision take him out of that moment, but in that instant, the Sight crawled into his head like vertigo.

He was caught in a current like nothing he had experienced before. The Sight pulled him into a roaring barrage of darkness broken by slivers of cutting light; it was a terrible, overwhelming silence pierced by sharp bursts of painful ringing. Everything burned; his entire being was ablaze. He could not breathe. He simply disintegrated into nothing, and the vision ceased.

"Ow—Raiden!" She pulled at his grip but could not free herself. He opened his fingers, and she yanked her hand away like an animal retreating from a trap to lick its wounds.

He composed himself before she could look up from rubbing her hand and see his wide-eyed, slack-jawed expression. She inspected her hand as she gave it a shake, opened and closed it.

"Sorry." He took a deep breath as quietly as he could. "I am not aware of my body when I'm lost in a vision."

"Jeez, I take it you didn't see love in my future."

Determined to forget the vision and avoid lying to her, he seized her sarcastic comment so quickly he didn't even think of what came out of his mouth.

He forced a chuckle. "What makes you think I didn't?" He swallowed back the taste of a lie, pushing back what he had seen and taking a chance down this lighter path of conversation.

She laughed. "Because I won't have anything to do with it," she answered. "I'm not particularly interested in love."

"Is there a reason?" He wanted to know.

Nicole paused. She huffed. "I don't want to be like my mom," she confessed.

"What do you mean?"

"She didn't want to be a part of our family anymore. I don't know when it happened exactly. They fought a lot, Mom and Dad. She started acting like she was surrounded by enemies, everyone was out to get her, scold her, criticize her, or embarrass her. We couldn't do or say anything right, especially Dad. When they told us they'd agreed to get a divorce—" Nicole shook her head, a tiny smile on her lips. "We were actually relieved."

"How long ago was this?"

"I was twelve—or thirteen, I think. About five years ago. It was strange at first. We seemed much happier as a broken family than when we were whole. Tony, Mitch, and I were happier with Dad, and Mom seems happier on her own chasing love. She's on her third husband, Daniel something or other.

"Everyone acts like love is this steadfast feeling, this un-fuck-ing-breakable bond, but I think that's a load of crap. It wasn't true, not for my parents. It wasn't even true for her and her own children. If love can't stand up to doubt and stress and insecurities, how strong can it possibly be?"

Nicole leaned her head back and gave a little groan of frustration. She lifted her head. "I'm not saying there isn't value in relationships. I just think some are worth more than others. I can't bring myself to hang my happiness solely on some person who might love me one day and walk away the next."

"You don't think it would be different for you? How can you know?" he challenged.

"I don't," she admitted with a shrug. "Not all of us have the luxury of seeing the future."

He scowled at her.

Nicole laughed. "The fact of the matter is I don't feel incomplete. I have my dad, my brothers, friends, and Bandit." She scrubbed the dog's belly. "I've never felt like there's some slot left empty. Honestly, the only time I ever felt deprived was before the divorce. Living with her when she was so detached felt far worse than her not being around. When your mother doesn't want to be your mother, it stings to have to live with her, attempt at bonding, feign niceties, always wondering if today she thinks you're daughter or foe. It was exhausting. But now ..." She concluded with a content sigh.

Nicole sat there across the bed from him, her hands resting on her crossed ankles. Her shoulders were relaxed, and there was an honest satisfaction in her eyes. Raiden sensed relief from her confession and wondered if she'd told anyone else before him. The sounds of the television downstairs were drowned out momentarily by a tremendous laugh from Mitchell.

Bandit sat up at the sound, ears perked up. Nicole encouraged him, "Go on, boy. Go get 'im." The dog jumped up and leaped from the bed, jostling Nicole and Raiden on the mattress.

Nicole's confession remained on Raiden's mind. He persisted. "You don't think there's any possibility that you're wrong?"

Nicole looked him in the eye. "I don't claim to know what love is or isn't. I just know that I do what makes me happy. What makes me happy today may not be what makes me happy tomorrow. But I do know I never want my happiness to depend on someone else loving me."

"I suppose as long as you can say you're happy, that's all that matters." Raiden wondered if he could live like that, caring only about each day as it came and doing what felt right. With glimpses of the future haunting his mind, however, he wasn't sure if he ever could.

"I used to live my life by the mantra 'maybe tomorrow.' Maybe tomorrow Mom and Dad won't fight, maybe tomorrow Mom will be happy with her life again, maybe tomorrow—ugh! What a waste." She shook her head again. "I've come to realize if you worry about if you'll be happy tomorrow, you'll miss out on today."

"I would like to live like that," Raiden mused.

Nicole folded her arms across her chest. "Why can't you?"

"I don't know. It seems almost … wrong to start something that's doomed to fail. You have that freedom of not knowing, but knowing pieces of my future takes that away from me."

"Oh, come on, you can't enjoy life along the way? You would really deny yourself something you want just because it might not last forever?" She looked at him, waiting for his answer.

"Isn't that why you don't want anything to do with romance?" he countered.

"No." She laughed. "I'm not willing to make promises I can't keep. I may want companionship and intimacy someday, but I'm not under the illusion that it has to be forever. The way I see it, sooner or later, it will fade, and I'll be free to continue on my own way without the burden of a broken promise or feeling like I failed somehow."

"You don't know what it's like to *know* where you're going to end up though," he said.

"Neither do you." Her voice shot up an octave with playful outrage. "Just forget the stupid visions. They might be different tomorrow—you said that yourself. You saw me dead right? And here I am."

He knew she was right, and he wanted more than anything for that fact to prevail. He couldn't be certain whether his vision of Nicole in the stream had showed her death, but he wanted to believe with all his heart that he had seen a terrible future and that it had been changed. In that moment, an alternate fate had existed for her, and she had avoided it. As long as that was true, he could believe those dark, unclear visions of her future might not come to fruition either, and that maybe his future might be different too.

Eighteen

Nicole looked at the clock on the nightstand: four-thirty. "Dad should be home soon. We'd better show our faces downstairs," she said, unfolding her legs and swinging them off the bed. She bounced onto her feet. "Let's find out what Mitch is making us for dinner."

Raiden stood to follow her, wondering if she could truly live each day without worrying about the future—especially now that she knew about the Council. If she couldn't prove to the Council that she wasn't a threat to either realm, she would have no choice but to fight. He certainly wouldn't let her face that alone. If she wasn't going to think about the future, then he would have to.

He watched her move down the stairs with ease, revealing no sign of the exhaustion that had plagued her only a few hours ago. Just a little sleep, and she was fully recovered. He supposed her tremendous power had everything to do with that. Her magic did not make her impervious to injury, and it did not spare her from its taxing physical effects. At the very least it would always be there to repair the damage it would inevitably cause.

There was a warm, inviting scent in the house, the smell of cooked meat mingling with aromatic spices.

"What's the chef's special tonight?" Nicole asked as she reached the bottom of the stairs.

"Chili," Mitchell answered from the middle of the living room where he lay on the floor with Bandit.

"Yum," Nicole sighed. "You're the best."

"I know," Mitch said, chuckling. "But you know what makes chili even better?"

Nicole rolled her eyes and gave Raiden a knowing look as he reached the bottom of the stairs. She mouthed her brother's answer as he spoke.

"Corn bread," he said.

She pressed her lips together in a firm smile and nodded. "What do I get if I make you your beloved corn bread?"

"I won't tell Dad that you disappeared for two hours and then spent the afternoon upstairs with Ray." Mitchell's condition was as nonchalant as if he'd desired a simple favor.

Heat bloomed in Raiden's face. They had done nothing; Nicole had been asleep the whole time.

"Deal," Nicole agreed easily, promptly turning on her heels and entering the kitchen with purpose.

Raiden kept up with her, dropping his voice low. "Does he think …?" He wasn't entirely sure what Mitchell was implying, which flustered him all the more.

Nicole laughed. "No," she assured him. "But it does sound a certain way, doesn't it? That's the point."

He nodded. "I suppose you're right."

"Of course I'm right. So, do you wanna help me make muffins?" She put her fists on her hips, betraying no hint of troubling thoughts.

Raiden grinned as a thought came to mind. "How about we make it interesting?"

"I'm listening." She tilted her head expectantly.

"We make these muffins without using our hands."

A grin spread across her lips. "I'm in. Let's do it."

Raiden acted mostly as instructor, providing the spells. "*Aperi* will open the drawers and cupboards ... Use *adme* to summon what you need."

Retrieving their bowls, utensils, and ingredients proved to be the easiest part. Mitchell wandered over, attracted by the sound of laughter. He watched, acting as a self-appointed referee, calling, "Hands!" every time Nicole attempted to use them.

"Come on. How hard can it be to measure cornmeal?" Mitchell teased.

"A hundred times harder than using your nondominant hand," Nicole said. "Now shush." She pointed her finger at the measuring cup this time, and its movements were more precise and controlled.

"Doesn't that count as using your hands?" Mitchell asked.

"It's literally my first day using magic," she said with a laugh. "Get off my back. Oh, I need the half cup." Nicole turned toward the drawer beside her. "Aperi." The drawer opened. She pointed at the measuring cup and said, "Adme." The cup jumped out of the drawer and into her hand. When she turned to close it with a bump of her hip, the drawer wouldn't budge.

"It's stuck," she said.

Mitchell laughed.

"I think your opening spell might have been too strong," Raiden said with a chuckle. "Try *agos.*"

"Agos," she said, and the drawer slammed shut, startling her.

"What's next?" Raiden asked, looking around at the ingredients strewn across the countertop.

"Eggs," she answered, lifting one easily from the carton with a flick of her hand, but she hesitated and let out a nervous laugh. *This could go very wrong*, she knew.

"Don't think too much about it," Raiden suggested.

"Wait, let me get my phone," Mitchell said, pulling it from his pocket.

Nicole held the egg suspended over the bowl.

She sighed. "Okay," she said. Raiden and Mitchell watched intently as she attempted to tap the egg against the counter but slammed it against the tile instead, pulverizing it.

Mitchell snickered. "Nice," he said, watching his phone record the incident. Raiden chuckled discreetly behind his hand.

"Wait, wait, let me try again." Nicole struggled to speak through her own laughter. Raising another egg over the bowl, she scrunched her face, concentrating on it. The shell burst into bits. All three of them were caught in a spray of exploding egg.

"Oops," she said.

Mitchell roared with laughter. "Aw, man! It's on my phone!"

"I haven't been this terrible in the kitchen since I was ten," Nicole said, wiping egg from her face.

"You'll get better at it," Raiden assured her as he pulled a section of shell from a lock of hair hanging in front of his eyes.

"Why don't you try?" she suggested. "I don't want to waste any more," she added with a guilty smile.

"If that's what you want." He nodded. With a subtle wave of his hand, two eggs drifted from their places in the carton, tapped themselves against the rim of the bowl, and split open. The contents of each shell plopped into the mixture below.

"Wow, someone's handy in the kitchen." Nicole nodded approvingly.

"It was just me and my mom. We were always together in the kitchen. I was a master at kitchen spells by age seven."

"What else are you hiding?" Nicole asked, folding her arms.

Mitchell returned from the sink where he had been carefully cleaning his phone. "Hey," he said, spotting the eggs in the bowl. "You didn't use your hands, did you?"

Nicole raised her hands. "I didn't touch a thing. Kitchen Master over here did it." She nodded toward Raiden. "Go ahead—show him."

Raiden complied. The spells were as fresh in his mind like he'd been in the kitchen with his mother yesterday. He gestured to the bowl, and the ingredients within churned without a spoon or whisk to mix them. Nicole and Mitchell stepped back and watched. To Nicole and Mitchell, it no doubt looked like he did it all with nods and hand movements, the spells unspoken in his thoughts as he worked.

The ingredients mixed themselves into a thick batter. Lids flew back onto their containers of flour and cornmeal and sugar. Every trace of spilled powder, liquid, and egg gathered together into a growing ball of filth, leaving the counters spotless. The growing glob of spilled ingredients moved, a tiny, shapeless golem rolling and inching its way toward the sink like a squishy little accordion. It tumbled into the sink, where Raiden's spell died and left it lifeless. In less than a minute, the only things on the counter were the finished batter and the muffin pan.

Mitchell clapped slowly with an approving nod. Nicole looked at him with a mystified gaze that made his face and chest bloom with heat. He didn't want to pry his eyes away from hers, seeing that light in them, but he didn't want to let them linger too long either.

"That was—by far—the coolest thing I've seen in this kitchen," she declared.

Raiden laughed. "That can't be a difficult feat to accomplish with magic."

"You'd be surprised by the things that have happened in this kitchen," Mitchell said.

"Hey, kiddos," Michael called from the front door. "Something smells great in here." He appeared in the entrance to the kitchen, hunger in his eyes as he followed his nose.

"Hey, Dad, you just missed the show," Mitchell said, dropping a hand on Raiden's shoulder.

"Is that so?"

"Raiden just went Marry Poppins on the kitchen." Nicole presented the immaculate countertops.

"Sorry I missed it … So, uh, I guess you've heard what's going on around here, Mitch."

"Yeah, yeah. I'm all caught up," Mitchell assured him with a nonchalant wave.

"Okay then," Michael said, his shoulders relaxing. "How did it go today, Nicole?"

"Fine. I picked up a few tricks," she answered, containing the truth behind a smile. She moved toward the wide kitchen drawer beside her brother, retrieved shiny silver scoop, and proceeded to scoop and plop batter into the muffin tin.

"Good," her dad said. Raiden could hear uncertainty in his voice.

"Dibs on licking privileges," Mitchell interjected, pointing over Nicole's shoulder at the bowl and scoop. Nicole finished and passed them over her shoulder into his greedy hands. "Oh, and you lose. Hands," he added.

"Ugh," Nicole groaned.

"Lost what?" Michael asked.

"We were making muffins without using our hands," Nicole answered as she slid the muffin pan into the hot oven.

"In that case it's probably best I wasn't here for the mess," he said with a laugh.

"You would have been beside yourself at the state of these counters five minutes ago," she confirmed casually.

"Was it worse than the Thanksgiving of '08?"

Nicole laughed. "No," she said as she set the timer.

"Then I think I could have handled it. Speaking of 'handling' things," he went on, rushing into a though that had clearly been on his mind.

"Yeah?" Nicole reluctantly invited her dad to continue, glancing at Raiden as though she might need his help. He had the feeling this was not an area where he could help.

"What are we going to do about all … this and school?" Michael waited with expectant eyes.

"To be honest, I haven't thought about school once today." She and Raiden exchanged a look that recalled the chaos of their little trip to Veil. Despite the conflict during their trip to Cantis, he couldn't help enjoying their moment of mutual recollection.

"Well," Michael said with a sigh, "since it's only Friday, we've got a couple days to figure that out."

"Great," she replied. Her attempt at sounding relieved was un-convincing to Raiden.

Nineteen

Nicole dropped a tea bag into each mug and watched the tendrils of crimson spread through the hot water for a moment as the little paper pouches sank. Carrying a mug in each hand, she flicked off the kitchen light with her elbow and proceeded to the back door with fluid strides. Not one drop of the herbal tea jostled over the sides of the cups. Raiden was outside, watching the portal anxiously. She reached the back door and paused for only a moment, both hands occupied and no way to turn the knob. Her dad looked up from the couch.

"Need a hand there?" he asked.

Before he could get up, Nicole commanded the knob to turn with a look. The door opened. "I got it, Dad. Thank you though." She turned and gave him a smile before stepping over the threshold.

Outside, she pulled the door closed with a magical tug. Through the French door, she caught a glimpse of her dad's bewildered face. It would take more than a day for him to get used to having magic in the family.

Raiden stood at the edge of the patio, squinting through the dark. She held out one of the mugs, her presence still unnoticed. "Hi," she said.

Raiden's attention shifted to her, and his frown turned into a subtle smile. "Thank you," he said, taking the mug from her. She wondered if what Raiden had said was true—if there was magic in everything. Could the scent of rose hips chase away fears? Or perhaps hibiscus petals and cinnamon bark could fortify the heart against worries and doubt.

Nicole clutched her tea close like a talisman against troubled thoughts. She couldn't let herself slip into that place; it would do her no good. Her heart pounded at the thought of the Council and the man they had sent—Sinnrick. It was strange having to think she had legitimate enemies and even stranger that she had no faces to go with their names. Dread formed a cold, heavy stone in the pit of her stomach, and all she could do—hoping it would do the same for Raiden—was believe the heat of her tea would soothe it.

Nicole needed to break the silence. "Do you think we could close the portal?" After all, she had planned on doing just that—and locking Raiden out of her life—mere hours ago.

"Yes, I'm sure we could, but as long as you're here, another portal will inevitably open. It might be a useless effort."

"Then we'll have to keep closing them," she thought out loud; her voice grew heavy with the understanding of how daunting that task would be. Not to mention, eventually they would slip up, someone would find a portal before they could close it, so long as her enemies knew where to look.

"Unfortunately, the Council knows about this portal. They knew about it before it opened. There is nothing stopping them from opening a portal of their own in Cantis if they cannot find one. It may not lead them to you directly, but it would get them close enough to find you," Raiden said.

"But if I wasn't here," she mused, "if there wasn't enough magic here, would they still be able to open a portal?"

"That I'm not sure of. I think it would be very difficult—near impossible," he said.

"It sounds like my only option is to leave." She looked into her tea as though her future was there to see if she just looked hard enough. "I know you said you'd help, but you can't spend your whole life keeping me away from these people."

From the corner of her eye she saw Raiden look at her and she was afraid of what he might say, so she filled the silence before he could. She sighed again; this time it turned into a groan. "How can I go to school like I have nothing better to do when I have portals to worry about, this whole magic thing to figure out, and dragons following me around?"

"Dragons? You mean it's here? You saw it?" Raiden searched the surrounding shadows.

"I met him," she corrected, "yes."

"Him," Raiden repeated with a dry laugh. "You two spoke?"

"Well, yeah. What do you expect me to do—ignore a dragon when he talks to me?"

"No, but I'd like to think that after what happened today, you'd have learned to have a healthy suspicion toward everyone, be they human or dragon."

"Relax, Raiden. It's not like he's going to be sleeping at the foot of my bed. Besides, he's not interested in my company." Her voice betrayed her disappointment.

"Nicole." He drew out her name in exasperation.

She mimicked him. "What?"

"It's a dragon, not a pet. You do realize that, right?"

"I know that. I wouldn't consider him a pet any more than I would consider you one." She hid her grin inside her mug, attempting to take a sip and squelch the idea. A dragon as a pet and Raiden as a plaything—she thanked the night for cloaking the vigorous blush spreading across her cheeks. When had her imagination become so bawdy?

Raiden huffed. "Let's just hope it's not around for very long."

"Would you stop saying *it*? Jeez, you sound like a psychopath trying to dehumanize a victim."

"A dragon isn't a human," he said simply, taking a sip of tea.

"You know what I mean—I take it you know about the debt issue?"

"Regrettably."

"You do realize it's a steep debt—Gordan was pretty serious about it."

"Gordan? Just how long was this conversation?"

"Not long enough." She shook her head and then turned an expectant look at him.

"Well, it's going to be hard to pay that debt with me around. I don't intend on sending you into any life-threatening situations again."

"Okay, stop right there." She put her hand up. "This is *not* a protect-Nicole competition, all right?"

Raiden scowled.

"You know what I think?" She punctuated her question with a sip of her tea.

"What's that?" his words preceded a dry chuckle.

"You're jealous." Her mouth twisted into a wry grin.

He gave her an incredulous glare. "Of what?"

"My dragon."

"*Your* dragon?"

She laughed. "Yes, *my* dragon. I think behind that prejudice of yours is a boy who always dreamed of having a dragon of his very own."

His cheeks flushed. "They aren't pets, Nicole."

"You know I'm right," she sang from behind her mug, but he didn't answer.

They stood there in silence, Nicole smiling in her mug and Raiden brooding into his. With every drink, Nicole grew warm for a lovely moment before the cold air penetrated to her core once more. She shivered, but this time, before she could take another drink, her eye caught the portal—or rather something peculiar beyond the portal. For a puzzling moment, there in the darkness, she could have sworn she saw a glow of light—*no*—it was fire. Her eyes went round as she realized she could see flames all around them, faint and transparent. It was a strange, ghostly light.

Her mug dropped from her hands and struck the patio with a

sharp crash.

Raiden's head jerked toward the sound. "Nicole?"

She whirled around and bolted for the back door without answering. She wrenched the door open and lunged inside, disturbing her dad and brother.

"What is it?" Her dad demanded.

"What's going on?" Mitchell asked.

"Nothing. I just need a book." Her words tumbled from her mouth as she hurried across the living room to where her backpack still sat beside the couch. She pulled the bag open, the zipper moaning. Her hands fumbled with the books inside until she found the one she recognized—the book about portals. "Don't mind me," she insisted breathlessly as she stood and ran back out the still-open door, hoping they would stay put.

Raiden was about to step into the house, and she nearly collided with him. Nicole took a moment to shut the door behind her to keep her dad and brother from hearing.

"What's wrong?" Raiden asked.

"We need to close that portal," she said, thrusting the book at him. "Now!"

He took the book, recognizing it. Nicole grabbed his arm and dragged him across the patio and into the yard before the portal. There, standing before it, his eyes grew wide, and she knew he could see the glow of fire from the other side too.

"The forest is burning." Nicole's voice wavered with sadness and shock.

"There's nothing we can do about that," Raiden said, opening the book and flipping through the pages hastily.

Nicole's heart sank. She felt in some way this was her fault— the forest burning, dying. Nicole saw it all with terrible clarity. The forest was ablaze, flames lapping up the great heights of the slender trees. The portal was a window into that horror, making it all vivid, but even all around her, she could make out the blurred flickering of flames. The fire drew nearer to the portal, until its heat finally poured through, spilling into her realm and enveloping them in a dry, blistering gust.

"Raiden," she said with impatience.

"I'm looking as fast as I can," he answered with strained words. "I need light," he said, snapping his fingers.

Just as his light bloomed, a blazing tree at the edge of the forest broke free from its roots. Brittle and burning, it fell toward the portal. Raiden, hunched over the book, did not see the fiery pillar coming at them. Nicole grabbed him by the collar of his shirt and yanked him aside as the charred canopy burst through the portal and struck the earth with a loud crack.

Raiden was not deterred from his search. "Here!" His hand clapped against the book lying open in the grass. They scrambled to their feet; Raiden scooped up the book.

"Read this." He indicated the spell set apart in the center of the page. "Together," he insisted, taking her hand. The words were just visible in the orange glow from the crackling tree.

They pronounced each word together. "Ahyde stig! Belucan gang! Forcierre eahtend!"

The roar of the conflagration on the other side of the portal shrank away. The incredible heat dissipated. The light from the portal twisted and contracted. The fallen tree was caught up in the closing portal, lost like debris into a sinkhole. As the portal closed, it created a vacuum, pulling at them where they stood. They leaned away to resist. Then, abruptly, it stopped, and they stumbled backward.

Just like that, the tree; the heat; and the raging, crackling moan of the fire all vanished. The sudden icy silence left Nicole and Raiden lying in the clover, eyes wide with astonished relief. She took a deep breath and let it out carefully. A bubble of laughter broke her silence.

"What could you possibly find funny right now?" Raiden wondered, the severity of the situation lingering in his voice.

"I don't know," she confessed, and that made her laugh harder.

To her surprise, he broke into laughter too.

At last she quieted herself. "Maybe we should call it a night,"

Nicole said.

"It certainly has been a long day," Raiden agreed.

"Feels more like a week," she said, suddenly weary.

They trudged toward the house, their heavy steps in sync. When they stepped inside, they found Michael and Mitchell intent on the television—far too intent, in fact.

"Are they …" Nicole looked closely, taking a step toward her dad. "Are they frozen?"

"It would appear so," Raiden answered, leaning in to study Mitchell. "What happened when you came inside?"

"They were fine," she insisted, her voice high. "I came in for the book. I was worried they might come outside when I shut the door—what did I do?"

"It looks like you simply paused them for a moment—without even thinking, no less."

"Yes, thank you, but what am I supposed to do?" Her voice grew more frantic.

"It should wear off sooner or—"

Michael and Mitchell both jumped, startled by the sudden appearance of Nicole and Raiden right in front of their faces. In turn, Nicole and Raiden were startled by their sudden movement.

Her dad clapped his hand over his heart. "Jeez! Where did you come from?"

Nicole smiled. "Sorry—from outside."

"How did you do that?" Mitchell demanded.

"Mitch," said Nicole, shaking her head at him, "just assume from now on that the answer is always magic."

Twenty

Raiden came down the stairs, raking his sleep-disheveled hair back repeatedly.

"Good morning," he greeted Nicole and Michael in the kitchen. There was an edge of embarrassment in his voice as he realized he was the last one awake.

It was seven thirty, and the first signs of daylight were washing the stars from the sky.

"Morning," Michael answered as Raiden stepped into the kitchen.

"How did you sleep? Any ghosts of girlfriends-yet-to-come visit you last night?" Nicole covered her grin with her coffee cup.

Raiden smiled broadly. "No visions at all, actually. I think I was too exhausted for even the Sight to penetrate my sleep. Not having a portal to worry about didn't hurt either."

"Tell me about it," both Michael and Nicole muttered in agreement.

With the portal closed and no need to worry about Moira or Sinnrick coming after them, Raiden could simply enjoy this odd place, this warm home with Nicole and her family.

"Care for some coffee, Raiden?" Michael offered, opening the cupboard door to take a third coffee cup off the shelf.

Raiden hesitated for an uncertain moment. "Yes, please." He pushed his hand through his hair one last time.

Michael poured the hot, black liquid from the large carafe into Raiden's cup and handed it over. Raiden dutifully lifted the mug to his mouth and took a sip. His brow puckered for an instant.

Raiden forced down his mouthful of coffee and nodded. "Thank you."

"Since that portal is closed, I guess that means you're sticking with us for a while, eh Raiden?" Michael revealed no trace of anxiety this morning.

"Yes, sir, as long as you still approve." Raiden held his coffee in a perfect imitation of Michael.

"There isn't anyone else around here who knows about all this magic stuff, is there?" he asked, chuckling.

Raiden caught Nicole glancing at him, and he wondered if Gordan had crossed her mind as well.

"No, sir," Raiden answered.

Michael clapped Raiden on the back. "Then you've still got the job." He checked the time over the stove. "I guess I better get a move on. I'm wrapping up a few projects today—with any luck—but I've got to drive out to the quarry for some more rock first." Michael raised his coffee in farewell before downing the last of it.

Nicole drank too, and Raiden followed suit with a reluctant look.

"Love you," Nicole said as her dad set his cup in the sink before giving her a quick kiss.

"Love you too. Stay out of trouble today," he said.

"We will," she said. "Drive safe," she added.

"You bet," Michael said with a salute before striding out of the kitchen.

The moment he was gone, Nicole turned to Raiden and said in a hushed tone, "You don't have to drink it if you don't like it. It takes some getting used to."

"It's not terrible," Raiden said, looking into the cup. "It's just …

bitter."

She laughed. "Here." She opened the refrigerator door and retrieved the carton of milk. After pouring a glug into Raiden's cup, she instructed, "Try that."

He obliged. "That is better."

"Careful," she warned as she returned the milk. "Before you know it, you'll be drinking it black, and you won't be able to survive a day without it."

Raiden took a deep, content breath and smiled. "This is—it's been a long time since I had a pleasant morning like this," he confessed, looking down into his coffee.

Raiden saw a shadow of guilt pass across her face and he wondered if he should keep those thoughts to himself.

"I mean that in a good way," he insisted. "Before, it was hard to remember I had a life like this once. It's easier to remember those brighter days here. I should be thanking you for that." He looked at her and for a second thought he saw her cheeks flush.

"I hope I'm not interrupting your romantic moment," a sleepy voice mumbled from the staircase.

Nicole rolled her eyes. "Good morning, Mitch."

Mitchell shuffled into the kitchen, his eyes squinting against the harshness of the lights overhead. "Nikki," he whined, leaning into her.

"Yes?" she asked.

"I'm too weak to make breakfast. I think my muscles are already atrophying. I need food." He drew out the last word, draped his arms around her, and hung on her shoulders.

She struggled to bear his increasing weight. "Okay, okay," she gave in, laughing. "Three bowls of oatmeal coming up."

☙

There was a bounce in Nicole's step as they walked outside, crossing the patio and he couldn't help noticing how easy it was to smile now. Too easy, it was surreal, he almost didn't want to trust it.

"If you had any idea what summer is like here, you would understand why I'd rather be outside practicing than inside studying the books," she said after Raiden suggested she do some more reading before they went back to experimenting.

He was skeptical. "How warm could it be?"

"Ever see an egg cook on the sidewalk?"

"That hot?"

"Yep," she said.

"Sounds like the Wastelands," Raiden mused.

"The what?"

"The Wastelands, where the dragons have been since the wars ended," Raiden explained, looking around the yard, casually searching for any sign of the dragon's presence. Nicole must have noticed.

"I think he prefers the roof," she said, looking up. He did the same, but there was no Gordan. From the corner of his eye, he saw her shoulders sag.

"What would you like to try today?" Raiden's voice brightened with satisfaction—no dragon to be seen.

"No flying today, thank you," she said, cringing.

"Why not some practice with the elements then?" he suggested.

"You mean like earth, air, water, and fire?"

"Yes, although I dare say we've had enough to do with fire." Raiden glanced at the spot where the tree had fallen through the portal last night. The ground was scorched, the clover blackened and dry.

"Agreed," she added with a stern nod. "Why don't you start us off then, *Master*," she added with mock reverence.

"Let's see." He straightened up and took a deep breath. "Crafian byre." His voice was strong and clear. For a moment, nothing happened. Then the light breeze grew stronger, rustling their hair.

"No way," she laughed over the wind.

"It will die down on its own eventually. It's not that powerful of a spell." He had to raise his voice. "But for the sake of demonstration—*Byre ablinn!*"

The wind shrank away to a gentle tug on their clothes.

"Can I try?" Nicole asked.

"Please do." He was just as eager as she was to see what she was capable of.

"What was the first spell again?"

"Crafian byre." His words were low and barely kicked up the breeze.

"*Crafian byre.*" As soon as the words escaped her lips, there was a sharp charge in the air, and wind hit them hard, sending them reeling. "How do I make it stop?" her shout was barely audible.

"Forwic byre!" Raiden said with as much force as he could muster.

Almost immediately, the gust stopped, leaving no more than the slightest breeze in the air.

A laugh slipped from her lips. Maybe the sound carried a trace of magic lingering in her mouth, an inadvertent spell that turned it to music and made it so infectious, pulling at the corners of his mouth.

"Whoa," she said.

He chuckled. "I should have seen that coming."

"I feel like I burnt my tongue," she said.

"Maybe we should try some exercises with water?" He motioned toward the pool.

"It's not exactly swimsuit season. I'd rather play with fire than get soaked." She eyed the clear blue water.

"We're not going to get wet," he promised. "These were some of my favorite spells growing up."

He stepped up to the edge of the pool with confidence. "Murum undarum," he said, and the water quivered below him. It swelled up shakily into a mound of water as high as his shoulders. Then it sagged, sinking back into the pool.

"Huh, that's odd," he muttered. "That wasn't anywhere near what it should have been."

"Hey, it impressed me." Nicole stepped forward to stand beside him.

"But it should have formed a wall." He frowned at the water. "I used the spell for fresh water. It should have worked—it always works."

"Oh, this is salt water," she said. "Does that make a difference?"

"Salt water?"

"Yeah," she said with a shrug, "to keep the pool clean without chlorine."

"In that case ..." He pulled his shoulders back and said, "Murum mare."

The water churned and lifted high over their heads in a thick wall. The water level of the pool shrank to less than half.

"Raiden!" She grabbed his arm. "Someone will see! Stop!"

The wall collapsed, crashing back into the pool, and a sheet of water leaped up in the aftermath. They turned their backs against the splash, hunched together, too late to escape it. But not a drop hit them. As Nicole threw her arm over her head as a shield, the water fell around them, sliding down through the air as if a glass sphere enclosed them.

They straightened up cautiously.

"We're not going to get wet," she said, mocking him.

"If I'm not mistaken, we're still perfectly dry," he said matter-of-factly.

"Yeah, you're welcome," she folded her arms and looked around the soggy yard surrounding the pool.

"That's not my fault. You broke my concentration."

She laughed. "Well, excuse me. Why don't we stick to less conspicuous spells that can't be seen over the walls?"

"Who's supposed to be the teacher here?" He folded his arms, trying to feign annoyance.

"Get teaching then."

"That's why I brought this." He pulled a book out from his pocket. It was the size of his palm. Then, with the flick of his wrist, it expanded to its proper size.

"You're a real show-off, you know that?" She snatched the book from his hand and shook it at him.

"I've got to enjoy my superior knowledge while I can, what with you making everything I cast look novice in comparison." A grin broke his attempt at a scowl, and he turned back toward the pool.

Nicole opened the book. Raiden stepped in close beside her and brushed several pages aside until he found the one he wanted. "There—try that one." He touched the spell on the paper.

The water in the pool still shook and sloshed, as rough as a miniature sea. Nicole read the spell out loud: "Ur felbeira." The command stilled the water into a glassy surface.

"Now this one." He pointed to another spell halfway down the page.

"Devireo." She read the word with uncertainty, but its effect was great. Frigid air spread through the yard. The wet clover stiffened. Droplets of water crystallized and crunched under Nicole's feet as she stepped away from the pool. Ice crawled across the surface of the water as the spell spread like a swift fog.

"Wow," her word was a warm, white puff in the cold air. "How thick is the ice?" She stepped back onto the cool deck, coated with fuzzy frost that crunched under her foot.

"I would guess a hand's breadth at least." He took the book from her hands, closing it as she left him standing in the frosty yard.

Nicole placed one careful foot on the ice, then the other, and let out a burst of delighted laughter—it rang with childlike joy and fear. "Oh my god—if this ice breaks I'm blaming you and your spell."

"You cast it," he countered. "You'll be fine."

"Mm hmm. Why don't you join me? If I go down, you're coming with me." She held out her hand in demand.

"Fine." He took her hand and stepped onto the ice. "Just to prove that I'm right."

She laughed.

"You know, I really hope you appreciate the irony of your failed prediction," she said.

"It was a sound prediction. You kept us dry after all." He smiled down at their feet as they took slow steps toward the center, their hands still clasped.

☙

The air in Cantis was hazy with smoke. A thin, gauzy layer of clouds hung in the air, and the day took on a strange, ambiguous light too dim to call daylight, too bright to call darkness. Moira peered out her window and wouldn't have known whether it was dawn, noon, or dusk if not for the old clock ticking the truth beside her.

The forest had burned through the night, and below the castle was a great black scar across the earth. The remaining trees, less than half of what had been, stood in patches in the dark, ashy expanse—straight, blackened poles standing defiant and bare. There was nowhere to hide any longer—not in the forest at least.

She wondered if perhaps the Council's man—the one mentioned in the discarded letter—had perished in the fire. Not likely—she knew better. Anything alive had the mind to flee a burning forest. No, she couldn't possibly be that lucky. There was work to do yet. Somewhere down there was a portal, and beyond that was everything she needed.

First she had to locate the portal. Then she would have to send a set of eyes to seek out the fera and her dragon. With a huff, Moira turned away from the window and swept across the chamber to her worktable, where a book lay open. The seeking spell there should reveal the location of the portal—they could be tricky to spot but were easy enough to find if one had the old spells.

Moira glanced at the page and found the spell to summon a seeker of portals. She only needed to read the words clearly in her mind as she waved her hand over the book to cast the spell. Like a ghost rising from the pages, a large, shadowy bird bloomed into being and swooped soundlessly for the open window. It flew through the air like a wisp of smoke, its tail trailing behind it in long ephemeral tendrils.

Moira followed eagerly, returning to the window and expecting to see the spell diving through the air toward the portal like a hawk to its prey. But when she spotted the portal seeker, it merely circled the sky overhead. For several minutes it circled, trapped in an endless search for the portal. Finally the spell died. The black, shadowy bird dissolved into vapor on the breeze.

"What?" she muttered in disbelief. How could there be no portal? There had to be a portal—the letter had said! The dragon was gone. Where else could the fera and the thief have gone with it if not through the portal? Her fingers curled into her hands, and her nails bit into the flesh of her palms. They had escaped through the portal, she was certain, and they had managed to close it.

When the skin under her fingernails screamed with pain, she took a deep breath and loosened her fists. This was not a failure—not yet. She would have to get creative. There had to be a clue somewhere, portals always left their mark, sometimes in mushroom rings, or large twisted knots in trees. She studied the remains of the forest again, fearing she might have burned the very sign she needed. Ever since the separation of Veil from the old world, portals had appeared to bridge the rift between realms—proof to her and her fellow members of Dawn that the worlds were still linked, that they were never meant to be severed from each other, not completely, and they would be whole again.

Again she sank into that nauseating thought that she could have burned away whatever sign the portal had left behind. With a resolute huff, she straightened herself up. She could not give up until she had the dragon recaptured, the fera obtained, and her stone returned to its rightful place—or until her master, Venarius, found out the dragon was gone and killed her for her failure. *Fail me again and I'll relieve you of this world*, she remembered his words with chilling clarity, but it was not her demise that frightened Moira. Her master had already taken her life from her. Without her beloved, what did it matter if physical existence came to an end? She'd long given up the hope that her master would restore him.

However, she hoped to have the stone with her when she died, whenever that day might be. If she succeeded in anything, then let it be recovering that beloved artifact of the life she had lost so many years ago. The need to hold that stone, have him with her one last time was all the drive she needed.

Her gaze drifted past the blackened scar that maimed the valley to the silent city of Cantis, its buildings untouched by the fire. Countless people had perished in those streets and beneath those distant roofs. Master Venarius had thrown away lives like rubbish. The loss of so many lives left an eerie void, a favorite playground of the death keepers. There were several such cities throughout Veil, left lifeless from the Dragon Wars—unsettling monuments to death that no living person wished to reinhabit.

With a wave of her hand, she dissolved into a wisp and flicked through space, shifting through the ether from the castle and down to the valley below. Her feet sank into the thick layer of ash.

"Othiewe grundhyrde," she said, raising her voice so that it carried far through the cold, gray silence. "I know you're here, Keeper," she called, knowing their kind all too well.

"This is quite an unexpected summons," the death keeper's chilly voice preceded his appearance. "You know the spells of necromancy," he commented with a distasteful tone—the keepers did not like the living who meddled in Death's affairs. He could not ignore that ancient call; however, luckily for Moira, this keeper was intrigued enough to show himself.

"I require your assistance," Moira said bitterly.

"What kind of assistance?"

"There was a man in my castle not two days past. He took something of mine, and last night that same man and his companion stole something else from me."

"Yes, the dragon." The death keeper waved his hand, dismissing her attempt at secrecy.

"Do you know this man?" she pressed, aggravation building in her voice.

"As well as you can know a man with a dormant heart. Raiden grew up in the rubble of your plans." He paced, circling Moira, appraising her.

Her eyes followed him and his slender form, which was not unlike the slight, burned husks of trees scattered around them. He had the uncanny look of a youth not yet come into manhood, his face still and his features delicate. It was a bizarre juxtaposition, such an ancient soul, his cold hardened tone, with a face of fifteen years.

"They are not my plans," she said indignantly. "But I need to know where he went," Moira said.

Amarth smiled. "What makes you think I know?"

"Come now. All death keepers are sensitive to living beings, especially in such an empty place as Cantis." Moira tried to make herself tall and was still shorter than the death keeper.

"While that is true"—he made a full turn around her and began his second—"there were quite a few interesting occurrences last night, with the arrival of someone new. He is also searching for Raiden. I doubt he'll have any more luck than you have."

"So the Council's man is here." Moira pursed her lips. "Where is *this* one?"

"You want to know so much," he said with a smile. "That one is searching the city. He's far from finding anything."

Moira let out a groan of annoyance. "Look. Raiden"—she pronounced his name angrily—"my dragon, and a girl were in this forest last night. They escaped through a portal that has since been closed. Tell me—did you see them? Do you know where the portal once stood?"

"An interesting trio, are they not? The girl was exceptionally intriguing," he mused.

"Indeed," Moira agreed through her teeth.

"I wonder what it is that makes her so peculiar, and so important to you," he said, making his price for Moira's questions clear to her.

Moira huffed, but what harm could there be in a death keeper knowing who the girl was? "She is the last of the fera. The Council seeks to take custody of her before—" She stopped herself. "That's of no concern to you, of course. You have your answer. Now I'll have mine."

"A fera," Amarth said, trapping a laugh behind pressed lips, yet somehow the sound still percolated through him and echoed in the forest. "They *are* a curious trio."

"The portal, Keeper. Which way was it?" Moira grew harsh with impatience.

"Right under your nose," he answered curtly, his shape fading into the dreary air, "at the base of the castle's cliff." His voice trailed away cheerfully.

Moira whirled around and aimed herself directly at the castle. Pulling up the hem of her robes, she ran with a vigor she had not felt for some twenty years. In minutes, she reached the edge of the burned forest. On the jagged, vertical expanse of the cliff, there was an irregularity: a smooth, even surface as though the rock had been heated to a liquid and then cooled. She reached out in fascination, touching her fingertips to the cold, sleek surface; it was almost like glass. She ran her hand over it, unable to reach the top, admiring the peculiar beauty.

A giddy laugh burst past her lips as a surge of triumph overtook her. Spreading her hands out before her, she summoned the book from her chamber. It popped into her waiting hands, open to the same page as she had left it. Cradling the book in the crook of her left arm, she flipped back through several pages and found the spell she needed.

The incantation she was about to speak once held great hope for the people of Veil in the early days. It was a way to return to the place they thought was still their home, and many had hoped they would return one day to find themselves welcome once again. People can only stand being shut out for so long. Generations had passed, and now most people felt Veil was their home, no one longed for the past anymore. The old world had become little more than a distant memory to most, and these days few people knew the spell to open portals. Who would want to return to a hostile, foreign place? Now people even feared the appearance of portals, worried that their safe haven might be discovered and disturbed. The Council did their level best to find and close every portal that opened, to preserve Veil's solitude. Dawn looked to the future—a future where the world was whole again. Things would be different. Moira swelled with pride as she uttered the words:

"Onhlid stig, unlucan gang, brycge gin." Her voice trembled with anticipation.

As though this place was still the weakest point in the barrier, the spot where the portal had opened previously quivered and rippled before her eyes. She bit back her excitement and turned toward the field of ash behind her. Her previous golems had been of little use to her cause, apparently no match against her adversaries. But now she knew whom she was dealing with, and she knew better than to expect a golem to overcome the fera and the dragon. She still needed something that could last long enough for her to observe them. This golem would have to be far more formidable. She appraised the expanse of burned forest, an abundance of material to suit her needs just waiting for her magic.

Twenty-one

Nicole clutched Raiden's hand for support. A pulse of heat rolled through her that she insisted to herself was just her magic moving through her as they stepped out onto the ice of the frozen pool. The air was cold and sharp around them, the tingling cold of the spell rising from the ice. She shivered despite the heat flushing her cheeks. She let out an anxious whimper and a nervous laugh as she stood with both feet on the ice.

Her foot slipped out from beneath her, and she jerked it back with a wobble, Raiden as her anchor. "We could really use a pair of ice skates right now."

Then a sweltering wave of hot air cut through the crisp, chilly day and rolled up Nicole's back. They turned together to see a colossal golem towering over them, pulling its hindquarters through a newly opened portal. The golem radiated acrid heat. The green clover beneath it shriveled and blackened. Its body was riddled with red-hot cracks threatening to burst with fire. In its massive black head, its eyes were two burning pits. The image of this burning monster seared into her mind.

The golem advanced, its form familiar but far more distorted than that of the golems they had last encountered. Its spine protruded from its back. Its long limbs were crooked. It appeared almost too massive to retain its shape—as though it had been drawn angrily by an unsteady hand. They backed away as it advanced. Nicole's mind froze on one thought: Raiden's sword was in the house, upstairs.

A massive black limb flashed toward them in a blur as she and Raiden jumped away from it. She fell toward the shallow end, and he threw himself toward the deep end. The golem's hand broke through the ice. A cloud of hissing steam burst into the air. Her hands slipped on the ice, and at her feet there was only slush. She kicked, trying to pull herself back onto the thick frozen slab. The whole surface of the water fractured around them before Raiden could get to his feet. The ice split beneath him, opening like a trap door and closing, he was gone in a blink like he had never been there—she let out a shout of dismay and the golem turned its burning eyes to her.

A giant twisted hand came crashing down next to her, narrowly missing as she rolled away. She fell into the water. The heat of the golem's arm spread through the pool. She swam in a panic, awkward in her shoes and clothes, toward Raiden. As she left the golem grasping behind her, the water grew colder. She could make out Raiden's blurry form pushing up against the ice, searching for a way out but it was still too thick and heavy to budge.

They met in the middle. A grasping claw came crashing into the water between them. They were tossed helplessly in the churning water. There wasn't a trace of ice left when they broke the surface. Wading desperately slow through the chest-deep water, Nicole could feel her magic building, her own fire within, and she imagined herself burning inside out like that monstrous golem, her eyes smoldering. She shook the image from her mind, she couldn't be afraid of the only thing that could help her.

The golem swiped the air, and they ducked. A yelp slipped past Nicole's lips as the creature missed. This thing kept swinging and missing as if its eyes were useless. Then how did it know where to strike? They scrambled and waded sluggishly to the edge of the pool.

But the crooked, blackened thing plunged its hand into the water again, catching Raiden and pinning him beneath the surface.

Her scream was sharp in her throat. She pulled at the hand, but it didn't budge in the slightest. It was too hot to hold for long, she was forced to let go. Its other hand grasped at her, catching her legs as she jumped back. She wrestled herself free. With one more awkward step, she was at the pool's edge, dragging herself out of the water. Her mind raced. She didn't know how to *use* all the power swelling with a panic inside her, how to fight something like this. With the kelpie, it had been mindless instinct.

Raiden's sword came to mind again. She had no spells for this—only desperate need. With every fiber of her being, she concentrated on that sword, demanding that it appear, summoning it with open hands. The flood of fire through her arms was so swift, so hot, that she thought her fingers would blacken and blister. To her relief, the sword appeared in her hands with a blinding flash, shining like a star, cool and soothing against her skin.

The golem wheeled around and swung its free hand at her, still clutching Raiden with the other. It had not seen her. No, it could feel her, sense her magic; she was almost sure of it. She fell back out of its reach, hoping it would pursue her and pull its other hand away from Raiden. It did not.

"Nicole!" Mitchell called from the doorway. His voice struck her heart with dread. She couldn't let Mitchell get hurt.

Without a second thought, her panic rolled through her and pushed him back into the house with a burst of magic that sealed the door shut. *Sorry Mitch.*

Her bones felt brittle, like the slightest movement would shatter them, but she had to move. Whirling back toward the pool, she closed her fingers around the sheath with a painful grip and grasped the hilt with her right hand.

The hilt's silver wings unfolded as she freed the sword and leaped back into the water. Her feet met the shallow bottom of the pool with a jarring force. Both hands on the hilt, she plunged the blade into the golem's wrist as deep as she could and wrenched it to the side. A deafening shriek cut through the air, piercing her ears. The golem yanked its arm away, and the sword went with it. She slipped under the water both to escape the sound and to retrieve Raiden. Her panicked heart tried to count the seconds that had passed—how long had he been down there? She caught his arm around her neck and stood him up. They resurfaced, his head hanging forward.

Her heart twisted itself into a knot of dread—*oh no*—a pulse of magic escaped her as she said his name. "Raiden," she snapped in his ear. He coughed, his weight still leaning against her, practically pushing her back down into the water, he was so heavy in his soaked clothes. He lifted his head and she let out her breath.

The golem's massive hand fell, severed from its wrist. Raiden's sword dropped to the ground into the soggy heap of soot. The golem swung at them with its remaining hand, swiping the air, striking the water. They ducked under the water and he pulled her tight against him before they slipped through the water and into the ether, falling onto the cool deck with a heavvy smack. More bits of golem flesh dropped from the severed limb, dispersing into lumps of wet soot.

Nicole heaved herself from the ground, and Raiden followed sluggishly. Her eyes fixed on the sword lying in the grass at the golem's feet. The golem straightened up. Then it hesitated. Its attention shifted, and it turned toward the house, seeking something.

Nicole sprinted for the sword, dropping down to avoid the golem. She slid across the slick, wet ground, and her hand closed over the hilt.

"Nicole," Raiden's voice called out as the behemoth came down on top of her.

She raised the sword over her as though it were a shield, and a panicked pulse of power surged through her. The golem's enormous form filled her vision and closed her in a dark shadow. The sword emitted a blinding flash. She heard another muffled shout from Raiden through the golem's mass; then, as suddenly as her world had gone dark, it burst into light.

A heavy rain of soot clumps pelted her as she rolled over and crawled awkwardly with the sword still in hand. Exhausted and stunned, she rolled onto her back with a sigh. Her heart was pounding in her ears—she could hear nothing else.

After a string of indiscernible mumbles, at last his voice came through to her clearly. "Nicole?" He sank to the ground beside her.

"Yes?" she said in a daze, her eyes blinking up at the clear blue sky.

"Are you hurt?"

As her gaze drifted back down to earth, she spotted Gordan standing on the roof. Their eyes met, hers filled with questions and his with—was it surprise or did she see concern on his face?

"I don't think so," she answered Raiden without taking her eyes off the dragon.

Gordan stood fascinated on the roof. He took a breath to ease the tightness in his chest as his gaze fixed on Nicole. There was more to Nicole than he had ever expected. He could still feel the charge in the air, her tremendous power that the golem had followed like a blind creature follows a sound. Given the circumstances, he had expected her to be afraid; but now that the threat was gone, the unmistakable tenor of fear still hung in the air. He understood. What he sensed was imbedded deep in Nicole's soul, a part of her long before this life. Most souls lived many lives, bore memories and scars that influenced and shaped them forever. There was a terror in her. Looking into her eyes he could see it clearly, an open wound from her past.

He heard a door open and a moment later someone stormed across the patio below.

"What the hell was that?" He turned around once, surveying the yard, his shoes squelching against the wet ground. His resemblance to Nicole was obvious to Gordan—he was her brother Mitchell. Gordan had heard the name spoken inside the house. His soul was young and unburdened—he was lucky.

"A golem," Raiden answered, picking himself up.

Mitchell beat Raiden to Nicole, offering his hand to hoist her to her feet.

"I'm fine." Her preemptive defense was feeble. Any idiot, even one from this realm, could see that was a lie. She was shaken and held herself up gingerly. He could see the pain in her movement, could feel a ghost of it in his own muscles and bones. Gordan had to give her due credit—for someone who knew so little about her own abilities, when the time came, she had trusted her instincts and came out the victor.

Her gaze drifted back up to him, and he understood the question there in her eyes. Why had he given up the opportunity to pay his debt? In all honesty, he had no desire to pay his debt so soon. He wanted the excuse to observe some more—and not just her.

Raiden's silence attracted Gordan's attention. Now there was an old soul. How many lives he must have lived to become so placid to the core. Such was the fate of old souls. The more lives a soul lived, the most it experienced, the more it could become jaded and they often did. Souls could bear so many scars that they struggle to feel. Raiden's soul was old indeed, perhaps one of the oldest souls Gordan had ever seen.

What stirred Raiden to life now? Nicole? Gordan couldn't help but wonder if Raiden could withstand that vast numbness alone. Would it swallow him up? Many ancient souls could be so callous from so many lifetimes and they could hardly feel a thing. Raiden was lucky to have found Nicole.

Maybe Raiden could bring a little tranquility to the deep-seated fear in Nicole, just as she managed to disturb the infinitely still waters of his soul. Oddly enough, Gordan looked forward to his debt-bound days in this magicless realm.

From where he watched on the roof above them, he could see plenty that didn't require his empathetic powers. There was concern and relief in her brother's hands as they helped Nicole to her feet and lingered.

"Thanks for locking me inside." Mitchell's words dripped with sarcasm.

Nicole's eyes were fierce with challenge. "What would you have done, Mitch?"

He answered with silence, a begrudging acceptance of her point. He prodded a pile of wet soot suspiciously with his foot.

"I thought the portal was closed; you said so last night," Mitchell said.

"It *was* closed last night," Nicole answered.

"So how did it get opened again?"

Nicole and Raiden looked at each other, the answer understood in their locked gaze. But they weren't the only ones who knew. Gordan wondered—was Moira baiting him, expecting him to take his freedom the first chance he got? Below him lay the second missed opportunity. But perhaps there was more to this unwelcome visitor.

"I'm not sure I even want to know right now, let's just get the hell inside and get you dried off," Mitchell said.

For a moment, Gordan wondered what it would be like to be one of them. Maybe it was all those years of solitude, or perhaps the human form was influencing him in a way he never had anticipated. He found himself wanting to be among them. He never once had longed to be with his own kind, not in all his years confined in that tower.

"At the risk of sounding like Dad," Mitchell said with a sigh, "maybe you to should stick to safer activities for the rest of the day—like working out." He nodded, approving his own suggestion.

"All right, Mitch," Nicole said.

Satisfied, Mitchell turned toward the house.

Nicole immediately looked to Raiden with a scowl. "We're not going to get wet." She imitated a man's voice.

A laugh erupted from Raiden's lungs as they crossed the yard and followed Mitchell toward the house.

The door clicked closed, and Gordan was alone once more.

☙

The images in Moira's looking glass went dark, leaving her with nothing to glare at but her own reflection. She had not expected that the golem would manage to kill Raiden—though it would have been a welcome outcome. Nonetheless, she had learned a great deal.

When the golem was attracted by the dragon's presence, Moira had been surprised to see it merely observing. She had expected it would take the opportunity for freedom and return to Veil, but it had not. It was clear to her that Raiden was not following the Council's orders—he was not their man after all. She almost laughed; he had defected, and the Council was none the wiser. Since he clearly wasn't obeying the Council, he might as well be assisting Dawn, and he could certainly be a valuable tool to her. What she had observed with the most zeal was closeness between him and the fera. She was so desperate to save him from the golem.

Her mind replayed the scene again and again. Moira was pleased by the dragon's unexpected reservations. It was fortuitous for her that it was inclined to prolong its debt to the girl. They remained a package that meant she could attain them both more easily. All Moira had to do was lure the fera to her somehow, and her escaped prisoner would have no choice but to follow.

But there still remained one snag in her plans: the other man sent by the Council. The death keeper had said he was wandering through Cantis. His mission to find Raiden and the fera was bound to intersect with her own, and she could not allow anything to interfere with her success. Before she could move forward, she had to be sure all threats to her success were nullified. First, she would have to find this man, and then she could set a trap for the fera and the dragon.

Twenty-two

Sunday morning, Nicole had just come in the back door when her brother tromped sleepily down the stairs.

Mitchell rubbed his eyes, noticing the sheen of sweat on Nicole's bare arms and face. "Were you out in the gym?"

"Yeah, I woke up feeling like I had two scoops of preworkout," she laughed. Her body had been buzzing with so much magic that her skin itched and she felt jittery.

He gave her a wide-eyed look of understanding. "Damn. Sounds like magic is messing with your system, huh?"

"I'm figuring out how to deal with it." She tried to brush off her own worry with a nonchalant tone. "Front squats sure seemed to help."

Mitch stopped in front of the fridge. "You don't know how lucky you are to have your own personal gym." He shook his head and sighed. "The rec center at school is a madhouse sometimes."

She walked into the kitchen. "You don't have to tell me," she said with a laugh. She pointed toward the shop outside. "I had to share that gym with you and Tony."

Mitchell scowled and hit her with a playful punch as she turned toward the coffeemaker with a satisfied laugh.

"Okay," he conceded, "but imagine that times a hundred frat guys."

"You poor thing," she said, feigning sympathy. "Are you still dating Samantha?"

"Nah, but there's a cute guy I see at the coffee shop in the afternoons," he said with a shrug.

"Where's Raiden?" She turned her gaze up to the landing atop the stairs.

"Speaking of cute guys," he muttered to her with a smirk and she gave him an exasperated look. "Upstairs, I guess. You down for epic protein pancakes?"

"Always," she answered, already climbing the stairs. She reached the landing and turned left toward Raiden's door at the end of the hall. The door was closed. By the time she reached the door, she thought it would be better to let him sleep. But before she could turn around, the door opened. She jumped.

"Nicole." He looked surprised and then relieved.

"Who else would it be?" She noticed his sleep-disheveled hair and held back a laugh.

He smiled.

"Since you're awake, Mitch is making breakfast," she offered, rocking back on her heels before turning back toward the landing.

He followed. "What are we having?" he asked as he descended the stairs behind her.

"Mitch's epic protein pancakes," Nicole answered.

In the kitchen, Mitchell was halfway into the fridge gathering ingredients. "Gotta feed the muscles if you want them gains," Mitchell declared, emerging from the fridge with milk and eggs as Nicole and Raiden entered the kitchen.

A puzzled look crossed Raiden's face. "What does that mean?"

"Here we go," Nicole said, shaking her head as she poured herself some coffee.

Mitchell set his ingredients down with a look of shock on his face. "'What does that mean?' Don't they have gyms where you come from?"

Raiden shook his head with further confusion. "Gyms?"

"Good luck with that one, Mitch," Nicole muttered as she retreated from the kitchen. Hearing Mitchell try to explain "the gym life" to Raiden would certainly be entertaining, so she figured she'd listen from the living room.

She took another sip of coffee before setting it on the table by the couch and lowering herself to the floor for a good stretch.

"Look, to be big, you gotta build muscle. To build muscle, you gotta lift heavy weights and eat—a lot." Mitchell gestured as if indicating his points in invisible boxes laid out in a row before him.

Nicole tried to contain her amusement as she stretched. Within seconds of her placing her butt on the carpet, Bandit advanced with a barrage of licks aimed directly at her face.

"Bandit." She leaned away to postpone the inevitable, but she was on his level, his turf; anything and anyone from the doorknobs down was fair game. She could not escape.

"Okay. All right." She rolled away, but he followed, tail wagging. Cringing with affection, she wiped the slobber from her face.

Before her dog could get to her again, she snapped her fingers in front of his nose. Like striking a match, the friction of her fingers conjured a tiny orb of light. A self-satisfied grin spread across her face, and her chest swelled with giddy pleasure—she was getting damn good with the light spell.

Bandit's eyes locked onto the light, his entire body tensed, prey drive activated. The dog snapped at the hovering orb, catching it in his mouth. Beams of light streaked through his teeth. Nicole fell back laughing, and the spell followed her, escaping the dog's mouth. Bandit gave chase as he did when hunting house flies.

Nicole lay there on her back, giggling as she made the light flit back and forth around the living room. Bandit kept his nose locked on target, scrambling after it, snapping at it every time he came close enough. At last she took mercy on her dog and called the little light back to her hand and made it disappear in her fist. The dog rushed up to her, sniffing her closed hand eagerly. She opened her fingers and let Bandit inspect her palm.

"See, it's gone," she said, but Bandit sniffed and searched her until she was forced heave herself off the floor to escape.

Since Raiden and Mitchell were distracted in the kitchen, she figured it was a good time to take a shower. Her workout sweat was already turning pungent. They didn't even look up as she made her way up the stairs, and she shook her head to herself, smiling.

But suddenly her smile went sour. This morning felt stolen from another life, as if she had no right to lighthearted antics in the kitchen or carefree moments of laughter. The portal was out there again, and their enemies were waiting on the other side. It was only a matter of time before trouble came looking for them again. She knew what she had to do—leave this life behind completely.

Once she emerged from the bathroom, she could hear the lower tones of Mitchell and Raiden's voices joined by her father's downstairs in the kitchen. It was familiar, having three male voices in the house again. The fondness pained her heart. The sweet, warm aroma of pancakes wafted up the stairs, and her stomach gave a ravenous grumble. Maybe just today she could enjoy this, the last few pieces she still had of her old life before this new existence consumed it entirely.

She dressed eagerly, jumping into a pair of jeans and a tank top before noticing the blinking light on her phone where it sat on her window sill.

A chorus of laughter rolled through the house, and Nicole looked out her bedroom door, anxious to join them. A quick glance at her phone revealed Roxanne's name along with a text message: *Are you sick?* The text was from Friday, and there was another from yesterday. *Hey, everything all right?*

There was a third text from late last night. *Nicole, if you don't answer me, I'm coming to your house tomorrow to make sure you're alive!*

I'm fine, Nicole replied in haste, sending that message before starting a second. *Wasn't feeling like myself Thursday and Friday. I'll be at school tomorrow. Promise.* She sent the second text and sighed, comforted by the knowledge that her friend slept in and that Nicole's answer would be waiting for her when she woke up. With that, Nicole slipped her phone into her pocket. She didn't know how to juggle two lives, not when one came with golems and portals and people out to get her, but she couldn't lose her best friend.

On her way out of her room, she grabbed the red sweater hanging from the open door of her wardrobe. Her heart was still reeling from the moment of panic. The last thing she needed was Roxanne showing up and demanding to know what had been keeping Nicole from school. Nicole didn't think she could keep everything that had happened a secret from her, but she had no idea how to tell her or if she should. The thought of dragging Roxanne down into her mess, into this alerted reality full of enemies, knotted Nicole's stomach.

Down in the kitchen, Raiden leaned against the counter, coffee in hand. Her dad stood in front of the stove, transferring a pancake to the top of the growing stack on a serving plate. Mitchell was wiping up the last smears of some spilled batter from the glass stovetop beside the burner where their dad was cooking.

"Is breakfast ready?" She peered at the stack of ready pancakes with hungry eyes.

"Pancakes are a go," her dad said.

"Yes." She raised a celebratory fist in the air.

"Come get them while they're still warm," her dad added.

She crossed the kitchen and pulled down several plates from the cupboard over the sink.

"What was all the laughing about?" she asked when Raiden appeared beside her with ready hands to take the plates from her. "Thanks," she said.

"Mitchell mentioned your dad flipping pancakes when you were kids. I asked if he could do it, and he said it was harder than it sounds." Raiden set the plates down on the counter, and they each took one.

"Then Raiden and Mitch both gave it a try," her dad continued the story with a chuckle.

"How'd you do?" Nicole asked as she took a couple of the large pancakes.

Raiden took a pancake, and there was a satisfied look on his face. "I flipped one."

"Mitch had a little trouble," her dad said.

"Yeah, yeah. Raiden got lucky." Mitchell wrung the sponge in his hand, rinsing out the last of his failed pancake flip. He scowled.

"Aw, don't be sad, Mitch." Nicole pushed out her bottom lip and put her head on Mitchell's shoulder for a moment. "Your pancakes are still the best."

"I know," he said with a confident shrug.

Raiden placed his plate of plain pancakes beside Nicole's on the counter.

"Do we eat them like this?"

"Oh, no." She shook her head with a grave expression. "This is where the endless possibilities begin. You can put anything you want on them."

He laughed at how seriously she spoke of pancakes. "Like what?"

"Butter, syrup—if you're boring." She scrunched her nose.

"You mean classic," her dad chimed in, claiming some pancakes for himself.

"Nut butter and bananas or yogurt and blueberries." Her voice lit up. "Or all of those things."

"Have you figured out how much she loves food?" Mitchell asked, stabbing the pile of pancakes and seizing four on his fork before dragging them onto his plate.

Nicole left her plate to retrieve her large jar of cashew butter from the cupboard. She spread some between her two pancakes and on top. Raiden watched as they all chose their toppings. Her dad sliced a banana and crumbled walnuts on top, finishing with a drizzle of honey. Mitchell showered his in cinnamon before dropping a few spoonfuls of yogurt over his stack and topping it all with chocolate chips. Nicole rinsed a double handful of blueberries and carefully released them over her pancakes. Her dad took some berries as well.

Raiden laughed. "I have no idea what to try."

"Here's a tip: there's no wrong combination," Mitchell said. He drove his fork down into the center of his food, claiming the mountainous breakfast and taking it to the table.

"Trust me, if you can flip a pancake, then you can garnish one." She raised her voice enough so Mitchell could hear, hoping to get a rise out of him.

Sure enough, he took the bait. "Everyone gets lucky, Ray."

Nicole cackled to herself silently, dropping her head back. Raiden finally spread cashew butter on top of his pancakes. Then he picked one of the brown-flecked bananas from the pair left on the counter.

"That's gonna tweak him all day," Nicole murmured between them.

"To tell you the truth," said Raiden, looking over at Mitchell and lowering his voice, "I may have used a little magic."

Nicole grinned. Then, in a second, she bottled it up behind a casually pleasant expression. "Your secret is safe with me."

Raiden topped his pancakes with honey. "There." He nodded with satisfaction and looked at her plate beside his. "I don't see how you can possibly finish all that."

She cocked an eyebrow at him. "Watch me."

They took their plates to the table, where Mitchell and her dad were already seated.

"What time are you hitting the road today, Mitch?" Michael asked.

"I don't know. Around two, I guess," Mitchell mumbled around a mouthful of food.

"Good. Then you can help us clean up that mess in the backyard."

Mitchell swallowed, forcing his food down a little too soon. "What? That's their mess." He wagged his fork toward Nicole and Raiden. "I never asked for portals or monsters or magic."

"And the rest of us did?" Michael sounded amused for a moment. "Like it or not, we got it. You're helping."

Mitchell exhaled with a low grumble, glaring at Nicole. She just smiled and batted her eyelashes at her brother. "Come on, Mitch. Just think happy thoughts."

He scowled and went back to his pancakes.

"I guess that means we'll be focusing on practical magic today." Nicole tried not to sound as pleased as she felt, but a smile cracked her mouth. Everything about this morning felt right.

Mitchell grumbled. "You can't just abracadabra that mess away?"

"Hey," she said, and everyone at the table looked up, "are we going to tell Anthony about all this?"

Mitchell's face twisted deviously, no doubt concocting some great prank to initiate their older brother into this new world they all lived in now. Their dad, on the other hand, clearly hadn't considered it. His expression turned to a quizzical frown, and he took a few moments to imagine that conversation.

Michael shook his head. "Let's not get ahead of ourselves. One day at a time," he said before taking another bite.

One day at a time. Nicole resisted the urge sink into the gloom waiting beneath the surface of this pleasant day. It took enough effort not to let the portal looming in the backyard drag her down into worry about tomorrow, hell, even an hour from now. She'd just promised Roxanne that she would be at school Monday. Her dad still thought some semblance of normal could be salvaged from all this chaos. Keeping it together, finding everything good in the spaces between the horrors while she tried to prepare herself for her enemies, was already all her mind could balance. School was the last priority on Nicole's list.

"Isn't it kind of pointless to close the portal again? We know Moira opened it. She knows where we are—she can just open it again." Nicole said as she and Raiden crossed the patio.

"We have no way of knowing what she's up to. She may have sent a golem, but she might not have any intention of coming through herself. It would be risky," Raiden said. "Leaving the portal open puts us at risk of Sinnrick finding it. Closing it might be pointless when it comes to Moira, but as long as she's waiting to act, it would be foolish to leave it open for anyone or anything else to discover."

"I guess you're right," Nicole said, *or until another one opens because of me.*

Raiden presented the book that had been tucked under his arm, flashing an encouraging—if slightly uncertain—smile before opening to the page they needed.

They recited the spell just as they had two nights before, but there was no sign of a change. They looked to each other with questioning eyes. Nicole stepped forward and reached out. Her fingers sank into the portal, disappearing. She yanked her hand back.

"It didn't work," she said with disappointment.

"That can't be right," Raiden said, shaking his head and looking down at the book in search of the answer. His eyes flicked back and forth as he read.

"Oh no." His words came on a heavy sigh.

"What?"

"It says the portal can only be closed from the realm where it was opened, we'd have to be in Cantis to close it."

"And that could be exactly what Moira is waiting for us to do. If we try to close it, she's potentially right there waiting for us," Nicole said with a groan. "So we just have to leave it?"

"It could be more of a risk to go through it now than to just wait it out and see who or what might come through next. All we can do is be prepared and hope it closes soon," Raiden said, closing the book with a disappointed sigh. "That's the best we can do."

Nicole took a deep breath. It was beginning to look like she would not have a single vestige of her life left to keep. "What would happen if I left—I mean I take my magic with me, would that help?"

"The portal would close sooner."

"Could she open a portal again if I wasn't here?"

"Without magic as a link she wouldn't be able to," Raiden said.

She sighed. "I think I better talk to my dad."

☙

"Dad?" Nicole took a reluctant step into his room, holding the letter from the Council Raiden had given her. She couldn't get his expression from her mind, his mouth firm with worry, fear in his eyes when he handed her the letter from her enemy to show her dad. The reluctance in his hand lingered in the paper. She understood. The trust that kept him here with them was still new and fragile, and it had nearly been broken once before by the Council's expectations.

She couldn't deny that reading their first letter made her a little cold, wondering if any of the things he told her could be beautifully crafted lies, if her sympathy was for something real or not, if he might turn around and end up being her greatest fear, someone she trusted who would leave her. But she kept those thoughts to herself, because the look on his face told her that was precisely what he dreaded might happen. The letter had the power to break this, whatever this was, his addition to their family, their home. The sadness in his gaze, the anxious tension in the silence as he stood there looking at the letter in her hands, made her believe him, but her dad would have the same doubts when he read this letter, she knew he would.

He sat at his desk looking over his supplier catalogs. "Yeah," he answered without looking up.

"I need to talk to you," she said.

Now he looked up. "What is it?" He frowned, no doubt hearing the weight of terrible things in her words.

Nicole wished she could spare him this nightmare. Her stomach churned with guilty nausea. He was already shaken by portals and magic, seeing monsters in his backyard and letting a stranger into their home to help her figure out how to control this chaos. Telling him about the Council searching for her, the dragon she had saved—or, as Raiden liked to put it, stolen—and the woman behind the golems waiting on the other side of the portal now out to get them both, it would push him further and she didn't know how close to the edge her dad was behind his composure.

He listened to everything she said with a stony expression, nodding occasionally when in agreement with her choices and frowning further when he disapproved. Disappointment was clear on his face when he learned about Raiden's ties to the Council and read the letter, but she did her best to share Raiden's story and capture the sincerity she felt in his words, the proof she had seen in Cantis, what they had both witnessed in his actions. Finally, her dad nodded, apparently weighing it all against Raiden's secret favorably.

Once Nicole finished explaining the dilemma with the current portal, the presence of her magic keeping it open, and the only viable solution that didn't involve facing an enemy, she took a deep breath and sighed. It took him a few minutes that felt like ages to respond.

"I can't say it's easy to just let go of the idea of you graduating ... but it is what it is, I suppose." He shook his head. "I know how hard you've worked in school, how smart you are, and all these obstacles are not your choice."

Nicole's eyes and nose stung with welling tears. She always tried so hard to make her dad proud, to live up to every success her brothers had made before her. Although that life was long gone, that Nicole still existed in her, and she was heartbroken with failure and shame.

The instant her dad spotted the tears, he was out of his seat and had his arms around her. "Hey," he said, "it's all right. We don't live in the same world we used to. We can handle this, we have no choice, right?" He attempted a laugh.

She was surprised and comforted to hear him say that.

"Besides, you have enough places you can go. Your brother in Ventura. Mitchell is in Tucson. You can stay with your aunt and uncle in Michigan. Your cousin in Oregon. We can make this 'on the move' thing work."

"Yeah," she said, unenthusiastically. She hadn't really stopped to think of it. She loved visiting her family, being in new places, but was that going to be the rest of her life, hopping between places, playing hide and seek with her enemies in another realm?

"You've always been smart and strong and determined. Things are going to change along the way, they won't go as planned, and whatever happens, if you keep on being the young woman you've become, I'll be proud of you."

He wasn't helping the tears stop. She nodded against his chest. She sniffed her runny nose and blinked back her tears. "I guess this means tomorrow we should go to the office and drop out?"

"I suppose so. You're eighteen, so you don't need me there." He was as calm as if they were discussing a doctor's appointment. Her not finishing high school didn't bother him because there was a much great fear he was holding in his chest. There were people after his daughter and none of the strangeness challenging his reality could scare him like that fact did.

"No," she answered, "I suppose I won't."

Twenty-three

Nicole opened her eyes to a familiar anxiety in the darkness of the morning, knowing it was Monday, time to officially leave her old life behind. That old, nagging urge to run grew restless in her legs, and her body fell into the routine as she shimmied back, feet first, off her bed and climbed down in the dark.

She had woken up in the middle of the night and seen the light on in Raiden's room. Part of her knew that some of his sleeplessness came from worrying about *her*. Now that his room was dark, she didn't think it was fair to wake him. He deserved his rest.

So she dressed silently in her room, pulling on a pair of leggings, socks, and running shoes. She donned a white shirt for high visibility and gathered her hair up into a high ponytail. With a pair of knit gloves to protect her hands from the biting wind, she was ready to hit the road.

Out in the hall, she placed her feet down in practiced silence. With just a little magic and hardly any thought, she glided over the spot where the floor creaked beneath the carpet. Every day, she grew more comfortable with the new sensations and reflexes that came with her magic.

Once at the front door, her hand found the key, turned the

deadbolt open, and pulled it from the lock. Just enough of the dim light from the streetlamp outside fell through the narrow window beside the door. There she untied her right shoe, threaded the key onto one of the laces, and tucked it beneath the crossed laces to secure it. She tied her shoe again and slipped out the front door. As the door shut behind her, she gladly inhaled the smell of cold and winter wood smoke outside. The brisk air struck her with urgency, the need to run, to warm her body against the chill.

"Activities done in the dark are quite often of a disreputable nature."

The cool voice came from the darkness, and she jumped.

"Gordan?"

"It must be dreadful to have such poor eyesight." His voice was right beside her.

She chuckled. "I manage with what I've got," she said, her voice trembling with the cold.

"Where are you off to at such a secretive hour?"

"Come along, and you'll find out," she said, thinking her grin was lost in the dark.

She left him behind, shifting from a standstill into an easy run with a single stride.

Gordan followed along the rooftops with lithe steps, following Nicole as she ran on the street below. Although her thoughts were beyond his perception, he could feel the very air pulse with her fear in every foot strike and beat of her heart. It seemed to recede beneath each streetlight and swell in the shadows in between, intensifying with each return like waves bringing in the tide. With the tension of her magic building in the air, he might have guessed what would happen.

As she passed beneath another cone of light from the lamp overhead, the bulb went out with a great spark, and the darkness slammed shut around her. She surged forward as though swept along in a wave of panic. The harder she ran, the farther she seemed to get from that lurking fear. At least it seemed she left her fears behind or maybe burned them away in exertion. Her anxiety faded into the recesses of her being until Gordan could no longer sense it. As he watched Nicole, he felt only fortitude carrying her swiftly into the therapeutic rhythm of her heart beat, breathing and stride. He knew the feeling well; he wished he could stretch his wings and fly toward the horizon. Perhaps in the darkness of the morning he could, just for a short time, while she ran.

He looked toward the east, seeing the subtle approach of the sun far sooner than human eyes would. There was time, almost an hour, before the sun's light washed over the sky.

℘

Raiden's body snapped upright in bed as he wrenched himself free of a vision. His chest was still aching with relief and adoration, his body flush with the heat of an embrace. He could smell sunlight and sand in the silver hair of his nameless companion. Now free from that vision, he sank into disappointment, his mind drifting to Nicole.

The sky through his window was almost the pale blue of day, but the house remained silent. For a moment, his heart raced, suspecting a predator nearby. While they slept, they were completely vulnerable. He did not trust the dragon to watch out for them—at least not for him. There was no telling what might happen if Sinnrick were to find the portal in the middle of the night. If he knew that this house was where he'd find Nicole, would he break in or just wait somewhere out of sight? And Moira—she had opened the portal and yet had done nothing since sending the golem. Would she risk coming through the portal herself? She seemed far more likely to keep sending traps and lures through the portal in an attempt to catch them off guard. He couldn't be sure which was the greater threat.

Out of habit, the first thing he did was dress. The soft loose pants he'd been given to sleep in were far too insubstantial, too comfortable. He could not get used to that luxury in just a few nights. The past several years, he had slept in the first layer of clothes he always wore. Granted, he was happy he no longer had to wear garments that had belonged to his father; still, he felt far too vulnerable in clothes meant only for sleep. So he stepped into the trousers Nicole called jeans and pulled a red sweater on.

Still barefoot, he left his room and treaded down the hall past the landing. Just before he reached the bathroom, the floor creaked underfoot. He cringed and hoped that wouldn't wake Nicole. Then he stopped, looking toward the dark doorway of her room. The air in the hall felt flat. He took a couple of steps closer to Nicole's room, and still there was no familiar trace of her magic in the air.

His heart gave an uneasy thump against his ribs, urging him into the room.

"Nicole?" His voice was caught between a considerate whisper and his anxiety.

No answer came. He threw his hand to the wall, striking the light switch. The room lit up, and from where he stood he could see only blankets on her elevated bed and a pillow unoccupied. The air fell out of his lungs, and he spun back into the hall. His footsteps thumped in the silence like a panicked heartbeat as he ran for the stairs, his thoughts on the portal.

As he came to the bottom of the stairs, a dim figure appeared in front of him—a white shirt visible in the darkness of the house.

"What's wrong?" Nicole's quiet voice nearly laid him out in shock.

He grabbed her shoulders and dropped his head for a second to let out a breath that was both a sigh and a laugh.

"Raiden?"

"Nothing." He shook his head and removed his hands from her shoulders.

Nicole reached for the wall, and with a click of the switch, the kitchen filled with light, stunning their eyes in a moment.

"Where were you?" He tried to answer his own question by studying her clothes.

"Running." She walked into the kitchen and set about making coffee.

He nodded absently, still dizzy from the sudden panic and equally abrupt relief.

"I was feeling a little anxious about school," she said.

"And how do you feel now?"

"Better—I guess part of me knew this was coming even days ago. It's just now I have to make it official, sign the paper, say good-bye to that whole life—to my friends."

"How much time do you have?" He looked at the clock; it was six forty-five.

"Couple hours. Enough time to shower, get dressed, have break-fast, and brood just a little more." She let out a laugh.

"You'll be fine," he promised.

"Right—this is the easy part. The Council is the hard part." She tried to sound unburdened by the fact. "Do you want to come with me? See what a magical place my high school is?" She let out a sar-castic laugh.

He smiled, keeping his relief to himself. Her suggestion put a sudden stop to the slow creep of worry that he wouldn't be with her in case anything from Veil might have arrived in the night. "Why not?" With that portal open he didn't want to let her out of his sight, and, frankly, he just wanted to be with her.

❧

"I thought we were going to your school," Raiden said, as they stepped out the back door, not that he really cared where they were going. He was content to follow.

"If you're going to get the full experience of what my days used to be like before you showed up"—she paused to smile at him—"then this is how we get to school." She pointed at the back wall of the property. "It's a tradition to hop the wall." She spoke with play-ful reverence.

"All right then. We just … go over the wall?" Raiden couldn't keep himself from laughing, unable to understand the reasoning, but she was smiling so what did it matter?

"Yep," she said with obvious pride. "We magicless kids have to find excitement and adventure anywhere we can, and nothing feels more badass than going over a wall like Indiana Jones every day."

"Who is Indiana Jones?"

Nicole laughed. "A fictional college professor-slash-treasure-hunter with an knack for using a whip."

"Oh." Raiden nodded but didn't feel less confused.

"Come on—and no magic, if you can handle it," she said.

"I don't use magic for every little thing," he countered.

"Okay," she said, grinning.

"Ladies first." He extended his hand.

"Don't mind if I do," she said before taking off. She at the wall and jumped, planting her hands at the top and hoisting herself up before throwing a leg over. She halted at the top, straddling the wall. "I gotta say, it's nice not having to do that with a backpack. What are you waiting for?"

Raiden stood there where she had left him, looking at her with an imperceptible smile on his face. He couldn't help wishing there had been more days like this in the last nine years—and that there would be more in his future. But how could he be that lucky? He felt like a thief with something that did not belong to him. It only occurred to him now that he wanted to keep her. Could he keep leaving the woman with silver hair on his pillow, pretending he didn't know about her, while he was with Nicole?

She laughed. "What?"

He shook himself from his thoughts. "Nothing," he answered as he broke into a steady lope toward the wall. Thanks to his height and long arms, he caught the top of the wall easily and heaved himself up with little effort. He sat himself down beside Nicole.

"That seems like an unnecessary effort just to get to school," he said.

"Unnecessary? If we were in a horror movie, a wall could be the difference between escape and a bloody death."

"I'm sorry, but what is a horror movie?" he asked, his words riding an exasperated sigh.

Nicole looked toward the sky and let out an amused groan as

she swung her leg over the wall and dropped down to the gravel below. She stepped onto the sidewalk, and Raiden followed suit. They crossed the street, making their way toward the cluster of red-brick buildings just beyond a car-filled parking lot.

"Movie is short for moving pictures, so you can capture scenes and events to watch later," she explained.

"Sounds pretty straightforward," he said.

As they made their way across the parking lot, Nicole tried her best to explain movies to Raiden.

He shook his head. "Imagine," he said, "solving all our problems in two hours or less."

"Yeah." Nicole laughed as she trailed her fingers against the chain-link fence. They followed the sidewalk toward campus.

There were hardly any other students walking in with them, and the lot was packed with vehicles. Ahead of them, the campus was quiet.

"Where is everybody?" Raiden looked around, seeing only two others making their way through the parking lot.

"In class. The bell will ring soon," she said.

People—other people. It hadn't crossed his mind until now. He hadn't been in a crowd of people since he was thirteen.

As they came to the first of the brick buildings, a crackling toll rang through the air. In a matter of seconds, streams of people poured from every door into the area around them. Raiden's lungs expanded and stopped. The number of students increased, surrounding them. His steps slowed, and his heart rate accelerated.

The din of student conversation met his ears: a familiar cacophony of voices. It sounded so much harsher than he remembered. He stopped and she bumped against him. His hand caught hers, a reflex to find an anchor. His eyes fixed on the gathering packs of students around them. From the corner of his vision, he could see her glance down at their joined hands, but he couldn't let go, he could feel himself slipping back to a place he didn't want to be. If he didn't let go, he would be okay, he wouldn't go back there.

The haze of human noise awakened something in the back of

his mind, fanning a dim memory into a flame. In his mind, the voices broke into screams and panic. He was back in Cantis nine years ago. The walls of their home had not blocked out those terrible sounds, not even when his mother closed him in that tiny closet to keep him safe. His breathing was shallow and quick, his heart racing.

"Raiden?"

Her voice broke through the phantom cries from his past. He could feel her hand in his, his grip so hard he realized it must hurt, but she didn't pull her hand away this time.

"I'm all right," he said. "It's just—the people," he struggled to explain, but she looked at him with understanding in her eyes.

"They're going to thin out soon," she said, tightening her grasp on his hand.

They proceeded more slowly into the students and the crowd spread out, dispersing toward the surrounding buildings. They passed beneath a high shade structure that sheltered outdoor tables. Raiden focused on Nicole's hand, his feet, their cadence, instead of the crowd. Then someone trailing a cloud of pungent cologne passed in front of them. Nicole scrunched her nose and stopped.

"What is it?" he asked.

"I think—" She waved her free hand in front of her face, holding her breath. She doubled over with the force of a sneeze. A wave of warm magic rolled out from her, a ripple of chaos. The metal picnic tables around them slid across the concrete, moaning and twisting, screeching and crashing into one another. Students screamed, leaping away from the tables—Raiden tensed. Everyone ran from the destruction, but lingered just beyond the wreckage in their shock and curiosity. Nicole and Raiden were left standing in the middle of it all like a meteor in its crater. His breathing hastened to match the tempo of his racing heart, but at least they weren't caught in the crowd of people any longer.

There was a remarkable silence, eerie in the presence of so many people. But it only took a second before the murmur of voices spread through the air.

Nicole tugged on Raiden's arm, and they ran, distancing themselves like some of the other students had done. He wondered if they seemed like just another pair of frightened bystanders. Would anyone make the connection—the two of them standing in the center of the destruction?

Across a large open cement courtyard, in front of a building with two small green lawns on either side of its entrance—the word Library clinging to the red brick above the doors—Nicole finally stopped.

"I can't believe that just happened," she hissed.

Raiden's mind was clearer now that they were away from the throng of students. "At least no one was hurt," he said, hoping that eased her panic as he took a deep breath to calm himself. "There's nothing we can do about it now."

Nicole let out an exasperated sigh. A loud pop and hiss startled them into each other's arms and then another pop and another.

"Oh no," she cried said as the water came down. In the nearby grass in front of the Library four spouts of water erupted from the lawn. Passing girls ducked and covered their heads, squealing as they scuttled away to protect their hair. Nicole and Raiden evacuated to a safe distance, suffering only a few cold drops.

For a moment, she closed her eyes and took a deep breath. While her eyes were closed, he was free to study her face. He could see just how long her lashes were lying against her skin and the scattered sun specks across her cheeks.

"Nicole!" someone cried. Raiden's attention jerked away from her to a girl jogging toward them, curly blonde hair bouncing around her shoulders. He looked back at Nicole, who went rigid. He grabbed her hand, hoping he could pull her back from whatever unease had seized her.

"Roxanne," Nicole said with a look of terror on her face. She covered it quickly with a smile.

"Oh my God—where *were* you last week?" Roxanne demanded with wide eyes, but her tone shifted immediately to excitement. "Did you see what happened to the picnic tables?"

Roxanne was so excited she didn't even give Raiden a second glance as he stood there beside Nicole or notice that he had her by the hand. She didn't even give Nicole a chance to answer the questions.

"They're saying the tables started moving and twisting on their own. I didn't see it. Did you?"

"We didn't see it happen either—just the aftermath."

Raiden tried not to show how impressed he was by Nicole's convincing disappointment.

Roxanne looked back and forth between the two of them. "We?" Her gaze fell to their joined hands.

Nicole presented him. "Rox, this is Raiden."

"Hi, I'm Roxanne," she said with a little wave.

"Nice to make your acquaintance," he said.

Roxanne's eyebrows shot up. "Did you just move here?"

"Temporarily," he said, but he didn't like the sound of that answer.

"Are you transferring to Cibola then?" she asked with an innocent smile. It was a perfectly logical assumption.

"Um." Raiden stalled, looking to Nicole for the answer.

"Yeah. Actually, we have some things to take care of in the office," Nicole said, allowing that vague truth do the lying for her. Raiden bobbed his head in approval.

"Oh, right," Roxanne said, nodding. "How do you two know each other?" she asked hastily before they could escape.

"We ran into each other the first day he was in the neighborhood," Nicole said.

Raiden cleared his throat to disguise a laugh that almost slipped past his carefully composed mouth.

"Cool," Roxanne said. "All right, see you in class then," she said with a wave and hurried off toward a nearby building.

A sigh of relief escaped from Nicole's lungs. "That sure doesn't make this any easier." She hung her head.

The fountains of water died down.

"You'll find a way to tell her," Raiden said.

"That should be a fun day," Nicole said with an ironic laugh. "Come on. Let's get this over with and get the hell out of here."

Nicole led Raiden around the building where the sprinklers had burst. They walked through the main gate of the school toward the front office. They came to a side door above which the words "Councilor's Office" hung on the red brick.

"Here we go," Nicole muttered and opened the door.

❦

Sinnrick stumbled over something hard in the darkness of yet another empty home in Cantis. He kicked the unseen object angrily. He had searched this entire city and found no trace of Raiden. Sinnrick was beginning to wonder if Raiden hadn't met his end somewhere out in that forest. Maybe he'd been killed by the fera. His sigh of exhaustion dissipated into the silence. The idea of a body search wasn't exactly appealing, not to mention that it wouldn't be easy if Raiden was no more than a pile of bones in an even bigger pile of ashes.

After wrestling the pack off his back, Sinnrick dug through its contents, searching for one thing in particular. At last he found the rigid object, a tin box no thicker than his thumb. A short leather strap fastened the case closed. He opened it, revealing crisp sheets of letter paper. The top of each sheet bore the Council's seal, and it was laced with a spell that had one purpose: to take the finished document directly to, and only to, the Council. If anyone intercepted one of these sheets, the spell would ignite the paper and destroy its information.

He removed a single sheet of paper and closed the case, rolling his eyes. It was a somewhat outdated method of communication. Sinnrick personally wondered if the distance between Cantis and Atrium was too great for the more convenient system, the vox channels, but they hadn't issued him a mask. He supposed the chances that he might not return from this assignment were high. Disposable men would surely be given the retired resources.

He shook the thought from his head.

"Report," he said, the key word that activated the magic in the paper. The seal shimmered with momentary light, and a subtle wave of warmth surged through the blank page.

"Sinnrick Stultus reporting from Cantis." He dictated, and the words appeared one after another. "The last known residence of Raiden Cael was sealed tight. I received no answer from within and could not gain entry. Furthermore, I have witnessed some unusual activity for a place presumably uninhabited. Not only were there class seven golems in the vicinity, but the forest here was consumed by widespread fire. I suspect this has something to do with the fera and that Raiden's absence could be related.

"I have since searched the entirety of the city and found nothing. I send this report in hopes to verify with the court seers if Raiden's future has indeed gone dark—and if so, I respectfully request permission to proceed with the task of locating the fera on my own."

His words filled the page almost to the end.

"Send," he commanded with a satisfied nod.

The page flicked into the air, folded itself tightly, and flitted away. Sinnrick—distracted by tucking the case of letter paper back into his pack—heard a faint tapping. He peered across the dim interior of the empty house to see the white folded paper through the darkness. To the left of the door, his report bounced and tapped against the window like a frantic moth trying to fly through the glass.

He huffed and crossed the room, taking care not to trip again. His hand closed hard with annoyance around the doorknob, and he opened the old, warped door with a yank. The hinges moaned. The letter ceased its attempts to escape through the window and flew out the open door.

Twenty-four

The door closed behind them. Nicole separated her hand from Raiden's at last and he was disappointed by how much his heart sank when her fingers slipped away. They stood in the silent office where a woman sat at a desk by the door. On the front edge of the desk sat a name plate: Patti Blanc. Nicole approached the woman, her fingers clattering across her keyboard.

"Hi," Nicole said. "I need to speak to my councilor about a dropout form."

Patti's attention seized on *dropout,* and she looked up abruptly to see who would say such a heinous thing. Her eyes lit with recognition when she saw Nicole, and she laughed.

"You're so funny, Nicole," she chortled and looked back to her computer screen, her fingers resuming their task. "Mrs. Sterling is in her office," she said, still smiling and shaking her head.

Nicole smiled and said, "Thank you."

Raiden, standing a step behind her, looked around the office. Behind him was a waiting area with a few round tables, each with a few chairs arranged around it. There were a couple of students waiting slumped in their seats. When Nicole turned away from Patti's desk, she nodded toward the available seats.

"Hopefully this won't take long," she said, drifting toward the open door across from the closest table. Raiden sat down where he could see partly into the small office. He could make out the front side of the desk within, picture frames lining the edge, but he couldn't see who was sitting behind the desk. There were two empty chairs, and Nicole chose the one closest to the door. She sat down.

"Hi, Mrs. Sterling," Nicole said.

"Hello, dear," a chipper voice greeted Nicole.

Raiden leaned in his seat but still could not see the woman behind the desk.

"I need to fill out a withdrawal form," Nicole stated coolly.

The voice of Mrs. Sterling laughed dismissively. "A withdrawal form? Whatever for?"

"To withdraw," Nicole said with a hint of annoyance at having to state the obvious, "from school," she added, in case Mrs. Sterling needed further clarity.

"I don't understand—you want to drop out?" Mrs. Sterling said the last two words with disgust. "But you're in the running for valedictorian."

"I'm aware of that," Nicole maintained her polite tone. Raiden could see her stiffen in her seat. The lights over his head flickered.

"Don't be silly. Why would you throw away all that hard work? You don't want to do that," Mrs. Sterling said.

Nicole straightened up in her seat and leaned her head toward Raiden; even from where he sat, he could hear the two pops of vertebrae in her neck. He cringed; Mrs. Sterling had no idea what Nicole was capable of these days, and she was clearly testing the boundaries of Nicole's patience.

"Actually, I do," Nicole said with a tight smile.

Mrs. Sterling's tone was patronizing. "Have you talked to your parents about this?"

"Not that it matters—seeing as I'm eighteen—but yes, my dad supports my decision, so I'd appreciate it if you would please get me the form I need." Nicole's voice was so calm Raiden almost expected her to snap at the woman.

There came sounds of a drawer opening, paper shuffling, and finally the crinkle of a crisp sheet of paper. Raiden saw the page appear in a slender, red-clawed hand. Nicole received the paper gently, though he could see the tension in her jaw.

"Really, dear," said Mrs. Sterling, her voice losing its sweetness. "You're wasting so much potential."

Raiden tensed as he watched. Nicole's jaw clenched, and suddenly every light overhead went out with a hum and a pop. Patti jumped in her seat behind her desk. Raiden's attention jerked back to Nicole.

"Whoops, that's unfortunate," Mrs. Sterling was chipper once again. "It looks like I won't be able to put this into the system now."

"That's all right. I'll return the form tomorrow when your system is back up," Nicole answered, mimicking Mrs. Sterling's sweet tone with a trace of venom as she stood up. No reply came, and Nicole excused herself.

The instant she passed through the doorway of Mrs. Sterling's office, Nicole's dignified stride turned into a furious stomp. "Got it," she said, holding up the paper. "Let's go."

Raiden hopped up out of his seat and fell into step beside her.

Back outside, the campus was all but deserted. Nicole sighed. He watched her shoulders sag with relief and felt the charge in the air dissipate as the door shut behind them.

"I always hated that woman," Nicole confessed with a laugh. "Well," she sighed, looking around. "I guess this is my chance to say goodbye. Wanna look around, see where I've spent the last four years of my life?"

"Lead the way," he said.

"This way." She waved her hand, and they walked side by side back through the main gate beneath the school sign that read, "Cibola High School, Home of the Raiders."

They passed the Library and the scene of Nicole's panicked waterworks. A man was hunched over one of the sprinkler heads, pulling apart the mechanism.

"Oops," she said guiltily, and they veered left through the open-air walkway between two brick buildings.

As they passed a rectangular planter with cement benches set into its sides, the scraggly branches of a bare thorn bush quivered. It sprouted leaves and countless buds that grew plump and opened in a great flourish of color and fragrance.

"At least you can say you made it a more beautiful place before you left," Raiden said.

"Oh yeah," she said with a laugh, "a few roses should make up for that mess I made of the picnic tables. We better keep moving, or it will take over the school."

As they passed a few doors, plaques on the wall indicating classroom numbers and Nurse's office. Nicole pointed to one, saying, "That's where I should be right now. English with Mr. Barkin."

They walked toward a set of locked gates that looked out on the road and traffic passing by the campus. Nicole pointed to a set of double doors into the building on the left. Raiden tried to imagine a life where he walked these halls everyday instead of the empty streets of Cantis, a simpler world where he was just another student within the gray walls, catching Nicole's eye in passing. Would they have known each other in that life? Would he have noticed her out of hundreds, realized how remarkable she is without being thrown into her life like he had been?

Nicole and Raiden wandered down the quiet corridor.

"You've spent four years here? Sitting in one of these classrooms every day?" He had the freedom to do as he pleased, go where he wished, read what he liked, pursue his own desires. Yet there was something appealing to him about the idea of this safe and consistent monotony Nicole had lived.

"That's right," she said.

Down the hall and around the corner came an electronic beep and a crackle of sound Raiden didn't recognize. Then a man's voice spoke for a few seconds, distant and fuzzy. Another voice replied near and clear.

Nicole dropped her voice to a low hiss. "Ugh, it's Joe."

Raiden lowered his voice too. "Who is that?"

"The school security guard. He'll hound us for being in the hall without passes and escort us to tardy-sweep."

"Here." Raiden took her hand and pulled her into a short hall perpendicular to the main one which led to an emergency exit. "Quick lesson in invisibility?" he murmured between them and stepped closer so that she backed against the wall. They were only inches apart.

"Sure," she answered.

"*Ungesewen,*" he said. The air grew warm for an instant, tingling against his skin as the spell settled around them.

The sensation was like a soft rain of dust. The tickle compelled Nicole to scratch her cheek, but then the heavy, shuffling steps of the approaching security guard met their ears, and she froze.

Joe appeared, his gait lumbering and slow. He walked right by them, a mere two feet away, even glanced down the narrow emergency exit hall and noticed nothing. Nicole let out a chuckle under her breath, but Joe stopped and looked again, directly at them. His suspicious eyes searched their general direction but never seemed to settle on anything. Raiden leaned a little closer, as though the closer they were, the more invisible they would become. Joe shrugged away his confusion and kept walking. They listened to his footsteps get farther until the sound of the door opening at the end of the hall told them the coast was clear.

Nicole held back a burst of quiet laughter behind her lips and sighed before lifting her gaze. Raiden's mouth spread into a satisfied smile. They were nearly pressed together—and he was intensely aware of it the instant their eyes met. His eyes were drawn to her smile, then—before he could think better of it—his lips to hers. He leaned in, and the space between them was gone.

Her warm lips against his sent a wave of heat through him. From her lips came a rush of magic that swelled within him, tingling and raising goosebumps on his skin. Overhead, the dull hum of the lights grew to a loud drone, and they grew brighter. A chorus of pops broke through his oblivious delight. Startled, they pulled away from each other. He heard Nicole's head thump against the wall. A laugh and a hiss escaped her lips as they both reached for her head. A shower of sparks fell from above. He caught her hand and he pulled her into a run away from the rain of shattered light. The hallway went dark.

They bolted down the hall and turned left at the end of the corridor. Caught up in a surge of adrenaline, they kept running. His heart was riding the high of that moment. Nicole steered them right at the end of the hallway, down a narrower hall lit by sunlight through the pair of windowed doors. They emerged from the building on the opposite side from where they had entered and were back beneath the great shaded patio where the tangled and twisted picnic tables sat—now wrapped up in orange tape fluttering in the breeze, a rather feeble warning for students to stay off.

At last they slowed to a stroll. Nicole laughed, rubbing the back of her head with her free hand. "Maybe we should go back home before I do any more damage here," she said.

"*We should go back home*" was all Raiden heard, and he smiled at that, realizing how at home he felt here in such a short time. As they passed the distorted aluminum monuments to Nicole's power, Raiden wondered if he truly understood what she was capable of.

಄

Gordan sat up when he heard the sound of feet on gravel beyond the wall of the backyard. Nicole and Raiden's voices preceded their appearance over the wall. They made it over with relative ease—for humans, that is. They crossed the yard, casting suspicious glances all around. He chuckled and lay back down, stretching his lanky form along the peak of the roof.

"You can rest at ease, for now. Nothing has come through the portal," he said, taking pity on them. Their tension in the air relaxed.

"Was that—"

"Thank you, Gordan," Nicole said, her voice breaking into a laugh as she cut Raiden off. "Would it kill you to admit he's nice?" she muttered, no doubt thinking Gordan wouldn't hear it.

"I don't know. That might be too much of a risk to take," Raiden said, a teasing tone replacing the genuine distaste Gordan had heard before in the tower. Beneath the hum of attraction, the humor, slight annoyance, Gordan detected far less mistrust in Raiden's heart, even if there was still a bitter edge to Raiden's acceptance of his presence. What an affect Nicole had on him, indeed.

Their voices drifted away into the shelter of the house. Gordan heard the door open and close. Nicole's sigh was so heavy he could hear it as clearly as her voice even from within the house.

"Funny, I'm free from school, and yet all I want to do is study something." Her laugh sounded sad to Gordan. "I think I'll start reading some of those books we brought back. Maybe there's something in one of them that will help me figure out how I'm supposed to deal with portals that won't close and people who have it out for me."

"Well, since you have a guard dragon watching the portal, there's no reason we can't get lost in books all day." Raiden's voice came muffled through the walls of the house.

"Exactly," Nicole said with warmth in her voice that he could feel through the walls and the roof. She truly did like knowing he was there. Gordan snorted and closed his eyes. Unlike humans, he could monitor the portal in his sleep with his keen senses.

Twenty-five

Raiden woke up Tuesday morning to a peculiar aura hanging in the air, prickling his skin. He didn't hear any of the usual sounds of Nicole or her father in the kitchen.

He eased himself up from his bed wearing only a soft pair of sweatpants and left the room. His bare feet were silent against the plush carpet of the hallway as he made his way to Nicole's door at the other end.

"Nicole?" He pushed the door open and looked in, startled by the sight of a shoe hanging midair in front of his face. Every object in Nicole's room was suspended, hovering almost motionless—shoes, articles of clothing, books, stuffed animals, a jewelry box, her sketchbook, pencils, a tiny wooden figurine. Some objects turned ever so slightly, rotating like planets suspended in space.

"Nicole." This time he raised his voice above a whisper. From below, he could only see her hand draped over the side of the mattress. He said her name again, urgency raising his voice as he tried to maneuver through the objects floating throughout her room.

Some things he could not avoid, bumping them and sending them spinning off through the air. Once beside the loft bed, he reached for her hand, hoping to wake her quietly. "Nicole."

Her hand closed around his like a trap with sudden—almost overwhelming—force. A jolt of magic rolled through him and the room like a ripple across water. His heart started when her charge of terror moved through him, so swift and brief he could think he imagined it, and he wondered if he had awoken her from a bad dream. Everything fell to the floor, clinking and thudding like a swift flurry of drums. The air cleared of the thick charge of magic. As quickly as her hand had closed, it opened, releasing him.

"Raiden?" Her hand disappeared, and she leaned over the side of her bed with sleepy lids hanging over her eyes.

"I was trying to wake you." He lowered his hand secretively, unsure if she was aware of their brief contact.

"Is something wrong?"

"No." He looked around the room. Not a single object was even an inch above the surface where it lay. "But everything in your room was"—he paused, looking for the right word—"floating."

Nicole blinked the sleep from her eyes, but they still looked troubled as she surveyed her room.

"Are you all right?" He watched her eyes, waiting for her to look at him.

She rolled away from the edge of the bed, disappearing from sight for a moment before she slid off the foot of her bed and climbed down.

He persisted for an answer, troubled by her silence. "Nicole?"

She lifted her gaze to his. "I spent most of the night thinking how stupid it was to try to sleep in my own bed like nothing was different, like I didn't have to wake up today and prepare for a life of running away from people I've never met—just because I exist." She finished with a sigh and a smile that wrenched at his heart.

"We don't have to leave right away," he said. "Are you going to tell your friend about all this?" He thought of his friend Caeruleus, leaving Cantis with his father unexpectedly. Raiden knew Caeruleus's father had been the reason he never heard from his friend that they were moving to the mainland, but he wished he knew why or at least had the chance to say goodbye.

"I don't know if I can tell her about the portal or the people after me. She wouldn't believe me, and even if she did what kind of friend would I be if I left her to worry like that? I'll figure out how to tell her I'm leaving," she said bitterly. "But I can't lie to her, so I don't know how I'm going to do this."

"You'll find a way," he said.

❧

The day was gray. A blanket of thick cloud pressing down on the world reminded Nicole how trapped she already felt. Being a realm away from her problems provided her with very little protection. It wasn't any safer than just hiding out in some hole in Veil—where the Council and potentially even a sadistic dragon-collector were out to find her. This realm was such a fragile sanctuary, safe only as long as the portal remained undiscovered. Moira had opened the portal to send her golem after them, and every day that passed without a sign of her made Nicole more uneasy.

Nicole was compelled by ominous thoughts to enjoy what few days of freedom she had left. It seemed inevitable—the day would come when she would have to run, leave the empty shell of her safe life behind her, and she feared it would come soon.

"What's on the agenda for today?" her dad asked as he shrugged on his Sherpa-lined leather jacket.

"Practicing outside," Nicole said with a shrug. Being inside the house made her anxious, knowing the portal was out there, even with Gordan around she felt better keeping an eye on it herself.

"It looks like it's going to rain," her dad said from the kitchen as he pulled his keys from his paint-stained work jeans.

"Then I'll practice inside." She caught the look her dad cast at Raiden shared for a brief moment, reluctance and a trace of doubt in his gray eyes. "Hey Dad," she said.

He looked at her.

"Remember when I used to go to those MMA classes with Tony?"

"Yeah," he said, looking a little confused by the subject change.

"Add magic to that—I'll be fine," she said with an encouraging smile. Whether he was worried about enemies on the other side of the portal or second-guessing trusting Raiden to be alone with her, she hoped that reminded him of the confidence he usually had in her. He raised a daughter who could look out for herself, she didn't want him to forget that in light of all this surreal uncertainty.

His confusion turned to an amused nod. "All right, love you," her dad said. "Keep it safe." He gave them both one last glance before turning to leave the kitchen.

"Love you too," she said, waiting to hear the front door open and close. "Better practice while I can," she said, eager to be doing something, to escape her thoughts that just went around and round, boring a hole in her sanity. She opened the back door and stepped outside.

She tromped across the patio and onto the grass. The cold air was welcoming against her skin. She stood listening to the morning, the occasional hum of a car engine driving down the street on the other side of the wall. The drone of Cibola's bell stretched through the air but today she felt like that sound couldn't reach her, not anymore. It was a relief to cut the cord. For the first time since Raiden arrived, she didn't feel caught between two lives and somehow that brought her a little sense of peace. As full of enemies as it was, she couldn't bring herself to wish this new reality away.

Even the energy condensed and buzzing in her core felt calmer today. With a heavy sigh of relief, she lowered herself down, banishing gravity with a thought before her butt could touch the dewy ground. She folded her legs, closed her eyes, and took another deep breath.

She heard the door open and close. Raiden's footsteps on the patio grew louder and then stopped.

"You're getting better," he said.

She opened her eyes and looked up at him. "For some reason it seems easier today," she said.

"Perhaps you needed a few days to settle. We *are* dealing with eighteen years' worth of pent-up magic."

"*We're* dealing with it, huh?" She folded her arms.

"Yes, *we*," he said, nudging her with the side of his leg. "I have to deal with it too."

She wobbled. A little cry escaped her as she righted herself, managing to keep from touching the ground. "Jeez, if I'm so troublesome, I'll let you off the hook and ask Gordan to help me instead."

He turned back to her with an appalled look. "Now hold on."

She leaned back in laughter, tipping her balance past center. With a helpless yelp, she fell back onto the cold, dew-covered clover. Raiden's laugh took the place of hers. Nicole scowled, calling a little magic out of her core. She thought of a simple summoning spell, silently dispersing it across the yard. The creeping magic drew all the tiny beads of dew into her waiting hand, where they formed a wriggling ball of water the size of a softball.

With a devious gleam in her eye, she held up the orb of water, prepared to throw.

He held up his index finger. "No," he said, attempting to sound stern and failing, with a slight smile in the corner of his mouth.

She squinted at him and then sighed. "*Devireo*," she said and the water grew colder, expanding, freezing into a cloudy sphere of ice. Her lips pursed with disappointment. "I thought it would be clearer."

Raiden gave her an impressed nod. "The books seem to have made a significant difference."

"We risked our lives to get those things. Like I'm not going to study every word," she said with a laugh. "They really are helpful. The one that explains how simple spells are more versatile than they seem, now basic spells can be manipulated, like the summoning spell with the dew." She held up her icy orb. "I liked that book."

"That's the most advanced book," he said incredulously.

She shrugged. "It's the most interesting, and I like the author's voice. He's less stuffy and patronizing than the others," Nicole said.

"Well, I'm sorry to say we won't be going back for more books anytime soon."

"Who needs books when you have a seer and a dragon?" The

cold ache in her fingers drew her attention back to the frozen globe in her hand. She passed it to the other hand to give her stiff joints some relief.

She had an idea. "What did you call it the other day? When I turned the wood into a stone."

"Transmutation," he said.

She nodded and looked at her solid ball of ice with an eager gaze. She wanted a glass sphere, clear and perfect, that wouldn't melt. Without fear or hesitation, she let her magic swell. It flooded her, and she guided it to the biting cold object in her hands. The warmth of her power thawed the ache in her fingers, and she resisted the urge to imagine the ice melting from that heat. Instead, she only allowed her mind to picture a perfect crystal ball. Her hands filled with hot magic, and then the orb grew hot, burning hotter until she thought she heard her skin hiss against it.

"Ow!" She dropped it, looking to her fingertips to see if the ridges and valleys of her fingerprints were still there. The ball fell to the ground, hissing on the moist clover. Steam drifted up around a pristinely clear crystal ball.

"Satisfied?" Raiden asked.

She couldn't answer until she placed her hands on the crystal. "Yes." The weight of it felt comfortable as she marveled at it, turning the sphere around. There wasn't a single flaw, and it almost looked like the crystal remained still and her hands moved around it.

Then, suddenly, the ball lurched from her grasp, and it flew, magnetized, into Raiden's waiting hands.

"Hey," she said, frowning.

"Since you've been reading the advanced book," he said, passing the crystal back and forth between his hands, "why don't we try something different today?" The ball halted, caught between his hands. Then he pulled his hands apart, and there were two identical crystals, one sitting in each hand.

She blinked the fascination from her eyes. "What spell was that?"

He lifted them a little higher. "Which one is real?"

She folded her arms. "You're giving me a pop quiz?"

"Yes." He looked her in the eye.

"What do I get if I pass?"

"The satisfaction of being right isn't enough?"

"No. What's the prize?"

He thought for a minute and looked up at the thick gray clouds covering the sky. "If you get it right, then we do whatever you want today, rain or shine."

"Deal." Nicole said with a devilish thought. *I'll make him sit down next to Gordan and watch a movie*, the idea formed laughter in her lungs but she bit her lip, holding it in as she stood up and studied the twin crystals sitting on his open hands. At first glance, there was no difference to behold. Her eyes fell into a motion like a metronome, back and forth, trying to see the slightest incongruence. A tiny drop of cold water hit her cheek, jarring her out of the hypnotic trap before her. She squinted at them, but they still looked the same.

She recalled reading the section on illusions before she went to bed. They were most convincing when looked at directly, even more so when touched. The senses could so easily be fooled. The more scrutiny you gave an illusion, the stronger its deceit proved to be.

She shifted her focus to Raiden, who stood there waiting with an expectant look and a smile in the corner of his mouth. She stepped closer. With a foot of space between them, she anchored her gaze to Raiden's blue-green eyes and took in all she could from the fringes of her vision. In her peripheral vision, she could make out both orbs where Raiden held them up, his elbows locked against his sides to support them.

The persistence of her stare broke his composure. "What?"

She laughed. "Nothing." With her eyes still trained on him, she noticed that the blurry shape of the crystal to her left seemed to waver, and there was a slight glint in the air.

"Do you give up?"

"Just to verify," she said, swinging her arms, "if I get it right, we do whatever I want?"

"That's right."

Several more rain drops struck her on her nose and forehead, on her scalp and her cheeks. Nicole leaned in close, squinting at him. She fought back her triumphant smile until she saw confidence spread across his face. Then she snatched the crystal from his right hand.

He dropped his left hand, and the illusion broke. The imitation crystal dissolved into particles of fading magic.

He sighed in defeat. "All right. You win. What do you want to do?"

Nicole almost told him her idea about Gordan, but standing so close to him, she couldn't help thinking about what happened yesterday. She wanted to taste that again, his lips and the rush of doing something dangerous—because wanting him surely was, maybe more so than her enemies.. Part of her knew that her only hope of keeping her sanity was to allow herself to live a little. She couldn't let her life crumble into a sad state of paranoia, just waiting for Moira to attack or for the Council to find her. There was no way in hell she could live like that, and—if the worst should happen—she sure as hell wasn't going to die without taking the opportunity to feel that rush as many times as she could. An army of golems could come today. Sinnrick could find them tomorrow. She could be standing before the Council next week. *If I die, why not have something good while I can?* He had someone else waiting for him in the future anyway. She didn't have to make any promises.

She let the crystal drop and stepped into Raiden, pulling him down by the nape of his neck. Adrenaline flooded her. Her heart hammered a terrified warning, *don't do this.* With his lips pressed to hers, she felt dizzy with exhilaration. His arms closed her in, locking against her back. A surge of heat and magic rolled through her, and she let it radiate freely, into the earth, into the air.

Across the ground, the folded clover opened, unfurling like the sun had come out. The rosebushes along the wall twisted and grew into huge, tangled masses laden with more blossoms than ever. Not even a low rumble of thunder overhead could shake them apart.

A biting gust picked up. The wind circled them. Another beast-like grumble came from the clouds. At last they broke apart, chests heaving with quickened breath. It was then she finally noticed the rain falling around them. They remained dry in a funnel of magic and wind. The backyard seemed to fade, and she could faintly see the forest of Cantis surrounding them.

The pounding of her heart in her head shook her out of her delirium. She realized her magic was pouring out of her, racing through her veins. The sight of Veil around them grew clearer, as though the barrier between realms no longer existed. The dull, rainy day parted like curtains, revealing the golden sunshine of a clear Cantis morning. The forest was blackened, bare, a field of charred, pointed trunks pointing upward into the sky. For a moment, she was frozen in shock.

In a sudden panic, she caught herself—they shouldn't be seeing Veil. She tensed every muscle in her body, seizing her magic and locking it deep inside her. Cantis vanished from sight, and the yard returned. The torrent of wind sagged to a mere breeze, and the rain came down on them in heavy sheets. The drops collected the magic from the air like tiny sponges, washing it away and delivering it into soggy earth.

Nicole let out a cry, her fear gone in the distraction of the downpour. They were soaked in seconds and Raiden hurried across the patio but she remained in the yard, throwing her head back and spreading her arms wide to welcome the pouring rain against the burning rush still pulsing beneath her skin. Icy droplets pelted her but couldn't wash away her fever. In the back of her mind she thought, *I've finally lost it.* Portals, monsters, dragons, enemies looming on her horizon hadn't tipped her close to the edge of sanity, but the exhilaration of kissing Raiden, feelings something she had been afraid of for so long, that might finally do it. The cold water was soothing against her skin with the conflagration of adrenaline and attraction still burning inside her. Maybe if she stood in the rain long enough, let the cold sink in through her wet clothes, she could smother that desire.

"Nicole," Raiden shouted through the din of the rain.

She opened her eyes and turned to see him, standing on the patio looking at her, waiting for her. She hurried across the patio and they ran for the house. Beneath the shelter of the house just outside the back door, they were safe from the rain and most of the wind. They turned back to look out across the yard. Another cacophony of thunder shook the sky, and they stood amazed at the sight of the dripping, gray world. The slanting rain drummed against the concrete of the patio, hissing in their ears like summer cicadas.

"Wow." The word escaped Nicole's lungs in a whoosh of bewilderment, both from the rain and from the rush of kissing Raiden. She was shocked by the sudden intensity of the rainfall and the fire of that kiss—or had that been her magic? She couldn't be sure what just happened. All she knew was that her head was spinning.

Raiden couldn't take his eyes off Nicole. His heart pounded in his chest, and he still hadn't caught his breath. Then she turned to him. Their eyes met, and they became two magnets, drawn together— her hands to his face, his to her waist. He shuddered with cold, but her warm lips set him ablaze. He felt her shiver and closed his arms around her, turned toward the door with her still caught in his embrace.

Raiden backed her against the glass of the door and fumbled for the knob, never breaking contact with her lips. When the knob turned, the door fell open under their joined weight, and they tumbled inside. They broke into laughter, minds giddy from the mingling of their mouths.

Bandit came bounding into the living room, diving between them and licking whichever face he could until they both rolled away to escape him. Nicole yanked off her wet shoes and tossed them just outside the back door. Raiden followed her example and shut the door. The boisterous rhythm of the rain became faint, echoing his heart through the shelter of the house.

Completely drenched and dripping, they shared an uncertain

glance, her face was flush with embarrassment as she turned toward the stairs. He followed, his skin itching to touch her again, but he supposed they should be more concerned with dry clothes—Nicole wrestled off her soggy sweater, and Raiden shook off his jacket as their feet thumped up the stairs in haste. A shiver rolled through him and he wasn't sure if it was the cold or the memory of feeling her against him.

They reached the top of the stairs, and when they turned toward their respective rooms, they turned right into one another. He felt trapped by her gaze. Her breath and her lips trembled with cold, drawing him back in to press his mouth against hers—*just once more*. He turned her around, his back to his room and her back to hers at the other end of the hall, with every intention of stepping away and letting her do the same. He couldn't seem to do it, though. She pressed herself against him until he backed toward his room, and her steps matched his. Their hands peeled off shirts and dropped them in a damp heap on the floor. He pulled her in, skin against skin. A shiver rolled through her body and then through him. There was a charge of magic in it and his chest was a frenzy of pounding and hunger.

Her hands caught the waistband of his pants. With a quick yank, she pulled his pelvis toward her, and he eagerly took hold of her hips before fhis hands followed the waistband of her jeans to the front.

His fingers pulled at wet denim and plucked the end of her waistband free of the button. She pulled her mouth away for a moment and a smile spread across her face. Stars, he couldn't resist that smile. He leaned back into her lips, pulled her in by the nape of her neck. Then a sickening vertigo struck him as the Sight seized his mind, throwing him into a terrifying and all-too-familiar vision of Nicole. The fluttering in his stomach turned to a dreadful nauseated churning.

He was on his knees before Nicole. A terrible whirlwind shrieked around them, burning his skin. She was oblivious to his presence, her warmth lost behind an eerie glow of magic in her eyes.

Her body arched, her mouth opened in a voiceless scream. He watched in dismay as she fractured, the power inside her rending her skin like paper. He couldn't bear it, he didn't want to see this, this wasn't really happening. *It's not real, she's right here in my arms*—desperately, he searched for reality, for Nicole warm and real against him. His senses strained away from the horrifying vision to the present; he felt Nicole's lips against his, the pressure of their bodies pressed together, cold water dripping from his hair. He pulled away, from Nicole, from the vision, breaking the contact between their lips and taking deep breaths to steady himself.

For the first time he could remember, he had stopped a vision—removed himself from it. For an instant, he was relieved, thinking he'd escaped and all was well again. He wanted nothing more than to chase the haunting chill of that vision away with her warmth, but Nicole looked up at him with no trace of desire in her eyes. Absolute horror had taken hold of her expression as she stepped away from him. Her eyes were dark with fear and her mouth slack with shock. He could see it in her eyes: she had seen the vision—no, she had lived it.

"Nicole." He spoke as if he were trying to sooth a frightened animal, knowing she might bolt at any moment. She was frozen where she stood, but he wasn't sure what he could say to make that nightmare disappear. He realized he knew nothing of the true horror of that vision—she did. How could he possibly protect her from that?

"I was—" Her voice trembled, and she lifted her hands to study them, to reassure herself that she was here again. Her hands shook. She opened her mouth but didn't speak—not that she needed to. He knew all too well what she had seen—what she had lived.

Raiden shook his head and pulled her into his arms. "Visions don't mean anything," he insisted. It was the same mantra he used to ease his own anxiety. It occurred to him then that he was attempting to comfort himself as much as her. "They don't mean anything," he repeated. But his words and his arms could not convince her and she pulled away from him, crossing her arms protectively against her chest. He let her back away from his arms and watched her turn toward her bedroom.

His gaze on her bare back went cold with guilt as he watched her walk down the hall, hugging herself against what she saw. He took a deep breath, pushing his hands back through his wet hair, and held it in his lungs, trying to understand how he could fix this.

Twenty-six

Sinnrick dozed, reclined in a large, plush—albeit dusty and moth-eaten—chair in some abandoned home. He was perfectly content to relax since he couldn't continue his mission until he received word from the Council. Although these dim, empty homes were rather depressing, he felt quite safe inside and comfortable enough to sleep even if there was potentially a lunatic fera out there burning down forests and making men disappear. *Poor Raiden*— Sinnrick wondered what fate the unfortunate man had met at the hands of the fera. Sinnrick certainly wasn't going to end up like Raiden. No way he would die before earning his wings.

The sound of flapping came from the fireplace, and Sinnrick lurched forward out of his cushy chair, unsure whether to expect a bird, or a bat, or a fera to come tumbling down from the flue. A sprinkle of soot dropped down from the chimney, and he fumbled to ready his standard-issue sword. Then out flew an envelope, stained black. It sailed across the room and struck him square in the chest, one of its rigid corners pricking him through his tunic.

"Ah," he hissed, rubbing his chest a moment before plucking the letter from the floor. He was both eager and annoyed as he tore open the Council's reply. His reprieve was over, but at least now he could get back to work, and the sooner he did that, the sooner he would be back in Atrium receiving his wings.

> Sinnrick,
> Our seers have indeed seen Raiden. He is alive. However, their visions of him are unclear. We suspect he is somewhere in the other realm beyond our Sight. The fera is known to be residing in the old world, and it is likely Raiden has followed the fera through the portal. Locate the portal. Find Raiden and the fera. Fortune be with you.
> Official Scribe of the Council
> The Courts of Atrium

Sinnrick groaned. The other realm—they had not prepared him for this. He had searched the entire city and hadn't found any portal. That only left the rest of the bloody island for him to search. With a sigh laden with apprehension, he crushed the message between his hands. As he left the silent house, he tossed the crumpled paper over his shoulder.

❧

Raiden stood heavy with shame in the hall until Nicole closed herself in her room. The sound of the door closing was a strike to his chest and he hated himself, wishing he could comfort her but knowing that the nightmare in her mind had come from his embrace. Raiden snatched up his wet garments and went to his own room. He hurled the clothes into the corner, where they slapped against the wall and slumped down into the hamper. He shoved the door and it closed.

He never knew visions could be shared like that—that a kiss could link someone to the Sight in *his head*. His fingers slid back into his hair and found a firm grip. Now she knew firsthand the dangerous potential inside of her. He could never take that back. His blood was hot. His heart pounded furiously.

After he changed into dry clothes, he stood at the closed door, his forehead resting against it helplessly while he tried to muster up the courage to open it and face Nicole.

At last, he sighed and wrenched the door open. The hall was empty, Nicole's clothes gone—not a trace of their interrupted liaison left behind. He made a point to take confident strides toward the landing, hoping to leave his shame behind him. From the top of the stairs, he saw Nicole sitting on the couch below.

Nicole didn't look up at him, but he was certain she heard his footsteps on the stairs. The house was silent, and it reminded him too much of his days before Nicole. As he came around the couch, he considered asking permission to sit beside her, wondering if she might not want him to. Fearing her answer might be no, he sat down—leaving a distance he hated between them.

Without a word, she scooted closer and leaned into him, resting her cheek against his shoulder and crossing her legs over his. He couldn't help the tiny smile that came to his lips. She chased away his anxiety with that simple gesture. Naturally, his gaze fell to her legs lying across his lap.

His eyes traveled the length of her bare legs from the sheepskin boots on her feet all the way up to the loose boxer shorts revealing the shape of her thighs almost to the hip.

Old scars laced her knees—the dark spot of a skinned knee, the brown line of a deep cut. Hers were the scars of childhood, adolescence, the kind that became fond memories. The scars he bore were ones of violence, fear, and survival—the kind that rend the heart deeper than the skin. He wanted to trace those marks on her legs with his fingertip. She shouldn't have to know scars like his, but he felt sure that was precisely what was coming for her.

Nicole drew in a long breath and let out a tremendous sigh. "I can say my curiosity about the Sight has been more than adequately satisfied."

"I'm sorry," he murmured—sorry that he hadn't known the risk of their intimacy, that he didn't have better control of the Sight, that nothing these past few days had changed the ominous future he kept seeing.

"It's all right. It could be better that I know," she said. "You have to understand what's at risk if you're going into a fight, right?"

"I suppose," he said hopefully.

"How can I avoid it?" Her voice softened with uncertainty.

He didn't want to admit that he didn't know the answer.

"You know," she said, "the day you came through the portal, I knew my life had changed, and I was glad. I never felt like that was my life anyway. It was more like this pattern contrived by parents and educational standards that I had to follow, step by step." She shook her head, and to Raiden's surprise, she laughed. "It's funny, because nothing's really different after all ... There are just different people out there who want to control my life now, and we're just sitting here on the couch like we have all the time in the world."

They were silent a moment.

"I should have left Sunday with Mitch, or yesterday," she said heavily. "I should be driving to Ventura right now."

"In a storm? That still leaves the problem that there's a portal out there now," he reminded her. "Leaving might be the best solution. But even if you do, any amount of time the portal remains open—whether it's an hour or a day once you've distanced yourself—is a window of opportunity for danger to find your family."

Nicole nodded slowly. "Maybe I can convince Dad to go stay with Anthony for a week or so, give the portal time to close and keep him away."

⁌&#x3;

Nicole's dad came home, the rain hissing behind him momentarily as he stepped through the open door. "It's really coming down out there."

Nicole and Raiden went silent as Michael walked into the living room. His shirt was damp, and the bottom of his jeans were dark with water. "I had to tell the crews to go home since we were doing mostly landscaping today," he said.

Nicole craned her neck back to look at him. "Hi, Dad."

"You two got caught in the downpour too, I see," he said, eyeing her wet hair and how close she was sitting to Raiden—she had pulled her legs away from his lap and folded them up against her.

Her cheeks flushed as she noticed her dad scrutinizing their closeness. "Yeah, it's no less than I deserve since it's my fault," Nicole said.

"As long as you aren't conjuring up storms in the house—and I can get back to work tomorrow—you won't hear any complaints from me," her dad answered with a chuckle.

"Isn't it weird?" Nicole said. "With portals and magic and dragons, rain still seems more out of the ordinary in Yuma." She laughed.

"Dragon?" Her dad straightened up.

"Gordan, actually," she said.

"Gordan."

"*Her* dragon," Raiden added with a chuckle.

"I told you about him—remember, Dad?"

"Of course I do. I guess it didn't quite sink in that there's a dragon *here*," He pointed down at the floor for emphasis. "It's not in the house, is it?"

"*He* is outside," Nicole said, suddenly realizing he was out in the rain. "On the roof."

Her dad ceased pinching the bridge of his nose and opened his eyes. His gaze traveled up to the ceiling.

"Dad," she said, getting his attention, "have you seen a dragon on the roof in the past few days?"

"No," he said.

"Then consider him an imaginary friend," she said, lifting her shoulders dismissively.

He laughed. "And here I thought I was starting to get used to this stuff."

"You have nothing to worry about from Gordan, Dad. He's like the ultimate life insurance."

"I'm not sure I even want to know what that means," her dad said.

"You don't," Raiden agreed.

Nicole shook her head, mirroring Raiden's sentiment.

"Well then, it appears we're all housebound for the day." She heard genuine relief in his voice and wondered if he wasn't glad to be home to chaperone. "You think Raiden can handle hot chocolate?" Her dad walked into the kitchen.

Raiden gave her a questioning glance.

She smiled. "Why don't you put on dry clothes first, Dad," she said with a laugh. Then her face fell flat as she thought of Gordan out in the rain again.

To Gordan their conversation was muffled more than usual by the drumming of rain against the roof tiles. He looked out into the distance, the reach of his keen sight impeded by the steady rainfall. The sudden storm finally eased to a moderate shower, the drops of water still plump and heavy.

Below him, the familiar whine of the back door met his ears. Only one pair of feet stepped outside, shuffling softly.

"Gordan?" Nicole called into the rain with reluctance and yet somehow with confidence—perhaps uncertain of her words but sure that he was listening. "My window is open"—she lifted her voice a little to combat the noise of the rain—"if you want to get out of the rain."

He could feel her presence linger, the subtle pulsing of her heartbeat through her brisk, humming aura hanging in the air. If she thought to say more, she changed her mind, and her footsteps shuffled back to the door. It whined open again and then clicked shut.

"My gratitude to you," he said under his breath.

He could hear their voices inside again.

"What were you doing out there?" Her father's words barely made it through the rain.

"Just appreciating the damage I've caused," she answered.

Gordan stood, unfolding himself stiffly. He always felt cramped in this form. How he wished to spread his wings, stretch his neck, move his tail freely again. A weighty sigh came from deep within. His breath was hot, and a tiny flame licked at his lips, lost immediately in the cold, wet air.

Still the rain came down. To think—a drizzle stoked into a storm by a simple kiss. He couldn't be sure when Nicole's magic was more powerful, when her life was in danger or when her heart was full to bursting with something bright. Gordan's footsteps made no sound as he climbed the slant of the roof to its peak and cut across to Nicole's dark window.

§

Nicole was dying to know if Gordan might be taking shelter in her room. She figured he'd rather not have company, and he probably wouldn't stay inside if he heard her coming up the stairs. The day passed, and she couldn't help glancing up the staircase at the landing every fifteen minutes. As difficult as it was, she waited until the rain finally dwindled to the faintest drizzle before she allowed her curiosity to pull her up the stairs and into her room. She didn't want to chase him out into the downpour.

The sight of the open window seized her lungs with joy. The orange and yellow flowered towel she had left was folded by the window; but when she touched it, she was pleased to find it was damp. She had to laugh at the thought of Gordan wrapped in the vibrant beach towel. Then her happiness quickly sank into disappointment. She just wanted to see him again, talk to him. There was no reason he had to be alone constantly, hadn't he had enough of it? She wanted to ask him how long he'd been locked away in that tower, and why he didn't want to get close to anyone. She couldn't help feeling like the moment she released that shackle, he became her responsibility.

Twenty-seven

Raiden was relieved when Nicole stole away upstairs. As the day wore on, he had become more and more anxious to check the portal. With all this magic Nicole constantly radiated, he wondered if the portal would ever close. He felt it would be best if Nicole left and he remained behind to watch the portal until it was finally gone.

With Nicole upstairs, he stepped out the back door. There was still a faint sprinkling of rain, barely more than a mist. His eye was immediately drawn to the gleam of the crystal ball lying in the yard where Nicole had dropped it. He crossed the yard and picked it up without thinking.

Seers used crystals like this, but he didn't know how or what the purpose was when the Sight came to seers without them. As he looked into the twisted shapes inside the crystal, he felt compelled to let in the Sight. He couldn't deny that it was an advantage he and Nicole had on their side. The thought of using the Sight struck a chord of fear in his chest. So far it only promised her demise and his failure and if he kept looking into the future his eyesight would slip away.

Shame flushed his body with an uncomfortable heat. He felt

selfish and cowardly. Now was not the time to worry about losing his eyesight. If he could help Nicole, he had to use anything he had at his disposal, no matter the consequences. He could risk going blind someday if it meant keeping Nicole alive—maybe the Council was why he kept seeing someone else in his future, maybe he could change it.

With a flare of determination, he peered into the crystal and welcomed the Sight. He braced himself for the jarring seizure of the impending vision. He was astonished when it came gently. He slipped into the vision as though he were stepping carefully into a pool, submerging himself in another moment in time. He knew he remained where he stood in the yard, but he perceived only the vision around him. For the first time he could recall, everything in the vision seemed to slow.

Instead of halting flashes and sudden pictures, he stood in a constant uninterrupted scene—only the clarity came and went, his sight blurring and sharpening in a perfectly timed undulation. Never had he experienced a vision so steady. He could discern some great corridor, the ceiling vastly high overhead, and there was a great commotion around him. Indistinct bodies moved around him, clashing violently.

At last he saw two people before him who instantly struck him as familiar; it took him one sluggish second to understand why. He knew them both, these two who came together in an embrace so fraught with fear and joy and overwhelming relief. The one whose face he could not see, her back to him, identity hidden behind a cascade of silvery white hair. The face he *could* see stopped his heart—it was him.

He was looking at himself, not old, not far in the future at all. The face he saw before him was scarcely any different from the face he had seen in the bathroom mirror that very morning. His stunned heart lurched back to life, its rhythm quickening. Before Raiden could escape the vision, he caught a glimpse of her as his not-too-distant-self held her at arm's length and she turned her face toward someone rushing by them. He caught a glimpse of white brows and lashes through her hair but that was it before she turned away again.

Raiden returned to the present, feeling so heavy for a moment that he thought his feet would sink into the wet ground. The crystal in his hands sparked such a surge of frustration that he hurled the ball into the portal. A gentle ripple stirred the air as the orb sailed into Veil.

He stood there seething. His intention had been to see something of Nicole's future, and instead he had received a painfully clear glimpse of his own. What little hope he had held that the woman was Nicole in the distant future was now extinguished. The vision couldn't be more than a year away, his face looked barely changed at all.

"Not all of us attain the futures we seek." Gordan's calm voice startled him. "I know that disappointment well."

Raiden whirled around to see the dragon standing uncomfortably close, an arm's length away. "How long have you been standing there?" Raiden took a step back.

"Long enough to see that vision in the crystal." Gordan nodded toward the portal and the ball that lay somewhere beyond it.

Raiden felt a nervous thud in his chest, as though another witness to the vision somehow solidified its inevitability. A few stray pinpricks of cold moisture fell from the sky, hiting his cheek.

"It seems appropriate to discuss why Nicole is not the one in that vision."

"With you? Why?" Raiden asked with distaste in his words.

"Because I share the same interest in her as you." Gordan did not flinch at the glare Raiden gave him. He clarified, "I am as intent on preserving her life as you are."

The tension in Raiden's shoulders eased only slightly.

"What do you want to know?" Raiden asked guardedly.

"Everything *you* know."

ᙓᖇ

Sinnrick couldn't help but tread carefully through the burned forest, with a kind of subconscious respect for the dead. The forest had been the only life left on the island of Cantis, and now it too was silent and lifeless like the city, like the old castle peering down at him from the mountain.

He sighed, unsure how much more of this place he could stomach. Any place would be better than here. Maybe that was the reason Raiden had disappeared into the other realm. Raiden might not be chasing the fera at all. For all Sinnrick knew, the man wanted out of Cantis—out of Veil entirely. The fera could still be lurking here in Cantis. After all, wasn't an empty place like this the perfect place to hide?

Sinnrick wandered aimlessly into the forest, not sure where he should start looking for a portal. Regrettably, the day they had discussed portals during his basic training courses, he hadn't paid much attention.

As he walked, he couldn't help looking up at the castle through the remains of the burned trees. That dark, looming shape watched him, and he felt he should reciprocate. His suspicious eyes took repeated glances upward as he walked until his toe collided with something hard.

"Ah," he hissed, dropping his gaze to see a crystal ball rolling sadly through the ashes of the cremated forest. He stooped to pick it up, brushing it clean. With a confounded frown, he scanned his surroundings, wondering how this seer's tool could have ended up here. There couldn't be a seer wandering through the forest like he was.

A hopeful idea struck him so suddenly that his heart reeled with adrenaline. This could only have come from a portal. His excitement instantly deflated with the realization that he still had one significant problem: there was every possible direction to choose from and no way of knowing which direction the portal could be.

He hung his head with a sigh and noticed that at his feet there was a trail through the ashy ground back to the place where he originally had kicked the crystal ball. He traced that path and placed the crystal down where it had lain before he disturbed it. He straightened up with pride as he looked down at his anchor point.

Then he saw it—a second track through the ashy dirt. He realized that if this thing had come through the portal, then that track would lead him right to it.

☙

Raiden fidgeted with discomfort as he confessed what he knew to Gordan.

"I received a letter from Atrium the day I met Nicole. They knew a portal would open and they wanted me to find the cause, the fera. They insist she'll compromise the barrier and they seem to think I'll jump at their word and bring her to them." Renewed irritation crawled up the back of Raiden's throat.

"I see," Gordan said with a nod. "It seems our understandings of the fera are quite different."

"You've heard of the fera?" Raiden couldn't mask his surprise.

"I've not heard any accounts of their nature, but I have heard the name mentioned many times, only I did not associate it with Nicole until now. I regret to say I know all too well that the Council is seeking the fera and that they have done so for some time."

A frown came quickly across Raiden's face. "How could you possibly know that?" He hadn't even told Gordan what the letter said.

"Because they are not the only ones who seek her."

Raiden had thought that nothing could strike his heart with greater pain than that glimpse of the silver-haired woman. Hearing that someone else out there besides the Council was after Nicole left him breathless.

"Who?" It was all he could utter.

"A man by the name of Venarius, the leader of a group that calls themselves Dawn." Gordan's voice lowered almost to a growl. "I have had the great displeasure of being his *guest* for the past decade. Most of that time I spent in the tower, but for a short time I was held on the mainland. While I was there, I overheard many things."

Nausea churned Raiden's stomach. He didn't want to hear any more, but he needed to know about this other threat. The dreary day around them seemed suddenly much darker.

"Do they know about Nicole? Do they know where she is?"

"While I was in his company, no one knew anything about this fera, who it was, or where it might be. But that was a decade ago. I can tell you this: whatever the Council knows, Venarius knows." Gordan's voice was solemn.

"But why?" Raiden shook his head, confused. "What does he want with her?" Impatience infected his words.

"Venarius spoke of protecting the fera from the Council, but what he intends to do with Nicole, regrettably, I cannot tell you. They prepared a secure location for me and moved me away from Venarius. I remained there until the day Nicole released me."

Raiden had thought his heart couldn't sink any lower, but it descended deeper still. A decade—Gordan had said he was a prisoner for a decade. "You said you've been in Cantis for ten years?" His voice shook softly.

"Give or take a year, I suppose. Counting the days that passed was all I had besides those cursed chains and stone walls." Gordan's words were bitter.

Raiden knew air was moving in and out of his lungs, yet he felt like he was drowning. The dragon had been brought to Cantis nine years ago—nine years ago, Cantis had fallen silent. *They prepared a secure location*—here standing beside Raiden was the very reason everyone he knew was gone, the reason his mother was dead? The idea that they killed everyone in Cantis to hide a dragon made his lungs shudder. A black haze closed in around Raiden's vision. His body flushed with heat, but his skin chilled with sweat.

As much as he wanted to hate Gordan, blame him, hit him as hard as his bones could withstand, Raiden had to swallow the lump of disdain and horror in his throat. If this Venarius person could kill an entire city of people just for the sake of keeping a dragon safely hidden, then Raiden could be sure he would go to any length to get Nicole.

"What kind of resources does this Venarius have?" Raiden hardly recognized his own voice, heavy with distress.

"That I do not know for certain. I can tell you he has eyes and ears in the courts of Atrium and a terrible hunger to succeed. From what I heard in that place, Venarius is nothing if not a man who gets what he wants."

Through the back-door's window, Nicole spotted Raiden and Gordan standing in the yard. Her excitement—and jealousy—at seeing Raiden and Gordan in conversation welled up in her with a great swell of buzzing heat. As she took one step toward the door, the power building in her broke free. It enveloped her, swept her up in a current of magic that whisked her through the door and across the yard. When she put her foot down, she was standing between them, bewilderment wide in her eyes.

"Whoa—hi," she said, astonished. It was the only thing she could say as she looked into the startled faces of Raiden and Gordan.

"Hi," they said.

She couldn't help but smile at their voices in unison.

"What's going on? Did I catch you talking about me?" she asked, her jovial tone fading as she sensed the tension between them. She was standing right in the middle of it.

Raiden hesitated.

"You did," Gordan answered readily.

She felt her joy wither, and a cold anxiety sprouted in its place. "Oh."

"It turns out Gordan knew something we didn't," Raiden said. "Someone else in Veil is searching for you."

"Venarius." Gordan spoke the name with ease and venom. "The same man who kept me in chains for a decade."

Nicole jerked her gaze to Raiden as her mind flooded with too many thoughts and questions to tease apart. She turned her eyes back to Gordan. "What does he want?"

Raiden's frustration was apparent. "We don't know."

"Well," she said, squirming a little where she stood, at a complete loss for how to react, unsure if she was even surprised by hearing this anymore. "Shit."

Nicole sighed and Gordan could feel her frustration balancing on a wobbly tightrope of fear in her heart. "I think it's time for a game plan. What the hell do we do?"

Her question hung in the air. The silence was oppressive and the space between them filled with tension. This dilemma was a tether linking the three of them together, and now they were all undeniably aware of it. Gordan could have sworn their hearts thundered in unison for a moment in that silence.

"Whatever we can do," he said with solemn acceptance, and he dared to look Nicole directly in the eye. "I am bound to you. Standing beside you is all I have to offer."

Gordan's sharp ear heard Raiden inhale deeply, and a surge of jealousy rolled through the air. Gordan looked to him but could not divine the thoughts that troubled Raiden—only his sudden dread was apparent. Yet strangely enough, Gordan sensed a spark of hope through the gloom coming from Raiden.

Raiden glared back at him. For a moment, they shared a look that escaped Nicole's notice. Gordan could understand Raiden's attachment. After all, Raiden had known her only a day longer than Gordan. He knew how quickly connections could take hold between two people.

Gordan watched an endearing rush of blood warm Nicole's cheeks. This girl had freed him without hesitation and had given him her loyalty without question. He had seen her obliterate a kelpie with her desire to live and conjure up a storm out of pure exhilaration. In only four days, he had come to know her in a way he had known only one other soul.

"Thank you, Gordan," Nicole said, "even if you don't have a choice in the matter."

She laughed, and the sound met his ears like soft music. Yes, there was something in her Gordan knew well, the predator turned prey, strong yet powerless. He wanted to shield her from that struggle. Now he knew why he felt so attached to her. They were kin.

Gordan knew that the day his debt was paid, the loss of that connection would wound him. The air became thicker with an expanding cloud of anguish, and his gaze returned to Raiden, whose face carefully masked what Gordan sensed. What troubled Raiden's heart so deeply Gordan could only guess. They both knew it was only a matter of time before either the Council or Venarius located the portal, and perhaps Raiden knew how that day would end.

❧

Sinnrick left the crystal where he had found it and made its original path through the dirt his own. He marched dutifully, expecting to step through the portal at any moment. As he walked, he glanced up again and realized he was heading directly for the castle. He was beginning to doubt whether that crystal really had come from the portal. Had someone up there thrown it?

He inspected the windows of the castle above, wondering if the crystal could have fallen so far without breaking. At last he came to the edge of the forest and onto the dirt track that led up to the castle above on the cliffs. He groaned. No portal, just a wall of rock.

In a moment of frustration, he kicked at the ground, stirring up a cloud of fine dirt into the air. He sighed with a hoarse grumble in his throat. Then something odd caught his eye. The settling dust swirled, churning in the still crisp air. He took a step closer to the cliff wall and felt the slightest breeze. His nose caught the scent of rain—a smell that couldn't have originated there in the burnt forest. Studying the cliff face, he noted the unnatural smoothness unlike the rest of the rough stone.

When he leaned in closer, a cool breath of foreign air rustled his disheveled brown hair. The portal seemed to sigh at him, and he grinned with triumph as he straightened up and reached out to touch it. His fingertips grazed the portal, igniting a startling charge that prickled his skin. He pulled his hand back, and the air rippled before his eyes.

"At last we meet," a feminine voice said behind Sinnrick.

He whirled around, his heart lurching into a frantic rhythm.

When he laid eyes on the woman, his immediate reaction was amused relief. She was slight. Her petite frame appeared almost burdened by the dark robes she wore.

He noticed her crazed stare. Before his puzzled mind could produce a question, she raised her hand and turned it with a sharp flick of the wrist. A sudden flash of red dazzled his eyes, and he was struck by an acrid spell. His muscles seized in pain, and a piercing ringing drowned out his thoughts as his body crumpled in agony.

☙

Moira paced her chamber. Her first inclination was to be rid of the Council's man and ensure he could not interfere with her plans. However, he could prove to be a valuable asset. She had the opportunity to provide her master with not only the fera but also a prisoner with knowledge of the courts—perhaps a bargaining chip if the Council cared at all about their men.

She paused at the window to look out over the burnt forest, the sun setting, sending long dark shadows across the forest floor. Below the portal waited. No doubt it was closing slowly, as all portals inevitably did because the two realms were constantly shifting around each other, perhaps still trying to separate completely. Everything that mattered lay beyond that portal—the fera, the dragon, and her stolen heart.

While the golem had allowed her to gather some valuable information, it now seemed to have been a mistake. They knew she was here, knew she sought them out. Perhaps she had ruined her chances—sealed her own fate when she sent that golem.

She could wait and hope the fera would appear as it had once before, bringing the dragon with her—but they might never come—or she could take matters into her own hands and go after the fera and the dragon. It would be a risk. Although Moira had witnessed the fera use its power through the eyes of her golem, there was no way to know how reliable her own magic would be to her in the other realm. Then there was the stone. She could not fathom how to go about finding it and capturing the fera at the same time.

There were too many factors to consider. Both the dragon and the Council's defector would try to protect the fera. If Moira was forced to kill the defector in the process, so be it, but that could prevent her from ever finding the stone he had taken. If the dragon stood in the way of obtaining the fera, Moira might have to be rid of it and hope her master wouldn't begrudge her the sacrifice. A pang of dread struck her. The Council's traitor surely had some inkling of the stone's value to Moira, he had taken it after all and he could use it against her again.

With a tremendous sigh that turned into a groan of dismay, she turned from the window and resumed her pacing.

Twenty-eight

Nicole woke up the next morning, her body humming, filled with warm magic. She wrestled herself free of her blanket to escape the building heat, sweat clinging to the small of her back. She rolled to the edge of her bed and eyed the window, which was open only a few inches. Relieving her body of a little magic and heat, she squinted at the window, and it slid open entirely. An eager breeze chilled the room, and she welcomed it against her charged skin.

For a moment, she sprawled herself out in her boxers and sports bra, letting the cold morning air cool her. She sighed, imploring the buzzing energy beneath her skin to calm, but she knew the only way to get relief was to release it. With a sigh, she turned onto her belly and slid off her bed.

Her room was dim, but she navigated every step from muscle memory. To her surprise, her foot brushed against a warm, furry body, and when she looked down, the black shape of her dog lay curled up in the middle of her bedroom floor.

"Bandit," she cooed with surprise. He usually slept beside her dad. In fact, Bandit had seemed far more attached to her than usual these past several days, which both pleased and baffled her.

The dog lifted his head at the sound of her voice and rolled onto his back, tail wagging. She scrubbed his belly a few times before resuming her task of dressing. With a chuckle, she tossed her sleep clothes onto the dog, and he simply lay there beneath the garments. She stepped into a red thong and then into a pair of athletic leggings. After she pulled on a fresh bra and a shirt, she gathered her clothes off Bandit and tossed them into her hamper.

A steady breeze flowed in through her window, carrying with it the scent of a wet world after the rain. She leaned out the window and looked up. The sky was clear, not a single streak of cloud to be seen across the deep blue of predawn. Stars were shining their last faint light before the approaching sun could chase them away.

"Good morning," a polite greeting came from beside her.

Startled, she lost her grip on the window frame. She nearly pitched forward out of her room and onto the roof. Then she spotted Gordan sitting on the slope of the roof beside her window.

"Gordan," she said on a breath of relief.

"My apologies." He stood and approached the window.

Alerted by Gordan's voice, Bandit flopped on the floor, clamoring to get up and over to the window. The dog came to her side with a curious nose raised to sniff the air.

"You have many protectors." Gordan nodded toward Bandit.

Nicole looked down at her dog affectionately. When she looked up at Gordan, she caught his gaze for just a moment. He looked away.

"You should not invest so much fondness in me, Nicole." His voice was distant.

"I think I have bigger problems now than getting attached to people I can't keep." Her words came with unexpected confidence. Her heart rate accelerated, and the air filled with an electric charge. The wild curls around her shoulders and the sleek black sheets of Gordan's hair floated in a brief absence of gravity.

Gordan revealed the slightest smile. "I hope I'm there the day you realize your enemies have far more to fear than you do."

"So this is where you spend every day—just lurking on the

roof?" she asked, climbing out the window to join him.

"I do not lurk," he said indignantly.

Nicole trod cautiously, placing her feet on the red tiles tentatively. "It's a decent view at least," she added, looking around with a nod.

"It's certainly better than the tower," he agreed.

"Is it really?" she couldn't help asking. "Aren't you just as much a prisoner here? You're stuck in another realm attached to someone who's just going to drag you into deeper shit than you were already in." She looked at him with guilt pinching her face.

"There are many ways to be a prisoner," he said. "I do not see repaying someone for their compassion as any kind of prison." He spoke with a cool tone as he cast his gaze skyward.

Nicole felt her face flush with heat. Her heart sped with relief and tentative joy now that he was finally letting her get closer to him.

"You wouldn't rather be free to go wherever you want—to fly again?" She raised her hand toward the faint stars.

"To be free," he said with a sadly ironic tone, "dragons have nowhere to go but the Wastelands. Freedom for me means I am welcome nowhere. Without my debt to you, I have but one place to go: among my own kind. Now that is a prison."

She smiled. "Maybe you can't go anywhere you want in Veil, but how would you like to travel around *this* realm and see new places?"

"You're inviting me," he said with a snort of amusement, "when I am compelled by my debt to follow."

"Why shouldn't you have a say in the matter? We're in this—whatever it is—together, aren't we?"

"I would be lying if I said I wasn't curious about how this realm has changed since the divide," he said.

"I'll take that as a yes then," she said cheerfully.

"Won't Raiden be thrilled," Gordan said with a devious smile.

Nicole laughed. "I can't wait to tell him. I guess I'll have to wait until he wakes up," she said with mock disappointment.

"He is awake—he has been most of the night." Gordan spoke matter-of-factly as he turned back toward Nicole's bedroom.

"How do you know that?" She turned around awkwardly and followed him with painfully slow steps, trying not to look down past the edge of the roof as she watched the careful placement of her feet.

"That man's restlessness permeates walls. Not to mention that I could hear his footsteps pacing his room incessantly."

Nicole was stunned to hear Gordan sound flustered, his cool composure broken. His outright annoyance almost made her laugh.

"Careful, Gordan," she said, swinging one leg into her room, "you sound like you're investing a lot of emotion into this situation."

Gordan gave her a sharp look but immediately wrenched his eyes away with a huff.

She chuckled, climbing into her room, where Bandit waited, tail still wagging. She left her room on light, eager steps and strode down the hall. Since Raiden's door was closed, she knocked, expecting him to answer swiftly. When there came no answer after a minute, she almost laughed.

"Raiden? Gordan said you're awake," she said.

She heard a sigh through the door and, finally, it opened. Her smile immediately went slack when she saw him. His brow was crumpled, his mouth stern, and his eyes were dark with some troubling thought.

"What's wrong?" she asked.

He softened his expression so fast that she thought she had imagined the gloom there a moment ago.

"I suppose I've just been letting myself worry after what Gordan had to say yesterday," he said lightly.

Nicole remained suspicious. She noticed he was dressed and wondered if he had even tried to sleep last night. Had his fear of visions kept him up, or something else? She kept her curiosity to herself, suspecting he wouldn't be honest anyway.

"You don't have to worry about Gordan. He said he can't wait to go on an extended field trip with us," her attempt at a joke fell flat.

His posture and voice were stiff. "That's great," he said, bobbing his head.

Nicole had to push past her confusion. Who was this Raiden, and where was the one she had yesterday? "Okay," she said, "what's going on?"

Raiden pressed his lips together for a moment. Then he smiled—it was small, but it looked genuine to Nicole.

"I've just been analyzing our options. I'm sorry to be so ... solemn."

"Trust me, I *get* feeling solemn right now, but I need a break from it and, I think, so do you," she said with an anxious laugh. "You're driving Gordan nuts." She leaned into his room to grab his hand. "Plus I miss your smile," she muttered quietly, dragging him through the doorway and down the hall.

"Where are we going?" he asked.

"To the roof," she answered.

"Why?"

"To watch a goddamn sunrise in case I die today," she said with a cynical laugh. She didn't release his hand as she pulled him into her room.

"How can you even joke about that?"

"Because," she huffed as she yanked her blanket down from her bed, "it would drag me down otherwise." She wadded the blanket up and heaved it to the window. "Come on."

She climbed out the window and added, "You too, Gordan. No hiding."

Raiden climbed out the window behind her. Carefully, she led the way from the west side of the house and up to the roof's peak to the other side where the eastern sky was already blushing with the approach of dawn.

As she unfurled the blanket, she wobbled, and Raiden caught her elbow. They shivered in the predawn glow, situating themselves close together and wrapping the blanket around their shoulders.

"Gordan," Nicole called with a soft but stern voice.

"I'm right here," he said, his voice coming from behind them.

Raiden fidgeted beside her. She found his hand inside their co-coon and laced her fingers with his. "I'm gonna need you both." She couldn't lift her voice above a murmur, because the truth of her confession scared her. "For the sake of my sanity, I need to have good things to hold onto—I can't let this crush me before the fight's really started—but I'm gonna need help remembering that sooner or later." Her through tightened; she was on the verge of tears. She couldn't let unseen threats turn her into a weak, frightened little girl. She would let them motivate her to prepare for a fight and enjoy whatever good things she could, but she would not let fear win out.

"I think I can do that," Raiden promised softly.

The cold seeped into their shelter through the blanket from the roof tiles beneath them, forcing them as close as two bodies side by side could be. Overhead the stars sank into the blush of dawn, and the three of them slipped into silence as they waited for the sunrise.

୧୬

Raiden trailed behind Nicole as they descended the stairs.

"I'll get coffee started," Nicole said.

"I think I'll go check on the portal," Raiden said, veering his strides toward the back door as they reached the bottom of the stairs.

He stepped out into the brisk golden morning and crossed the yard with a purpose. A ring of toadstools had sprouted in the clover around the portal, revealing its presence. Raiden reached out, his fingertips meeting a gentle resistance as though he were pressing them against a sheet hanging from a clothesline. The portal would not yield, and Raiden's hand persisted, advancing several inches before he finally broke through. Half his fingers disappeared from sight. With a pang of unease, he removed his hand from the portal.

The signs that it was finally closing brought no relief. Since his conversation with Gordan yesterday, a terrible realization had been festering in Raiden's thoughts. He had to do what he could to help

Nicole the most. Of the three of them, he was the only one with access to the Council. If he waited too long to return, they may not trust him, he might lose that advantage.

For now they thought he was one of their own. He could lead Sinnrick away from the portal. He could walk right into the courts of Atrium and learn what the Council knew, all they were planning. But that meant leaving Nicole. She already understood that she couldn't stay here, hiding in her own backyard. While she left home behind, he would hopefully lead her enemies away from her trail. Gordan insisted that whatever the Council knew Venarius would know as well. If that was true, misleading the Council would prove doubly valuable. He would just have to convince Nicole to proceed with the plan without him. At least she wouldn't be alone; she had Gordan.

He wanted terribly for there to be a better plan, one that would allow him to stay, something that could benefit her more than a set of eyes and ears among the enemy. But unless Nicole wanted to spend the rest of her life running, they had to have a plan that would eventually bring down the Council and Venarius as well. They were dealing with enemies with more resources than they could even imagine. Bringing down enemies that big was more likely from the inside than fighting head-on.

He inhaled deeply, pushing his fingers back through his hair. It felt like he was being torn in two—he wanted to be with her, but he wanted to protect her. His best chance to do that was to go. The sound of the back door opening and closing drew his attention away from the portal.

Nicole crossed the patio and the stretch of green ground that lay between them. He goaded himself—if he were strong enough, he would tell her here and now what he had to do. He would say his good-bye, perhaps with a kiss, and leave. The portal was closing, after all, and that meant it was time for Nicole to distance herself from it.

"Everything all right?" she asked.

He closed his eyes, breaking away from her questioning gaze for a moment, long enough to steal himself for what he was about to do. When he opened his mouth, he lost the words and huffed, taking a step closer. He caught her neck in his hands, guiding her lips to his. Like before, their contact was electric. A surge of her magic rolled into him through their joined lips. It was a rush of exhilaration, of utter delight and giddy surprise.

☙

The pulse of Nicole's magic moved through the portal and into Veil, washing over the remains of the Cantis forest. It spread like a healing balm in the soft light of a hazy morning, moving through the blackened trees. The winter air grew charged and warm as a spring day. New growth sprang up from the soot-coated earth, tiny green sprouts rising through the ashes. The bare ravaged trunks of the trees trembled with life, regenerating their branches.

Up on the mountain, that same warm magic wafted into Moira's chamber like a contented sigh. She rushed to the window, folding herself over the sill in her haste. Below, like an emerald wave rolling over a black beach, the forest was revived.

Moira marveled at the spectacular display flowing from the portal directly below her—*the fera*. The magic in the air was raw, unrefined. Every charm and trinket in her chamber buzzed with strength. The cabinet rattled with its overcharged contents. Her bookcase shook with the restlessness of the long-unread tomes on its shelves. Then a low, metallic moan hummed in her ear, and she turned to her worktable behind her. There lay the massive shackle once worn by the dragon. It was useless to her, its curse broken, no more than a hunk of rusted metal. Again it shuddered, emitting a low resonant tone. The remnants of the broken curse were resurrected, mended by the fera's magic in the air.

When she reached for it, the charge of the curse and her own magic ignited a spark of black light. She yanked her hand back and grinned with terrible glee. If she hoped to catch and detain a powerful prey like the fera, Moira would have to use the fera's own power against her. The wasting curse fed on the physical energy of its victim. It had left the dragon devoid of any strength. All the fera would have to do was touch the cursed metal to feel its effects.

Moira's only problem was that this shackle was far too big. While contact alone would make removal near impossible, Moira couldn't risk the possibility that it could be lifted off. Before she could use it against the fera, she had to carefully reduce its size. It was a simple spell for anyone when cast on any old object. However, on an object bearing a powerful curse, the task became far more tedious. Shrinking the shackle without affecting the curse would take some time, but certainly no more than a day. She set herself to work eagerly.

ᑯᓄ

Raiden's heart raced. His body burned. This was what he needed: his lips against hers, her touch, her warmth, her peculiar kind of cynical joy. If he left, he feared he might lose himself to that old numbness. Could Nicole revive him again if he sank back into that place?

He broke their warm connection. Looking into her rich, amber eyes, he realized it didn't matter. He'd give up those feelings to keep her alive.

"Wow," she said with a dazzled smile and a laugh. "Okay, then."

The bewilderment in her voice and blinking gaze struck him with affection. He laughed quietly. He wanted more time with her, to memorize her, her face, her voice, her lips. He wanted the comfort of her company a little while longer—one last stint of peace, and dare he say happiness, before he walked away from her. He shuddered at the thought of willingly going back into that state in which he had spent so many years, of reporting to the Council as his father had done.

"Forgive me," he said, his selfishness betraying him. He knew time was slipping away. Every hour he remained with her could be the difference between maintaining the Council's trust or earning their suspicion; but he needed just a little more time with her—half a day, one last night. How much could a few extra hours possibly matter? He could leave the next morning—first thing, he assured himself. "I've been worrying too much," he said, concealing the truth with the truth.

She sighed, and he watched her whole body relax. "Well, stop," she said. "Do you see any golems? Moira? Sinnrick?"

"No," he answered with a reluctant grin.

"Is fire raining from the sky?" She put her fists on her hips.

"No," he said through a laugh.

"Then calm down. We've got packing to do—pretend we're going on a vacation. We can go over some defensive spells and maybe have fun in the process—got it?" She grabbed his shoulders and gave him a playful shake.

"Okay, okay," he said. "You're right."

"Thank you," she said, beaming. "Let's go look through the books. Maybe there's a spell to help you relax," she teased, turning back to the house.

He shook his head, unable to resist the smile she so often brought to his face. He would try to do as she said: enjoy today and not think about tomorrow.

Twenty-nine

Gordan exhaled in exasperation. Even on the rooftop of the small building behind Nicole's house, he could still sense them with exasperating clarity. Every day he spent in this realm, he became more attuned to Nicole and Raiden, more sensitive to the deepest facets of them.

Yesterday this had been purely intriguing. Today, however, Gordan would have preferred the dank isolation of the tower to Raiden's incessant turmoil. Gordan's sense was keen enough to ensure he experienced every moment of contentment and each dreadful return of Raiden's shame, fear, doubt, and anger—but the limitation of his sense denied him any real understanding. He was dragged through the agonizingly circular state of Raiden's emotions without the clarity of knowing the tormenting thoughts that caused it all.

All bloody day this continued. All day Raiden seemed to be at war between misery and happiness in Nicole's presence, battling some haunting thought. Gordan was so aggravated by Raiden's inescapable duress that he nearly caved under the need to know the source. He had been especially tempted when Raiden was torturing himself, pacing alone in the yard.

There had been some relief after Nicole spoke to Raiden, and

265

for most of the day he seemed calmed, almost happy. But as the sun sank in the sky, that cancerous agony in Raiden's chest returned. As infuriating as Gordan's unwilling empathy was, he couldn't deny that it was still far more pleasant than the exile he had known back home in the Wastelands. Even his decade of dark imprisonment had seemed but a few months in relation to life in the Wastelands. Perhaps it was the influence of Raiden's emotions pervading the air, but Gordan felt himself worrying. He liked it here. He enjoyed being around Nicole and even Raiden. In fact he could happily bear his debt forever, but he knew painfully well that the day would come when his debt would have to be paid.

He sighed. He was most definitely turning into Raiden. All Gordan could do was take each day as it came and hope that today Nicole would relieve Raiden of his distress—and save Gordan from the burden. It didn't take an empath to see that those two had an odd way of balancing each other—and even a complete idiot could see the physical attraction. He was just glad his ability didn't make him susceptible to their more physical urges, or he would truly have gone mad by now. The weight of their past lives and the trials of this one were enough for him.

The rich colors of sunset traveled across the sky like spilled blood, staining the few streaks of clouds overhead with robust pinks and reds. From outside he could hear the sounds of dinner, voices mingling together, dishes tapping and clanking. There was quiet contentment in the house again, and Gordan could finally relax, hoping against all odds that Raiden would actually sleep tonight and allow him to do the same.

Gordan stood up, eager to relocate to his usual spot and settle in for the night. With a few strides and a jump, he sailed across the space between the workshop and the house. He slept beneath Nicole's window, where he could intercept any intruder attempting to slip inside and hear any threat that might enter her room from within the house. Before he knew it, his body grew heavy with exhaustion. He didn't suppose it was from the last twenty-four sleepless hours, he could go quite a long time without sleep. But Raiden's emotional state during that time had drained him immensely, surely Raiden too was tired enough to sleep.

Sometime while he dozed, Gordan felt Nicole enter her room. He could feel the darkness of night around him without opening his eyes and hear Nicole's heartbeat from his place outside her window. He listened to that rhythm as it quickened ever so slightly with her climb onto her bed and as it slowed with impending slumber, lulling him into the depths of sleep as well.

❧

The creak of the bedroom door opening made Raiden's heart lurch forward, throwing him upright. But he knew that form even in the dark. Her long curls seemed wilder than usual as she crossed the room and crawled onto the bed. Without even a whisper she buried her face in his chest. His heart pounded anxiously as she settled down with sleep-heavy movements.

There was a charge of magic in the air carrying dread, slithering into him and down his spine. He could only suppose some nightmare had disturbed her slumber and lingered in her heart. Who haunted her dreams? The Council? Venarius? Enemies whose faces she didn't even know. He felt the tiniest shake of her head against him—as terrible as it felt to know nightmares plagued her sleep, he was glad this time he had not been the catalyst of these troubled thoughts in her mind. Instinct moved his arms around her. Was he a horrible person for feeling a little grateful for that bad dream, for the chance to be her safe haven? Comforting her comforted him.

This was the first time he had held her sleeping in his arms, the first time their slow breathing mingled in the same bed. Getting to know this small bliss was bittersweet, he would want it again, but he had made his decision. He would hold her while he could and leave when the sun came up.

Raiden's arms tightened around her. Her breathing slowed, and her heartbeat settled into a peaceful rhythm and his own fell into sync. Each time he felt his arms slacken, he forced his eyes back open—treading the dark sea of unconsciousness, trying to keep his head above those waters. He could sense the Sight in the depths of the darkness, waiting for him to sink below the surface. He wanted to know what lay ahead for them and he didn't. He wanted to close his eyes, but he wanted to be conscious of this as long as he could.

A deep sigh interrupted the shallow cadence of her breathing. His own breath turned to a stone in his throat. Not much more than a week ago, his life had revolved around retribution—justice— half a life's pursuit and planning only to botch his ambush and ob- tain a stupid stone. Stealing it had made him feel powerful for a moment; he had been capable of taking something she treasured in return for her taking all that he loved. How quickly that stone had become meaningless—revenge turned bitter—now that he had Nic- ole and couldn't keep her.

For ten years, he had wanted to feel something—anything— and revenge had seemed like the only way to regain the freedom to live and feel. How could he, when that chance had been taken from his mother and everyone else in Cantis? If he got justice for them then he could live without guilt, at least that's what he thought then. He hadn't needed the permission of ghosts to live, he needed his own.

At last he had what he really needed, and now he had to let it go. He would have to walk away from what he loved. His heart seized at the thought. It was a dreadful realization to have, to let that word ring in his head. *Stars*, he tightened his arms around her, *I love her.* It would be more difficult than having her taken away from him, because it required his own action, his own strength, to put that distance between them.

The faint glow of dawn proved what he feared: the night would not go on forever for his sake. The sun had heard his silent promise and rose now to hold him to it. Leaving Nicole to her peaceful sleep, he eased off the bed. He reached for his sword and the clothes he had worn the day he came from Veil—his father's clothes—from under the bed.

Removing the shirt he wore felt like shedding part of himself. He felt exposed and raw. He did not want to don his father's clothes again, not the day he had to leave Nicole. No, he refused. He was not that man, would not be that man. He could not let that man live through him in any way. He kicked his father's clothing back under the bed and dressed in his own.

The fastest he could bring himself to move was no faster than a crawl. He wanted every last moment he could steal with Nicole, even just glancing at her while she slept. Then a wave of cowardice washed over him, and he considered leaving without waking her. He didn't feel strong enough to look into her eyes and say good-bye. Only the thought of being like his father kept him from sneaking away.

There was one last thing before he could slip out of the dim room. He opened the top drawer of the bedside table and plucked the stone from its hiding place. If he was going to leave, perhaps he could lure Moira away from Cantis and let the empty city rest in peace at last. If he could trust the books on portals, without Nicole's magic in this realm, opening a portal would be all but impossible. So no matter who came to Cantis with plans to open a portal, they would find themselves at a dead end. Nicole's family would be safe, and she would be somewhere her enemies wouldn't be able to find her.

Pushing the stone into his pocket, he went downstairs to wait for her to wake up, hoping that time away from the sound of her breathing would be enough for him to figure out what to say and how to steel himself to do what he had to even if she begged with her honey eyes.

Raiden felt welcomed downstairs by the scent of coffee beckoning him into the kitchen. As he descended, he inhaled deeply. Although he hadn't yet come to appreciate the drink like Nicole and her father, Raiden had grown to love the smell. He would miss it. He would miss everything about this home.

Michael stood in the kitchen holding his mug of coffee and reading the newspaper spread out on the counter before him.

Michael looked up from the columns of text. "Good morning, Raiden."

"Good morning," he replied, lifting his voice over his self-loathing.

Michael spotted the sword on his back. "Expecting trouble?"

"No," Raiden said with grave sincerity. "No, I just need to return to Veil. I have some business to take care of there." He leaned the sword against the wall beside the back door.

"Oh." Michael nodded without further question, either because he felt it was no business of his or because a part of him knew he wouldn't want to know. "Well, I'm sorry to see you go."

Raiden smiled through a painful twinge of disappointment in his chest.

"Does Nicole know?" Michael asked with a protective edge to his words as he glanced up at the landing.

"No. I still have to tell her."

Michael sighed and put his coffee down. "I like you, Raiden. I was scared I might be making a mistake when I invited you to stay, but you proved me wrong. I appreciate all the help you've been to Nicole, but my daughter deserves far more than someone who will leave when she needs them."

"I—" Raiden tried to respond but had no words ready. Michael's gentle tone hit him hard. He wanted to explain—why it was better that he leave for her sake, that he understood all too well that she had already felt the pain of being left once, that he knew that pain too and it made this decision unbearable, but how else could her enemies be stopped from coming after her?

"Listen. I like to think I know Nicole pretty well, better than most people. It's not hard to see the way she looks at you, and to be honest, that's been the strangest part of all this—stranger than the portals and dragons and magic." He smiled to himself. "She's never been boy crazy, so I dare say this is genuine. I want to see her happy, whatever that entails. You're welcome in this house, in this family, Raiden—but you are not welcome to break her heart."

"I wouldn't dream of it. I have every intention of coming back—if you permit me." Raiden felt his heart pounding in his ears.

"That's up to Nicole," Michael said, picking up his coffee before taking a sip and dropping his eyes back to the newspaper.

A pang of anxiety rang out in Raiden's chest. If he walked away now would she allow him to come back?

Nicole started upright—the hair on the back of her neck standing alert—expecting to find herself in the presence of some enemy, surrounded by faces she didn't recognize. She was in Raiden's room—alone. *Oh no, did I really?* She thought that had all been a part of her dream—her enemies had been bringing her house down around her and she couldn't find anyone, not her dad or her brother, or Raiden while it all fell apart. She remembered climbing out of bed to make sure he was still there. Her eyes swept the room, every corner. No Raiden. For a dreadful moment she thought this was it, she was finally waking up to find it was all a dream. Her eyes fell on the open drawer, the only thing out of place. Slipping halfway off the bed in the process, she dove for the drawer, pulling herself up and the drawer farther open at the same time. It was empty. She considered returning to her room to see if Gordan was outside her window.

In the hall, she peered through the open door of her room at the other end of the hallway, part of her fearing that someone might be in there waiting for her. But she shook off the idea, urging her steps toward the stairs. Less than a minute of paranoia, and she was already exhausted by it. How could she possibly live with it every single day? She relieved to see Raiden downstairs at the breakfast table, dressed and ready for the day. Then she spotted his sword leaning against the wall beside the door.

Her dad was in the kitchen, and she wondered with a pounding heart if he had spotted her coming from Raiden's end of the hallway a minute ago. Heat flooded her cheeks even though their night in the same bed had been spent only sleeping.

"Morning, Dad," she said sheepishly as she shuffled into the kitchen.

"Good morning, kiddo," he said and gave her a hug with one arm.

Nicole detected tension in the air as she poured herself some coffee in the mug left for her on the counter.

"Well," her dad said and downed the last swallow of his coffee and set the mug in the sink, "I better be off." He planted a kiss on Nicole's cheek before leaving the kitchen.

"Raiden." Her dad acknowledged him with a nod as he passed from the living room to the front entry.

Nicole was puzzled by her father's tone, not unlike the one he used after being disappointed by her or her brothers. She scrutinized the frown on Raiden's face as she waited to hear the jingle of her dad's keys and then the opening and closing of the door.

"What's going on?" she asked, a nervous laugh sneaking out as she realized she was still in her boxers and sports bra thanks to her haste to see Raiden was still there.

"I have to leave," he said with a harder tone than usual.

Her chest went tight, but she managed to keep her reaction inside, *people don't stay, why should he be any different?* She tried to insist it didn't matter. "Okay—for good?" A tiny part of her hoped he would say yes and prove her right.

"I'll come back."

"When?"

"I don't know." He spoke with quiet agony audible in his words.

Drawing in a long breath through her nose, she huffed. "Are you going to be super vague about everything, or will you just tell me what this is about?"

"It's about you."

"Seriously, can I get more than three words at a time? What do you mean?" Panic, fear, and thoughts of her enemies pumped adrenaline into her bloodstream.

"Between the Council and this Venarius person, you can't expect to run forever, waiting for one or both of them to find their way through a portal. I have the opportunity to get close to the Council. I can mislead them and Venarius, sabotage their plans, maybe find a way to bring them down from the inside. If I want to take advantage of that, I need to leave now, before they suspect that you and I have formed an alliance."

She crossed her arms firmly against the slight chill in the house and her annoyance. "So basically you think it's your responsibility to solve my problems for me?"

"Yes, as a matter of fact, I do. As the only one with the ability to get close to the Council, it *is* my responsibility."

She shook her head. "No. This is my problem, not yours."

"I'm not asking your permission, Nicole."

"What happens if you show up and they decide you're a traitor? Then what? What good can you do if they lock you up? I don't give a shit where you think you'll be the most beneficial to me. As it stands, we're three against who knows how many. With numbers like that, any plan that divides us is a bad idea."

He closed his eyes and took a deep breath before stooping to grab his sword. She stood there in dumbfounded silence as he opened the door and walked outside. Not until the door closed did she jar herself out of her trance. Throwing the door open, she stormed out after him.

"Raiden!" She choked out his name through the lump of fear in her throat. "Is that really what this is about? Or do you just not want to stay?"

He whirled around. "Of course I want to stay. Do you think leaving is easy for me? I never wanted to be this person."

Her heart tightened into a knot. "Then don't be."

A sigh escaped his lips. "I keep having that vision."

"Vision? You mean about the woman?"

He hesitated. "That's not the vision I meant. The one of your future."

She knew the one—she flinched, remembering. He sighed—it sounded guilty.

"If that isn't torture enough—yes, I still see that woman, and it kills me a little. I'd rather it was you. No matter what I see, it all seems to point us in the same direction—you into oblivion and me into someone else's arms. I'm going to do whatever it takes to change those visions."

His words seized her heart. She knew what he meant, but she refused to let those words form in her mind. They'd known each other for only seven days. Just because she kissed him didn't mean she was signing up for some forever, to take the place of some silver-haired fantasy woman.

"Do you want to stay or not?" she asked, not wanting to think of his indirect declaration hanging in the frigid mourning air as she stood there shivering.

"Yes," he said heavily.

"So stay. It should be that simple." She took a step back toward the house, hoping to pull him back and also wondering if it was wrong of her. They were pulling on a rope between them, arguing about being together, he wanted the future and she wanted now.

"Nothing about this is simple. It never was." He stepped closer to her.

"Then stay because I'm asking you to. Because something is bound to go wrong. Because the three of us together are better than two here and you alone." She tightened her crossed arms against the cold of the morning as she trembled in nothing but her boxers and her sports bra, her feet aching against the cold cement.

"Anything else?" he asked.

"What else is there?" She played dumb.

"Are you too afraid to admit it or just stubborn?"

She didn't answer.

275

"Maybe it's only been a week, but I dare say you feel the same. You don't have to admit it. I still intend to keep you alive."

"Don't. Don't do that—don't treat me like I'm some fucking damsel in distress. Stay and help me fight."

"I know you can fight for yourself—you're a natural and you don't need me here to teach you anything—you have the books. And you'll have Gordan. What more help can I give you here?"

She knew what it was like to be punched in the stomach. She had dared Mitchell to do it once. This was worse. Raiden had laid down a point she couldn't counter.

"We both know the bigger threat is in Veil," he said.

"Dammit, Raiden—" She would not say it. She would not be that girl who thinks she's in love, whose world spirals out of orbit in order to revolve around someone else.

He looked at her with a pained smile. "Forgive me for being selfish." He trapped her face in his hands and pressed his mouth to hers.

Her lips ignited, and the fire spread, wild and fast. Even her feet freezing on the cold patio caught fire. Then, just as suddenly, he released her. She sealed her mouth shut with a scowl before her tongue could betray her with foolish words.

Before he turned away, his gaze spilled into hers. She countered his turquoise stare with guarded eyes.

At the portal something was very different. The clear window revealing Veil was no more than a shade. Her eyes could barely make out the forest beyond, and for a moment she thought she saw the shapes of canopies atop the trees, but she knew the forest had burned—she let the confusion pass. The portal was fading as Raiden had said it would. It was time for her to leave as well.

Leading with the sword in his right hand, he leaned into the portal, passing slowly with visible effort and a grimace on his mouth. With one last glance over his shoulder, he gave her a faint smile, and then he was gone. She stepped off the patio and into the wet clover to look through the portal, everything was faint, Raiden was little more than a silhouette.

"It's closing." Gordan's voice hit Nicole's ear like icy air. She jumped but did not look away from the portal. "You know the sooner you leave, the better. If you aren't here, another portal cannot open."

Gordan was right, of course, but she had to pack and tell her dad it was time. She wondered how would Raiden find her when he came back—if he came back?

Although the dew on the clover-carpeted ground bit at her feet and froze her toes, she could not take her eyes off the portal, waiting for him to change his mind and come back. She shuddered from the cold, straining her eyes to see through to Veil. *Turn around,* she thought, her face pinched against memories in her heart.

Thirty-one

Raiden staggered forward into the night beyond the portal. He focused on his grip around the cool metal of his sword. He would not think about the look in Nicole's eyes or the taste of her lips. The warmth of that kiss lingered—he shouldn't have done that—tempting him to turn right back around.

In his attempt not to think of Nicole, it was no surprise that he found himself thinking about his father. He wondered what had crossed his father's mind the day he left. Had he thought to turn around? Was there a cloud of anxiety churning in his chest, telling him how wrong it was to leave? It took all Raiden's effort to keep his feet firmly planted on the ground so they would not take him back to the portal, but they would not move forward either. Leaving once hurt enough; he didn't think he had the strength to leave a second time. He couldn't risk going back when he had come so close to caving in to Nicole's objections.

One deep breath gave him the power to take a step away from the portal. Each step seemed easier the farther her got from her. Although he feared distance would bring back the numbness, he would have to turn that into strength. The numbness would be his ally again, help him stomach his role in the courts, pretend to be loyal to the Council. There came a high-pitched hum before a bolt of crackling energy struck him between the shoulder blades. A wave of acid spread through him, sweeping him up in a fiery current. He didn't even feel himself hit the ground.

When the tide of agony receded, it left him aching, lying with his cheek against a cold, hard floor. He opened his eyes to a lit chamber and a pair of slippered feet. The fog in his mind cleared, and a harsh voice cut through the ringing in his ears.

"The fact that you stole something precious from me is reason enough to kill you and do it slowly."

He pushed his forearm against the floor with a cringe, rolling himself onto his back. His whole body twinged with the remnants of acidic magic. He didn't know what spell Moira had used against him, but he could feel the impact of it still stinging between his shoulder blades and its effects tensing his muscles in sudden spasms. Moira leaned over him, robed in tattered silk and velvet. From where he lay on the floor, she seemed like a black pillar, dull blonde hair spilling over her shoulder and bound in a single loose band.

"Did you think this imitation would fool me?" She held out her hand long enough for him to make out the stone he had stolen— no, it was the replica Nicole had created. He had almost forgotten. Moira threw it down. The stone shattered, and he closed his eyes as the tiny fragments pricked his face.

In an instant, her composure snapped. "Because of you, it's all gone! He's gone, the dragon's gone, the fera." Then suddenly her face softened and her voice sweetened, her self-control regained. "But I must thank you. With your help, I've come to see the importance of removing all obstacles before proceeding. I made the mistake of letting a few filthy survivors hide in their holes for ten years, but I won't make such a grave error again. Because of you, I know where the fera is hiding. I know that the Council has located her and that they had someone else here in Cantis looking for her."

Had? Raiden wondered what fate had befallen Sinnrick.

"What do you want with her?" Raiden's words were a struggle, but he had to find out if he could. Why did they all want her so terribly?

"Not a thing. I simply wish to return the fera to its rightful owner, which I never could have done if you hadn't come thieving into my life. You have proven to be quite the lucky charm, my dear. Not to mention that you just saved me the trouble of coming after you myself. When the fera comes looking for you, I'll have her *and* my master's dragon once again. Everything as it should be."

Raiden sank into her words, into the cold, stone floor. If he had stayed with Nicole, Moira would have had to come to them, the three of them, and she wouldn't have had a fighting chance.

☙

Gordan wondered how long Nicole would stare at the portal, shivering and disappointed. Then something flashed in her eyes. She let out a cry and whirled around toward the house.

"What? What is it?" All he sensed was a surge of adrenaline and magic in the air.

He trailed behind Nicole. She didn't answer him as she threw open the door, running into the house. He stalled at the threshold while she ran up the stairs. The black dog wandered past him into the yard like he wasn't even there. From outside, he could hear her rummaging through her room for several minutes until she reappeared on the landing dressed in her shoes, pants, and long-sleeved shirt and clutching a soft red hooded-jacket.

Before she could take one step down the stairs, she disappeared like a candle flame in the wind and blew through him, shifting through the ether. As sudden as a wisp, she flickered onto the grass outside, her stride toward the portal uninterrupted.

"What do you think you're doing?" Gordan turned around and strode across the patio.

"Going after him—"

"The portal is barely open as it is, Nicole. If you leave, it will close for certain, and you could be stuck in Veil where, I assure you, your enemies will easily find you."

"It's not about me right now." She shoved an arm into her

sweater.

"He's right about his plan, Nicole. You know he is. He's the only one who can get close to the Council—that might be your only chance at winning this fight. You'd risk that because you aren't finished arguing?"

"No." She shrugged her red coat onto her back and led her approach into the portal with extended arms. Her muscles trembled against the portal's resistance. "But I will risk going there to help him—if that dumbass is still alive."

Gordan was astounded. "Wait—can you see through the portal? What did you see?" She pushed farther into the portal, and he felt terribly heavy, as though his stomach had filled with sand. The last thing he could allow was Nicole to go. He did not want to pay his debt today.

"I don't know," she said hurriedly. "He was there. Then there was a red flash, and he just … dropped. Then he was gone." Her voice broke, and Gordan could feel how heartsick she was. She turned her eyes away from him, but he caught the glisten of fearful tears.

Before Gordan could gather his thoughts, both her arms were shoulder deep, and one leg was already through the portal.

"Nicole, stop. If you do this—"

"I get it, all right? It's dangerous. I'm still going." She clenched her teeth and forced her way through.

"No! Nicole, you don't understand—" The instant she pulled the last of her body through the portal, the debt that bound them together seized him, yanking him toward her as though a single step had taken her a thousand miles away. With a violent jerk, he slammed against the portal, but it would not yield.

Without Nicole, there was essentially no magic left—at least no source significant enough to weaken the barrier. Her absence would only expedite the portal closing. If Gordan wasn't wedged halfway between the realms—a veritable doorstop holding the passageway open—the portal very likely would close immediately. Neither Nicole nor Raiden would have a way back. Gordan was no fera. A dragon alone couldn't breech the barrier between the realms, but he hoped he would be enough to keep this portal open long enough for them to make it back.

He attempted to push himself away and managed to put a few inches between the portal and his nose. One elbow sank slightly into the portal, and exasperation rumbled in his throat. He collapsed against it, his face meeting the resistance as though it were a wall of glass. All he could do was pray to the Fates that Nicole found Raiden soon. He didn't want to be the first being to learn what happened when a portal closed around a living thing.

A frigid gust welcomed Nicole as she forced herself through the portal. She zipped her hoodie closed and pulled up her hood. She squinted through the darkness, her eyes blinded by the sudden lack of sunshine. As she blinked, the starlight finally permeated the night, and her vision adjusted.

She saw no sign of Raiden.

"Raiden." An edge of harshness in her voice cut through the silence as she strode toward the trees. Something caught her toe, and she lurched forward, unable to stop herself from falling. An angry huff stirred the dirt around her nose and mouth. She rolled herself over, propping herself upright.

A gleam near her feet met her eye—Raiden's sword. She snatched it off the ground. Clutching the sword in her hand, she scrambled to her feet. Where was he? A swell of fear washed through her.

Her heart skipped into a panicked tempo. "Raiden?"

As if in answer to her call, a terrible sound cut through the air: a hoarse, unbearable scream pulled her gaze up to the castle looming overhead. Another agonizing cry drifted down from above, carried on the cruel wind. Of course—Moira had been waiting. Nicole clung to the sword, sinking into the dread of that sound.

Her body felt heavy, her heart like a stone weighing her down. Even if she had been good at flying, she didn't feel capable of getting even a foot off the ground. Unfortunately, it was fly or take the long way up following the dirt road, and she feared Raiden didn't have that kind of time.

The warm charge of her magic rushed through her. Gravity gave way, and her heart nearly burst with triumph. She escaped the earth. Then a cold, harsh gust slapped her, flinging her onto her back. For a second she lay there stunned, the air knocked from her lungs. Her grip on the silver scabbard did not slacken. She took a deep breath and eased her aching body upright. Wind whistled around her, carrying swirls of ash, hissing like laughter.

Terror stung her eyes, and the icy wind made them water. Each minute she wasted, Raiden came closer to his last. With a resolute sigh, she slung Raiden's sword onto her back and turned toward the dirt road. It was the only option she had left. She eased into a run. Her legs would have to bear the task. With guilt thick in her chest, she hoped to hear that awful scream once more—at least then she'd know he was still alive.

Thirty-two

Nicole rounded the bend where the road turned around the base of the cliff. At first it sloped upward gradually. In the faint light of the stars, she could just make out the multiple switchbacks of the road as it made its way up to the castle. A pang of dread ran through her heart, but she pushed her legs on. Keeping her eyes on the road ahead and trying not to think of how far she had to go, she thought only of moving her legs.

As the incline grew steeper, her legs burned. The building fire in her quads seemed to ignite a surge of magic. She had—albeit accidentally—ether shifted before. She hoped that she could do it again. She had to for Raiden's sake. The heat of her magic grew so intense that she felt like her very substance was as light as a flame. The wind caught her up like a kite, and she streaked through the darkness in a blink.

Suddenly the ground beneath her was level, and her momentum was far too much to overcome. She tumbled into the castle grounds, her heart racing with exhilaration. Sprawled on her back, she panted. Lying against the cold earth assured her she was solid once more, although she felt like she was spinning. Once she caught her breath, she rolled over onto her hands and knees and sprang to her feet. Her first few steps were a stumble, but at last her head cleared and her balance steadied.

Raiden couldn't move. Every nerve in his body had to be gone by now, burned away. The stone floor numbed his cheek and chest, but the rest of him burned. He wondered if this was anything like what Nicole had felt in that horrible vision of her future. Maybe Gordan could help her learn to control the tremendous power she possessed. She deserved to find comfort in her magic, not fear. The weight of his wretched failure seemed to press him farther into the floor. He wouldn't make it to Atrium, wouldn't be able to interfere with the Council. Nicole would have to spend her whole life running—trying to avoid and prepare for the day she would have to fight. The cold floor offered some relief to his aching body, but it was useless against his torturous thoughts.

"Why hasn't she come yet?" Moira demanded. Raiden knew she wasn't addressing him. "Where is the fera?"

Moira did not exude a sense of danger to him. Mostly she struck him as … undone. Her hair was unkempt, and she blinked with frantic rapidity. Occasionally she threw her gaze over her shoulder toward the corner when there was nothing there. She was quite able to cause pain, and he knew firsthand how capable of a killer she was. But he could not fear her. He only wondered how long she would keep him alive in an attempt to lure someone who would not come.

Again her head snapped around, but this time she rushed to the corner. She yanked down a moth-eaten curtain, revealing a tall crystal looking glass. From where he lay, he was unable to make out the image in the mirror before Moira blocked his view.

"Moira, why was the mirror concealed?"

The voice Raiden heard was level, calm, bordering on utter indifference. There also seemed to be the slightest note of the sort of critical derogation that came from countless years of uncontested superiority. The man who spoke did not hurry his words with his impatience. There was, however, audible disdain in his use of

Moira's name—some past disappointment that lingered, perhaps. He sounded like a dissatisfied mentor hardened by years of deficient pupils.

"I beg your forgiveness, Master. It was not my intention to—"

"Never mind. I only need to know the dragon's condition and inform you that you will be receiving a guest. He will be arriving soon."

"Why—sir—if I may ask?"

"Because I need someone reliable in Cantis to take care of another matter."

"Have I not proven to be reliable, sir? The dragon—"

He cut her off, "Is only safe because I had you rid that miserable island of its inhabitants. There isn't a soul left who could possibly meddle in my affairs. You are a mere formality."

So Venarius didn't know his dragon was gone. Raiden inched closer to listen. Moira wrung her hands together behind her back.

"I only wish to be of as much help as possible. I could assist."

Venarius sighed. "Our ears in the courts tell me that the Council has located the fera. They already have two men there. But it seems the fera is hiding in the other realm where their seers cannot See. They have not yet heard news. I'm sending our own man in hopes to make contact with her first."

"It is fortunate, then, that you chose Cantis for the dragon." Her knuckles were white.

"I'm well aware. I'll decide who's best to send tonight, and they should arrive sometime tomorrow."

"Of course, sir."

Silence permeated the chamber.

"Moira?"

"Yes, sir?"

"The condition of the dragon." His expectant tone made her sway, or maybe that was Raiden's vision blurring.

"As well as usual, Master."

Raiden thought he heard Moira swallow. There came no response, and he imagined Venarius scrutinizing her face. But her sigh said otherwise. Venarius departed without another word to his unstable subordinate. In a split second, the cowering woman whirled around, casting a crazed stare straight at him. He didn't flinch.

"I know you have feelings for the fera. I saw for myself through the golem's eyes. Why hasn't she come looking for you?" Her voice grew into a sharp shriek.

"Sorry to disappoint you," he said painfully, "but she won't be following me. The portal is closing, and she's long gone." He couldn't stop the stiff smile that spread across his dry lips.

Her mouth twisted with a sneer, and he knew what would come next but instead a soft jingle rang through the chamber. Moira cocked her head and then looked back to the mirror. No one called. Instead the glass reflected the crumbling entranceway.

Nicole paused to look up at the castle and had to remind herself to keep moving. She spotted a lit window high above. Raiden was in there. She advanced anxiously up the steps to the entrance. The narrow twin doors seemed to grow taller as she approached. As she stood within reach of the handle, the doorway leaned over her. Her hand closed around the twisted iron, and it felt like ice against her skin. She pulled with all the traction and strength she could muster, and the giant door creaked open just enough for her to get inside.

In the looking glass, Moira and Raiden watched Nicole squeeze through a narrow gap between the two doors. Moira waved her hand in front of the mirror, and the image closed in on Nicole.

Disbelief fell from Raiden's lips before he could stop it. "No."

When she turned her gaze back to him, eyes alight with triumph. A chuckle bubbled up her throat, escalating into a roar of laughter that churned Raiden's stomach.

"You were wrong, dear," she said. "You would have been better off if you had just done as the Council told you. You could have been revered and rewarded in Atrium by now."

"Rot in hell, hag." He heaved each word painfully from his chest.

She laughed again. "After you, my dear. What were you planning on doing with a fera anyway—keeping her for yourself? You have no idea what she's destined for. What makes you think an insignificant wretch like you could have changed her fate—or yours, for that matter?"

Air would not fill his lungs. His heart raged against his ribs with furious force as he sank deeper into his pit of failure.

Down below in the once-grand entranceway, any trace of fabric, tapestries, or carpets had disintegrated years ago. What remained of glass in the windowpanes was clouded and gray. Faint moonlight, feeble and dreary, snuck in through tiny gaps in the dry vines clogging the windows. Even Nicole's most careful steps shuffled through the darkness, echoing louder than she expected.

Moira had to know she was in the castle. Nicole expected a flood of golems, a sea of black forms with claws, to come spilling into the corridor from the darkness ahead. But nothing happened. Each moment of stillness compounded her anxiety. Was Moira too busy torturing Raiden to notice or merely watching with cat eyes as Nicole wandered the maze, a mouse losing her nerve? Nicole hoped with a shudder for the latter.

The long muscles in her legs tensed with the struggle of keeping her steps as careful as possible and resisting the urge to break into a run. The fastest way to find Raiden and get out was to throw caution out the vine-choked window. Raiden didn't have time for the safest route. His best chance was the fastest.

All she could do was guess her way through the castle and hope common sense and luck would get her to Raiden in time.

A brittle crunch under her foot made her jump, and her tiny gasp filled the cavernous corridor. Her gaze fell to her feet, and she spotted a dried vine. As she waded through the shadows, more dead vines snapped. The floor, walls, and even the ceiling were increasingly covered with the carcasses of plant life. It appeared as though not even these plants could survive Moira's presence. The deeper she went, the darker the corridor became. No windows lit her way as she delved farther into the inner passages.

Finally, she couldn't tolerate the darkness any longer. She grew leery of the shadows, of the disadvantage, of sneaking around feeling afraid. With a sharp spark of magic, she set the hall ablaze with light. It was as though every shadow caught fire and withered away, leaving a strange, yellow-gray glow that spread through the castle until every last corner of darkness disappeared. It was an eerie illumination that could barely be called light.

Ahead of her, the hallway was a tunnel of dead vines, choking the thresholds of open doors. There were no furnishings, as though everything had been consumed. Confidence possessed her stride, and she didn't look back as she ventured down what looked more and more like the throat of a beast.

She didn't bother checking rooms; what she needed to find was a staircase. Her pace hastened as the effects of her magic faded and the shadows regenerated, creeping in around her once again from corners and crevices.

Thirty-three

"Fascinating. I never thought I would see one of the fera—and here she is. The last. So unassuming," Moira murmured. "I wonder how she will handle the confounding spell—oh, I could just watch her. Imagine not only delivering her to Venarius but knowing infinitely more about her than anyone else—to be useful again."

Raiden shuddered. He would have preferred torture to lying there while she leered at Nicole through the glass.

"Sadly, time is not on my side today." Her mutterings were clearly not meant for him.

He finally regained feeling in his limbs. He struggled to push himself up. The exertion made the floor pitch, and he fell back onto his chest and cheek. His vision fogged. Just moving required every bit of his focus, yet he still needed to keep his attention on Moira. She rummaged around the room sporadically until finally she stopped, her hands having found the object of their search.

He couldn't make out the item in her hand until she came closer. At last he managed to sit up and strain his eyes to see what it was. He recognized the shape of the thing: an iron shackle.

"Would you like a taste?" She sneered at him, leaning over and touching the shackle to his heart. Too sluggish to avoid it or swat her hand aside, he cringed as the iron bit his skin even through his clothes. His chest went cold, his ribs felt brittle, his lungs ached, and his heart tightened. The cancerous magic spread, feeding on what little strength he had left, pulling it out through his heart and leaving nothing but piercing weakness.

She removed it. Almost immediately, the effects receded. He was by no means capable of standing, but what little strength he had returned. Moira straightened up with a smug smile. The cursed metal did not seem to affect her to any degree. Only the maker of a curse would have such immunity.

"Enjoy that? It worked wonders on the dragon until you came along."

He couldn't be sure if it was his imagination or the Sight; suddenly he saw it—Nicole with the iron band around her throat as it had been around Gordan's, locked up like an animal, captured, claimed, waiting to be used—but for what?

His chest felt hollow. Nicole's terrible fate, his future without her—by walking away, he had led her right into it. There was no recovering fast enough, no strength for any spell that might help him. He was desperate to alter that future. So maybe changing part of it would be enough to affect the rest. Only one thing came to mind, to take away the leverage she had to use against Nicole—him.

"You don't need me. She's already here. What reason is there to keep me alive?" He spoke quietly, hoping to sound weaker than he knew he was. His voice was all he had left.

"Soon enough, dear. But I need your help first. You don't think she will allow me put this around her neck, do you?" She laughed. "That's where you come in."

The blood drained from his face, leaving him lightheaded. "I would never do that," he growled through his teeth.

"Oh, don't be stupid." Moira set the shackle down. The iron scraped against the grains of the wooden table. "Puppetry is far more trouble than it's worth. Strings too often become tangled or broken." A few steps away, she stopped in front of the fireplace and grabbed a fistful of soot. "I only need some blood for a little project."

If he could only get away—his body might not be capable, but perhaps he could ether shift. It was foolish. He wouldn't get far, maybe as far as the hallway, but that would be far enough if there was a window nearby. The window in the room was too close. Moira could stop him there. So he set his mind on the distance between himself and the hall, called on all his strength and energy, and then slipped into the ether.

Never before had he felt so out of control. The usual tremble of air around him seemed to shake madly, jerk, and throw him back out a mere step away from the door. He staggered against the door frame and lurched toward the hallway. Then a sharp force struck him in the shoulder, throwing off his balance.

Moira's soft slippers whispered across the stones. He hissed, inhaling through his teeth as she gripped the hilt of the dagger in his back. His torn flesh screamed as she wrenched the cold blade from his body.

"This should do." Her voice was clear and lighthearted as she shuffled back to the table where she worked.

The shadows built up a resistance to Nicole's magic. She had to chase them back with more frequency, setting a charge of anger to them like a lit match to gasoline. Every time the darkness burned up into that dim haze that wasn't quite light, and every time it revived faster than before. She counted her steps as she went. At thirteen, she pulled the sword off her back and hugged it to her chest. At twenty-seven, the vines looked thicker than before. At forty-three, she hadn't seen a door for a while. At seventy, there was nowhere to turn. One hundred. Just the hallway behind her and the hallway ahead of her. One hundred fifty. It seemed quieter than before. She didn't hear her footsteps striking stone or crunching vine. She looked down to see dirt beneath her feet.

That couldn't be right. The stone floor was gone. The corridor went black again, and she set her magic to it in a panic. It ate away the shadows more slowly than usual. Her heart stopped. There was no corridor, no ceiling, no walls, no vines underfoot. She wasn't in the castle anymore. There was only a forest—not even a forest—an infinite tunnel of trees extending in front of her.

She spun around only to find the same sight. Trees, tall and thin in the fuzzy light. The shadows did not return, and for a second she wished they would, as though they would bring her back to the castle—but that didn't make any sense. The last thing she wanted was to wander down that endless path. Turning toward the trees, she decided she would rather enter the forest even if it was teeming with kelpies. She didn't care. Someone wanted her to walk along that path. Well, she refused.

When she turned ninety degrees, somehow the wall of trees in the corner of her eye wasn't there. Instead she turned to see the same path walled in by forest on each side. Panic flailed in her chest, and she turned exactly ninety degrees again—but there was the path instead of the trees.

"No," she cried, turning over and over, back and forth, only to see the same path, the same trees, turning with her

She sank toward the ground, crouching over her feet, pressing her palms into her eyes and her face into her knees. This couldn't be happening. She had to find Raiden. He could be dead already. Because of her—all their problems were because of her. The sword caught between her torso and her legs was cold and comforting. It was real. Yes, she had something real to hold on to.

Frustration expanded in her chest. This was all an illusion. Of course—she remembered the passages she had read about illusions. She could beat this spell. With her eyes still closed, she stood up, swung the sword back onto her back and moved forward, blind, her hands extended in front of her. They hit something solid, but it wasn't a tree; it was stone. Eyes still shut, she focused on the feel of the sword on her back and the rough, cold wall beneath her hands. She kicked something wooden, and she skirted around it, never taking her hand from the wall or opening her eyes.

Her fingers ran over rotten wood. Then, several paces farther, she felt the wall turn a corner, and she tripped on the bottom step of a staircase. She gasped. Her eyes snapped open. Stairs. Sprinting up a flight of stairs had never felt so effortless. Her heart pounded with elation. She felt like she'd won, defied the maze. Any minute now she would see the glow of light, the room where she'd find Raiden. She ran.

Before she reached the top, she heard the echo of a cough tumble down the hall toward her. The scuffling of her eager footsteps nearly drowned it out. Taking the final steps two at a time, she halted when she saw a choice of two hallways. Holding her breath, she waited. A triplet of short coughs drifted down the corridor, catching her ear like a hook and pulling her into a run. Of the few doors she saw ahead, only one was closed, and she set her sights on it. She did not rein in her speed until she reached the door, catching the handle to stop herself. The latch opened, and she practically fell into the chamber.

Against the opposite wall sat the bulk of a grown man, his head hanging forward. Outside a gibbous moon was rising, and its light fell in a soft stream through the window. The man at the other side of the room was concealed in shadow. She pitched forward, crossed the chamber, stepped through the faint light, and at last she could see—he was not Raiden.

Her legs carried her forward out of instinct. With timid steps she drew closer, stooping down and reaching to touch his shoulder. The thought that he could be dead twisted her stomach, but his head snapped upright and he snatched her hand. Her heart struck her ribs hard, and she yelped.

"Who are you?" His eyes immediately softened as they took in her features. She wondered if, for a moment, he had thought she was Moira.

"Nicole." She blinked at him, wondering how much a name really mattered right now. But out of habit she returned the question anyway. "Who are you?"

"Sinnrick Stultus."

The name struck her heart cold, and she noticed her hand was still caught in his grip. When she looked into his eyes, brown and unchanged, she saw no recognition in them. He had no idea who she was. His expression only told her that he was relieved to see someone who wasn't Moira.

He reminded her so much of her brother—light brown hair, cunning eyes that could not be dulled by exhaustion. She had no time to help him, but if she didn't then she might as well be killing him herself. Cursing herself silently, she gripped his hand better and pulled him to his feet.

She was curious. "How did you get here?"

"I'm on assignment. The Council sent me to locate a colleague named Raiden. When I arrived, it seemed there wasn't a soul on this miserable island. Then the whole forest went up in flames, and I thought it might have to do with him. I never found anyone. A couple days ago—maybe it was yesterday; I can't remember—some woman appeared in the forest, and next thing I know I can barely move, left here to rot, I presume."

She took notice that he did not mention the other part of his mission—finding the portal and the fera.

"Can you walk?" she asked hopefully.

He took a step and sagged toward her, nearly dragging her to the floor. Resisting his weight, she managed to prop him up. "I'll take that as a no."

"What are you doing here?" Sinnrick allowed her to put his arm around her shoulders, and he swayed a little.

"I'm looking for Raiden too," she answered cautiously, her heart like a trapped hummingbird in her chest. Why should she be scared? What could he do to her in his current state? The man couldn't even walk on his own.

"The Council send you? Should've known they wouldn't have much confidence in a fresh recruit," he muttered, his face right beside Nicole's ear.

"Come on," she said.

"If you're looking for Raiden, does that mean he's somewhere in this castle as well?" Sinnrick asked.

Nicole answered with a grim nod. His question made her heart swell with anxiety, drumming the brisk cadence that her anxious legs yearned to match. With each step she regretted her decision.

"I hope we're not too late," he said.

Nicole scowled, thinking it wasn't too late to just leave the sorry bastard to fend for himself. Distress had her magic churning, and it erupted suddenly. The walls around them trembled. Fine grains of sand drifted down over them, and the grinding of shifting stone hastened their strides.

Once the rumbling ceased, their pace relaxed.

"It's a wonder this place is still standing." Sinnrick's easy tone sounded forced, and the tension around them only increased.

Nicole remained silent, but Sinnrick insisted on talking.

"You weren't sent here by the Council, were you?"

"No." Her mind had no capacity for creating lies, not while Raiden monopolized her thoughts.

"You must be the fera then," he said.

She stiffened, unsure if she should keep walking with him.

Sinnrick kept talking. "You must trust him a lot to be here looking for him. I can hazard a guess that he wasn't going to bring you to the Council." He chuckled. "I thought he might have found something better for himself in the other realm. I didn't think it was the fera—imagine that. At least now I know why the Council never heard from him. But how did he end up here?"

"We—" She stopped herself, hearing a shuffle down the hall. The sound was almost drowned out by their footsteps.

They halted, and the slow, heavy tempo of a third pair of feet met their ears. The hall turned no more than twenty feet ahead of them. Sinnrick glanced over his shoulder, and Nicole craned her neck to see but there was no one.

They watched the path ahead, tensing further with each step that approached. The hall was dim. The bleak stones seemed to turn everything to shades of gray. Even Sinnrick and Nicole looked colorless in so little light. When a figure pitched forward and stumbled into their line of sight, Nicole wrenched herself out from under Sinnrick. He wavered without her support.

She sprinted down the hall. She knew that form, knew the width of his shoulders, his disheveled hair.

"Raiden," she gasped, stopping herself short of colliding with him. "Are you okay—how did you get away?" Her words tumbled frantically from her mouth.

He swayed, placing his hands on her shoulders to steady himself.

"Can you walk?" She put her hands on his forearms, wondering how he could have escaped when he could barely stand. Then her hand brushed against something cold and rough—iron hanging on his arm. The touch of it turned her stomach; it was hauntingly familiar. She recognized the dreadful touch of Gordan's shackle instantly, reliving that moment in the tower unexpectedly.

She recoiled from the draining sensation and felt guilty for pulling away from him. Something wasn't right. His hands gripped her shoulders too hard, strangely strong for someone so weak. And he hadn't said a word. Her stomach twisted into a knot, and her heart struck her ribs in warning. The more she tried to pull away, the crueler his grip became. Shoving him, she broke free and stepped back, bumping against Sinnrick, who had managed to make his way down the hall on his own with the support of the wall.

"What's wrong?" There was audible confusion in Sinnrick's voice.

The sword seemed to call her. It guided her hand to the hilt as Raiden's hand went for the metal circle hanging on his arm. As his hands opened the hinged iron ring, she freed the sword. The blade rang through the silence, and its light cut through the shadows, revealing Raiden's face, ashen gray with golem eyes.

"That's not Raiden," she said, wondering with a pang of nausea where the real Raiden was.

The doppelganger lunged forward, thrusting the open shackle toward her. As he leaned into the light of the sword, his irises glowed, smoldering pieces of coal where the turquoise pools she knew should have been.

Instinctively, she swung the sword. The blade was impossibly light in her hands and met the slightest resistance. An inhuman shriek ripped through the golem's throat, its mouth spreading open back to its ears. The heavy sound of iron clattered against stone, echoing down the hall. For a moment it staggered back, clutching one arm with the other, retreating partway into the shadows.

Securing the sword more firmly in her grip, she stood her ground. It came back, charging. She held the sword tight and raised it like a bat. It lunged. She swung. She closed her eyes in the last instant, unable to watch the sword strike what still looked like Raiden.

The blade made contact, lurching to a stop in the golem's head. Its body dropped to the floor, limp, pulling the sword and her down with it. Her hands remained locked on the hilt. She yanked frantically to extract the blade from the cloven skull. *Not Raiden's, it's not Raiden*—she shook her head, refusing to look. Her Raiden was alive somewhere. He was here—he had to be.

The sword came loose, and she stumbled back. Sinnrick caught her, barely keeping them both upright.

"Nicely done," he approved.

Nicole panted, her pulse reeling. Her thoughts were sluggish with shock. Her body hummed with adrenaline. Sinnrick took her by the arm and guided her another step away from the slumped form of the golem on the floor.

He let out a stiff laugh. "Glad I'm on your side."

Before she could smile, the golem sprang up from the floor on all fours—looking even less like Raiden than before, head misshapen, limbs too long, spine hunched. It caught Sinnrick in its arms, hands grasping his face. It wrenched his head around, and the sickening snap met Nicole's ear.

She screamed and swung the sword. Sinnrick slumped to the floor. The golem's half-split head rolled, a monstrous, openmouthed grin on its face. A second later it sunk into a pile of ash over Sinnrick's body.

Her whole body shook. Her hands could no longer hold onto the sword. It fell, clattering to the stone floor, the blade's sad cry ringing through the silence. She could not tear her eyes away from the body at her feet, couldn't escape the tremor of horror moving through her. Before her lay the fate of those who chose her side. The thought stopped her breath. Every hair on her body stood up, and the air in her lungs went stale. She gasped for fresh air.

Forcing her eyes closed, she broke the trance of poor Sinnrick's corpse. With her face and eyes turned aside, she crouched and searched blindly for the sword. Her fingertips brushed the skin of his arm, still warm, and she jerked her hand away. She found the sword, snatched it off the floor, and bolted down the hall in the direction from which the golem had come. Her heart turned into a cold lump of guilt as she left Sinnrick behind.

Around the corner she came to another stairway. She was fast with fear, blazing up the steps, grateful for the burn in her quads and the labor of her heart and lungs. No pain would be as much as she deserved for Sinnrick's life. He'd have been better off alone, better if she had left him in that room. When she reached the top of the stairs, she ran. The urge to cry Raiden's name expanded in her lungs, stifled only by the reluctance to waste a single precious breath that she needed to run.

Thirty-four

Moira threw a pewter goblet at the mirror, shattering the glass. Raiden shuddered at the sight of Nicole running, her image fractured. The Sight rolled in like bile rising in the back of his throat, and he resisted more disjointed visions.

"I'll do it myself," Moira said with a sneer. She spun on her heel toward the door, her form twisted into the air, and she was gone.

This could be his only chance. He refused to let the pain or the complete lack of energy in his limbs keep him on the ground. A small puddle of blood had pooled around his shoulder, thick and slick under his limbs. His arms shook like the ground quaked beneath him, but he would not let them buckle. His legs felt full of sand. They were not the legs he knew, but he had to make them work. He had to move. When he straightened up, a breath of disbelief flew from his lungs, and his balance wavered. The door was only two paces away.

He was grateful to put his foot down after the effort of picking it up. One more step. His hand reached for the support of the door frame. Then something struck him hard, this time from the front. His head reeled. He lost his grip on the frame. The sound of her yelp hit his ears, and the impact of her body pummeled him.

They toppled to the floor, his muscles screaming, his ribs near breaking with every sharp pound of his heart. A thrum of dread hummed in his heart. He had led her here, and if she stayed trying to save him, she might leave this place was as a prisoner.

"Guess that makes us even," he wheezed through the pain, remembering that day they had met in a collision.

She gasped.

"I'm so sorry," she said breathlessly. Her voice soothed his aching heart. With frantic haste, she pulled herself away from him. He would have gratefully let her stay, no matter how fervently his sore body protested under her weight. Her hands eased him upright, her touch like a balm to him.

Her head pivoted back and forth, wide eyes taking in the room, lingering on the blood-smeared floor. Her gaze snapped back to him. She studied his face, taking in the pallor of his skin, the shadows under his eyes.

The concern in her eyes melted into an angry glare that glistened with wetness. "The only reason I'm here is to tell you you're an idiot," she said.

The scowl on her face only made him smile. She took his arm and draped it around her neck. Shifting back onto her heels, she heaved him upright alongside her.

Then the realization struck him. It was suddenly clear to him now how this path would lead him into the arms of another. She would save him at the expense of herself. He couldn't let her.

"We won't make it out of here, Nicole. Not like this." His hoarse voice scraped against his dry throat and he pulled his arm away, standing unaided on his unstable legs. What could he tell her to convince her? She would have to believe she wasn't leaving him to die. "Moira thinks Gordan owes his debt to me. I'm bait. She won't kill me."

"Until she realizes he isn't. We're leaving. Now."

"Where is Gordan?"

"I don't know—back home. Raiden, come on," she said, pulling on his arm.

"She won't let me leave as long as she thinks Gordan will come to help me. You have to go get him."

"We can't lead him right back here to be locked up again," she said.

"Remember what you said about the three of us together being better than apart? We need his help this time, Nicole." Speaking, breathing, standing, all composed a symphony of anguish in his chest.

"I'm not leaving without you." She slipped her arm around his back, but he would not move.

"No," he said, wincing. "We won't make it out, not without his help. Please, trust me. Go get Gordan."

She shook her head. "I can't. I can't leave you here."

"Dammit, just this once, would you not argue with me?"

Moira flickered through the air and found herself standing in the hallway with a pile of soot and a body at her feet. She sneered as she looked down her nose, not seeing the man, only searching for her iron collar. The hard, black curve of iron half buried in the ash caught her eye, and she bent down. A wheezing breath whispered through the man's lips.

She straightened up with a contented sigh and then lifted her foot and placed the bottom of the soft slipper on his broken neck. With a leisurely movement, she leaned her weight onto the neck underfoot and put him out of his misery with a snap.

Nicole huffed through her nose. Those eyes of honey bore into Raiden's heart. All he could do was hope she would not spot the deception in his eyes. To his surprise and relief, she leaned away, her gentle hand trailing along his back. Her hand slid down his arm, then caught his hand, clinging to his fingers.

"The sooner you two get back, the sooner you can yell at me." He twisted his mouth into what he hoped would be a convincing smile. His hand slipped out of hers, dropping to his side as she took one step back, still unable to turn her eyes away from him.

"Oh, please don't go yet," Moira cooed behind Nicole in the hallway.

Nicole spun around. His heart sank. He was too late. Moira flicked her wrist as though swatting a fly, and a force blew past Nicole, throwing him off his unsteady feet. A sickening sensation rolled through him as he slid along the floor back into the middle of the room. The fresh haze of Moira's acrid magic lingered in his muscles, causing tiny spasms and leaving a metallic taste in his mouth.

"Come in. Stay a while," Moira said.

Nicole looked back at him, her eyes measuring the distance between them, but she did not turn her back to Moira. Nicole took cautious steps backward, moving toward him. Moira matched her pace, strolling into the chamber. She paused a moment to turn back and wave the door closed. She tapped her index finger against it. The wood creaked with the swell of magic, and the space around the door filled with a momentary glow. They were sealed in, the three of them.

As Nicole backed up to him, Raiden noticed his sword slung across her back. With careful ease she removed the sword and then turned just enough to present it to him.

The silvery white metal fit into his fist, and he took hold of it with renewed strength. Nicole pulled him to his feet. Somehow the cool metal pulled out the pain, absorbed the remnants of Moira's magic. He felt steady on his feet again. Nicole released the sword to his possession and turned back to Moira.

"I think we can come to an arrangement here, don't you?" Moira spoke as she stepped away from the door confidently.

"What kind of arrangement?" Nicole asked.

"No!" The force of his voice induced a cough, and he failed to sound as severe as he had hoped.

"He's useless to me now, but I'll let him live if you agree to stay."

This time Nicole whirled around with a fiery glare in her eyes. They screamed every word she didn't utter. Her gaze burned into him for only a second before she turned back to Moira. In that moment he saw the muscles of her neck relax with sudden confidence.

"That's two for one. That's not a fair trade." Nicole took on the defensive tone he knew well by now.

Of course—Moira didn't just want Nicole. She wanted Gordan too. And if Nicole surrendered herself, she condemned Gordan to the same fate. There was no chance she would sacrifice that dragon alongside herself. Stubborn as always, she had to save them both—Raiden didn't know whether to adore or hate her right now.

"He's not worth that much to you? Fine, I don't have to give him up. It matters not. You'll stay here either way. I merely thought you might want the opportunity save him; that is what you came all this way for, after all. But if you prefer to do this the difficult way, then I will enjoy punishing him later." Moira circled them, assured by her seal on the door.

Raiden tried to stand beside Nicole, but she still placed herself between him and Moira, pushing her hands into her jacket pockets. Then she turned to him with a fire in her eyes and her lips pressed together in determination. He understood; they both knew Moira wouldn't honor any trade, fair or otherwise. She had no intention of letting Nicole leave this chamber.

She dropped her wide eyes and his gaze followed to see her hand emerge from her red sweater with a familiar stone cupped secretively in her palm. She pressed her lips together before she turned to Moira, now at the back of the long, rectangular chamber.

"Would you let him live for this?" Nicole pulled her fist from her pocket and revealed the stone.

Moira's nonchalance broke into a frantic stare and an anxious twitch. She was too slow to compose herself; they had seen how much she really wanted it. Maybe enough to get them out of this.

"What you want for what I want." Nicole closed her hand around the stone, and Moira made a tiny lurch forward. "Should I take that as a *yes*?"

Moira's face twisted.

"Well, then you're going to have to come and get it."

Nicole wheeled around and sprinted for the door. The seal on the door emitted a force that pushed against her. The closer she got to it, the slower her progress became. She reached out as her stride slowed, coming just within reach. Her hand burned bright with magic. With the smallest touch of her fingertip, the seal shattered. The barrier broke. The door cracked off its hinges and crashed into the hallway with a bang. Suddenly, with no resistance, all Nicole's effort to run shot her forward like a bullet.

Moira shrieked as Nicole disappeared with the stone trapped in her fist.

Thirty-five

Nicole ran without a plan, no route ahead of her. *Just run,* she implored her legs even though she was running on empty. Moira would follow. Getting her away from Raiden was good enough. But now she didn't know what to do. Handing the stone over to Moira wouldn't work.

She caught sight of large double doors ahead. They had the look of escape, of an exit that might lead outside. She skidded to a halt and caught the massive curled handle. The rusted hinges moaned as she pulled, but it barely budged. She placed a foot on the other door and pulled again. It opened. A tongue of icy wind licked her face as the door swung wide. Outside—freedom—this was her chance.

A red bolt of heat crackled through the air, hitting the door as Nicole ducked and lurched through the archway. Splinters flew past her ear. She charged into the wind without a second thought as a wave of heat rained kindling down around her. The force lifted her off her feet for a brief moment. Her legs kicked in the air, but she hit the ground running, staggering forward.

The thick, golden light of the rising sun stunned her eyes, drowning out the path before her. Throwing her arm up to block the sun, she saw a familiar shape: the dungeon tower across the valley like a massive black rook in the dawn. The stone bridge beneath her feet extended between it and the castle. Then she saw the terrible gap near its center.

Nicole threw herself backward, falling back ten feet from the broken end of the bridge. Her legs shook as she returned to her feet. The feral wind swirled around her with vicious strength, pulling at her clothes, nudging her toward the edge. She knew she hadn't gotten any better at flying since her last attempt. She wasn't sure which she would rather face—the savage gales or the bloodthirsty woman on her heels. Which was more likely to kill her?

For some reason, she felt like she had a better chance with Moira than she would fighting the wind, at least while she still had the stone. It went against Nicole's instincts to move toward the woman—who came stalking across the bridge with murder in her eyes—but so did getting any closer to the broken edge behind her.

All she could do was stand her ground and hold up the stone, ready to throw it. Moira froze just beyond arm's reach of Nicole and the stone.

"Give it back. You'll hurt him," Moira stammered.

Nicole cocked her head. Her arm slackened. *Him?* This woman was mad.

"What do you mean?" Nicole had to raise her voice over the howl of the wind.

"My master stole him from me. And then that thief took all I have left of him," Moira spat. "I can't lose him again." Her voice trembled with despair.

Confused, Nicole looked down at the stone, wondering if it had really been a man once or if it was just the object to which Moira had chosen to attach a sad delusion.

"Then let us go free." Nicole tried to keep her voice steady.

"Don't be so naïve. There's no such thing as freedom. Not for you. Even if I let you go, you would still belong to him. Venarius will find you. He will not be stopped."

Nicole froze, terrified by her words for just a moment.

In a blink, the stone disappeared from Nicole's hand and popped into Moira's.

"My dear, you might be the fera, but I know a novice when I see one," Moira said with satisfaction curling her lips. "I've studied for years, and even with your raw power, you are at a disadvantage."

Nicole grinned, pulling another stone—the real stone—from her other pocket. "Am I?"

Moira's expression fell stricken, and she looked down at the stone in her hand—the illusion dissolved. Fury contorted her face. Her eyes flashed back to Nicole. Moira threw the shackle as Nicole hurled the true stone down against the bridge. The stone shattered, splintering into a glittering puff just as the collar clamped shut around Nicole's throat, knocking her off her feet.

"No!" Moira's shriek rang out, echoing endlessly between the mountains. She dropped to her knees, diving for the remnants of the stone, but they were whisked away on the wind. She stood slowly, unfolding herself.

The weight of the iron collar anchored Nicole down, heavier than something of its size should have been. She watched through distorted vision as Moira took two steps to the side of the bridge. She swayed there in the wind.

"My love," she sobbed before letting herself fall.

Nicole chocked on her shock through the pain spreading out of the collar, not believing her blurry eyes. Moira was gone, but the pain of the shackle kept building. She locked her fingers around the rough metal, kicking her legs uselessly. The curse spread, a tide of fire in her neck that spilled into her grasping hands. It crawled through her, filling her chest, creeping down her legs and up her arms. Her bones felt as heavy as blackened iron and as fragile as glass. The slightest movement took all her effort and rattled her body with pain. One hand inched around the iron ring. Each tiny movement was torture. There was a latch somewhere, she knew. All she had to do was open it.

At her very core her magic burned, a whisper, faint as a distant star. As the curse spread like a plague through her body, her own power flared, sending a wave of relief washing through her. As quickly as it came, it passed, and the surge of agony returned. Yet another flare of soothing magic swept back the curse. Again, agony radiated through her from the cursed iron. It was a battle between two opposing waves, each pushing the other back to its origin.

Raiden leaned on his sword, using it as a walking stick and cursing his lethargic legs. He stumbled into the hallway, slamming against the wall before he managed to make the turn, panick rising in his chest. The longer he held the sword, the quicker his arms drained of Moira's magic still festering in his system. Each step grew steadier if not stronger. He was by no means at his best, bruised, bleeding, aching, but he could see straight. He could command his body at last.

An eerie breeze drifted through the corridor, carrying the sound of a distant scream. He lurched forward into an unsteady run, one hand clutching his sword, the other prepared to catch the wall in support.

When he came to the gaping threshold, a gust of frigid air struck his face. For a second he sagged against the door frame to keep from toppling over. His eyes fell to the scattered remains of the doors and followed the debris out onto the bridge. Leaning into the wind—it was cold enough to numb his aches and pains—he let go of his support and ran.

The sunrise dazzled his eyes, and even when he shielded them, at first he could see no one out ahead of him. His vision was still not clear enough to see so far. As he neared the end of the bridge, he could see a figure lying on the stones. The bridge shuddered beneath his feet. A fog of charged air rolled toward him, raising the hair on his neck.

"Nicole," he called, fighting to stay on his feet.

His body slowed against his will, and the sight before him became painfully clear. Her back arched in pain, hands grasping at her neck, her lips parted. Her eyes were open wide, dark with magic, devoid of the Nicole he knew. A swell of power surged from her, shaking the stones of the bridge, flooding the air with raw, crackling energy.

His sword's faint glow suddenly blazed bright in his hands. The ache of his muscles shriveled into nothing as Nicole's magic washed over him. The blood-clotted wound on his shoulder tingled, healing. In the back of his mind, the Sight grew a thousand times harder to resist. It rushed forward, seizing him with a strength that scared him.

He saw Nicole, countless glimpses of her—smiles, scowls, moments holding her, talking, laughing. She was alive, those eyes of honey bright as ever, not clouded with magic. Her presence was warm and loud; it was breathtakingly real. His heart reeled in those moments.

Then the Sight cast him into another place with debris under his feet. Nicole was just out of his reach, eyes dark, back arched. Great stones fell around her. Her magic devoured all sound, all light and shadow, until it consumed her as well.

Raiden broke free of the vision. He fought to stand. He chose to have a future with Nicole in it, and he would, no matter the costs. She was so close, no more than ten steps away. Her scream cut through the air, the sound warbling and distorted by magic, twisting and echoing. Then, somehow, over the roar of the wind and her piercing scream, he heard the click of the latch.

Her hands, red and hissing, wrenched the shackle open. An acidic vapor rolled through the air as the curse broke, and the surge of Nicole's magic waned. The wind died down to a whisper. Without the force of the wind and Nicole's magic pushing against him, Raiden collapsed onto his hands and knees.

The heavy iron struck the stone bridge with a clang that rippled through the stillness followed by a barrage of coughing. She stirred, rolling onto her hands and knees. He let himself sag with relief, painless but still utterly exhausted. The two of them heaved themselves to their feet on wobbling legs, catching each other's eyes.

"Hi." It was all he could think to say.

"Hi." Her raspy answer was punctuated by a cough.

Then a sickening sound stopped his heart—the gritty shifting of massive stones. Nicole looked down at the bridge beneath her and then back to him. They lurched forward, toward each other, staggering into a run as the stones shifted and gave way beneath her feet with a terrible, low, scraping moan. She fell with the stones, diving for the edge as he did for her.

Thirty-six

Nicole fell, reaching for Raiden. Her hips struck the stones. Her body folded against the edge, her torso barely made it, legs dangling. Her waist ground against the stone, and there she stopped. Their hands knotted together. Her neck still burned with every movement she made. She lifted her head, raising her face to Raiden's. His grasp and his weight were all that prevented her from slipping off the bridge.

"I've got you." His strained voice gave away his bluff. The way his arms trembled, she knew he had no strength left to pull her up.

The smallest flare of magic felt like knives running through her. Her body couldn't take any more abuse. She had to use her legs. She kicked to find a foothold and only dislodged pieces of the crumbling structure. A stone fell away, pulling her farther over the edge. The sound of grinding stopped her in cold fear. Their eyes met. She held her breath.

Beneath them the stones gave way, and they fell, two bodies and a cluster of great stones. Terror rattled inside her chest; not even a gasp escaped her. Their clothes rustled around them. Her grip on Raiden's hands tightened, her nails digging into his skin. Their arms were stretched straight between them, preventing them from drifting apart. Then a glint of light struck her watery eyes.

Behind Raiden, a strange light trailed through the air. Between his shoulder blades, feathery shadows unfurled like a parachute. Suddenly his decent slowed, and gravity yanked her down, testing their grip. She swung at the end of his arms, and he cried out in pain.

Silver wings spread before Nicole's eyes, but she couldn't make herself understand. They fell but more slowly now—gliding in their descent. Raiden pulled her against him.

As they neared the ground, they were drifting rather than falling. They hit the ground in a tumbling heap, landing in a thick pillow of ash and dirt. Nicole rolled across the ground and sat up dizzily, brushing dirt from her face and searching for Raiden. A few feet away he lay sprawled on his back, unmoving.

"Raiden?" She crawled frantically on her hands and knees to reach his side.

He didn't respond. Her gaze fell to what lay spread beneath him—wings. They were real. The incredible wingspan had to be no less than ten feet. Where had they come from? Each feather shimmered like a mirage. She reached out and touched the silky plumage, light as air. She had to wrench herself free from her dreamy disbelief. No time to marvel at wings. Strange things had become commonplace in her life, after all.

Even the slightest movement of leaning over him sent chords of pain ringing through her body.

"Raiden," she said. His eyes didn't move beneath their lids. "Raiden!" Panic erupted from her voice.

He jumped, lurching upright and wincing. His hands jerked toward her and caught her arms. The terror of falling lingered in his eyes for a moment until they focused on her. Nicole sank back, releasing the dread from her lungs.

Reaching over his shoulder, his fingers probed the wings. His puzzled eyes and slack mouth mirrored the surprise on her face. When his gaze dropped from her eyes to her neck, his mouth turned into a frown. He reached out and his fingertips grazed her neck.

The ridges of his fingerprints were like sandpaper against the tender red skin. She managed to turn her cringe into a smile or at least a grimace.

Neither of them spoke. She couldn't think of a thing to say. So they secured their hands to each other's forearms and struggled to get their legs underneath them. They shook and swayed on their legs like newborn foals. The great silver wings hanging from Raiden's back faded to a faint light, folded back between his shoulder blades, and disappeared entirely.

She reached around his back, searching. Her fingers brushed against scrapes and cuts, torn layers of fabric—but no wings.

"I can still feel them," he said. "I guess the Council doesn't think I'm a traitor, or else they wouldn't have bestowed their great honor on me." There was malice in his voice.

She pulled her hand around from behind his back and took his hand. "We're alive because of those wings—who cares where they came from?"

"I do. It's what they signify—they think they can command me. They think they own me."

"This coming from the guy who wanted to play double agent this morning! Let them think whatever they want," she said with a bitter laugh. "Your life doesn't belong to the Council or the Sight—it belongs to you. So quit bitching. I want to go home."

A chuckle broke past his frown. "All right."

They followed the trail they had left along the ground. Above, the sky was clear and blue in the early sunlight. Scattered, not far off, was a field of the massive bridge stones, each sitting in a crater. A silvery white gleam reached out to them from a pile of broken trees and massive stones.

The hilt of Raiden's sword—its metal wings emitting a soft, lunar light—stood upright, the blade in the ground as if waiting patiently to be retrieved. He did not sling it across his back but merely let it rest against his shoulder as they hobbled on through the forest. What should have been a short walk seemed endless. Raiden, who had been so sure-footed in that forest days ago, stumbled and tripped on every rock and root. Their feet were heavy, their legs barely able to lift them for each step.

Raiden refused to let her go, and not because he relied on his arm around her waist to stay upright. His head throbbed, his back stung, his shoulder—though the wound had partially healed—still ached.

"I was ready to hear the end of your song, Raiden." The cold, eerie voice preceded Amarth's appearance as always, and Raiden pretended not to hear.

"I was hoping for anyone else's after Moira—her song is so dreary. To be quite honest, I'm rather intrigued by hers." Amarth nodded his head toward Nicole as they passed by him.

Raiden didn't flinch at the mention of Moira's death. His chest did not fill with relief, or joy, or even satisfaction. He just wanted to get back home, as far from Veil as he could.

"You should have taken my advice, Raiden. She'll be the end of you. Chaos and death are her only destiny. You cannot change that."

Watch me, Raiden wanted to growl.

"I can only lead you to the stream. But I can see you'll not drink. No matter. I will just have to wait. If only you could see what I see, Raiden. You have no idea what lurks in her."

Amarth seemed to pause for Raiden's response, but he would give none.

"Farewell, then. I will be seeing you soon. Oh, and by the way, you might be pleased to know your song has quite changed. I hear your mother in you again, but it has taken on a melody much like your father's."

Raiden stopped. His body went rigid.

Nicole reversed her last step. "You okay?"

He nodded. "I just need to catch my breath."

Nicole turned her face into his chest with a sigh of the same sentiment, revealing just how exhausted she was.

"Let's keep moving," he murmured, easing back into a steady pace.

She fell back into step beside him, oblivious to Amarth's haunting predictions. Raiden shuddered again, hoping it only seemed like a shiver against the cold. Even when he kept the Sight in check, he could not escape outside forces trying to tell him where he and Nicole were headed.

Ↄ

Gordan had never been so overjoyed to hear the bumbling sound of human footsteps. Crashing through the forest like drunks, their strides were uneven and staggering. Still, he recognized Nicole and Raiden's presence. He knew their breathing, their heartbeats. He hadn't realized how well he knew them until now.

To anyone else it would have seemed a peaceful morning, serenely silent, but not to him. This was the first time he had heard the crushing of his own bones. The portal pressed all around him. Most of his lower half was still back in Nicole's backyard. His right arm, shoulder, and half of his torso—neck and head included— were all in Veil.

He could feel Nicole getting closer as the force pulling him toward her eased little by little. At last he ceased slipping slowly through the portal. However, the relief was minor compared to the tremendous pressure that continued to compress his rib cage. When Nicole finally appeared, he wasn't sure whether he would want to embrace her or strangle her.

Nicole and Raiden were oblivious to the world around them, focused on the ground while they worked together to walk. They were a sight. Raiden was pale and haggard. Nicole was shaken, and a red ring burned around her neck—it summoned a phantom of pain from his memory, resurrecting the curse within his deep scar for a fleeting instant. She might not bear a scar like his, but they would be forever bound by the memory of that iron collar and its corrosive curse.

It wasn't until they were only a few feet away from the portal that she finally noticed him.

"Gordan." Her voice was a nearly inaudible rasp.

He knew that feeling too, could feel the curse in his own throat when she spoke. His anger died. He could not be mad at her. Raiden, on the other hand, was the reason she had gone running off into Veil, so Gordan felt free to hate him for the time being.

"Nice of you to hurry back. You look like you've thoroughly enjoyed yourselves." He said lightly through his shallow breaths, but he couldn't keep his gaze off Nicole's neck.

She smiled, lifting the heavy corners of her mouth, and it felt genuine to him.

"At least the portal is still open." Raiden looked him up and down.

"Not for much longer." Gordan strained to speak.

"What do we do?"

Nicole's rough voice pricked his heart. Gordan wished he could have been there to spare her from the very fate she had rescued him from. But with a twinge of guilt, he was glad he still owed his debt, that he still had reason to stay with them.

Gordan reached his arm as far as he could, offering his hand. "Just pull," he said, concealing his true desire with those words. Since the day she had saved him, he had wanted to touch that hand, so unassuming, strong, kind, loving, courageous—that hand she laid against his face, the first gentle touch he'd known in centuries. It was dangerous to indulge such a whim. She took his hand, and he couldn't help adoring the feel of it in his. He couldn't help but feel this moment would hurt him someday.

Nicole obeyed like a sleepy child, pulling on his arm. But he did not budge.

Raiden grabbed her wrist. "Stop. Don't pull him."

A scowl formed fast on Gordan's face.

"We can't just leave him in there," she said. "It'll crush him, or worse." She shuddered.

The distress in her voice coaxed a tiny smile from Gordan's mouth. How familiar this all suddenly seemed.

"No, I mean we should be pushing. He's keeping the portal open. Once he's out, it closes."

"Oh." She looked at Gordan's exposed head, neck, and shoulder.

"But we have to make it through too."

"Then it's time to get close and hold tight," Raiden said, nudging her toward Gordan.

Raiden sandwiched her between Gordan and himself. Gordan hooked his one free arm around her, and she cinched her arm tight around his neck. Three individuals were now one entity caught in the portal, one combined source of magic that could hopefully push back through.

Hoping to tip the scales toward the other realm, Gordan focused on his left arm with the intention to revert to his natural form. The spark of magic to transform pulled him, all of them. Slowly at first, but with every bit of his body that returned to the other side, the portal loosened. He could feel Nicole's arm sinking with him through the portal. With her arm through, the magic on the other side increased, and they slipped farther. She adjusted her arm securely around his torso as he pulled his head out of Veil.

Only his right arm remained, caught around Nicole, immovable. He dug in his heels and leaned hard away from the portal, dragging her after him. Arm, shoulder, head—she came through gasping. As her upper body emerged with Raiden's arm clinging to her waist, the resistance slackened further. Gordan positioned her arm around his neck and his arm around her rib cage and then pulled. The rest of Nicole and Raiden came falling through, knocking Gordan off his feet.

Into a shower of warm sunlight washing through the chilly air, they fell on top of one another into the lush green bed of clover, their chests rising and falling with exertion and exhaustion. Lifting his arm over his eyes, Gordan could see it was partly transformed—scaled, clawed, the bones doubled in size. Not even Gordan with his keen hearing noticed Nicole's brother standing at the edge of the patio until he spoke. Gordan wondered how long Mitchell had been standing there, perplexed by half a body trapped in midair.

"You know, I'm not sure I even want to know." Mitchell shook his head.

The three of them rolled away from one another. Gordan sprang up on nimble legs, holding his arm slightly behind him, letting it shift back into human form. Nicole and Raiden moved each limb with noticeable effort, leaning on each other, wincing and grimacing as they got to their feet. They both straightened up, a symphony of aches and pains percolating the air and tingling Gordan's skin.

Nicole turned, whipping the back of her hand against Raiden's chest. "Still think that was a good idea?" Her voice was a raspy whisper.

Raiden hissed, laughing through the twinge ignited by her furious smack. "I've learned my lesson," he said, chuckling.

"Good," she said, Gordan watched Raiden's amusement pinch with guilt at her grating whisper.

"I'm sorry," he said, his tone sinking into deep sincerity.

Gordan felt Nicole's annoyance soften at Raiden's tone, but she wasn't about to let him see how relieved she was that he was back, how scared she had been. The loudest ache ringing through the air came from Nicole's heart.

"I'm not coming after you next time, jerk," she warned, her rough whisper far from threatening.

"Well there's not going to be a next time," he promised. "I'm not going anywhere."

Gordan shook his head. Even as a soul reader, there were some things about these two he just didn't understand. He could feel it—she loved Raiden as much as Raiden loved her. Did she not understand her own heart, or was she pretending not to?

"I have a feeling I missed a lot this week," Mitchell said, shaking his head as he turned toward the house.

A smile fought to break out from behind Gordan's lips. Mitchell had the right idea: retreat. The calm was restored for now. The portal was closed. He wanted to return to his spot on the roof, settle back into this new strange life of his. He recalled being taught when he was very young that debt was a liability to be avoided. His kind no longer spoke of the blessing it could be. He had always been intrigued by the idea. The night he was bound by the debt, he had felt a sort of satisfaction at finally having his curiosity satisfied, but he never had expected to find himself bound to Nicole by anything more than that debt. Now here he was, stranded in the other realm with an extraordinary girl and a seer, happier than he had ever been among his own kind—even happier than before the wars.

He thought he must be the first dragon ever to hope his debt would go unpaid for the rest of his days. It was a selfish wish, but he wanted Nicole's life to be peaceful so that he could stay. It was just his luck that this marvelous girl—who was so determined to save herself and anyone she met—would have such a troublesome path ahead of her. Sooner or later he would have to save her. There was no contesting that fact. When his debt was paid, he would have to return to the Wastelands, to exile. He would miss her. He might even miss Raiden. But until that day arrived, he would gladly go wherever they might lead him.

www.ccrae.com

facebook.com/ccraebooks

Twitter @ccraesunshine

Instagram @ccraebooks

THE GEORGIA POETRY PRIZE

CHRISTOPHER SALERNO, *Sun & Urn*
CHRISTOPHER P. COLLINS, *My American Night*
ROSA LANE, *Chouteau's Chalk*
CHELSEA DINGMAN, *Through a Small Ghost*